Sunbeams at Twilight

(A Life's Echo-Second Edition)

A Novel
By
Lana Lynne

Second Edition
Published by: Forget Me Not Romances, a division of Winged Publications

Text: Lana Lynne

Design/Cover Design: Cynthia Hickey

Manufactured in the United States of America
History: First Edition Published by Venture Galleries, LLC. (prior ISBNs: ebook ISBN: 978-1-937569-15-0 and paperback: 978-1-937569-17-4): First Printing 2012 and Second Printing 2014. Permission given by Venture Galleries, Caleb Pirtle III, to transfer to new publisher January 27, 2018 with all rights reverted to the author.

ISBN-13: 978-1-946939-65-4

ISBN-10: 1-946939-65-X

Dedicated to the Echo of
My Mother's Life in Mine

Author's Acknowledgements and Notes

*Sunbeams at Twilight (subtitle: A Life's Echo) (*First Publication: First printing 2012, Second printing 2014; Second Edition 2018*)* is a work of fiction. All characters are fictional except those historical figures woven into the story due to the time-period. I have referenced the real life figures interacting with my characters in my endnotes. The interactions with my characters are fictional. My research of the setting and Reconstruction period of this novel has been extensive in order to give my characters authenticity and my readers a portal into the past. Any errors or adjustments made to facilitate the flow of my fictional story or the needs of my characters are my own. I have utilized endnotes throughout the book to give the reader a chronological listing to references that will allow the reader to study more on a historical figure or historical events mentioned. In addition, an extensive list of my research resources is given. There are no quotes from any of these. I traveled to Boston, Massachusetts in 2000.

At the time, I didn't realize it would become one of the settings in a novel of mine. Thankfully, I took time to appreciate the rich history while visiting. My husband and I traveled to Washington DC in 2010 to do research for this novel. We decided to go by train to get into the period. Although, I know today's rail travel is very different from the train travel of my characters, I relished the experience. We stayed in Georgetown and embarked on a research trip unlike any of my previous ones. I want to express my gratitude to the librarians at the Kiplinger library and the Historical Society of Washington DC. Their directions, guidance, and assistance were tremendous. We visited as many of the museums and saw all we could of our National Mall. The memorials to our soldiers still bring tears to my eyes and patriotism overflows in my heart. As I wore an MIA bracelet as a child during the years of the Vietnam War, the wall of the names of those sacrificing their lives caused me to read them in solemn silence. Our two days at Arlington are cherished memories.

The tour of Arlington House blends the history of a special

family, as well as our nation. It provided a unique historical perspective. The respectful walk through the Arlington National Cemetery held the echo of the lives of those resting there. I have included a list of the places we visited pertaining to research for this book in the Research Resources section at the back of the book. If I had to name the one museum, taking me by the most surprise and providing me with invaluable perspective and knowledge, it would be the National Museum of Health and Medicine. At the time of our visit in 2010, it sat behind Walter Reed Hospital. (It moved to Maryland in 2011.) I encourage all to visit. Of Course, the National Museum of American History and the National Museum of the American Indian were very informative. I gained insight into the homes and lifestyles planned for my characters during my tours of Tudor Place and the Dumbarton House. There are things you can only learn from visiting the places you choose as settings. I am grateful for all the kindness and insight of the people I met. The trip helped me to capture the Washington of 1874 still woven within the fiber of present day.

Some of my readers asked me what happened to two of the characters introduced in my second book, *Trails of Change (subtitle: A New Sunset) (*First Published in 2010; *Trails of Change (subtitle-A New Sunset-*Second Edition coming in 2018*)*. Many wondered what happened to Hallie Price and James Hawkins after they traveled from Indian Territory to Washington DC close to the end of 1867. I knew but didn't share until the first publication of *Sunbeams at Twilight*. This is indeed their story, but it broadens into the story of many diverse and conflicted characters. As the author, one of the minor characters from my second book captured my attention: Corporal Edward Rigby or Eddie to his friends. This is also his story. Many life-changing events have occurred for these characters since the readers last encountered them. The first chapter introduces us to them in the summer of 1874 while also providing a poignant glimpse of memories encapsulated in friendship, love, faith and grief; the elements of life.

There are many impacting people in our lives, and we still hear them echo even after they leave this life and go on before us. You will soon read of the echo of James's life throughout these pages. The echo of my mother's life is present every day for me.

Her faith, love, character, and encouragement are forever with me. I hope you are able to name the echo of at least one person in your own life.

    Lana Lynne

          2012 and 2018

Chapter One

PAIN REVERBERATED FROM the year-old arrow wound located beneath his right shoulder blade. He helped the other men clear the debris of limbs from the track. Once finished, he rolled his shoulders and arched his back to get some relief.

"How long do you think this will delay us, Lieutenant? Our boss wants us to pick up his new stallion on time."

Lieutenant Edward Rigby met the gaze of one of the two young cowboys who cleared the last of the obstacles in front of the train's engine. He wiped the sweat from his brow as he gestured toward the man who approached them.

"I'll defer your question to the engineer there."

The young man nodded and ambled forward to meet the railroad man with his friend in tow. The thirty-year-old soldier next to him shook perspiration from his hair and replaced his cap.

"Those boys kind of remind me of James and you a few years back," Sergeant Case said.

The lieutenant grimaced. "Try a lifetime ago. Let's get back on board."

They accepted the thanks of their fellow passengers outside of the rail car with formal nods. The conductor wasted no time and ushered them to their seats. Eddie Rigby shook his head as the sergeant next to him settled into a slumber almost as soon as the train shuttered and started building momentum. His eyes followed the young ranch hands' awkward but companionable progression to their seats at the opposite end of the car. Their eagerness

1

embraced this journey as an adventure. He remembered those same emotions when James and he left for war.

Eddie looked away from them. The movement of the land dashing past his window reminded him of the ongoing passage of time. His mind skimmed past his youth to a more somber time—a dark day during his last trip to Washington—five years ago when he was a sergeant.

One moment flashed in his mind above all the rest: in the foreground, a timeless picture of the last figure beside the gravesite. Most people would replay the faces of the president, his cabinet members, and all the military fanfare involved in honoring his best friend's life; however, those fell into the background.

~~~

1869

The woman made a single silhouette in black as evening painted the sky with darkening blue-gray shadows seeping like spilled ink, deepening the canopy to cobalt. He returned for one last goodbye after seeing the major and Mrs. Hawkins to the wagon. The graveside scene stopped him in mid-stride. A few sunbeams lingered, slanting through the branches of the solitary tree close to James's grave, illuminating the dark figure of Hallie in her mourning dress. In sharp contrast to the snowy ground, she fell to her knees. Words, displays of emotion, or any action deserted him. Reverence reigned, thankfulness coursed through his veins, and memories of the years of friendship with James replayed. His life would have been so very different if they'd never met. Yes, Sergeant Edward Rigby felt sure a life of crime would have surrounded him if not for his friend.

A final prayer left his lips before he lifted his head to find Hallie still beside the grave, the beams of light now faded. Her life would also have been very different without Boyd Richards and James Hawkins. Eddie sighed as he crossed to her.

"Hallie, it's time to go," he said in a soft voice.

She looked up with a mixture of sorrow and peace on her face as she reached for his extended hand without saying a word.

~~~

He hadn't seen her since that cold day in February 1869.

The years ebbed away without him returning to Washington. He managed to advance in military rank but sunk lower in the guilt he felt in not honoring his last promise to his best friend.

Lieutenant Rigby shook himself out of his reverie at the sound of a baby's cry. He looked across the aisle of the train car to find a well-dressed but tired looking mother trying to console her infant. Rail travel made journeys faster even with the unforeseen delays like today. Walking from car to car remained unstable for even the most sure-footed, and little ones found travel tedious in any fashion. Eddie smiled as the infant calmed in submission to slumber. The weary woman gave him an apologetic smile but directed a tender look at the peaceful face of her son. The pair had amazed him during the journey. The baby wailed just a couple of times. The mother dozed with the baby on her chest or with a protective hand on his back as he lay on the seat beside her during the night. More grumbles came from his seatmate than the infant.

The rumbling, bouncing rhythm of the train jostled Eddie's stocky form. His army uniform felt more confining in the small seat he shared with the other soldier next to him. Their return to Washington, along with the few original troops who served under Major Ronald Hawkins at the fort in Indian Territory back in '67, came after a marked delay. How had the years and diverse travels sped by leading to 1874? Some of the military detail met their demise at the hands of the Indians. The rest went to Kansas and Nebraska to work with the railroad extensions.

"Hey, Lieutenant, how much longer will it be until we get there? You're the only one I know who's made this trip back to Washington on the rail," Sergeant Nathan Case inquired.

Eddie pulled out his pocket watch and glanced past the sergeant to look out the window.

"Well, Mr. Case, from the way the land is changing and given the time, I'd say about three more hours."

His longtime friend and fellow soldier groaned, interlocked his fingers across his stomach, and scooted down in the seat.

"I might as well get some more shut eye," he said.

~~~

Memories once again overtook Eddie. His previous musings pondered the greatest day of grief in his life. Now, they went to the telegram from Hallie that brought him back to Washington to see James one last time. He knew something was wrong when he first received the wire. Normal correspondence came in the form of thick, informative letters in Hallie's handwriting as dictated by James. The miracle of his friend's survival with paralysis following spinal and neck injuries during the Civil War still amazed the medical community. As James had always managed to recover from his periodic episodes of illness since being injured, Eddie allowed himself to breathe and live a normal life after his transfer. His heart had jumped upon receiving the wired notice:

"Eddie" stop "Come home now" stop "James is ill" stop "Hallie"

The telegram came from a woman not given to hysterics. He knew her as a plainspoken woman to the point of blatant honesty. Before she became a caretaker for his best friend, James Hawkins, she worked in Texas as a soiled dove at a saloon. A common acquaintance of the Hawkins family and Hallie brought them together: Boyd Richards, a cowhand for Joe Kennedy, recommended her as an unlikely nurse for James during his family's period at a fort in Indian Territory. It had changed all their lives.

Hallie came to a relationship with the Lord and started training with Dr. Jones, the fort's doctor. She became his assistant at the hospital once the Hawkins family returned to Washington D. C.

Eddie's mouth formed a grim line at the memory. After a moment of hesitation, he went to his superior with his request. It received an initial denial, but they sent for him the next morning. The commanding officer had received another telegraphed message, this time from Major Hawkins in Washington. It granted Eddie clearance for six weeks of leave.

~~~

No, he couldn't dwell on those last days that he'd managed to share with James and the Hawkins family. Guilt slammed into his gut. Eddie squeezed his eyes shut, willing his mind to skip past it. He shifted, bumping his seatmate.

"Will you stay still, Rigby? I was just starting to get some shut eye," Sergeant Case grumbled.

Nathan must really be sleepy to forget protocol. Eddie grinned even as he gave a gruff reply, "You forget yourself, Sergeant."

One blue eye popped open as a sheepish smile crossed the offending soldier's face. "Sorry, Lieutenant. Doggone it, Eddie, it's still so easy to remember when we were just youths entering the war."

Eddie elbowed his friend. "Forget it, Nate, go to sleep."

The sergeant adjusted in the seat a few more times before slow, even breaths indicated sleep. Eddie gazed at the trees blurring past the window as the words he'd uttered for his friend's eulogy came back to him:

"I've been asked to speak to you today about my friend, James Hawkins. As I pondered, two lines came to me: Matters of Consequence, People of Importance. James truly helped me, and I know many of you, to define those things in a brand new way. This world defines Matters of Consequence as things, which are socially and politically successful, whereas James defined it as anything the Lord deemed consequential. Therefore, in the light of eternity, everything is consequential. Now, as for the second item, People of Importance: the world defines it as people who have social and political success. Many of you fit this definition, but don't worry; James would have included you in his definition because God doesn't leave out anyone." Many people in the congregation had shared smiles as he continued.

"If James hadn't held those views and hadn't been so yielded to being used by God before and after his accident, I wouldn't be here, and many of you wouldn't either. He reached out to me, shared his life, his faith, and his family. I've never been the same. James personified a yielded life. That's why he's the most important man I've ever known on this earth. As we all gather here today, let's ask ourselves how yielded we are."

~~~

What a hypocrite he'd been to make such a speech and leave Washington without keeping his promise. He scooted down in his seat and put his hat over his eyes. Hours later, after the train dropped his fellow soldiers in Washington, he changed trains to continue his planned journey to Boston. He'd requested his full period of leave in order to attend to all the long-neglected people in his life and to take time to make some important decisions.

Eddie found Julia's place of business after lunch the next day. Once inside the establishment, they directed him to wait for his sister in a small alcove of a sitting room. He'd been waiting about ten minutes when he heard a familiar voice through the curtained doorway. *It was Hallie! What was she doing here?*

"No, Julia, I won't do that. I've had two men give me opportunities to get past that time in my life, and even if I don't believe in myself enough to finish my present course, I know that I owe it to them, especially James. You know your brother called James the most important man he'd ever known. I have to agree, but in the end, the good Lord gets the credit. I know, I know, you're too cynical to hear those words."

Both women laughed, a pronounced pause followed. Hallie's voice resumed after the painful silence.

"Well, you know where to find me if you change your mind one day."

"I still don't understand why you care, Hallie, but I'll keep it in mind." Julia's voice held a hint of amusement.

"Goodbye, Julia Rigby, I have to finish a few more things before my train leaves."

Hallie's footsteps sounded, and then the door opened and closed.

Lieutenant Rigby stood when his sister pushed the curtain secluding the alcove aside. This visit made the second time he'd seen her since the end of the war. The first time he came to see her, she sent him away.

Julia now wore a bright blue satin dress with a low neckline. Her curly blonde hair cascaded from an ornate comb on one side. Her rouged lips and cheeks weren't garish. Small lines appeared at the edge of her cynical green eyes as she flashed a practiced smile.

"Well, soldier, I . . . ," Julia started but faltered.

As their eyes met, memories flowed.

~~~

Abandoned

They'd struggled since their mother left them. The less than maternal exit took place the day after a letter notified their mother of her husband's death at sea. At the time, fourteen-year-old Julia and eleven-year-old Eddie struggled the first year. They lived on the streets until Julia secured a job with a tailor. He rented them a room off the small shop. Their temporary security ended after two years when he closed the shop due to ill health. Eddie performed odd jobs, picked pockets, gambled, and fought for money to feed them. Sometimes he could only bring home enough food to feed one of them. At those times, he flashed a broad smile as he entered the empty room in the burned-out building and said he ate his on the way home. She proclaimed him the best brother any girl could have. However, over the next year, she became withdrawn and abandoned him.

～～～

As Eddie looked at her now, the sense of disbelief, betrayal, and fear coursed over him once again. The hollow memory of when he called her name to an empty space. He'd run through the streets looking everywhere for her.

The curtain on the alcove opened again and the powdered woman motioned for Julia. He shrugged as she scurried out with a mere apologetic smile. What difference did it make? He took a seat on a velvet chair and rubbed his hands on the fake vestiges of wealth; mere illusions and disillusions. He preferred his present reality. Thanks to James.

He leaned his head against the chair back. Julia's abandonment led him to his best friend.

～～～

Meeting James

The reality of the second abandonment embittered him. His activities for daily survival fluctuated on both sides of the law. By the time he turned seventeen, Eddie's street education turned him into a stocky young man capable of winning most fights—some for money and some just for the fun of it. During the next two years, he developed a true business as a gambler. For a time, he also won every card game. While other young men his age attended the prestigious university in town, he made a living that provided him a roof over his head until his luck changed. He became reckless and returned to the streets, ready to take chances to survive. The thin line blurred when he borrowed money from a dangerous man.

The unsavory characters in the man's employ came to collect when Eddie had just lost his last cent gambling one night with a group of students from Harvard. He always made money off these elite young men until that evening. The funny thing: the young man who won the game didn't want to play cards. No, those university gents viewed the evening as a last outing together before classes started. Eddie had smirked as the group of friends convinced their man to try his hand at cards. It seemed a religious objection to gambling restrained the brown-haired youth. Eddie leaned back with total confidence when James Hawkins sat down at the table.

No, it hadn't taken long for him to realize his underestimation of this opponent. The intelligent, azure-blue eyes twinkled as he raked in the last of his winnings and excused himself from the table. Each of his friends also chose to bow out of the game at that point. Then the most astonishing thing happened. James stood and started counting out money to his friends. The man returned the amount each had lost, and the group laughed as they left with smiles thrown Eddie's way.

The barkeep shook his head and guffawed with a shrug at Eddie. He stood, after a few moments, in the grim realization of his loss, and exited into the temperate night air. A slow perusal of the street didn't find anything out of the ordinary until he noticed the carriage to the side of the building as a voice called his name.

"Mr. Rigby, we do hope your night at the table was profitable. Our employer is in need of repayment at this time."

The hefty man stepped from the carriage, followed by another man of equal stature. They moved to stand in close proximity to Eddie. He cocked his head to the side and displayed his most charming smile.

"The night isn't over gentleman. This round didn't go so well for me, but I still have a few more establishments to frequent tonight and tomorrow evening. Tell Mr. Sullivan that I'll have his money for him by Monday."

The men stepped a breath from him with ugly smirks on both of their faces. "Now we do want to be fair," one said. "I think we'll take you down to the authorities and report you for not paying your debt. Then after the law deals with you on this matter, as well as a few other crimes we may be able to report on your behalf, you'll still be responsible for repayment. We can take years from you, my boy."

Weariness settled on him, and he met their eyes in even regard. "Why not just kill me?"

They laughed. "Now where's the fun in that? You have no family to speak of, and no one would miss you. No, Mr. Sullivan wouldn't profit from your disposal." The smiles disappeared, and they flanked him, taking his elbows. "Let's go."

A soft whistle came from the shadows, drawing the attention of the trio. A man leaned on the wall with one polished shoe crossed over the other. As they turned, he pushed himself forward in a nonchalant stroll toward them. Recognition coursed through Eddie, and he felt trepidation pierce through him. He didn't need this, a college boy involved in the darkest business of Boston.

"Get out of here, Mr. Hawkins. This doesn't concern you," Eddie sneered.

The young man removed his hat and played with the brim a bit before he returned all the expectant gazes. "You are indeed wrong, Mr. Rigby. This matter is of definite concern for me. Gentlemen, I am a student of the law and consider you allowing me to accompany you to the police an extreme favor. My family holds social esteem in both Boston and Georgetown, so I know Mr. Sullivan wouldn't mind your allowance for this opportunity to witness the apprehension of a real criminal. This man gave me an enjoyable evening of cards for which I was about to repay him. How much is his debt? The amount I am about to bestow on him may help defray the sum to be reported."

A definite air of disbelief surrounded Mr. Sullivan's men and they laughed, but sobered as James Hawkins waited with a look of utmost sincerity on his face.

"Mr. Evans, tell the gentleman what he wants to know, and let's be on our way to see this settled."

Eddie couldn't believe his eyes or ears as this new acquaintance produced the original amount put in the game.

"I will need a receipt for this," James said.

The man called Mr. Evans continued to assist Eddie inside the carriage. "I'll give you one once we get this scoundrel to the police."

Young Mr. Hawkins retrieved the money in question with an air of utmost calm. "Then you will understand my desire to hold it until we can make the transfer official."

Mr. Evans grunted as James stepped past him into the carriage.

The situation perplexed Eddie and filled him with suspicion. He shook his head and received a confident smile in return.

Once at police headquarters, things became even more unbelievable. James Hawkins sent a messenger for his brother-in-law, who turned out to be a judge and a former lawyer. Judge Thomas Jackson had married James's sister, Amelia. The police took the statement of Mr. Sullivan's men about his debt, and James Hawkins made the reduction of the amount with a receipt given in the presence of witnesses. When asked if he could pay the remaining amount, Eddie admitted to his close to non-existent funds. Therefore, the police prepared to throw him in jail. Inability to pay his debt in full and a few other petty crimes Mr. Sullivan's men attributed to Eddie appeared to doom him.

At this juncture, a very sleepy looking young judge stormed into the situation. Irritation followed the judge's initial relief to find Eddie in trouble instead of James. By the wee hours of Saturday morning, they made an informal determination with a formal decree planned for the next week. As the one *proven* wrong involved nonpayment of a debt, and a debt of a somewhat circumspect nature, Eddie didn't go to jail. The terms involved secure steady employment with repayment made from his initial earnings. The decree disallowed further contact or business between the stated parties. Eddie would make the payments owed Mr. Sullivan through the court.

Eddie mumbled his thanks as they exited. It achieved a reprieve, but he'd no idea where he'd get a steady job. Anyone in his neighborhood could have told the judge about the sporadic nature of his past employment. He hunched his shoulders as he turned to head down the street.

"Mr. Rigby, where are you going?"

He turned around at the sound of James's voice.

"I'm free to leave, aren't I, Mr. Hawkins?"

"Yes and no. Yes, technically, but not if you are to satisfy your future employer."

He smirked. "Who would that be? You?"

"Certainly not; I am to be at college. No, you'll be working for my family. The man who maintains the upkeep of their home and gardens is returning to my grandmother's employ in Georgetown, and they are seeking a replacement. Of course, you will take over his living accommodations."

Judge Jackson leaned over to whisper in his brother-in-law's ear. James kept his gaze fixed on Eddie as he responded. "Yes, Thomas, I *am* sure."

The judge then turned toward Eddie. "I hope you realize the opportunity you're being offered and don't take it lightly. Know this, Mr. Rigby: I will personally escort you to the jail myself if you so much as sneeze in the wrong direction as you deal with the Hawkins family. I have only been part of their fine family for a year but have long admired Lieutenant Ronald Hawkins, this young man's father, as well as his late grandfather, General Stephen Hawkins. These names mean nothing to you, but they will. Now, I'm taking both of you in hand and escorting you home. James, I don't know what you'll do once Amelia and I move to Washington in the spring."

As time passed, both Eddie's perspective and life evidenced a drastic change. He started out in the small carriage house behind their home. James came home most weekends and sought him out to accompany him on outings, including church on Sundays. Their friendship developed, and his family soon started asking him to take his meals with them. Before the end of winter in February of 1861, he became a Christian and moved into Amelia's former chamber on the second floor. Then the talk of war became a reality, and they made obvious decisions. The war arrived about a month before his twenty-first birthday. James left school to join the army and Eddie with him.

~~~

Yes, Eddie had gone with him. Too many memories . . . he missed his friend. Eddie opened his eyes and shook his head as sister swept back into the room.

The practiced expression on her face faltered and he stood.

"Eddie, what are you doing here?" She asked with a slight quiver in her voice as she approached him.

"Hello, Julia," he said in a voice modulated with tenderness. He gathered his older sister to him in a hug. She softened and collapsed against him for a brief moment before she pushed away to move to the velvet settee.

She sat with a flourish. "I sure hope Hallie didn't tell you to come rescue me, little brother, because I'm where I want to be."

He frowned and resumed his seat on the large mahogany and velvet chair. "No. How do you know Hallie?"

She smiled with candid amusement. "Hallie has visited me as often as possible since a few months after their return from Indian Territory. She has this crazy idea about me becoming a seamstress and dresser for this theater company. Isn't that a laugh? Me—take a cut in pay to become respectable."

Eddie's frown deepened as he fixed a puzzled stare on his sister. "Do you really like what you do here?"

She smirked as she answered. "Little brother, *like* has very little to do with what we may have to do in this life to survive. I worked in a few darker places before Miss Amanda took me on as one of her girls. This is a clean and respectable place. The clients aren't just anyone off the streets. We have soldiers, senators, judges, and lawyers."

"Julia, didn't you ever think about getting married?"

She laughed.

"No, thank you. In my observation and experience with the many married men who frequent this place, that institution is a lie. What's so laughable is that the men think they're actually good husbands. I wish more men would tend to their wives and lives with the quality of care they want others to think they do. You see, little brother, most of these men want people to think so well of them, but few are willing to expend the effort needed to make it true. Women like me see their true natures. Their wives get the lie. Marriage? Not for me."

Eddie just stared at her and felt sick. He remembered the sweet girl Julia had been and the dreams she used to share. He thought about Hallie's suggestion and knew it could get Julia back in the right direction.

"Julia, do you remember when we used to talk at night after you finished your day at the tailor's shop?" he asked, crossing to her and squatting in front of her.

Her expression reflected caution mixed with interest.

"Yes, why?"

"Well, you used to talk about owning your own dress shop. You'd show me your drawings, and I would design plans for the shop, remember?"

She gave a brief smile and reached out to play with the curls on top of his head. "Those are the times I still think about at night." She paused, letting her hand drop and grimaced. "But I let you down, Eddie. It was hard after Mr. Yancy closed the store."

He reached out and lifted her chin. "Sis, I was mad at you for a long time, and then I grew up. You did what you thought necessary. It made me tough, and then along came James. He showed me friendship, and since I've known the good Lord, I've forgiven everything a long time ago."

A slight mist moistened her eyes, but her expression became guarded at the mention of God. She stayed silent for a moment, and Eddie glimpsed a sadness he didn't understand as she responded.

"Did you know I met James once after they returned? Yes, I actually went to Washington to meet him and to ask about you. Anyway, Hallie shared her story, but, Eddie, I'm not letting go the way she did. It's taken me too long to get to where I am. I can refuse clients and take the ones I want," she said, straightening her shoulders.

Eddie sent up a silent prayer. His eyes studied her. They'd missed so much in each other's lives these past years.

"Julia, were you safe during the fire in '72?"[i]

She blinked at the change in subject. "Well . . . yes. It was on Kingston and Summer Streets to start and then took down most everything on Summer, Washington, and State streets. It even reached the waterfront, but we were safe here. It was frightening, but you know they lost more in Chicago in '71.[ii] Believe me, that was on everyone's minds."

"We had hoped the country would improve after the war," he said. "Those fires and the Wall Street issues last year have caused the country to continue to struggle."

"Well, at least you have a secure position in the military. Private businesses haven't done so well around here."

He frowned. "I know, but I might consider some other options."

She placed a hand on his shoulder. "Now, don't do something foolish, Eddie."

He grinned and stood. "I won't. How about you? Do you need money?"

She laughed. "No, darling brother. It doesn't make sense, but men will pay for basic needs. Stop, Eddie. Don't look at me that way. Anyway, I'm fine."

He dropped a kiss on the top of her head, crossed to the chair, and retrieved his hat.

"Julia, I've returned to Washington to work for a time, so I would like to see you —away from here. Would it be agreeable for me to pick up my sister for lunch?"

She stood and tossed her hair over one shoulder. "Not this week. Why don't you send me a letter and let me know when you'll be in Boston again? We can arrange to meet and maybe take a day."

He exhaled a deep sigh, wishing things were different, and nodded. "I'll do that, Julia. Think about Hallie's idea. If you're interested in truth, dare to be the Julia you were before life turned this direction. Few have someone interested in helping. Hallie knows this and is trying to be that someone for you."

Julia smiled but nodded. "Hallie is an unusual woman. I truly admire her."

She reached up to smooth the front of his uniform with a thoughtful expression as she fingered the buttons for a moment before looking at him.

"I went back to the old neighborhood to find you once. Old Tommy told me the family of a Harvard boy had taken you in. I was sad but glad all at the same time. Then, when you came to see me that one time after the war, I wanted you to cut all ties with me. Your new family could help you get to a place in life that held better opportunities."

"Julia—"

"No, Eddie, I've learned many things since that day. First, I never want to be without you, at least, coming in and out of my life. Old Tommy came to me when you joined the military. I held my breath as they listed the names of the dead. Then, I heard your friend was injured, and I went to his parent's home to give my regards. His mother was kind enough to let me read your last letter. She wrote to me when you came home. Therefore, when you came to see me, I expected you and planned my demise in your eyes. She wrote me again when all of you transferred to Indian Territory. Second, I've learned about my many limitations, but the people I love must not be restricted by my limits."

The first part of her admission overwhelmed him, but he couldn't fathom the nature of the latter part. He hugged her for a long time before pulling back.

"Julia, I don't know what to say. I'm sorry for my anger and hurt. Please forgive me. We have many things to talk about. Think about Hallie's idea."

She smiled and returned his hug. "You grew into a real handsome man, Eddie. Mum would have been proud. I'll wait for your note."

Eddie wanted to take her with him. His heart felt ready to burst with the desire to take care of his sister.

"I love you, Julia. Don't forget how special you are."

"Get out of here, Edward Rigby. I'll ruin my face and won't get any business." She laughed as he raised his eyebrows and stroked his chin. "Go."

He bowed and planted another kiss on her forehead. She blew him one as he reached the curtain at the entrance of the alcove. "I love you, little brother. Write soon."

~~~

Hallie Price Hawkins waited at the train depot in the heat of the July day. Her restless thoughts whirled in a collage of hopes and memories. Julia Rigby—tough and hardened. She could understand many facets of the woman because of her previous life in Texas. However, Julia's resignation and comfort with her status didn't lend consideration to anything else. Hallie tried to be objective in her recall of her first meeting with Boyd Richards—what crack in her facade of self-assured soiled dove had he seen? She hadn't even realized one existed until his letter arrived. It offered the opportunity to go to the military fort in Indian Territory. How had he ever conceived the idea of her becoming a nurse for his friend's grown son? She'd re-read the words multiple times before she could admit the truth: she wanted a different life.

A bittersweet smile danced across her face as she thought about the past few years. Only God could have attended to the details paving the way to her present life. It held more joy and deep grief than she could have anticipated. What a gift. She didn't regret one second, except for losing James. Even as she thought it, she recognized the half-truth. She had and still loved him enough to let him go.

She bowed her head, shut her eyes, and sighed as the emotions washed over her.

~~~

James

Loving James: *how* unexpected yet natural it had been. In the beginning, a strict caregiver and patient relationship mixed with intense respect, which developed and evolved into friendship. Then they became closer after she accepted Christ, and a friendship tinged with a common faith developed.

He always encouraged her to grow in her knowledge for a future in nursing. Dr. Jones and he provided volumes of medical books compiled since the war. They held the information gleaned from the care of soldiers. James also shared important literature with her from Dickens and Walt Whitman to her always and still favorite writings of Louisa May Alcott. She'd read Miss Alcott's *Hospital Sketches*[iii] multiple times.

However, nothing prepared her for the last evening before they left the Fort. James's best friend, Corporal Eddie Rigby, told her James wanted to see her and had taken her to where he lay in the bed of a wagon just outside of the gates. He rested on carefully positioned blankets and bags with his wheelchair positioned next to the wagon. After Eddie left them alone, James asked her to come watch the sunset with him. She crawled in beside him, and it felt so different. For the first time since she met this twenty-seven-year-old man who had suffered a spinal cord injury during the Civil War and survived, he asked for something for himself—a kiss. He'd never given or received one from a romantic aspect at that point. They thought never to replicate their special exchange— so pure and innocent. She remembered thinking it felt like her first real, genuine kiss.

She'd been married before the war, but not in a union of love. Her husband died as a soldier, and she went on to choose a scandalous career in a saloon. Plenty of men but no love. Therefore, the wonderful and unexpected kiss with James surprised her, but held no hope for a future.

They made the move to Washington D.C. The trip proved hard on James, and he'd become ill by the time they arrived. His doctor advised immediate hospitalization, but his mother refused, stating the infections and illnesses in the hospital threatened James's recovery more than nursing him at home. Hallie knew and followed all the regulations from the Sanitary Commission's[iv] guidelines set during the Civil War. The doctor gave his reluctant agreement but enlisted the help of another colleague. The man had trained with him in Pennsylvania before the war. Hallie learned a lot from both doctors during that time. She postponed her training with Dr. Jones at the hospital in order to commit to James's care day and night.

After his recovery, she noticed James's open looks of affection whenever she tended him. He tried to keep up their friendship and encouraged her pursuits at the hospital. At his insistence, his mother took her to literature meetings. Many of the meetings took place at his grandmother's house in Georgetown. She met Louisa May Alcott, the author, who gave her much insight and encouragement about nursing. Even though Miss Alcott suffered from a weaker health due to having Typhoid Pneumonia[v] during wartime nursing service, she remained an unrelenting supporter.

Then one Sunday after they returned from church with his parents, he asked her a question. His father had just left the room after they put him to bed for a rest. Hallie straightened his covers and as her hand trailed the side of the mattress, he shifted his hand to intercept her fingers. She stopped, her eyes finding his with a questioning glance. His blue eyes held a tender, serious light. He shifted his hand again, and she enfolded it in hers.

"James, what is it?"

He smiled in his endearing lopsided way. A painting of him

as a child showed the same smile. His mother told her it made it hard to scold. In that moment, the gentle way his eyes glowed paired with his smile, caused her heart to race.

"Will you marry me, Hallie?"

Shock winded her; then a nervous laugh escaped but stopped midway at the still earnest look on his face.

"James, you know that's impossible."

He tried to squeeze her hand with his limited strength, shifted his head, and sighed in frustration. "Why is it, Hallie? I have a job consulting on Indian affairs with our government. We both are of well-attained ages. We share many common interests and, more importantly, the same Savior. I also have two advantages for you over other men." The slight grin he gave disarmed her.

Hallie quirked an eyebrow as she grinned back at him. "James Hawkins this had better be good as you know I never plan to marry again. What are the two advantages?"

He regarded her in grave candor. "You would never be put upon by me as you would be by other men due to my physical limitations; and you are almost guaranteed to outlive me," he said without rancor. However, it made Hallie mad.

"How dare you say that to me, James Hawkins? That's the most insulting proposal. My reasons have nothing to do with your work, our ages, or your so-called advantages. We're from different backgrounds. I'm your caregiver, and your parents would never approve even if I considered it." She paused when he smiled at her last words. "I mean, I mean, of course it's impossible as I said. Now, good night."

She went to the door and turned at the sound of his voice. "Do you know when I decided to ask you to be my wife?"

"No . . . Oh, James, do stop talking about this." Soft exasperation mixed with expectancy reflected in her voice.

His eyes never glanced away from her. "It was when I was so sick —and, no, it wasn't like so many patients who fall in love with their nurses. You know I had that opportunity before you came into my life. No, I'd awaken in the middle of the night and could hear you breathing on the cot beside my bed. I enjoyed your presence and prayed. During those hours before dawn, I knew each moment could be my last, and I wanted *you* with me at the end. It sounds morbid, but it's not, Hallie. The realization that you are the person I'm most content with gave me pause and hope."

Hallie felt torn between the urge to go to his side or continue to her chamber. Confusion reigned as she shook her head and slipped out the door.

Over the next months, he continued to ask. James never pushed or demanded. He continued his twice-a-week appointments at the White House, daily meetings in his father's study, and his lunches with his mother, which some days included Hallie. They discussed literature and her hospital training.

Then one early summer night in his mother's garden—June 1868—changed things. She sat on the bench as the last beams of sunlight gleamed through the bushes and stirred an interplay of highlight and shadows on the flowers. James sat in his wheelchair in front of her. She shut the book she'd read to him.

"Well, I think we're losing the light. We'll have to wait to finish this tomorrow," she said, glancing up to find him looking past her toward the now darkening sky. A chill went through her. "James?"

After a weighted delay, his azure gaze left his distant regard, and he smiled with contrasting sadness in his eyes. "Hallie, I want to apologize for making such an irritant of myself this past month. It's just . . . I never thought of having the opportunity to ever find love after my accident. I told myself it should never be an option. Then you came into my life, Hallie, taking me completely by surprise. I may not have the right, but my heart has the love that I want to share with you," Gentle emotions tempered his voice until he stopped and cleared his throat. He straightened his shoulders and continued in a firm tone. "However, after much reflection, searching prayer, and consideration, the conclusion is: it's time to cease this pursuit. It just isn't fair to you. I am so selfish. Do you know I almost planned to give you a ring and beg your hand three weeks ago at you birthday celebration? As I watched you enjoy the presents from everyone else, I just couldn't. That's why I had Mother add my name to their present." James closed his eyes and shook his head. "To think of how you must have felt. We arrive in Washington with my illness marring the Christmas season, celebrate as the New Year arrives, and you assist me with my slow recovery. Then I try to change our relationship. You are trying to be my friend and an excellent, professional nurse with the reward of a love-struck man you don't want as a suitor. I bet you have regretted not returning to Texas with Mr. Kennedy's men." He laughed without humor. "You probably wonder where the James Hawkins you first knew has gone. Well, I'll tell you. He became the same as all the men you have dealt with—selfish. It's humbled me to realize *that* part of me is still present."

He looked up, and Hallie found she couldn't speak. He didn't understand and so she had to say it. Her throat constricted. "James, I . . . I love you. That's why I've refused your proposals." Her dark gaze met his.

Even as a look of confusion passed over his face, the warm light she'd seen in his eyes started to glow. He shook his head. "Please explain, Hallie, and then I have something to say."

Hallie had spent many nights reviewing her life and praying. In light of her past life and his family's social status, their complicated situation held a dilemma for her.

"James, I've never been a woman to really care what other people might say or think about me, but I don't want to cause your family name to be compromised."

His eyes never left hers as he frowned. "Hallie, no one in Washington outside of my family knows about your past, and even if they did, it's your past. Who you are at present is what is important. You have established yourself as a competent nurse and have impressed Dr. Jones with your intelligence and aptitude for learning during your days of service at the hospital. My mother and father are pleased with your detailed care of me, as am I. Most of all, you have become a Christian woman who cares for others. Your ability to deal with difficult situations has been an asset. How could you think you're not worthy of being a part of this family? Hallie, if anything, everyone is wondering how I could be so blind to not see the treasure under my own roof."

"James, do your parents know how you feel?" she asked, resisting the impulse to reach for his hand.

His gaze held pointed intent. "Yes, they do." He quirked his eyebrows as he challenged, "Any more objections, Hallie?"

An uncharacteristic shiver of nerves passed through her. "Do they approve? How will this affect my work? I still want to be your nurse. Wait—James, please tell me—what do you want."

"Hallie, please take my hand and look at me," he commanded in a gentle fashion. She complied and his fingers grasped hers with their limited strength. His eyes locked with hers. "I want to marry you. We both know the harsh realities of my condition. Our marriage will not be like most others. My war injuries have forever changed my life; however, God spared me, and it would be wrong not to share the love He's given me for you. You are such a surprise in my life, Hallie Price. I had finally matured to a place in my life in which I could deal with my handicaps and look beyond myself to others. I just never expected you. The kiss we shared at the fort the night before our return to Washington was perfect—a cherished, golden gift, which I never thought to replicate. Then we came home, and I got sick. Death knocked, but God stopped it again. My love for you grew each day. I knew if I lived even one more day, that I would want it to be with you. There's just one problem."

Serious hurt and concern filled his eyes. She squatted down in front of him. "What is it James?"

His flashed a bittersweet smile. "Now that you have confirmed your love for me, it is inevitable; I will break your heart."

"Why? How?" she asked as blood pounded in her ears.

"Because I'll leave you alone when I die."

She couldn't see his face as the sky continued to darken. "No, James, you could never break my heart. You and God have restored my heart. When you have to leave this life, it'll hurt my heart, but that's just a result of the tragedy of this world. James, I just turned thirty-two years, and I can honestly say this is the first time I've truly been in love. Believe me when I say there were many unexpected—oh, what's the word you taught me the other day—serendipities along the way."

He tugged a bit on her hand. "Hallie, please sit on my lap. I need to hold you for this next part."

Hallie took her time as she stood, secured his chair with bricks in front of the wheels so it wouldn't roll, and eased onto his lap. Her eyes adjusted to the darkness, and she could see his smile in the moonlight.

"Hallie, Price, I am a twenty-seven, let us just say an

almost twenty-eight-year-old man who sits here with little to offer you besides my name. It's a good name, and my family does approve of me offering it to you. You may not realize that I do have some money of my own. It's ours, as we may need it. You do not have to continue as my nurse, but if you want to, I won't protest." His fingers squeezed hers. "Hallie, will you do me the honor of becoming my wife?"

Hallie nodded as tears coursed down her cheeks. "Yes, James, I would be honored."

His hand shifted to caress her arm. Their eyes met and she bent her head to kiss him—as sweet and tender as the first one. She lifted her head in wonder. His warm breath brushed her face.

"I love you, Hallie," he said in a hoarse voice.

Her heart soared as she cupped his face in her hands. "I love you with all my heart, James."

She smiled and then kissed his forehead. He chuckled with delight, moving his head to look at her.

"You can do better than that. Come here, Hallie."

She knew his eyes twinkled, even in the darkness, and bent to accommodate him. They filled the kiss with the depths of their feelings.

"I never knew how real love felt until now," Hallie said in wonder.

James kissed her again. They might have stayed in the garden all night if his mother hadn't come to look for them.

Susannah Hawkins looked a little embarrassed and flustered, but she laughed with delight for their happiness. "I can see I'm going to have to help Hallie stay focused now that you've reached an understanding," she laughed, going to hug Hallie who had jumped out of James's lap upon hearing Mrs. Hawkins's voice.

"Come on, dear, let's get James to bed and *we* will talk."

James rolled his eyes at Hallie as they entered the house, and she hid her smile.

~~~

A hot puff of wind blew dust into Hallie's eyes, causing her to blink and return to the present. She smiled as a man tipped his hat.

"Good day, ma'am."

"And to you, sir. Do you have the time?"

He pulled out his pocket watch. "One-thirty."

"Thank you."

"You're welcome."

Hallie checked the bag at her feet, fanned her face—grateful for the shade of the depot. She dabbed at her face with her handkerchief and returned to thoughts of the past, this time to the period right before James's proposal. He'd been intent on an important reconciliation.

~~~

Forgiving Amelia

James worked an impressive wonder after he recovered from his post-travel illness. He asked to see his sister as soon as he regained enough strength to go on day outings. Amelia Hawkins Jackson hadn't spoken to her family in over a year. She insisted James be left at the Soldiers' Home instead of moving with his family to the fort in Indian Territory. Amelia hadn't wanted him to live at her home so he could take the government position offered to him. Embarrassment over his condition stopped her.

James had refused to admit to the hurt his sister's selfishness and lack of compassion caused him. In fact, he'd agreed to the Soldiers' Home, but his parents never considered it. All ties had remained broken with Amelia since that time.

James presented himself with Hallie and his parents at the home of Judge Thomas and Amelia Jackson one Saturday after lunch. His older sister bore a strong resemblance to him, and Hallie knew the woman couldn't deny their relations if seen together in public. They originated from Boston; however, her husband's job took them to Washington right before the war. Now, they lived in Georgetown,—rumored as a soon-to-be official part of Washington. Their maternal grandparents had always lived in Georgetown. Mrs. Eula Adams, their now widowed grandmother, resided just a few blocks from Amelia. The gracious, elder woman had visited the Hawkinses with regularity since their return. If the proximity to the White House and the capitol hadn't been an issue for James, they might have moved in with her.

Hallie had known many women like Amelia. All so self-righteous and controlling, focused on importance linked to social status, the need to tailor all the aspects of one's life visible to the social eye as perfect and free of scandal as possible. If Amelia had felt ashamed of her brother—a brave, injured war hero—Hallie knew the details of the past life of her brother's nurse were sure to mortify her.

The Jackson's two children, eight-year-old Robert and three-year-old Clara, hadn't seen their uncle or grandparents since the family chasm developed. That day, young Robert, preempted the butler and answered the door. A look of astonishment, followed by rapid delight, danced across his young face and diffused any feeling of trepidation.

"Grandmother! Grandfather!" he cried and flung himself at his now less than dry-eyed grandparents.

They hugged. After he disentangled himself, he turned toward his uncle. Caution and uncertainty emanated from his young body until James grinned and asked, "How about a ride in your Uncle James's chair, Robbie?"

"I won't hurt you, will I?"

The boy asked in such a grave manner that Hallie couldn't keep herself from leaning over James's shoulder to say, "Hello, Robert, I'm Hallie, your uncle's nurse, and I assure you it's just fine to sit on his lap." Robert climbed onto his uncle's lap even before she returned to her standing position.

The stoic butler stood back with his mouth ajar as Hallie pushed James's chair past him. All eyes turned toward the stairs at the sound of Amelia's voice.

"Edgar, who—" The woman's face went very pale. "Robert, get off of Uncle James's lap this instant." She hurried down the stairs. Robert gave his uncle a quick kiss on the cheek and ran toward the parlor.

"Hello, Amelia," James said with his eyes twinkling, "I'm still kicking and so it seems are you." He laughed at the initial irritation on her face but sobered at the brief look of shame that followed.

She seemed incapable of speaking to him and turned toward her parents, who looked like unwelcome guests instead of family.

"Mother, Father . . . it's . . . good to see you. I heard you had returned and am glad your time in that savage place was not unbearable," she said with her hands clasped in front of her.

Judge Thomas Jackson entered the foyer followed by Robert. "Major, Welcome home." He shook hands with his father-in-law. He stepped back and inclined his head toward them. "Mother Hawkins, James." His eyes didn't acknowledge Hallie.

Thomas Jackson, a robust man with graying hair that made him look older than his deduced forty-plus years; ten years older than Amelia, who—according to James—shared Hallie's age.

Hallie saw something in this couple—something she never wanted for herself: a union built on social convention. It baffled her how the daughter of Susannah and Ronald Hawkins could be so different from the rest of her family. However, it made her wonder if James's injury may have altered these wonderful people whom she'd come to love. Perhaps Amelia offered a reflection of what had been, and the rest of the family had let God adjust them to the reality of unchangeable circumstances.

"Thomas, I see Robert found you," Major Hawkins said.

"Please forgive our unplanned visit. James wanted to see his sister," Mrs. Hawkins said.

Hallie wanted to scream and say something to bring Amelia to her senses. *How dare she make her parents and brother feel so unwelcome? Judge Jackson showed more kindness toward his in-laws than his wife did.*

"No, think nothing of it. Please come into the parlor."

Hallie pushed James to a warm spot next to the fireplace beside a brocade chair. James turned his head toward her. "Hallie, please have a seat."

His brother-in-law gestured toward the chair. "Yes, Please, Miss—"

She smiled. "Price, Hallie Price."

Major Hawkins seated his wife on the sofa and turned to make formal introductions. "May I introduce James's nurse, Hallie Price? She came to us at the fort and has done an excellent job."

Amelia's eyes held skepticism as they assessed Hallie. "That's strange. I heard James was sick upon your return." Then a brief look of guilt crossed Amelia's face as she realized the comment revealed her awareness of her family's activities.

"That was in no way Hallie's fault," Mrs. Hawkins defended. "Amelia, if you had ever cared to learn the details of your brother's condition, you would realize what a miracle it is that we still have him."

James's mother looked angrier than Hallie had ever seen her. The petite woman flashed indignant brown eyes at her husband and rose. "Ronald, James, this was a mistake. I will not sit here and watch my daughter start clawing at Hallie when she has nothing but selfishness and a lack of love for her brother. I would like to leave now."

Major Hawkins's eyes scanned the room as he took his wife's elbow. Grimness etched into his face as he said, "Thomas, I will not say more than how much this saddens me. Would it be permissible for Robert to see us to the door?"

Amelia placed her son in front of her with possessive hands on his shoulders. His young eyes widened and looked to his father who nodded his acquiescence. Robert started toward his grandparents, but then looked back at his Uncle James, who winked at him with a reassuring smile.

"Go on, Robbie. I promise that I'll treat your mother as you would your sister. We love them even when they irritate us."

The little boy seemed to sigh in relief and almost skipped to grab his grandfather's hand.

"Father, Hallie and I will join you shortly," James said.

The major nodded at his son and left the room with his wife and grandson.

"Judge, I hope you will allow me to speak freely for a moment." James started and received a nod from his brother in law. Amelia Jackson's lips tightened and she held her rigid posture as her brother began. "Amelia, I have always looked up to you and loved you. You were always so present for me until after the war. I admit it has baffled and hurt me. It has almost been like you were mad at me, and it would have been better to have a dead hero for a brother than a living cripple."

Hallie felt even sicker as she saw the woman pale, confirming the truth of her brother's words, as did the look of distress and embarrassment on her husband's face. James grew silent. Hallie caught a flash of hurt as it passed over his face. He bowed his head for what seemed an eternity as everyone waited; then he looked up, and his sister gasped at the tears on his face even as he smiled at her.

"Amelia, I forgive you. As terrible as your feelings and reactions have seemed, I know they're honest and no one can fault you for that. There was a time when I wished the same thing had been my fate. I just hope you'll try to find out how proud you can still be of me. The Judge can confirm the good name and reputation I've made on the hill.

"The difference is *now*, by coming here, I have made our reconciliation public for you, and you can have a public association with me. I am sure your friends will be able to congratulate you. Since these things are of value to you, I will provide them." He waited for his sister to meet his gaze. "Just know those things no longer matter to me. Relationships and helping change circumstances for the better in this world are my status symbols with goals far beyond this world. You matter to me Amelia, as do Robbie, little Clara, and your husband."

The room filled with painful silence. Amelia Jackson twisted the handkerchief her husband provided and dabbing her eyes as her brother finished.

"James, I . . . I . . . ," Amelia said

Hallie stood, circled behind James's chair, and pushed him forward.

Thomas Jackson stuck his hand down and squeezed his brother-in-law's shoulder. "James, you are welcome in our home and at my office any time. I would like to meet next week, if possible. There are some matters of policy and business I wish to discuss with you."

James inclined his head. "Of course, Thomas, I look forward to it."

"Miss Price, it's nice to meet you." The judge nodded to her, and she smiled.

Hallie pushed James to face his sister. His hand shifted forward.

"Amelia, look at me, and take my hand, please."

His sister's hesitancy dissolved as her eyes locked with his. Amelia's tears fell in earnest.

"James, what a shallow woman I have become. It was easy to get past until now. Seeing you . . . how could I have been so uncaring? I used to carry you around when we were little. You, my precious, so very special brother, were always so full of promise and plans for the future. You were supposed to take on the world and achieve more than any of us. I'm *so* sorry." Her voice caught and her husband came to put a comforting hand on her shoulder.

James let his own tears fall as he squeezed his sister's hand and gave her an endearing smile. "Come to see me. We'll have one of our debates about current literature. Mother and Hallie have tried to fill your shoes, but they don't have your lawyer-like skills."

They all laughed and Amelia leaned forward to kiss her brother's cheek. The group then moved to the foyer just as a much-disheveled young nanny descended the stairs with a screaming toddler on her hip.

"Mrs. Jackson, I quit. This child's inquisitiveness is excessive for her age. She's into everything."

The young woman pushed young Clara at her mother as she nodded to Thomas.

"Good day, Judge Jackson. I'll send for my things."

The blonde woman left in a huff of youthful indignation. Hallie had to give Amelia credit for having the instinctive reaction of a loving mother. She consoled her little girl with soft words of reassurance while rubbing Clara's small back.

The child calmed and laid her head on her mother's shoulder as she sucked her thumb. After a moment, the child's wails subsided and her small blue eyes noticed Hallie and James. Her head popped up and she pointed.

"Who dat, Momma?"

Amelia smiled. "Why, that's your Uncle James, Momma's brother, and his nurse, Miss Hallie."

The small eyes widened. "Nuse? Unca James sick?"

Thomas reached for his daughter. "No, sweetie, he isn't sick. He fell down very hard during the war and hurt himself."

Clara stuck her thumb back in her mouth as she eyed her uncle. A smile started as she reached both arms towards James.

"I want my unca."

James gave his niece a broad smile. He glanced at Hallie and she stepped forward.

"Here, Clara, let me put you on his lap. His arms can't reach up for you."

Once Clara landed in her uncle's lap, she turned to face him for a thorough appraisal. Once finished, she leaned over to place a wet kiss on his cheek. James looked as delighted as his niece did. Everyone laughed.

The door opened and Robert entered. "Excuse me, Father. Grandfather asked me to get Uncle James and Miss Price," he said and frowned at his little sister. "Clara, you should get down. Uncle James has to leave now."

Clara's chin started to quiver. "No!"

Amelia looked at her husband. "Perhaps, Robert and Clara would like to go home with James and my parents for the rest of the day. We need to discuss a replacement for Miss Donovan."

Robert's face filled with joy, and he ran out the door to fetch his grandparents.

When Major Hawkins and his wife entered the house of their daughter for the second time, a much different reception awaited. Amelia flung her arms around her parents.

"I am so sorry," she said.

Within moments, plans developed for Robbie and Clara to go to their grandparent's home for the afternoon. Amelia and Thomas would come to collect them that evening.

~~~

Elizabeth McDonald

The afternoon passed in a whirlwind of childhood exuberance and wonder. Clara and Robert delighted in their grandparents' houseguests, Mrs. Elizabeth McDonald and her grandson, Charlie Scott.

The older woman and small boy had traveled with them from Indian Territory. They met the Hawkins after Indians attacked their home, killing the boy's father and kidnapping his mother. A friend, Boyd Richards, negotiated her release from captivity. However, Molly Scott had a mental breakdown after her ordeal that necessitated placement in an asylum after coming to Washington. Young Charlie Scott loved his new friends.

The youngsters turned each adult in the house into playmates, including Major Hawkins. Charlie's grandmother, Elizabeth McDonald, took charge whenever vases came close to toppling or if they endangered the draperies. Laughter swirled throughout the halls, up the walls, and to the ceiling. It gathered all occupants within its echoes, transforming everyone.

Hallie hadn't been around children much, and it refreshed her. It caused the eternal child who still lives within each adult to surface. James's laughter echoed throughout the house. The afternoon removed years from his countenance. Mrs. Hawkins leaned over at one point to interject, "Hallie, look at James. Now, *that's* my boy."

Amelia and Thomas arrived in time for dinner. Following introductions to Mrs. McDonald and Charlie, Hallie caught Amelia watching the grandmother and grandson. After dinner, the judge's wife pulled her mother aside, and they asked Mrs. McDonald to join them.

Hallie leaned over to James. "What's that all about?"

His shrewd eyes studied his mother and sister for a moment. "I'm going to surmise that my sister has found her new nanny," he said, quirking an eyebrow as he looked up at Hallie.

"What? Do you mean, Mrs. McDonald? She can't. She has Charlie to tend, and Molly's care still needs to be overseen if she's ever going to come home."

James grinned. "Hallie, you really should not be alarmed. Once my sister gets something into her head, she will be as accommodating as possible. She'll move mountains to make sure things are to Mrs. McDonald's satisfaction. Besides, I think it may be just what little Charlie needs. He'll have Clara and Robbie to play with each day."

Hallie snorted. "Well, it's Mrs. McDonald's decision."

The details worked out with deft precision and everyone seemed satisfied by the end of the night.

~~~

Hallie emerged from her reflection when the porter touched her shoulder. "Excuse me, Miss, I wanted you to know the train was delayed. It's coming, but it may be an hour off schedule."

Hallie smiled in gratitude. "Thank you." She glanced around at the other waiting passengers for a moment. She sighed and fanned herself. These trips to Boston to see Julia tired her, but she remained convinced of the necessity. Her mind went to when she first met Julia Rigby in 1868. The woman brought more than herself the day she knocked on the Hawkinses' door. She'd come to meet James and check on any updates on her brother.

Hallie glanced at the diverse people in the depot; strange how lives formed connections that forever changed the dynamics for so many others. Hallie compared the events of that pivotal day with today's meeting with Julia. Her heart hurt for the woman but knew only Julia could make the decision to change. Many had. Of course, the circumstances differed. Like for her friend, Molly Scott. James had thought a lot of her.

Hallie stood and stretched her back. She paced a bit, but soon resumed her seat. These memories—often too tender to revisit—stayed pushed aside by her responsibilities. They continued to rush back.

~~~

Molly Scott

Mrs. McDonald had worked for the Jackson's for about two months when a messenger sent for her during the middle of the day. Almost a week had passed since her last visit with her daughter. Molly had spoken just a few times since their arrival in Washington. Most visits consisted of Elizabeth talking while Molly stared into space. The message notified Elizabeth of a change in Molly's condition. It requested a quick response.

Amelia expressed shock and trepidation once informed by her new, but now valued nanny, of the situation. However, graciousness prevailed and she released Elizabeth for the rest of the day and even watched the children on her own.

A few hours later, Elizabeth McDonald sent for Susannah Hawkins. The doctors requested Molly go home to be with her son and mother for a few days. It seemed she'd asked the nurse, "Where am I?" during breakfast the day after her mother's last visit.

The doctors had met with Molly. She remembered the Indian raid and parts of her brief period of lucidity at the fort but still had blank spaces, especially the periods of trauma during her captivity with the Indians. They didn't feel her ready to go home on a permanent basis but felt she needed a better environment than the frightening asylum. Her son's presence might facilitate more recovery. Therefore, Susannah assured Elizabeth of welcome in their home if Amelia and Thomas had objections.

However, the Jacksons asked to meet Molly before they decided. The small blonde-haired, blue-eyed woman touched their hearts, and they agreed even with reservations present.

Charlie showed reserve around his mother at first. He pulled away and hid behind his grandmother. Extreme sadness reflected on Molly's face. Young Robbie went to her with a big hug of welcome. Charlie then dashed out to claim his mother with a love-filled hug of his own. Hallie cried, as did everyone present.

Molly's traumatized mind, which shut out the rest of the world, often depleted her. As she attempted a tentative venturing out, none wanted to cause her to return to the place of locked isolation.

It took a period of alternating a few days with her remaining family and the rest of the days at the asylum with the doctors each week for the first month. After that, she saw the doctors one time a week. She gained some weight, and, for the first time since the tragedy in Indian Territory, Molly Scott came home.

Hallie and James grew to like the diminutive woman who showed a dry, quick wit and a tender heart. It became apparent she always expected the best; therefore, she'd met the face of brutality unprepared. They loved her gentle soul. She fought with low self-esteem and self-confidence at first.

In James's opinion, Molly's life didn't have the right emphasis. He knew she struggled as the result of a situation not of her making; however, she knew the Lord, so a life of promise still awaited her. He talked to Hallie and Amelia about an idea he had for something to help not just Molly but many others. The idea started after Julia's visit and grew in design as he had his father make some inquiries. James managed to find the support of many in the community. They continued to work out the details of the venture after he asked Hallie to marry him.

Amelia befriended Molly, much to the early dismay of her prominent friends. However, as Molly started accompanying her to luncheons to raise funds for James's project, the ladies started to see potential in the tragic young woman.

Molly started taking a more parental role with Charlie again. Therefore, Hallie requested that they ask Mrs. McDonald to take on the care of James for three afternoons a week after his proposal. Of course, Hallie retained primary care. The schedule allowed her to progress with her time at the hospital with Dr. Jones, join Amelia and Molly for matters concerning the project, and have more relaxed time with James.

~~~

Some of the restless passengers paced in front of her, but neither their impatience nor the noise of the depot reached Hallie. Memories brought a smile to her face as the swirl of recollections moved to their wedding day. That wonderful, summer day in August of 1868.

~~~

Their Marriage

Hallie wore a dress fashioned of ivory lace by Mrs. Hawkins's life-long friend who owned a small dress shop. Major Hawkins gave her away and then stood beside his son and son-in-law at the crowded church. She became a member of a prominent family that day. The well-ensconced family moved within the fabric of community, politics, and society in general. However, of all the impressive people Hallie met after the ceremony, none of them meant more than the men who had served with James during the war. They shared battle stories and escapades foreshadowing the man James could have become without his injuries. He would've gone on to a position of prominence, probably as a senator, and they would never have met. His original post-war path planned a return to Harvard. All these things went through her mind. Then a small voice inside her said, *But look at all he has accomplished as he is now.* He held a position of respect and made positive changes in many people's lives.

James looked so handsome in his suit with his muted-brown hair trimmed and groomed. The glow in his azure gaze brought tears to her eyes and quickened her heartbeat. Their eyes never left each other as they exchanged vows except in prayer. All could see their love. The absence of James's best friend, Eddie Rigby, saddened them, but he remained in Kansas on military assignment.

They returned home after the reception where Major Hawkins assisted Hallie in putting James to bed. The full day had exhausted him. Hallie knew not to expect a normal wedding night.

So she prepared for the evening without expectations beyond sleep in the same room. However, as she prepared to leave to change into her nightgown, James stopped her.

"Hallie, your things have all been moved to our chamber. You don't need to leave to change."

It then occurred to Hallie—as an unusual flush crept up her face—her new husband still desired to share what intimacies they could, even just watching her change into her nightclothes. Hallie made a decision. She knew James's physical limitations. It had seemed better not to frustrate him in this area. She realized her mistake.

Hallie locked the door with the skeleton key, laid her gown on the foot of the bed, and then disrobed without shame in front of her new husband. Neither spoke. The soft flicker from the oil lamp couldn't match the love between them. James's eyes sparkled with moisture as she crossed to the bed and then widened as she ignored the nightgown and slid in beside him. Hallie moved to his side and met his waiting lips. She'd never felt such a wonderful, mysterious connection to anyone in her life. They kissed and shared caresses as possible, talking and sharing in the discovery of one another as husband and wife. Then Hallie slipped out of bed to don her gown. She blew out the lamp and slid in beside her husband to sleep. He moved his arm.

"Come here, Hallie. I used to dream of having a wife to sleep with her head on my chest."

Hallie smiled in the darkness. As she settled on his shoulder in the comfort of the darkness, listening to his strong heartbeat, his voice rumbled against her ear.

"I want to end this special day with a prayer of thanksgiving."

She turned her head to kiss the bottom of his chin in agreement and shut her eyes in reverence. Deep emotion colored James's voice:

"Father God, Hallie and I praise you for your grace, mercy, and love. Only you could have worked out the details bringing us together. I thank you for the time you have given us to this day and for this very moment we are now sharing. Our time, our days are in your hands. We won't look back or too far ahead. I promise to cherish her every second we're given. If I ever get enmeshed in the things of this world, please remind me and forgive me. Hallie is a gift so far above anything I could have hoped or imagined coming into my life. I am so glad she became a choice for me. Thank you, Lord. Please bless our rest. In Jesus' name. Amen."

James finished and then turned his head to rest his chin on her forehead. "I love you, Hallie. Good night."

Tears coursed down her face as she turned into his shoulder. "I love you, James."

The peace of the night enveloped them in its peaceful shadows of slumber.

The golden days and months after their nuptials shone like a sunrise over a wheat field or the brightest rays glistening off the ocean. James gained weight. They both blossomed. Each flourished in their individual work, as well as the joint work done on James's project—now an active endeavor of a handful of very influential people within Washington and Georgetown. Each day became fuller than the last.

At the end of five months, they held the ribbon cutting ceremony for his project. It seemed the perfect start to the New Year. The Hawkinses returned home full of smiles and satisfaction. Major and Mrs. Hawkins helped Hallie get James to bed as usual and then retired for the evening. Though exhausted, the day's events exhilarated Hallie.

"James, did you see Molly's face when you made her co-director?"

"Do you think she's ready?"

"Yes, she—" Hallie stopped, noticing sweat on his face. Now winter, the room held a chill even with the warmth from the fireplace. Her nursing instincts alerted, and she crossed to feel his neck and forehead.

"Hallie, stop. It has been an unusually busy day. I didn't get my mid-afternoon rest. That is all. Now come to bed. It's time for prayers."

Hallie complied with reluctance, but as James closed his eyes in prayer, she sent a silent one of her own heavenward.

Close to dawn, overwhelming heat awoke Hallie. She flung a hand over her own sweaty forehead and opened her disoriented eyes. Noisy breaths came from the other side of the bed.

"James!"

She rolled over and reached for him. His skin burned her. She kicked off the covers and scrambled out of bed. She ran into the hall without stopping for a wrap. Her gown billowed as she ran for the room of her in-laws.

"Major! Susannah! Come quickly."

Candlelight flickered and James's parents soon followed her back to him. Hallie lit the lamp and began her medical assessment. James opened his feverish eyes and smiled at her.

"Hallie, it's fine. Don't look so serious."

She bent and gave his forehead a quick kiss before turning towards his father.

"Go get Dr. Jones, please."

The major nodded and left the room.

Mrs. Hawkins left and returned with more rags and cool water.

Dr. Jones returned with Major Hawkins within the hour. His lips compressed into a grim line during his examination of James. He looked up at the family surrounding the bed as he removed his stethoscope from his ears and inclined his head toward the door.

"James, we'll be back in a bit," Hallie said, brushing his sweat-soaked hair away from his forehead. Once in the hall, Dr. Jones released a deep breath as he met the expectant eyes of the Hawkins family.

"We've been here before, so we know James and God have a way of overcoming things, but I'm going to be frank. This time could be different. His lungs are congested, and I need to watch his output carefully. His kidneys have worked well to this point, but he has some swelling, which may . . . well, I will not speculate. Hallie, I know it will be a waste of my breath to ask you to allow Mrs. Evans from the hospital to take over for you, but I do want her to take over primary care. You are too emotionally involved."

"Dr. Jones, I can—"

"No, absolutely not, Hallie." He stopped her and turned toward James's parents.

"Susannah, Major, it's too risky to move him to the hospital at this point, so I'm afraid we must treat this house even more like a hospital than before." His expression broached no argument. "That means no visitors except for immediate family and no children. We cannot risk further infection. Mrs. Evans will take over the excellent sanitation habits Hallie has in place."

Hallie nodded. She looked at Major Hawkins. "I'll send a wire to Eddie."

He put an arm around his wife.

"Write it out and I'll send it. His commander will not be inclined to release him, but I'll try to get clearance and follow-up with his change in orders by lunchtime tomorrow. He needs to come this time."

A long night followed.

James drifted in and out of a feverish delirium. Hallie and her mother-in-law stationed themselves on each side of his bed. The doctor scheduled Mrs. Evans to arrive in the morning.

The next evening, Hallie breathed a sigh of relief.

"Eddie is on his way, but it will take at least a week by rail, so we need to pray," Major Hawkins said.

James opened his eyes at the sound of his friend's name. "Is Eddie coming?"

His father crossed to the bed. "Yes, son, so you get better. Let us make this a holiday for him, and I will take responsibility. Anyway, it's time to bring him to Washington. It will take a bit of doing, but you let me concentrate on that chore. You just get better."

James gave a weak smile. "Yes, sir." He turned his head. "Hallie, Mother, I want you ladies to go rest. It will not do me any good to have you two getting weaker from a lack of sleep. Please. Mrs. Evans is here. I love you both."

They each kissed him in turn and complied with his request.

The days seeped into each other. Hours of prayer, care, and cherished time of visiting spent. James's color improved and his fever broke toward the end of the week. Eddie's arrival coincided with these events.

As Hallie enjoyed lunch with James, the door burst open.

James laughed and then started coughing as he asked, "What are you wearing, Eddie?"

Hallie got him some water.

"It's your own fault, Hawkins. I come rushing here—weary and dusty from the train, but at least respectable looking in my uniform. Some woman named Mrs. Evans tells me you can't have any visitors. Thankfully, your mother intervened, and then she promptly rushes me inside to where your housekeeper prepares a bath. I tell you they would have bathed me themselves if I hadn't protested. If that wasn't bad enough, the clothes left for me after I bathed aren't from my gear. They're items I left at your old house in Boston before the war. They'd been stored at your grandmother's house with your family's things until they returned. Anyway, as you can see, they no longer fit. I'm not that scrawny young man anymore."

The pants fit so tight he didn't need the attached suspenders to hold them, and the woolen shirt stretched thin over his muscled arms and chest. The buttons threatened to give way at any moment. At least the worn, brown shoes fit.

"Oh, Eddie, welcome home." Hallie laughed as she crossed the room to hug her husband's best friend.

She didn't *see* the two friend's eyes meet as Eddie pulled her into a tight embrace, but she felt the emotion in the air shift and surmised the exchange. Eddie disentangled his bulky form.

"I think I've been had. You don't look sick to me. If you wanted me to come home for a few laughs, you could've warned me. I think I even saw a gray hair this morning," he said, stepping around Hallie to advance to James's side. He thumped his friend's shoulder with his fingers.

"You'd better be glad I can't get out of this bed and whip you," James joked. He turned his gaze toward Hallie. "*Sweet* wife, come here and kiss me, then please excuse us for a few minutes."

James smiled, but she knew he had much to say to Eddie.

"Very well, *my husband*, as you're much better today. Dr. Jones will be so surprised when he visits this afternoon," she said, crossing to the opposite side of the bed to comply.

"You two are enough to make me regret my disdain for matrimony," Eddie said with a smile.

Hallie squeezed his hand on her way to the door.

"Enjoy your visit, but don't allow him to become too long winded. We have to make him rest."

The twinkling eyes sobered. "Not to worry, Miss Price, oh excuse me, I mean, Mrs. Hawkins. I still can't believe it. James, you even managed to get married before me." Eddie smiled again.

Hallie shook her head and left. She knew part of what James wanted to request of Eddie in case he didn't continue to recuperate, but more remained. She surmised her husband's intent to take care of as many of the things and people within the realm of his responsibility as possible. Ultimately, he would leave all of it in God's hands; yet James felt God expected him to do his part.

She wouldn't ask James what he discussed with Eddie. If he'd wanted her to be privy to all of it, he would've asked her to stay. Nothing else mattered except his present improvement. He had little to no fever, but she wanted his urine output to be better and continued to encourage more water intake. Her mind remained so focused on his systems that she didn't notice Dr. Jones on the staircase until he spoke.

"Hallie, how is our patient today?"

Her direct regard met his. "His fever is down, he's alert, and he demonstrates increased stamina with a slight increase in his appetite. However, his output is still low."

The doctor nodded in satisfaction until the last. "Any swelling? Have you watched his diet?"

"Yes, I gave the cook strict instructions."

His kind eyes studied her for a moment. "Hallie, I'll go check him. You still haven't been resting. Now, don't deny it. Is Mrs. Evans with him now?"

"No, Eddie arrived a little while ago, and they're visiting."

The doctor rocked back on his heels. "I'm glad Sergeant Rigby made it. Actually, this will give me a moment to talk to you about a matter that has been on my mind. I discussed it with the major, and he feels you should make the final decision. Let's go down to the parlor."

Unease knotted Hallie's stomach as they descended the curving shiny oak staircase.

The doctor crossed to look out the window at the snow-covered lawn for a moment. He turned and crossed to sit across from where Hallie sat in a chair by the fire.

"I want to preface this by saying how pleased I am about James's current status. He appears to be mending. Although, I cannot say he's well until more of his systems become functional again. I hope what I am about to request will not be an opportunity for yet some years. Please try to think as a nurse and not as his wife for now. Also, know that James and I have discussed this, at his request, I might add, and he wants it done."

Hallie's voice stopped him, "You want to do an autopsy if James dies."

He heaved a sigh, "Yes. Most of the reports we have are on soldiers with spinal injuries who didn't live through the hospitalizations. The opportunity to examine his injuries—how and if they changed during these years—could teach us so much. Unlike many of the unlucky ones, James never had surgery. His were not bullet wounds, and his father forbade it from the time of his injury even while in the field hospital."

Tears clouded Hallie's eyes. She straightened her shoulders and gazed into Dr. Jones frank and earnest hazel eyes. "I'll agree under these conditions. *You* will complete the procedure with Mrs. Evans's assistance. Also, I want it treated like a surgery instead of an autopsy. The incisions must be precise and less invasive. No one at the funeral should ever have a hint it of it."

The doctor scratched his graying head and nodded. "Agreed, but I have one question. Why Mrs. Evans? Young Mary McWhorter would benefit from being part of this, as would you, if it was a different patient."

"No, young Mary will make a fine nurse, eventually. However, she doesn't view the soldiers with the injuries in the same way as Mrs. Evans. As a field nurse during the war, Mrs. Evans addressed soldiers with respect and honor. That's how I want James treated if that time comes."

Dr. Jones reached over and covered Hallie's hand. "You have my word. Now, I'm afraid Sergeant Rigby will have to allow me some time with James. My schedule is more pressed without my two best nurses at the hospital."

He smiled and rose. "Please go find Mrs. Evans, and tell her I need her assistance. I'll send Sergeant Rigby to you."

Hallie found Mrs. Evans visiting with Mrs. Hawkins in the kitchen. She gave her the doctor's message. The matronly woman with a well-weathered face and a will of steel rose to excuse herself.

"My son is being given the best care possible. Please know I include you in that statement, Hallie," Susannah Hawkins said.

Hallie walked behind her mother-in-law, placing her arms

around her shoulders as she bent to kiss her cheek. "Thank you, but I know Mrs. Evans and Dr. Jones are in a different category. They're pioneers of medicine who are trying to assure no medical lessons from the battlefields are lost. I share your esteem of their skills. It allows me to concentrate on being the wife James needs me to be right now." She squeezed Susannah's shoulders one more time and moved to sit at the table. A sip of the warm coffee her mother-in-law rose to pour for her seemed to spread a little comfort and fortitude through her weary body. She closed her eyes, but opened them at the sound of a familiar deep tenor voice.

"Is there enough for another cup?"

Mrs. Hawkins smiled and crossed to the curly haired man in the doorway. "Certainly, Eddie. I bet you're hungry. There is some pie to calm your appetite until dinner. Knowing you, it may take two slices." She led the man considered her second son into the room. He sat across from Hallie as Susannah moved about the room. The silver knife chimed on the china as she cut the slices of pie and the china cup tinkled on the saucer.

"Here you are." Mrs. Hawkins placed the pie and coffee in front of him with a look of warm affection.

Hallie shared a smile with her mother-in-law as Eddie finished one slice and started on the second without any dalliance.

"I might need to go and beg Mrs. Riley to start dinner early," Hallie said with a laugh.

Eddie looked up with a short-lived look of guilt. "No, no, this is fine. It's just I haven't had any pie like this since I left the fort. Mrs. Riley didn't make this pie, did she?"

Mrs. Hawkins gave him a pleased smile. "No, I did. I hoped you would arrive today."

He grinned and took a sip of coffee. His large hand held the cup around the rim instead of by the delicate handle.

"How does he seem to you?" Hallie asked.

Eddie glanced from one woman to the other as he returned the cup to its saucer. "He seems fair, but there's something different this time. Hallie, I hope you can explain it to me. Dr. Jones and his nurse ran me out of the room so quick that I couldn't pull one of them aside."

Hallie glanced at her mother-in-law. "Dr. Jones needs to examine him before we speculate, but I think something is happening with his kidneys," she responded and covered Susannah's hand with her own. "Now, I don't know if that's the case."

The older woman didn't speak for a few moments. She then reached for Eddie's hand. "Let's pray right now for healing and God's plan for this family. Eddie, please."

Emotion roughened Eddie's voice as the words rolled from his lips.

Three nights later, James's fever hadn't returned and his lungs sounded clearer; however, something remained wrong with his kidneys. All prayed it resolved. A catheter placement soon followed. She helped Mrs. Evans bathe James at bedside after bidding Eddie goodnight. The older nurse made a quiet exit, leaving them alone.

"How's the most cherished lady of my heart?" James asked with his lopsided smile aimed at Hallie as she came to his side.

"Brimming to overflowing with my love for you," she returned, caressing his cheek.

He returned her loving gaze. His azure regard caused her to catch her breath as love, grief, and hopeful longing mixed within a single moment.

"Come to bed, Hallie. I want to lay in the darkness and talk tonight," he directed with tenderness.

She'd returned to sleeping on a cot in the room since his illness and frowned. "James, I'll disturb your rest, and I—" She stopped at the look in his eyes. "All right. Give me a moment to dismiss Mrs. Evans for the evening."

She returned and changed into her nightgown. The golden light from the lamp captured the love on his handsome face as she turned down the wick, extinguishing the flame. She lifted the covers with care, checked his catheter, and slid in beside him. His voice echoed in the darkness as she came home to the familiar place by her husband's side, sighing as she laid her head on his shoulder.

"Hallie, I want to talk to you, and please listen before you interrupt me. My life has been very blessed from the beginning to now. I have very few complaints or regrets. How could I? I loved my life prior to the war, and I received an extension on life past the war, which many of my comrades didn't get. As I lay here, quite possibly at the end of my days on this earth—No, now, you promised to listen, Hallie," he stopped as she raised her head and then waited as she returned to her former place. She heard his voice falter,

"What I have left at this point are some hopes and prayers: Hallie, go to Jared and try to explain things as best you can. Try to find a way to keep my promises to him. I'll leave it to your discretion for when to introduce him to Eddie; I talked to Eddie today about "Hallie's House." He's in awe of what we've established with the help of the community, but he still has military responsibilities. God's timing will prevail and we . . . you need to wait for it. Hallie, please embrace my parents as yours forever. They love you and share my pride in your accomplishments. Go forward in your nursing, and explore the opportunities from our project to see where God might take you. He really does have wonderful plans for you with or without me, sweetheart.

"All that said, Hallie, I want to thank you for becoming my wife. The last six months have been the happiest of my life. Due to our travels and my illness, last Christmas was rough, but I loved this Christmas with the whole family together. I had joys, sorrows, contentment, but pure happiness remained missing until I found it with you.

"Watching you discover your purpose in life has delighted me. Oh, Hallie Price Hawkins, you must keep moving forward. I've been almost gone so many times, and we've known that the next one might be the last. If this isn't it, please remember this because I'm so tired my mind might not remember it as well next time," he laughed, but then grimaced.

Hallie rose up. "James, are you hurting?" She peered at his face in the darkness.

"Hallie, it's fine."

Their breaths fanned each other's faces. Breath, life, and love flowed in the space between them. As their eyes adjusted, they could see each other in the muted shadowed forms as if at twilight.

"Oh, Hallie, I love you so much. I ache with missing you, and I'm not even gone. Kiss me."

Tears coursed down Hallie's face as she kissed his forehead, followed by his cheeks, nose, and finally his lips. She pulled away and looked at him.

"James, you're my true love. God disproved all my theories about men by allowing us to fall in love. I knew what a good, Christian man you were before we married, but the husband you've been since our marriage has shown how genuine you are. I'm so grateful for you and am not ready to let you go. *Please* don't go, James." She dropped her chin and he kissed her forehead.

"It's not in our hands. You have to be ready and willing to embrace life without me. You have a great capacity for love and partnership. Don't harden your heart. Stay pliable in God's hands. Promise me, Hallie."

Hallie didn't want to listen anymore. She wanted to go to sleep and wake up with him healed.

"James, I promise that I'll always love you and will seek God's plan," she whispered and kissed his lips with the utmost tenderness.

She curled up against him and heard him take a breath of contentment.

"Now, I'll pray us to sleep," he said.

They prayed together, and she heard him say, "I love you, Hallie," as she drifted to sleep.

She slept better than she had in weeks for the next few hours. A little past midnight, Hallie awakened. A stillness filled the room that caused her heart to race. She lay motionless against James's side. As she allowed her senses to acclimate, the absence of the comforting sound of her husband's heartbeat reached her. She clutched close for a moment. Silence. *No!* She sat up and turned.

"James. James!" No movement. "No. No," she whimpered as she sprang out of bed, padded to the door and into the hallway.

She knocked on the door of the room next to theirs and entered the darkness. Mrs. Evans awoke, grabbed a wrap, and lit a lamp to return to their room.

Mrs. Evans placed the lamp beside the bed and examined James. She shook her head. Hallie could see James hadn't awakened and gratitude filled her aching heart. She crossed to him as Mrs. Evans left to alert the rest of the family.

She hummed a hymn, stroking his hair away from his forehead. She bent to kiss him. His parents and Eddie arrived as she straightened. Susannah emitted an anguished cry and crossed to her son. Hallie stepped out of the way and cried as she watched James's mother cradle his head against her. Major Hawkins went to stand behind Susannah and bent to hold her as she held their son.

Eddie stood stunned and helpless. Hallie found she couldn't move. Everything seemed unreal and too real at the same time. Hallie had a vague perception of Eddie as he moved to the foot of the bed, touched his friend's feet, and returned to take her in his arms. Numbness overcame her. After an uncertain amount of time, Dr. Jones arrived.

The rest of the night and week—even through the funeral—remained hazy images to her.

It took a month to function beyond a surreal level again. The strangeness of grief—just when she thought her emotions stable, something tipped it again.

~~~

Hallie hadn't let herself dwell so fully in recollection in the five years since James's death. The maze of memories created a barrier from the presence of someone in front of her. It took a soft touch on her hand and a pleasant, modulated tenor voice to direct her back to the present.

"Hallie?"

She looked up into the slanted, smiling green eyes of the friend James had loved like a brother, Lieutenant Edward Rigby. Everything slowed as her brain registered the train pulling into the depot, steam billowing from the locomotive engine behind the stocky form of their dear friend.

Hallie stood without a word and, for the first time since the day of James's funeral, bowed her head to cry. She didn't see the smile fade from Eddie's face or the tears on his cheeks, but she felt the strong arms go around her in comfort.

As the steam from the train swirled around them and people began to disembark, they stood apart within an oasis of friendship and shared grief. It seemed like an eternity or maybe just a moment; nevertheless, the echo of the life of James Hawkins reverberated throughout their very beings.

The conductor called, "All aboard."

Eddie took Hallie's elbow, bent to get their bags, and guided them to the train.

Chapter Two

HALLIE MANAGED TO compose herself as they found seats on the train. She slid in beside the window and waited for Eddie to fit his stocky frame into the space beside her.

He grimaced, "My body is tired of trains. My sparse regiment arrived in Washington, and I boarded another train headed here to see Julia; too much of a quick turnaround for me. Sergeant Case took my gear for me."

"I must have left right before you arrived at Julia's. I visited her today."

Eddie nodded. "I know. Actually, I was behind the curtain of that parlor by the door. Hearing your voice startled me, and I didn't say anything. Forgive me?"

"What? Edward Rigby! Of course, I'll forgive you if you promise to never do that again."

He held up his hands. "Promise. I thought you'd be almost to New York and ready to take the boat by now. I'd come to the station hoping a train might be ahead of schedule."

"Not ever. Mine was late, but I'm glad now you're here. So, update me. Your letters have been scarce of late."

A shadow crossed his face for a moment. He gave her a guilty look offset by a smile. "I know. Writing hasn't been a priority lately. I even got a letter from a nice young lady, which I never answered."

Her eyebrows rose, "Really? All right, details now. Who is she?"

He laughed. "Do you know Miss Mary McWhorter?"

Shock lifted her eyebrows. "Mary McWhorter? How do you know her?"

"Well, she met me before the war when she was very young; however, she never took any notice as she had a girlish affection for James. Anyway, it seems she heard me speak at James's funeral and now finds me of interest. Her father must be someone influential because I got a letter a week after I returned to Kansas. I wasn't interested at the time. So, you know her?"

Hallie smirked, "Yeah, I know her. She comes from a good family. Her father is an attorney. Mary is a nurse at the hospital and plans on entering nursing school in Connecticut this autumn. She's in her twenties and very pretty. Now, you must know, she hasn't been without interested callers."

She wanted Eddie to find someone. He'd led a solitary life outside of the Hawkins family.

"Well, does that mean it's not a good idea to call on her?"

"No, no. Listen, she'll be home this weekend. I'll invite her to lunch and make introductions." She patted his hand and his face brightened.

"You'd do that for me?"

"Of course, I would. You're like family and my friend, right?"

Eddie scanned her face. "Right."

Hallie licked her dry lips at the realization of the substantial passage of time since they'd last seen each other. His responses to correspondence became limited after James died and then ceased altogether during the past year. They had much to discuss, so she dove right in to the first topic on her mind.

"Was Julia receptive to you?"

He shook his head at the change in topic. "Yes, I plan to come back and take her to lunch next week. Once I report in, I have at least one-week's liberty. Now, I want to know about you. There was a delay on mail reaching me for a while, but I did get your last letter two days before I left. It sounds like Hallie's House and nursing are keeping you busy."

"Yes, a little too much at times. It's been tough since the

economic collapse in '73[vi]. Our contributions have dwindled. I'm not sure how the neighbors have felt about our vegetable garden, but it feeds us well. Molly and I are co-directors as we await the director to arrive. Once he's able to take his position, I plan to go to Boston to finish nursing school. Major Hawkins tells me we should have an answer about the gentleman soon."

No knowing flicker crossed his face as he interrupted her. "How do the Hawkinses feel about that?"

She smiled. "Actually, they have encouraged me to pursue the position. Susannah is so busy with Amelia. They're involved in community and church activities. Young Robbie and Clara keep their weekends lively. Major Hawkins may delay his retirement or run for congress."

Eddie's eyes widened. "Congress?" Then he laughed. "James would've loved that. Well, good for Major Hawkins. Congress needs to investigate more of the railroads. Although, I think the accountability is better now. I'm considering a position with the railroad if I resign my military post, as it's now an option."

Hallie studied Eddie for a prolonged moment before responding. "If you take the position with the railroad, where would you be?"

He blew out a deep breath and met her steady gaze. "That's the thing. I'm not sure. Hallie, in some ways it's a good time for that. I mean, I have no family depending on me right now. The way the railroads are growing, the best place to be is out west." He paused and turned his gaze toward the window where the dimming sky flickered by them. "You know, I got into Boston last night but didn't want to interrupt Julia at work in the evening. I just walked around, but didn't talk to anyone. Our old neighborhood is so poor and sad. Then I see Julia today, and she's still sad behind all of that hardness and flash." He turned back to meet her eyes. "She said you were trying to get her to consider working with a theater troupe. I might stay and get a small house in Washington if she did that. Otherwise, she doesn't need me, and it would be better for me to go west. I'm tired of the military, Hallie."

"Eddie, there are a few things you still don't know. Consideration of these may give you other options," she said.

He gave her a wan smile. "Are you talking about me

working at Hallie's House?"

She nodded. "So, you do know? Well, it's partly that. James did leave you that opportunity."

He rubbed his hand over his face, and she saw his weariness. She covered her own yawn as his green eyes opened.

"Eddie, I think a rest would do us both good at this juncture. We'll talk more later."

He nodded. She smiled and shut her eyes, sliding a little lower in her seat.

~~~

Eddie had hoped to stave off his weariness until they transferred to the boat, but his eyes grew heavy a few minutes after Hallie succumbed to a nap in the seat next to him.

Memories, fears, grief, and desires always mixed within dreams. For a soldier, times of sleep were often where the myriad of unbelievable horrors experienced in the past replayed. The subconscious found the freedom to release things suppressed and denied during the light of day. After the Civil War, Eddie had dreaded night; he would seldom sleep an entire night as explosions, fallen comrades, regrets, and guilt ravaged him. Thankfully, he could turn to God in prayer during those wee hours. Without the Lord, madness might have overtaken his mind. The years in Indian Territory had shown him a different enemy and a different type of warfare where the rules for one side differed by a wide chasm from the other. The unexpected and unanticipated intricacies of negotiations with these diverse people caused many misunderstandings of treaties. Eddie had learned to deal with the post status of any hostile encounter much better than during the war until his transfer to Kansas and Nebraska.

The government had regulated much of the Indian Affairs at that point, but not all. Some of the generals[vii] made substantial errors in judgment. These cost the lives of the men under their command, including a few of Eddie's friends.

An unexpected skirmish after his return to duty following James's death now provided the plethora of substance for the underpinnings of Eddie's nightmares mixed with bittersweet memories. The two years following his best friend's death had been the hardest and most unexpected of his life. His commander in Kansas had prevented his original plans to return to Washington within the year, even with the efforts of Major Hawkins on his behalf, in order to fulfill his promise to James. Instead, everything swirled out of his hands, and then the hands of those in authority over him lost their control as unforeseen events unfolded. The current reason for his return to Washington stemmed from the far-reaching repercussions. No one outside of Indian Affairs in Washington knew about the details of Eddie's experience except for Major Hawkins. The government kept the incident from public scrutiny. Eddie's patrol received orders to capture a group of escaped Indians, but things had gone array.

"Eddie, wake up."

His eyes opened to Hallie's concerned face. Adrenaline pumped, and his heartbeat raced for a few seconds before he could bring himself back into the present. He ran a hand over his sweaty face. Hallie handed him her handkerchief.

"Thanks," he said, sitting up as he dabbed his forehead and upper lip. He looked out of the window and then propped his elbows on his knees with his head down.

Hallie reached over to retrieve the wet hankie. Her cool hand felt the back of his neck.

"Do you want to talk about it?"

Her soft but firm voice told him she could handle the re-telling, yet he couldn't. He smiled and shook his head.

"Thanks for the offer. Not now. I know there will be a time when you'll be privy to the tedious and shocking details, just not now."

No sign of offense registered on her face. "Whenever you're ready, Eddie. I'm just curious about an odd word you called out."

He frowned. "What did I say?"

Her eyes pierced his in unwavering examination as she said, "Sunbeam."

He flinched as if slapped.

No! No—too many things lacked resolution. His eyes turned from her perceptive gaze to seek solace in the darkening sky through the window. He wouldn't lie; just defer for now.

He turned guarded green eyes on her. "It does sound odd unless you were there—in the place causing these dreams."

Her eyes never wavered. "Eddie, I won't push you. Just know how much everyone in the Hawkins family loves you. You have a family."

His words tumbled out before he could stop them. "I need to talk to James." He expected her to flinch; however, she only nodded with a smile.

"I understand, but since we can't, at least he left us each other."

He sobered. "That's what he wanted."

She reached over and took his hand. "I'm glad you're home."

He frowned as he stroked her hand with his thumb.

"Am I? Hallie, do you realize home is something of an illusion for me? The streets of Boston were my home until I found one with the Hawkinses in the same town. The row house the family had as a residence in Washington when James died is no longer theirs. They live at his grandmother's house in Georgetown. I visited that home just once with James. It's not home."

"Eddie, you must have learned by now—people make a home, houses are mere shelters. However, I'm not referring to the Hawkinses' house. I meant Hallie's House. James wanted it to be a home for both of us. I, I meant—"

He cut her off with an understanding smile. "Hallie, I know what you meant. It's just reluctance at managing a house full of women in difficult circumstances causing me to hesitate. Why James felt I should hold a position like that is a puzzle."

Hallie withdrew her hand and gave him a playful slap on the arm. "Oh, Eddie. Your position is more of managing the financial and administrative aspects—the parts I dislike the most yet have been handling. As I still work at the hospital during the afternoons, the house has succeeded because of Molly. She's a terrific asset with managing the women and running the day-to-day aspects of the house. We have Ian, an older Irish gentleman who works as a handyman and anything else needed as far as errands and fetching supplies. We have one young man who lives in the former servant's quarters off the kitchen. He's an ex-soldier with an artificial arm and leg. His family wanted nothing to do with him when he came home as they work as fishermen. He's bitter but working at the newspaper. Let me tell you how surprised some of the irate husbands or men acquainted with our boarders are to find out how fierce Micah can be. Molly doesn't have to worry about any of them storming the doors to retrieve the women with him there. We don't have servants. Each woman completes an aspect of the care of the house and the cooking. The toughest part is the counseling and finding them jobs. The church supplied a nice young man who just started in the ministry to help, but the ladies seem reluctant to take advice from him. They much prefer Molly or me. Therefore, you see, the women won't overwhelm you. In fact, it's *they* who'll be apprehensive, but we need you there. Truly we do, Eddie. Especially as I'm about to leave to finish nursing school in the Roxbury neighborhood in Boston this autumn, I started last year, but had to leave before graduating because of things with Hallie's House. Don't be shocked, but James's sister took over things in my absence but became ill. She's fine now. I have only three more months of training before I can graduate. Have you heard of Linda Richards?[viii] She was the first nurse to officially graduate from an established school—the New England Hospital for Women and Children. I went by there when I arrived yesterday to see Dr. Susan Dimock[ix] and everything is arranged. I want it to be official. It's a promise I made to James. Dr. Jones told us official nurse training programs would happen. During the last year, three started. I preferred Boston to New York or Connecticut."

His mind raced as he took in all she'd shared. He stopped her at this last part. "Wait, you're leaving? I thought you just agreed we could be there for each other, my dear friend." He tried to chide her in a playful manner but a serious edge lingered.

She laughed "Very true, but Eddie you'll be there for me by allowing me the freedom to now go to Boston without the need to come home every weekend and deal with the administrative duties. I'll be gone for the one session, and I don't leave for weeks. In a way, it might be an advantage for you. No one in the house can run to ask me when they need to ask you."

"Whoa, I haven't said that I'm leaving the military or not taking the railroad job instead."

Hesitancy showed on Hallie's face. "Well . . . you will . . . because, although I don't know the details of your last talk with James, I do know his wishes and the reason you have accumulated a salary over these years of absence. It's time you started earning it and fulfilling whatever obligation you made to James."

A quick flash of irritation, guilt, indignation, and anger went through him. Leave it to Hallie to get to the point—one of the things he'd disliked about her and then grown to respect. He compressed his lips to keep from telling her she had no right to talk to him that way.

"Hallie, excuse me for a moment. I need some air. It's much too warm in here." He stood and inched past her before heading for the door leading outside to the small-railed landing on the back of the train car. *Sunbeam*. His heart ached in a moment of honest anguish. He shut his eyes, took a deep breath of the evening air, and said a prayer. The soothing sound of the train passing over the rails and the breeze in his face caused him to linger there for longer than he intended.

Black had bled into sky when the conductor opened the door and said, "Sir, we have lit the lamps. Would you like to come back to your seat now?"

Eddie made his way back to his seat, trying not to meet Hallie's gaze as he squeezed past her to take his seat. Her rich voice bridged the silence first.

"Eddie, I want to apologize. Both of us have had many experiences since James died. I had no right to speak to you that way. The liberty I took came from the knowledge of our common tie to James, but it doesn't dictate your life choices. You must choose, just as I'm making choices for myself. We would love to have you as part of Hallie's House, but if it's not right for you, then I'll pay you your back pay and start interviewing others for the position. In fact, I should have done it about six months ago, but Major Hawkins requested I wait. It's time to find our paths. James meant well; it's just he's not here dealing with all the changes and obligations."

Eddie sighed. "Hallie, give me two more weeks, and you'll have your answer. Fair enough?"

She nodded. "Fair enough. Now, are you hungry? Julia always has their kitchen make me a travel meal when I visit. They always send too much." She reached into the small satchel she carried. "Let's see—we have chicken, bread, cheese, and a couple of slices of cake. We'd better eat. It won't be long before we get to

New York and change trains."

Eddie grinned. "I should have dashed into a restaurant before coming to catch the train. It's just my thoughts raced after my visit with Julia, trying to find a way to fix things for her."

Hallie extended the cloth napkin she held like a bag loaded with food. He smiled as he took it and opened the folded edges on his lap.

"Eddie, you can't fix things for her. We can give her opportunities, but *she* must decide to take them. Keep praying and visit her again." Hallie took a small bite of her chicken as she waited for him to finish chewing and respond.

"I already promised to take her to lunch. It'll be later in the week before I can go back to Boston. I have to check in before my official leave of duty can start. This is just a couple of days of liberty. My meeting with Major Hawkins and the War Department is a priority. All decisions about my future hinge on the outcome of the conclusions reached with those gentlemen." He waited for her to ask for clarification, but she didn't. Instead, she bent her head to get a bite of bread and cheese.

They ate in silence for a few moments. He shook his head in disbelief when she reached down and produced a corked bottle of milk.

"We'd better share it before it spoils," she said.

He watched her take a swig and remembered, as she passed the bottle to him, a time in her life when sharing a bottle of something stronger with the men in the saloon where she'd worked in Texas would have been normal. The creamy milk tasted so good to him. He heard Hallie clear her throat and laugh as he sputtered.

"Sorry, I didn't mean to drink so much."

Her boisterous laughter covered any discomfort he felt. "You left me a couple of swallows. No, it's good to watch you enjoy something."

He wiped his mouth with the back of his hand before passing the milk back to her. She took another sip and passed it back to him.

"You finish it. I think my cake needs to be saved for later."

Her eyebrow shot up as he hesitated; then he took the bottle. "Thank you, ma'am."

"You're welcome, Lieutenant Rigby."

He finished his dinner, including his cake, and drained the last of the milk from the bottle. Hallie held out her hand for it and stowed it in her bag along with the napkins. As she straightened, he couldn't keep from heaving a deep breath. Things weren't how he wanted them. Never plan too far ahead. Meet the sunrise with arms open, bask in the awe of the sunset, but don't overlook the treasures swirling around you between the two. Accept endings and beginnings as necessary parts of this life. He'd thought he knew those things when he'd returned to duty after James's funeral. Then unforeseen events had unfurled to teach him in unimaginable ways. Even this unplanned time with Hallie, qualified as one of those treasures. His eyes narrowed. He studied her, noting the differences made by time. Thinner in her face with just a slight more angular line to her profile. It made her doe-like eyes more of a focus. He reached over and kissed her on the forehead.

"Hallie, you're working too hard. I can tell even without being there to watch you."

He watched a brief tender look cross her face before a wry grin took its place. He moved back in his seat.

"Eddie, just tell me how awful I look. Goodness knows, everyone has always thought me older than my years."

"I never did. I told James you couldn't be more than four years older than the two of us after meeting you that first night. He wasn't sure until his birthday when you clarified things," he said.

She smiled. "I'm a mere three and a half years older than you as you were a few months ahead of James. Now, I can see you'll need guidance as you start courting Mary McWhorter. Don't discuss age even though she's much younger."

"Courting? Who said anything about courting? I'm just investigating possibilities. How about you? It's allowable for you to step out again. The mourning period has more than passed."

The smile that had lifted her full lips and caused a sparkle in her eye faded. "Eddie, don't. You were forthright about your interest in Mary because you're ready for a relationship. We're not in the same place in life. All the things in my heart, my grief, my love for James are mine. I have no plans to let any of them pass. Others don't understand. I need you to understand. I need you to allow me to be myself. It's important to me."

Everything inside of him went still.

"Why is my condoning something James was against so important to you? He didn't want you to become a Dickens' character."

Hurt and something else crossed her face as she turned away. "That's not fair."

"Fair? I think we both know James Hawkins was quite fair in his judgments. Not always, what we wanted to hear but always based on love and honesty. I know his last wishes for you, just as I know his last wishes for me. The odd thing is neither one of us have either been able to or chosen to completely honor those wishes. Believe me; guilt reigned for a long time on me about that. Hallie, look at me."

He caught his breath as she turned with tears on her cheeks. "Hallie, please listen to me. I've come to realize so many things since my last conversation with my friend. First, he voiced his hopes for our lives with all the information and knowledge he had at the time. Second, God had much more information than James did. He had paths for us with people and lessons for us beyond James. That's why we're where we are today. Third, our paths have crossed again. I don't know what that will mean, but I do know God gave James insight because we're sitting here tonight. I'll make a deal with you, Hallie Hawkins: I'll be your best friend. That means honesty, support, and unconditional love even when we disagree. The one thing capable of altering our relationship will be when and if we ever find a new life companion, and even then, we'll remain friends, just adjusted in respect to the wishes of the spouses chosen. If you're so inclined, is it a deal?"

She wiped her face and searched his. "I'll hold you to that Edward Rigby."

He nodded and hit the arm of his seat like a gavel on a block. "Good. Now, since we're about to make the train transfer— that would be better skipped to go directly to the boat, if I had my choice—I have a suggestion. As soon as we get on the new train, you use my substantial shoulder as a pillow and get some rest. Let me navigate us through the rest of the journey. Trust me to get you there, and just relax."

"You're dealing with a self-reliant woman here. That may be a tall order."

He smirked.

"You can do it, and we'll both be the better for it. Now, *there's* the depot."

~~~

The rest of the journey—with its many changes—passed with a nice compatibility. He caught up on Molly Scott's recovery, young Charlie, and the Hawkins family. Hallie shared a small description of each of the ladies at Hallie's House, as well as the success stories of the women who had moved out on their own.

It turned out he knew the ex-soldier, Micah Gallagher, who lodged at Hallie's House. 'Smiling Micah' had served in Eddie's infantry company during the war. The red-haired youth had made everyone laugh even after his injuries. He'd made jokes. The man Hallie described didn't match his memories. It seemed his time at the soldiers' home before coming to Hallie's had changed him. His family's rejection had broken him. Eddie hoped Micah might be open to rekindling an old friendship.

Hallie nudged him and pointed out the window. He could see Major Hawkins standing on the platform, waiting. The train shuddered to a stop. Eddie gathered their few items in one hand, and they joined the queue of people in the aisle.

Once the shuffled flow brought them to the steps leading down to the platform, Eddie took her elbow and helped her descend. He sidestepped a few fellow passengers before quickening his pace to guide them out of the throng and toward the uniformed man smiling at their approach.

The sound of the deep, granite voice stirred strong emotions. "Welcome home, Lieutenant. Sergeant Case notified me of your arrival and concurrent departure to see Julia. I've taken the liberty to check you in at headquarters. They know you are on official leave until after we meet with the War Department."

Hallie turned with a puzzled look that Eddie met with a smile and a shrug. However, as she turned to hug the major, he sent a warning look over her head to the man he viewed, not only as his superior, but also, as a father figure. The older man's eyes flickered as he mouthed, "Oh." Therefore, the man assumed Eddie had told Hallie everything, and maybe he should have. He shook his head and received a nod as Major Hawkins released his daughter-in-law.

"I'm glad the two of you got to travel together, Hallie. We had some surprise visitors last evening who I think you'll welcome. They are staying with us, and we would like you, as well as Eddie, to join us for dinner this evening."

"Really? I guess I must wait until then to find out the identity of these guests?" Hallie asked, laughing.

"Of course. So you'll come. How about you, Eddie?"

"Yes, thank you, Major Hawkins," Eddie said, "I wonder if we might have time to visit in private today."

The major shook his head. "We'll see to it tomorrow morning. First, I have a little more work to do so we can be ready for all our dinner guests tonight. You need to go and get settled at Hallie's now."

Eddie frowned. "Hallie's? I sent all but these few things with the sergeant. Don't I need to travel out to that mosquito infested fort?"

"No, actually, I arranged for you and the few returning men from my original company to stay in the barracks in the middle of the city until we decide on the best place for a dispersed diplomat or discharge. You men should have returned to Washington a year ago, but we'll discuss the situation more tomorrow. As for you—due to the special leave granted at this time—the arrangements are a little different. I believe Hallie has kept a room for you all this time. Haven't you, my dear?"

Eddie closed his eyes to shut out the scrutinizing stare Hallie now locked on him. "Yes, yes, I certainly have," she said after a prolonged pause.

Major Hawkins smiled in satisfaction, seeming to enjoy Eddie's discomfort. "Eddie?"

"Yes, sir, but I'll need to retrieve my things from Sergeant Case because I'm sure he held on to them for me."

"He did, at my allowance, I might add," Major Hawkins answered, lifting his chin.

"Of course, sir."

Eddie hated the complications and conflicted interests. He already regretted his less-than-forthcoming conversation with Hallie on the train. A strong hand landed on his shoulder, and the major leaned forward to speak next to his ear with a voice choked with emotion.

"Son, let it go for a while. You're finally home. As you come to dinner tonight, allow yourself to just be Eddie Rigby, the best friend of my son, and in our eyes, a son in your own right."

The lump in his throat prevented more than a nod in response. Major Hawkins gave him a hardy slap on his back and took the bags from him. Eddie offered Hallie his arm, and they headed for the buggy where a driver awaited them.

Eddie looked at the changes in the city as the buggy took them through town. Flashes of when he marched with the troops down Pennsylvania Avenue overtook him. All the regiments had looked so noble and splendid, blue uniforms so sharp and new. Not many had sought Washington as a residence—except for politicians and those from old families—due to its close proximity to squalid conditions in many areas. The war changed a city with a former Southern slant for life. Major Hawkins wrote him about all the physical changes made during his years away, including Shepherd's[x] vast work on improving the roads and the city in general. Many grumbled at the inconvenience during the process, but now the consensus leaned more toward satisfaction. He shut his eyes. The buggy bumped along, and Hallie related the details of her visit with Julia to the major.

As she talked, Eddie allowed a light slumber to overtake him. The conversation of his companions sounded discernible but distant in the realm of his light rest. Major Hawkins interrupted a few times to ask questions. They discussed a few unfamiliar names. It might take him a while to learn all he'd missed and to meet all the people now sharing in the daily lives of his friends. He opened his eyes after he heard one name mentioned several times.

"Who's Jared?" he asked.

Hallie looked startled. "So, you're awake. Well, I think you may be about to meet him."

The buggy pulled to a stop in front of a large two-story house with an ornate wooden sign reading:

Hallie's House
Established by James and Hallie Hawkins and Community
1869

Eddie jumped down and turned to assist Hallie. The major tipped his hat and then answered Eddie's salute. The driver placed the bags on the porch and returned to the buggy.

"Susannah and I will expect you by six-thirty this evening. Dinner will be at seven o'clock," Major Hawkins said.

Hallie waved and walked toward the porch, leaving him to follow. They'd no sooner reached the steps than the door opened and two boys—followed by a pretty, blonde woman—almost knocked them down as they rushed through the mahogany framed entry.

"Jared Hawkins Rigby, you give that boot back right now!" the young woman shouted.

"Yeah, Jared, it's mine," whined the smaller of the lads.

Both boys looked about eight or nine. The one who held the boot and smirked must be Jared. He had curly blond hair and brown eyes full of mischief.

"No! Charlie has played inside with it and that puppy all morning. They both need to come outside. We're usually stuck inside most of the week. Since we got the day off, I want outside. Besides, you should be grateful. If my uncle weren't coming home today, we would both be at the Jacksons."

The young woman looked above the boys' heads to where Hallie and Eddie stood.

Eddie recognized her—Molly Scott. He glanced at the boy with the smaller stature—Charlie. Her son had grown. His glance returned to the other boy, and his eyes widened. Both women watched him.

Jared turned. "Hey, Mrs. Hallie, how's Julia?" he asked with a grin.

Hallie frowned. "Jared, what have I told you about that?"

The boy rolled his eyes. "How's, Ma?" Then, without waiting for a reply, his eyes narrowed as they moved to Eddie. "Is this my Uncle Eddie?"

Those words punched Eddie in the gut. His emotions went through the entire gamut: surprise, shock, joy, anger, and betrayal—with the last the most pronounced. Why hadn't Julia told him he had a nephew? Why had the Hawkinses not written him about Jared? Moreover, if James had known before he died—

"Eddie, take your time. It's a lot to digest. I promise to

explain everything to you," Hallie said in a quiet tone, "but he is your nephew and has anticipated your arrival these past years. You *should* have met him after James died. Just remember, his feelings must come before your own."

He gave her an accusing look, but he turned with a big grin on his face.

"Yes, Jared, I'm your Uncle Eddie. I'd love to shake your hand," he said, removing his hat.

Jared grinned back and stuck out his hand. "Your hair is like mine. Mr. James said I'd know you because we look alike."

Eddie worked to keep the smile on his face. So James had known. He couldn't think about it. Instead, he looked at young Charlie who watched him with uncertainty.

"This can't be Charlie Scott," he said with mock shock. "He was such a little boy when I last saw him. You're a big boy now."

Charlie stuck out his chin. "I'm nine. I don't remember you."

"That's all right. I bet your mother doesn't remember me either, but it's nice to see you both again," he said, looking from Charlie to his mother.

She blushed. "Actually, I have one fleeting memory of you at the fort, but it wasn't until I saw you today, and you have forgotten meeting me at James's funeral. I couldn't bring Charlie around James when he was ill, so I didn't welcome you then. Welcome, Corporal, I mean Lieutenant."

Eddie had forgotten her young age at the time of the Indian raid on the Scott's family farm—not more than nineteen. That meant she'd now reached her mid-twenties. He frowned and tried to remember. A vague recollection of someone on the church pew with Mrs. McDonald came to him.

"That's right. Please forgive me. Thank you."

She turned. "Boys, let's go get our baths. We have a special dinner at the Hawkinses' tonight."

"Baths!" Both boys exchanged looks of horror and ran in the wrong direction.

Molly threw up her hands and hurried after them.

Eddie put his head down and took a few deep breaths. He turned to find Hallie waiting with grim understanding on her face.

"Eddie, come into my office where we can talk and even yell if you need to," she said.

He nodded and in a display of half-hearted gallantry, gestured toward the door. He waited as she preceded him into the house. His mind focused on the fact that his sister and friends had withheld his nephew from him. He didn't notice the interior of the house or the people moving up and down the staircase who stopped to watch his and Hallie's entrance.

Hallie opened a closed door, lit an oil lamp, and motioned him inside.

"Please have a seat, Eddie," she said, moving to the chair behind a plain wooden desk.

He shut the door with reluctance and complied. The atmosphere made him feel like a child called before the teacher. He hadn't felt this angry since he left school at the age of eleven. His eyes flashed.

"Now, this is the Eddie I first met at the fort. It turned out you had a reason to be cautious about me. You must think you have reason now, but if you'll let me give you the story from the beginning, I'll save you a lot of embarrassment," Hallie said.

"Embarrassment? Why should I be embarrassed? This had better be some story. Go ahead," he returned.

She waited for a minute as if anticipating another outburst. When she seemed satisfied, she folded her hands on the desk in front of her as she began. "We'd been home for three months when Julia brought Jared to meet us. She decided to keep him after his delivery instead of taking him to a children's home. She'd never been pregnant before and had a little uncertainty about who the father was. Although she thought she *knew* because . . . well . . . that can wait until later. Anyway, Jared had been living at the brothel with her. All the women there helped raise him to that point. They're all his mothers in his young mind. At the time of her visit, Julia had come to Washington to enroll Jared in a school for boys as a toddler. The school didn't welcome them. Therefore, she came to the Hawkinses for help. Sure, she'd thought ahead when she gave Jared his middle name of Hawkins. It created the potential of relationship. Now, get that look of disgust off your face. Until you're a female in Julia's situation, don't judge. Let me continue. Julia didn't ask for financial help; she needed us to take him for a time as the school wouldn't admit him until he the age of four years—if they approved his application. She paid for all his expenses. Once the school accepted him, she paid the tuition for his schooling each year until he changed to public school to be with Charlie. The Hawkinses let him stay with them until he entered the private school. Then he came to live here after James's death. James wanted to write you immediately, saying how excited you'd be to have family; however, Julia stated she'd take Jared back to Boston with her if he did that. She didn't want you to come home and jeopardize your military career because of a decision that she'd made. We planned to tell you following your return to Washington. James and I got to know Jared. James told the boy all about you. He promised him his uncle would come home soon to meet him. But when you came home, James was sick. They didn't allow any children, including Jared, into the house at that time due to potential infection risks. Molly and Charlie moved into the Hallie's House, so Jared stayed with them those weekends. No young children came to the funeral, so you didn't meet Jared there. Please forgive the Hawkinses and me. Our grief-filled minds couldn't see past the loss of James. You left right after the funeral. Once my mind started to function again—during the terrible after calm—you weren't there. I received a letter from Julia inquiring if you had returned and met Jared. Of course, I told her no and asked if I could write you about him. She remained adamant and reiterated that she'd only allow it when you returned for good. Now, the story and the people in it aren't without fault, but Eddie no one wanted to hurt you."

Eddie heard the words in a surreal haze. "Hallie, I know you're used to handling men, but try not to handle me."

She bowed her head and then met his gaze. "Go ahead and lash out at me. It won't change anything. Once you're able to get over your self-pity and selfishness, you'd better consider a few things. Why would the Hawkinses, James, or I help Julia or Jared if we didn't love you? I travel to Boston three times a year to give Julia updates, and she sends funds for Jared's care. The economy has been horrible, and things haven't been easy. Jared is a healthy and happy boy who could really use you in his life right now. He isn't much younger than you were when your mother left, so you might take that to heart and see if you can help him. As for me trying to handle you or any other man, you don't know me at all. My father couldn't wait to get rid of me once my mother died. His answer—my first husband, who saw me as someone to warm his bed and complete the chores he didn't like. As I'm barren, no children made those years better. After he died in the war, I chose the life of a soiled dove. Even then, I wasn't handling men, just trying to control my own life. I'd been at the saloon for a few years when Ted Dalton walked through the door with Boyd Richards— the first man I'd met who simply wanted to have a real conversation with me. He listened to my story and then left. I praise God for sending him because he led me to James, who led me to Him. I'm still not perfect, just forgiven. If God can forgive me, I hope you can." She stood and came around the desk to stand beside him. He refused to look at her. "Eddie, the office next door is yours. It's been waiting for you. The board has wanted to hire someone else, but it was part of James's original proposal. They have agreed to wait until the end of the year before amending it. The salary has accumulated from opening day and saved for you even in these difficult times. I've performed your duties and received no pay. James left his savings and inheritance from his grandparents to me, and I have my nursing salary while I'm here. I have saved, as there's no pay while finishing nursing school." She stood. "I have something to see to and then must get ready for the dinner tonight." He kept his eyes down. She sighed and crossed to the door. "No matter what you decide, please attend tonight. You do owe the Hawkins family that much. Besides, I have the feeling you have your own secrets. Please know I'm here when you're ready to talk."

After Hallie left, Eddie pondered all she'd said. Her words stung in places, yet he couldn't deny their truth. In the end, it all came back to Julia. He released his anger over her abandonment when he left Boston, but today's discovery fanned the embers of his anger. He loved his sister and seeing her . . . He ran a weary hand over his face and then did the first sensible thing he'd done since they arrived at Hallie's House: he prayed.

~~~

Hallie had just started up the stairs when she heard Eddie's voice.

"Hallie, wait a moment, please," he requested as he reached the foot of the stairs.

She sighed and retraced her way to meet him on the last step. His worse-than-anticipated reaction to Jared shook her. Although she understood part of it, she wouldn't tolerate his verbal attack. Some of the ladies who now found shelter in this home had suffered physical and verbal abuse to a devastating degree. A hint of it laced Eddie's words, but she didn't put him in the group with those men. However, from what she knew of Eddie's childhood and adolescence before he met James, it—

"Yes, Eddie?" She looked up and marked the slight redness of his eyes. She relaxed a bit.

"I just wanted to apologize for my pitiful reaction. Jared is my nephew. That's the best welcome home present." He gave her a sheepish grin.

She just nodded and waited.

He shut his eyes and twisted his hat in his hands. His green eyes pled with her as he looked up to her vantage point on the step.

"Hallie, I had no right to make a personal attack on you. No right. Please forgive me."

A picture of him and James came to mind. "It's been a long couple of days, Eddie. Let's go back to where we left things on the train."

A thankful smile lit his face. "I'd like that. Thank you. Now, where's that nephew of mine?"

Hallie inclined her head and looked toward the second floor. "Probably giving Molly fits about wearing his Sunday clothes to dinner. Go on up, I'm sure he'd be pleased for a bit of a rescue. One warning: Don't let him fool you. He's got a bit of a scoundrel in him at times."

Eddie laughed. "Good—he wouldn't be my nephew if he didn't. Would it be all right if I took him with me to pick up my things at the barracks?"

"Of course, he'll love it. Just be sure and be on time for dinner."

She laughed as he took the steps two at a time. "Second door on the right. Be sure to knock."

Eddie gave her a little salute. She watched as he approached the door, knocked, and entered. She then headed to her own room to get ready.

~~~

Eddie heard Molly Scott's voice call, "Come in," after he knocked.

Molly glanced up with a slight grimace. Jared squirmed as she tried to fasten his collar to his shirt.

"Jared, hold still," she said.

"Here, let me." Eddie stepped in between his nephew and the tired young woman.

Jared stilled as his burley uncle's hands finished the task.

"There. Now, the trick is to endure the wearing of it," Eddie said with a grin and a wink.

Molly took the more compliant Charlie by the hand. She faced Eddie with a grateful smile.

"Lieutenant, it seems you always come to my rescue," she said, then at his puzzled look, "My ma told me how you helped look after me at the fort. I wanted to thank you."

Her heart-shaped face now showed expression, and her blue eyes no longer held the former trance-like stare. He noted the beauty of the restored young woman. He hoped life held many good things for her and little Charlie.

"What can I say? I'm good at rescuing pretty damsels." He delighted to see her redden and added, "You're very welcome, Mrs. Scott."

Jared's voice drew his attention. "Hey, Uncle Eddie, don't you have to bathe and change, too?"

Eddie laughed. "Yes, I have to suffer your fate, except it'll be a clean uniform for me. I'd like you to go to the barracks with me and meet my friends. I can get ready there and pick up my things to bring here for my visit. Would you like to come along?"

A smile encompassed Jared's face. "Sure! Can I, Mrs. Scott?"

Molly laughed with delight. "Certainly, just go easy on your uncle and stay clean for dinner, okay?"

"Yes, ma'am."

Jared headed for the door, and Eddie tipped his hat and dashed after his nephew. He caught up with him on the porch.

"Hey, hold it a minute. I hope you weren't planning on

walking. It's a ways to the barracks, and you'll mess up your dress duds. I'll check with Hallie on the best place to catch a hack or a streetcar."

Jared rolled his eyes, placed two fingers to the corners of his mouth and whistled loud enough to make Eddie's ears tingle. After a few moments, a sturdy old Irishman with a thatch of graying red hair appeared in a wagon at the front of the house.

Eddie eyed his nephew. "Now, how did you do that?"

Jared furrowed his brow. "Ian's job is to wait for my whistle every day." Then, as Eddie gave him a look of skepticism, he grinned. "Not really. I knew you must've asked Mrs. Hallie's permission, and she would have Ian ready to take us."

Eddie nodded, stroked his chin for a moment, and then squatted in front of his nephew.

"Well, as you are *my* nephew, I can take you with me anywhere that I like once your mother and I have a discussion. However, as you *are* in the care of Mrs. Hallie, I'll keep her aware of my plans and won't interfere with you when you're at school."

Jared's brown eyes studied him for a moment. "Uncle Eddie, does that mean that you plan to be around here to see me?"

Eddie smiled, "You'd better believe it."

Ian cleared his throat. "Would the two of you be minding the time? We best be going."

Jared dashed off in a second, "Beat ya!"

Eddie ran to catch him and clambered into the wagon a second behind his nephew.

~~~

Hallie laughed as she dropped the curtain back into place over the window in her second-story bedroom. She turned as Molly rushed into the room and passed her to the window.

"The rest of the ladies were crowding the front windows downstairs," she gasped.

Hallie quirked an eyebrow. "My, my, our lieutenant has sure caused quite a stir. Molly, please come button me." She turned her back toward Molly. The smoky blue silk dress with the black velvet trimmings remained her best. James had commissioned a seamstress in Boston to design and make it. His mother had provided the measurements as he'd done it as part of her wedding gift. She adored it, but the multiple buttons from the back neck to the waist challenged her, and she found it impractical for daily wear. She'd worn it the night of the dedication of Hallie's house; the last night James left the house. She remembered the way his eyes had glowed in admiration as she descended the stairs to where he waited with his parents that evening. He said the blue hue set off the sheen of her midnight hair. Even though he often declared her beautiful, Hallie hadn't believed it until that night. She came close on her wedding day, yet that day seemed so surreal nothing external could reach her heart except James's love. However, the night of the dedication differed in its vibrance. The authenticity of the strands of love and trust woven into a strong marriage validated every look and word they shared. She'd received his admiration and reflected it back without hesitation.

Molly reached the halfway point with the long line of buttons and paused. "Lieutenant Rigby has the house in a state. I don't think anyone considered the mysterious and long awaited director would be so handsome."

Hallie turned. "Handsome? Eddie?"

Molly gave her an incredulous look. "Yes—Hallie, please tell me you can at least acknowledge a handsome face and a strong form on a man."

Hallie turned forward and Molly resumed her buttoning task. "Well, I really haven't thought about it since James died. Especially, not about Eddie. You see we didn't start out exactly liking each other. Now, he's a friend. He can be very charming . . . he is . . ." her voice trailed off as she considered the impact this could have on the house.

"There, all done," Molly said; then, as Hallie turned, she added, "Lovely."

"Thank you, Molly," she said and then frowned. "We mustn't let the ladies lose their heads over Eddie. If he does decide to take the directorship, they must view him as a director, not a potential suitor. Besides, he's shared his intentions of calling on Mary McWhorter."

Molly sighed. "Very well. I'll share the news with everyone."

Hallie looked at the pretty young woman in the green taffeta dress, which a family in the community donated to the house. So young to be a widow, especially under such tragic circumstances.

"Molly, I've never really asked you about your relationship with Hank. Was it a good marriage?"

Molly's eyes widened, and then a reflective smile appeared. "Yes, it was, Hallie. Hank was about seven years older than I was. We met during the war when his regiment stopped by our house. His parents died before the war, so he came directly to my house at the end of the conflict. We married and moved to Indian Territory because Hank wanted to make a life for us in a new place. He felt suffocated in town after the war. My mother loved Hank and chose to sell our family home to go with us. You see, my father died when I was ten. Starting the farm was hard, but I loved it. We were expecting Charlie when we first moved there, and once he arrived, it made things even better. It satisfied me to work beside my husband, knowing the outcome took care of our family. I miss Hank and our life together."

"Do you think you might marry again?" Hallie asked.

"Yes, I'd like to. The little apprehension I feel is due to my breakdown. Will I ever be able to let another man touch me? Not because of Hank but because of the Indian that hurt me. The doctors seem optimistic, but I'm not sure. What if I snap again? All these things churn inside of me, but then a small voice seems to say, "Trust me," and it must be the Lord urging me to try. I'm going to trust it'll be someone very special who's placed in my life because Charlie is also involved. How about you, Hallie? Will you marry again?"

"No, I don't think so. You know my story, and then there was James—the closest thing to perfection in a man and husband for me. Anyone else would be unable to reach his level in my eyes," she said with a knowing smile.

Molly reached to take her hands. "Hallie, please don't take this the wrong way. Don't compare others with James. He truly was unique and special for you just like my Hank matched me, but they're gone. It's natural to make small comparisons, but no one can take their places. God doesn't send replacements. He sends individuals. Sometimes, it's because He knows we need them, they need us, or both. If God sends you someone who stirs your heart again, don't ignore him, Hallie. After all, your heart belongs to

Him first." She gave Hallie a firm hug. "Well, I'd better go find Charlie. You need to hurry as well. I forgot to tell you that a note arrived this morning from Mrs. Hawkins. She's sending a carriage for us this evening."

Mollie departed and Hallie drifted to the dresser where her evening bag lay. As she retrieved it, she checked her reflection, lingering a moment longer than usual. She laughed and crossed to the door. Never self-indulgent, she refused to start now.

~~~

Elizabeth McDonald answered the door at the Hawkinses' residence. She smiled with a twinkle in her eyes as she took Molly's and Hallie's evening bags and wraps.

"Good evening, Grandma," piped Charlie.

"Why, don't you look grown up, Charlie," exclaimed Mrs. McDonald, hugging him.

"Please take these things to the study as fast as you can, and come back here. I want to introduce some very special people. Actually, you've met two of them before, but you were too young to remember."

Charlie's eyes widened. "Oh, boy, I'll be right back."

He dashed off and returned before the three ladies stopped laughing at the enjoyment of his youthful excitement. Mrs. McDonald displayed a secretive smile as she turned toward the closed doors of the parlor.

As the doors opened, the small group observed seven people engaged in an animated conversation, which ceased upon their entrance. All heads turned toward them, and the four men in the group rose to their feet.

Hallie's heart leapt at the sight of the familiar faces of three of the guests. She gave a broad smile as she moved ahead of Molly.

"Boyd Richards, you are indeed a sight for sore eyes, as is your lovely wife," she said, and then glanced at the man beside the piano stool. "Billy, you sure have filled out into a full grown man. My, my."

A flush of red crossed the young man's face. "Good to see you, Miss Hallie."

A tall, beautiful woman rose to stand beside the handsome

golden-haired man Hallie had first greeted.

"Miss Hallie, I mean, Mrs. Hawkins, it's so good to see you," she said as she leaned to embrace Hallie.

"Lucy Kennedy Richards, don't call me anything except Hallie. Now let me look at you. Yes, I would say marriage agrees with you. Of course, I don't see how it couldn't. Next to my James, you've got the best man I've ever met."

Then something unexpected happened as she met the golden gaze of Boyd Richards: tears sprang to her eyes. His smile faded, and he exchanged glances with his wife and pulled her into a warm embrace.

"Thank you for sending me to James," she said over his shoulder.

"I'll second that," Major Hawkins interjected, smiling at them and then at his wife.

"So would I," a tenor voice said.

"Me, too," a child's voice added.

Hallie pulled back and turned to find Eddie and Jared entering the parlor. Boyd stepped forward with his hand outstretched.

"I see your rank has increased since we last met. It's good to see you again, Lieutenant Rigby."

"And you as well, Mr. Richards." Eddie shook his hand and then pulled Jared in front of him. "Jared, I'd like you to meet Mr. Boyd Richards."

Boyd grinned as the solemn lad reached out and up with his hand. "Hello, Jared, it's nice to meet you. I'd like you and your uncle to meet my wife, Lucy. You can call her Mrs. Richards."

Lucy Richards lowered her tall frame and flashed a dimple as she smiled at Jared. "It's lovely to meet you, Jared." She straightened and inclined her head toward Eddie. "You also, Lieutenant."

Jared looked way up as he reached to take both of them by a hand with him in the middle. "Come on, I'll introduce you around."

Boyd and Lucy shared the smiles of everyone in the room while Jared led them to Molly and Charlie.

"This is Mrs. Molly Scott and her son Charlie. We're friends."

Molly had tears streaming down her face, and Jared let go of the hands of his new acquaintances to hug her.

"It's all right, Mrs. Scott. He's not as scary as he looks."

Molly laughed a bit through her tears and shook her head. "No, no, Jared. I'm not afraid of Mr. Richards. You see he's the man who made the Indians let me go."

Jared had been told the story by Charlie, who didn't remember on his own, but from the events recounted by his grandmother. Once Jared came to live with them, Charlie told him how the brave cowboy stood up to one of the captured Indians and demanded he return to his tribe to arrange for the release of Mrs. Scott.

"Oh," Jared said in awe and sank down beside Charlie, whose eyes were as wide as an owl's on a dark night.

"Mrs. Richards, I'm so indebted to your husband," Molly said.

Lucy stepped forward and gathered her in a hug as Boyd said, "Mrs. Scott, I'm just glad God has restored you to your family. Your state saddened me when we made our return stop at the fort. You've remained in our prayers."

Mrs. McDonald moved to stand beside her daughter as Lucy moved back beside her husband. Molly leaned against her mother.

"We both thank you."

Charlie pulled on his grandmother's skirt. "Grandma, if this is Mr. Richards, where are the other cowboys you told me about? I want to meet them, too."

"Well, dear, all the rest are in Texas except for Billy over there. He's the one who played the harmonica for you."

The boy's eyes went to the young man who moved forward from his place beside the piano.

"That can't be Billy. He's too old. You said that cowboy was just a boy himself." He frowned with irritation.

His grandmother smiled. "I said he wasn't more than a boy himself at the time. He's actually about a year younger than your mother if I'm estimating right."

The sandy haired man in question looked startled as his multi-hued eyes darted to Molly Scott, who looked taken aback. Their gazes locked for a second. All witnessed a moment of unexpected flustration between them.

Billy's Texas drawl appeared to turn Molly's cheeks a pretty shade of pink. "I wouldn't presume to ask your age, ma'am. It's nice to see you again." He glanced down at Charlie.

"You sure have become a big boy, Charlie. I remember you liked my harmonica both times I met you before. Your ma wasn't much for talkin' the last time I saw you at the fort." A gentle smile played on his face as he looked back to Molly. She returned it.

"That was a time of many lost memories. I regret that," she said.

Charlie stepped forward with evident boldness. "You got that harmonica with you?"

Billy threw a grin toward Boyd and the man seated behind him. "Yeah, Boyd and Ben wish I didn't at times."

The dark haired woman on the sofa spoke with bright joy. "Billy is the best harmonica player I've ever heard. We love for him to play."

Susannah Hawkins stood and spoke in a subdued voice to her husband, who nodded at her. The major turned toward the group.

"I am afraid we have not adhered to protocol. Susannah reminded me that not all introductions are complete. We introduced Amelia and the judge when they arrived. They are off playing with the little ones, but I digress. Boyd, I'll simply introduce your family, and if you wouldn't mind imparting the names of my extended group to them, it will go a little more quickly."

Boyd stepped to the middle of the room. "Of course. I've talked about your group here so much I think it's just a matter of putting faces with names."

The major came to stand beside him. "Everyone, I would like to introduce Mr. Boyd Richards, his wife Lucy, his brother, Ben and his wife, Marie. As you've heard, this young man to my right is a friend of theirs and works with them, Mr. Billy Cooper."

Ben's gruff voice interjected, "He's family."

Major Hawkins nodded and then continued. "I first met Boyd in Arkansas in the autumn of 1866. He had traveled there with his two friends John Wilkins and Marcus Johnson who were finally returning home after the war.

"They had worked cattle for a brief period with the Pierce brothers after the war. I served as part of a military escort accompanying Boyd, Mr. Johnson, and his new bride back to Texas.

"Then later the next year, I crossed paths with Boyd in Indian Territory at what remained of the Scott's farm."

He paused and sent an apologetic look toward Elizabeth and Molly.

"Anyway, Boyd and Billy were both on a cattle drive for Mr. Kennedy, Lucy's father, and then they came back to the fort on their return trip."

"Being on that drive changed my life. The trail led to a reunion with an old friend and foremost meeting James. He led me to the scriptures, but that trail also led Hallie, the Scotts, and Mrs. McDonald to a new life and me to the Lord," Boyd said.

Hallie moved to stand by her mother-in-law, who reached for her hand and smiled with glistening eyes. "God has used the echo of James's life to connect so many of us," she said.

The doors burst open. Thomas and Amelia ran after two toddlers new to the Hawkinses' household, followed by their children. The little boy and girl in the lead looked to be about the same age, twins no doubt.

They both had golden hair very much like Boyd Richards. Lucy Richards started forward.

"Henry Arthur Richards, Amanda Rose Richards, you know better than to run in the house," Lucy admonished them with a frown.

The two three-year-olds stopped short at their mother's reprimand, as well as the awareness of all adult eyes in the room. Their golden brown eyes widened and they hurried to hide their faces in their mother's skirt. Lucy's frown disappeared, and she sent an apologetic look at the Judge and Amelia. Judge Thomas Jackson laughed as he watched Boyd swing young Henry up into his arms.

"Don't concern yourself, Mrs. Richards. Robert and Clara have had a grand time with your children. I think they just needed to find some familiar faces."

Jared and Charlie hurried toward fourteen-year-old Robbie, who seemed grateful to be relieved of his duty as a babysitter.

Nine-year-old Clara hovered behind little Amanda, smiling as Lucy Kennedy hugged her daughter.

"Clara, thank you for playing with my twins. I know they've had fun," Lucy said as she freed one arm to beckon the little brown haired girl to join Amanda next to her. Clara's azure blue eyes sparkled as she leaned in to hug the tall lady.

Hallie never ceased to be amazed at how much the little girl resembled her mother and late uncle. Just a toddler when they returned from Indian Territory, Clara had sucked her thumb as she sat on James's lap.

Major Hawkins cleared his throat and held up his hands as Mrs. Franklin, the cook there since Mrs. Hawkins's childhood, entered the room. Eula Adams, Susannah Hawkins's mother, had passed a year earlier. Mrs. Adams had invited her daughter and son-in-law to move into her house after James died. She said she got lonely as a widow. The home in Georgetown held many sweet memories, including Mrs. Hawkins's childhood and the family gatherings for holidays during James and Amelia's childhoods. The Hawkins family needed the solace of a home place after James died. It remained their home.

"I believe our meal is ready. Please make your way to the dining room. Just follow Mrs. Franklin."

The group milled to the elegant table and found their respective places marked with cards.

Hallie surveyed all the faces of the unique gathering of a Northern family and friends with a Southern family and friends. Only God could have designed the relationships present between all those gathered at the table.

Every head bowed without hesitation as Major Hawkins said grace to bless the meal. Hallie looked across the table as her eyes opened and found Eddie smiling at her. He inclined his head towards his nephew who sat to his right and mouthed, "Thank you." She gave him a broad smile. This once orphaned man didn't take the treasure of family for granted. "You're welcome," she mouthed back, and then Jared's attempts to reach across for a big bowl of potatoes broke their gazes. Eddie intercepted him and spooned some on the boy's plate.

Pleasant conversation interwoven with laughter circulated the room as they dined.

"So, Lucy, what venture has brought your family for this visit north? I don't think it's just to see us," Hallie said.

Lucy smiled and shook her head. "No, seeing you is an extra pleasure. Ben and Boyd's cousin, Andrew, has brought their aunt to Virginia. She moved to England to be with family after their uncle died. However, it seems the weather there has been too damp for her. Therefore, his cousin has invested in a home in Virginia, which he wants all family to use. He travels to the states once a year on business. Ben and Boyd hadn't seen their aunt since they left Georgia when Boyd and his late wife Nancy married. Still awkward youths at that time, and Ben just a boy." Her brother-in-law sent her a frown, followed by a smile that she returned as she continued, "Anyway, they arranged all the rail travel, and we arrived a month ago. They've had a great reunion."

"I bet his aunt is so proud of her nephews," Susannah Hawkins commented, shining a smile on the Richards brothers.

"She sure is. They're such extraordinary men." Marie Richards beamed.

Ben tried to frown but failed at the love twinkling in his wife's eyes. "Oh, Marie."

"You told me your cousin is a lawyer. Is the law his exclusive area of interest?" Major Hawkins asked.

"No. He has invested in multiple properties and also serves as an envoy for the English government," Boyd said.

"Really? Is he involved in Parliament?" Judge Jackson asked.

"I try to keep him off politics in our discussions as he'll offer his opinions for hours, but I do believe he definitely keeps company with, as he would say, 'that sort'," Boyd answered with a grin.

"Then instead, let me inquire about your business, Boyd. How's the farming and horse ranch enterprise?" Major Hawkins asked.

"Expanding, surprisingly, given the tough economic times. Lucy's father has been an asset since they moved across the road from us a year ago. His years of successful ranching made him a man of knowledge, which we needed. Some of the cattlemen had a few difficulties a couple of years back, and Mr. Kennedy among them. There's also the Jason variable." Boyd paused and looked at

Lucy, who wore a grim expression.

He continued, "Lucy's brother is an intelligent man trained at MIT in all the areas of science and agriculture. This did help the family not to have as much loss as they could have when the cattle markets dipped. He has transformed their ranch into a large farm and has expanded into exportations. Let's just say he wanted credit for his part in salvaging the family fortune to the extent that he wanted his inheritance early. In other words, he wanted to transfer the ranch into his name.

"His best friend is Mr. Kennedy's top cowhand, Ted Dalton. You met him at the fort. They're ruthless men. Now, don't think Joe Kennedy is weak. He actually planned for such a calamity, as it were, by buying the land in East Texas prior to Lucy's and my wedding. Furthermore, he made sure he listed it as Lucy's inheritance and had papers drawn that prevent her brother from ever making a claim. Then he made the settlement of the arrangement with his son to include retention of all their livestock." Boyd reached over and took his wife's hand. "Now, we're a farm and a cattle-horse ranch. There are too many details to discuss. Let's just say, God is faithful, and we're doing well at this point."

Major Hawkins smiled. "Glad to hear it. How are Marcus and Florence?"

Boyd's face grew somber. He sent a smile tinged with sadness towards his wife. Ben and Marie had grown silent and watched Boyd. The other adults also watched the golden-haired man. His deep southern drawl drew attention; therefore, all noted his delayed response.

His direct gaze returned to his host.

"Well, first, not to worry. They're for all-important purposes, just fine. It's just that they'll move back to Arkansas upon our return. Marc's father hasn't been in good health this past year, and they made a hard decision. They have become family." He stopped and Lucy Kennedy continued.

"There will be emptiness in our lives without them. As Boyd has written Mrs. Hawkins, they have two children, Alan Lee Johnson, age six years, and Elias Richard Johnson, age two years. Our children, along with Daniel and Martha's: Emily, Ezra, and Esther, will miss them. Richard, Florence's brother, reminded them of their promise to return home one day. Now, don't get me wrong, it's the right thing to do. Marcus wouldn't be able to live with himself if he didn't go. It's just hard. We're hopeful they'll return to us one day."

Major Hawkins frowned. "I see, yes. Forgive me, but I believe Marcus had two younger brothers who must be in their twenties by now. Could they not stay home without necessitating a move by Marcus and Florence? I mean they should certainly go and stay for an extended period. It just seems a shame to leave the life they have built in Texas."

Boyd nodded. "My thoughts were definitely on those lines; however, certain complications prevent it."

"Such as?"

"Do you remember Florence's younger sister, Alice?"

The older man leaned back with his brow furrowed. "Was she the little blonde who had Marc's two brothers trailing after her?"

The two men exchanged a grin. Major Hawkins shook his head. "So, tell me, which one of the Johnson brothers did she pick?"

"Will Johnson had that honor last year. The problem is the other brother, Jack. Yes, he's a man now, but still the baby of the Johnson family, and he found it too painful to stay home once Alice chose his brother. He's now working for the railroads, that is, whichever one has work at the moment. Needless to say, his mother is distraught. Will and Alice are living with Marc's parents. It should be enough for Marc and Florey to come for that extended visit, but it's not. Will even blamed Marc for Jack having the courage to leave home due to Marc's history of *running around places.*"

Susannah Hawkins's soft, firm voice drifted through the room with the clarity and wisdom of a mother who had endured much in life. "Mr. Richards, I mean, Boyd, please forgive me for offering an opinion, yet I feel I must. Meeting the people in Rockport, Arkansas really affected my husband, especially the Johnsons, the Cushmans, and you. He told me about the sacrificial friendship and love shone by your friends, Marcus and his new wife, through their agreement to come to Texas to help your brother run your farm. You could not bear to do it yourself after the death of your first wife. Is that right?"

Ben Richard's gruff voice responded. "Yes, ma'am. Marcus and Florey helped to save our farm. Martha, Daniel, and I had a hard go of it with the drought that year. They stayed. Marcus promised me he would be there for me at least until God brought Boyd home."

Boyd stared at his brother with haunted eyes. He swallowed hard.

Mrs. Hawkins nodded and then drew Boyd's attention. "Then it's time for them to go home. God sent them for a season of need and restoration. Their children need to be within the reach of their grandparents' arms." She smiled at her two grandchildren who sat at the small table by the window with the Richards children and Mrs. McDonald. They chattered in the excited oblivion of childhood as the cook served pie.

Boyd bowed his head for a moment. He looked up and gave his hostess a respectful gaze. "You're right, ma'am. I owe them more than those on this side of heaven can understand."

Billy Cooper's cheerful voice broke the melancholy. "This apple pie is almost as good as yours, Lucy. It has me feeling downright content. If everyone would humor me, I think it's time for some music. I've a mind to play my harmonica."

Hallie smiled. *Thank goodness! Time for some levity.* "I think that sounds delightful. Susannah, would you play for us?" Her mother-in-law played their mahogany pianoforte well.

Mrs. Hawkins nodded and rose. "It would be a pleasure; however, I have one condition. Hallie, you and Eddie must sing for us."

Hallie's eyes widened and flew to Eddie, who displayed an indulgent smile. He didn't seem in the least hesitant.

"Of course. Now if Hallie sings like James, our guests may want to pass," he teased.

Hallie's mind raced. She and James had spent many happy evenings listening to Mrs. Hawkins play. Once he learned she had a lovely voice, he requested she sing on those evenings. They laughed together when he'd joined in one night. James often said the Lord surrounded him with angelic voices to cover the discord of his own. Mrs. Hawkins told her how James and Eddie often sang in those early days of friendship before the war, but Hallie had never heard Eddie sing. They both sat in silent grief during the hymns sung at James's funeral.

She shot Eddie a look of challenge. "I think you may owe me an apology. Let's go see, shall we?"

Everyone stood, and then Molly, Amelia, Mrs. McDonald, and Eddie corralled the children in the direction of the music room.

Major Hawkins escorted his wife to the bench behind the pianoforte and then found a seat of his own. Hallie positioned herself to the side of the instrument and turned with an eyebrow raised as she waited for Eddie to seat Jared beside Molly and Charlie. Billy positioned himself on the opposite side of Mrs. Hawkins and winked at Charlie who smiled back.

"What's your pleasure, ma'am?"

Hallie leaned to whisper in Susannah's ear. She gave Billy a look of apology. "Mr. Cooper, you wouldn't happen to know Mrs. Julia Ward Howe's *Battle Hymn of the Republic?*"[xi]

Billy's eyes caught those of Lucy Richards, and they smiled. He moved his gaze back to Hallie and his hostess. "Being from the South, we prefer to call it *"Mine Eyes Have Seen the Glory"*[xii] and it happens to be the first real song I learned on the harmonica. You see, I salvaged my Pa's harmonica from our burned house when I was thirteen. I taught myself to play all the tunes I could remember from him and then picked up some here and there. Then later, after I came to live on the Kennedy ranch, I met Miss Lucy. When she came back home from college in the East, she took me to church. One day she stayed late and played the song by Mrs. Howe on that old piano. I listened real hard and practiced until I could play it."

Hallie turned with wide eyes. "Why, Lucy Kennedy Richards, I never knew you played the piano." They laughed and Hallie added, "Of course, we weren't more than acquaintances before, were we?"

"We were more acquainted than the other town ladies found respectable, but I didn't care. You were so kind to make sure Ted made it back to the ranch before my father had to come and fetch him. I enjoyed our brief visits," Lucy said.

Amelia Jackson cleared her throat in a not so subtle effort to communicate how inappropriate she felt the conversation had become. Mrs. Hawkins rolled her eyes and placed her hands on the awaiting keys. As soon as the first chords resounded, haunting harmonica tones interwove with singing, enthralling everyone in the room. Then Hallie's smooth alto blended with Eddie's strong tenor in perfect harmony, enrapturing all.

Hallie's heart soared and knew James smiled down at them. Emotions coursed through her eyes and met Eddie's as the last words echoed and the last notes vibrated the instruments. No eye remained dry, and all hearts swelled as the song evoked spiritual, emotional, and nostalgic reactions.

Joy sparkled in her eyes as she surveyed the silent room. Marie beamed as she leaned against her husband. Boyd had his arm around Lucy, who held two sleeping toddlers on her lap. He bent to kiss her on the head as she reached up to wipe away a tear. Even Amelia seemed overcome.

The judge adjusted his daughter on his lap and cleared his throat. Charlie just stared at them. However, Molly's face stopped Hallie. Her eyes looked past Eddie and focused on Billy Cooper.

Oh, dear. This could be bad. Hallie knew the look of a smitten young woman, and Molly wore it. Jared started clapping at that moment and broke the spell. Everyone joined in the accolades.

Major Hawkins walked to the piano, clapping, his eyes bright with emotion. He clamped a hand on Eddie's shoulder.

"It's been too long, son," he said with pride.

"Thank you, sir," Eddie said in a choked voice. He coughed and ducked his head.

The major didn't linger and went to shake Billy's hand.

"Very nice, young man. It was wonderful to hear you play again."

"Thank you, Major."

The seasoned officer then turned and placed his hands on his wife's shoulders. "Susannah and Hallie, you were superb. I think this would be a time for the gentlemen to adjourn to my study to discuss politics and the state of our nation's affairs. This will allow the ladies to talk about us," he paused to give a smile to each of the females present, "Hopefully, to list all of our virtues."

Laughter filled the room as Major Hawkins turned to engage Billy in conversation while they made their way to the music room door.

Eddie didn't move away with the other men, and Hallie

turned with a puzzled expression.

"Eddie? You aren't allowed to stay at our hen party." She laughed and then became disconcerted at the way he watched her with a gentle light in his eyes. An audible sigh of relief escaped her when he grinned.

"Why not? I know it'll be a lot livelier than the bear party next door. No, I just wanted to concede your triumph. I'm sure James much preferred listening to your melodious voice than mine. Hallie, you've always managed to surprise me."

To Hallie's dismay, her face grew warm. She much preferred the off-kilter friendship they'd developed to this pointed admiration. She gave a loud laugh.

"Oh, Lieutenant Rigby, I surprise myself at times. Thank you."

He shook his head as he gave her his signature self-deprecating smile. "You have my admiration, Mrs. Hawkins," he said in a somewhat mocking tone. "Now, if you'll excuse me."

Neither one realized Susannah Hawkins remained on the stool behind them, watching their exchange with interest. Hallie jumped at the sound of her voice.

"It's more than acceptable for you to have male admirers again. The mourning period is more than satisfied, daughter-in-law."

Hallie put her hands to her cheeks, pressed, and tried to calm the trembling of her hands as they straightened the sheet music on the pianoforte. A flash of anger then coursed through her but soon diminished as she looked into the kind eyes of her mother-in-law.

"Susannah, Eddie is a friend," she said.

The older woman's eyebrows went up in slight disbelief. "Then why retreat into formality?"

Hallie gave her a frank look. "Because he needs to know that's all I want. Besides, he's about to call on Mary McWhorter."

Mrs. Hawkins raised an eyebrow. "That girl must have had her father use his connections to locate Eddie at his post. Although that had to have been either right after he returned from the funeral or within the last six months since—" A startled expression appeared on her face. "I mean . . . the troops at the post were given many assignments away from their headquarters, and this delayed their reception of letters."

Hallie felt a sense of unease settle in her stomach. "Eddie did stop answering his letters for quite a while."

"You know the military. Anyway, back to Miss McWhorter. She has always been determined, even as a child. Here's an interesting bit of history, my dear. When James and Eddie marched off to war, she was still a girl of twelve years. She came to tea with her mother one day during the war and informed me of her intention to marry James one day. With Eddie right beside him for months before the war, I never heard her admire him until the day after James's funeral. Just something to consider."

Hallie frowned as she watched her mother-in-law cross to help Mrs. McDonald usher the children out of the room. She turned and found Lucy Kennedy waiting a few feet away. The blue-green eyes sparkled, and the dimpled smile flashed as Hallie faced her.

"Hallie, that was the most breathtaking performance. You know I heard you sing once in Texas. I was in town late at the newspaper and passed the saloon on my way to meet my father at Mr. Sigman's office. He'd told me to wait for him at the newspaper, but you know me. Your beautiful voice caused me to stop. Ted came out right after and escorted me to my father."

Lucy Kennedy had always treated Hallie with kindness even when the respectable ladies of the town wouldn't spare a look her way. Many also whispered about the headstrong and smart young woman. She'd returned home without finishing college in order for her brother to attend school in Boston.

Jason Kennedy—how that young man came out of such a wonderful family remained a mystery to her—a selfish and ruthless man even as a youth. The first time he visited the saloon proved one time too many. He hurt young Erma and left bruises.

Hallie then decreed that none of her girls would have to deal with him again. His father's position as one of the most respected and influential ranchers in town didn't matter.

"Thank you, Lucy," she said, moving to take her hands.

Lucy squeezed her fingers and then looked down for a moment. "Hallie, this is none of my business, but I feel this is something you need to hear. It was hard for me not to overhear your conversation with Mrs. Hawkins, and I want you to listen to me. Boyd and I went to talk to Brother Moore about our engagement. He talked with us about his concerns due to knowing Boyd would always love his late wife. I told him of my confidence in God's ability to give Boyd more than enough love for me if He'd brought us together. Hallie, it's been more than either of us expected. Boyd is the most wonderful husband and father. I've never felt like a replacement for the wife he lost, nor are our children substitutes for his first son who died. The human heart is capable of more love than can be imagined when we let God have it. You are the Lord's, so please don't limit your future."

Hallie didn't want to hear her words, just as she hadn't wanted to hear Molly's earlier that evening. She crossed to a small case on a table nestled in a shadowed corner and retrieved a small ambrotype[xiii] picture. As she handed it to Lucy, her eyes became moist.

"This is my James—taken on our wedding day."

Lucy's eyes softened as she gazed on the glimpse of their euphoric day frozen in time. Hallie wore a detailed lace dress and stood beside James's wheelchair. His handsome and guileless face frozen in time.

"Boyd had hoped to introduce James to me but warned me off getting too fond of him. He was a dashing man. You both look so happy even though you aren't smiling. Why do photographers tell you not to smile? Susannah planned to show me his photograph."

Hallie took the picture back and held it to her heart. "Yes, we were happy. He was so unlike anyone I've ever known. It's just—"

Molly's voice interrupted them. "You two come over here. I have questions about Texas."

Hallie laughed and Lucy smiled.

"Just think about it, Hallie," Lucy said. She turned and made her way to the settee where Marie sat. Hallie returned the picture to the case and returned to the group. She found a chair across from where Molly sat beside Amelia and Susannah who had left the children in the care of Elizabeth McDonald.

"What would you like to know, Mrs. Scott?" Lucy asked.

"Well, I kind of know about yours and Boyd's story from

the letters Susannah received and shared. I'd like to know about the farm, your other friends there, and how Marie met Ben."

Lucy looked at her smiling sister-in-law. "I'll let Marie tell their story."

Marie sparkled. No one could be around her and be sad. Her enthusiasm knew no bounds, especially when it came to the subject of her husband.

"He didn't think well of me for years. We first met as children, I mean. They left Georgia and bought their farm after Boyd and Nancy married. My father brought my sisters and me by to offer assistance if they needed it. My mother died when I was young, and Nancy treated me so nice when we met that I'm afraid I made a nuisance of myself, visiting often. Ben scowled at me and never would talk. Boyd showed more tolerance as Nancy liked my help. I have three other sisters and wasn't missed much at home. Then the war came and Boyd left to fight. Nancy liked me to come over even more and after little Sam was born; she asked my father if I could stay for a few days at a time, especially after those soldiers came and took Ben off to war. Things got to be very hard for her as the months passed. Soon, my pa agreed for me to live there. He checked on us every couple of days until the time of the fever came. My entire family got sick, including me. We were sick close to a month. My pa took me home in hopes little Sam wouldn't get sick. I got well and two days later, my pa brought me over to the Richardses' place.

"Ben had gotten there and found Nancy dead in the house and Sam buried under the tree—a horrible day. My pa helped Ben bury Nancy and then took me home again. I tried checking on Ben, but he wouldn't talk to me. Then Boyd and his two friends, John and Marc, came home—terrible. Ben would open the door and tell me to go home whenever I stopped by. I've never seen a man so grief stricken as Boyd, and his friends so close to death. They looked like skeletons. Once they were strong enough, the three left again. Ben had a soldier friend who came to help him with the farm for a time, but he soon returned to help his own family.

"The good Lord saw fit to send Martha and Daniel to Ben at that point or he couldn't have made it. A drought came. Ben had to adjust to his first artificial leg, such as it was. Anyway, time went on, Boyd returned with Marcus and Florence Johnson—the missing piece needed to make the farm a success. Boyd left to run cattle again.

"With the Johnsons there, Ben could return to schooling lessons with Mr. Penney. Once I passed my teaching certification, I asked to teach Ben, but Mr. Penney wouldn't allow it until he retired two months later. I can't describe my excitement when the time came. However, not Ben; no, not the least bit. It took me months. After Lucy came, Billy started noticing my friend Mattie and me. It seemed to make Ben consider me more, and here we are."

All the ladies laughed. Molly leaned forward. "You mentioned Mr. Cooper also took notice of your friend Mattie. Have they been courting?"

Marie and Lucy shared a smile.

"No, she gave Billy a little heartache when she chose Adam Creel. They married two years ago."

"Billy hasn't had an easy life," Hallie said. When all the women looked at Hallie in surprise, she felt the need to clarify. "He would come to town with Ted and the boys. Now, don't look like that. He liked to *talk* to me, nothing more. Just like when I met Boyd for the first time—only conversation over lunch. Now Lucy, forgive me, it wasn't from not trying. That man of yours would tempt any woman. Oh, Amelia, quit looking shocked. That was a lifetime ago."

Mrs. Hawkins nodded. "There are indeed many lifetimes within a lifetime. Boyd issued that same sentiment to me in one of his letters. It's just hard to move out of one into the other as our circumstances change."

"That may be true, mother, yet I contest Hallie's blatant discussion of her past life. I would be ashamed," Amelia stated as she sat up straighter and clasped her hands in her lap.

"Amelia—" Hallie started but stopped as Marie Richards enthused.

"Excuse me. How else do you want her to discuss her history? Yes, it's an appalling profession; however, it was her life. We all make mistakes. I would rather someone talk with candor about it, rather than lie and pretend it never happened. It seems to me, Hallie isn't prideful about her past. She just accepts it with recall of the more pleasant and proper interactions she's had, such as with Billy and our Boyd. Besides, she would have to be blind not to find the Richards brothers handsome." Marie smiled at Lucy and Hallie.

"Well, I can't abide it. James is not honored in her discussion of her past." Amelia sniffed and dabbed at her nose with her handkerchief.

Susannah Hawkins frowned at her daughter. "Amelia, James knew Hallie much better than any person here. He told me on more than one occasion how refreshing he found her candor. So don't choose to be offended on his account."

Hallie felt the impact of her past anew. "Amelia, God has healed the hurt and forgiven the sin from my former life. However, there are scars within, which make me ever grateful for His mercy."

Amelia gave her a haughty stare for a moment, and then faltered as all eyes turned on her.

"I'm sorry, Hallie. Well, I guess it's time to go check on my children."

Her sister-in-law rose and Lucy Kennedy squeezed Hallie's hand. "I'd better check on my two also. We'll visit more tomorrow. I want to come and see Hallie's House."

Mrs. Hawkins leaned over to give her a brief pat before turning a bright smile on Molly and Marie. "I think we should all have an outing to the milliner's shop tomorrow. Putting on a new hat is always a boost."

"Lucy and I aren't used to new hats. Such a treat," Marie said.

Hallie smiled and nodded in agreement, but continued to look at the door where Amelia and Lucy exited.

~~~

The ladies didn't hear the door open during Amelia's scathing reprimand of Hallie nor had they known Eddie Rigby listened through the cracked partition to the responses. He shut the door as Lucy and Amelia started towards it.

Lucy Richards smiled at his approach as they exited the parlor and responded, "Of course," when he begged forgiveness and asked to speak with Amelia.

The graceful, tall woman smiled with a flash of a dimple as

she started up the stairs.

"Yes, Eddie? What did you need?" Amelia inquired with irritation.

"I was on my way to get Mrs. Scott for young Charlie and happened to hear the end of the conversation in the parlor."

"And?" she asked with a lift of her eyebrow.

Eddie remembered the first time he'd met Amelia as a youth—vibrant. She and the judge had just married. If she hadn't been married, he would have made a fool of himself with his puppy-like adoration. While self-indulgent, she never spiraled into meanness. "As James isn't here, I felt the need to ask what's really bothering you?"

Her blue eyes, so like James's, flashed with anger. "Waifs, beggars, and prostitutes. Why my brother had the proclivity to bring those into our family, I will never know. And now, his past relationships have brought confederate rebels here."

Eddie saw Major Hawkins step out of his study and close the door. Amelia's look of angry disdain shifted to her father and back to him. He frowned and stroked his eyebrow in thoughtful regard.

"Let's explore those incredible statements, Amelia. I acknowledge my former status as both a waif and a beggar; however, I never asked anything of your brother. He offered me help and provided me the opportunity to make something of myself. The rest he left to me, and I've managed it pretty well. On the topic of prostitutes, James never sought out any one of that ilk. It's true my sister went that way, and she sought out James as the closest thing to me for Jared. There again, she's never asked for financial help from your family and has paid for Jared's care and schooling. The other former soiled dove is Hallie. Once more, not someone sought out by James. Mr. Richards sent her, as he saw something in her that waited for a better opportunity in life. God ordained the rest, and Hallie has continued to work hard. I'll not speak for your father regarding the Richards family, yet they were friends before James met Boyd. Here's another correction needed: The Richardses come from one of the most influential Southern families in Georgia, and Lucy Kennedy Richards is the daughter of one of the most respected ranchers in Texas. It all boils down to the fact that you're angry at yourself for wasting so much time being ashamed of James, and now he's gone. We're reminders of how much he accomplished. "

"Why I . . . " she sputtered and then burst into tears.

Major Hawkins's mouth formed a grim line as he came to take his daughter in his arms.

"Let it go, Amelia," he said and nodded dismissal to Eddie over her head.

Eddie sauntered back to the music room. The delightful sound of female laughter—especially the wholehearted signature laugh of Hallie Hawkins—made him smile as he opened the door. The memory of a different laugh resounded, reminiscent of the mixture of the wind blowing the reeds of grass near a river. The turmoil of the past pulled at the present. It gave him pause. He hoped his plans to call on Mary McWhorter didn't result in disaster.

The time had come to make a more normal life. He decided this before he boarded the train from Kansas. Now that he knew about Jared, it gave him even more incentive. His nephew needed him. Life events had happened, and he learned to flow with them.

However, after the incident that detained him and brought him home, he wanted to decide his direction for once. A nudge of conscience penetrated him even as these thoughts circulated in his mind.

He smiled as all eyes turned at his entrance. "Ladies, I hate to disturb your pleasant conversation. Please pardon me."

"Yes, of course, Edward, how can we help you?" Mrs. Hawkins responded with a fond smile.

"Charlie is in need of his mother. He took a small fall upstairs during play. His grandmother sent Jared to get you, but he came for me instead."

Molly stood. "Is he hurt?"

"I understand he has a large bruise and a small cut," he said. "It winded him a bit, but that's it."

She sighed in relief and smiled at the other women. "Please excuse me. It has been a lovely evening. I think it's time to bid all good night. If the lieutenant doesn't mind, I think it's time to take Charlie home."

Hallie rose.

"Molly, I'll gather Jared and go with you."

Eddie shook his head. "No, Hallie, you can stay. I'll accompany Mrs. Scott and the boys."

Mrs. Hawkins stood, taking control of the situation. "Ladies, thank you for a wonderful evening. I'm sure it's time to put all children to bed. Good night, Hallie, Molly, Eddie. I will see you tomorrow. Marie, let me see you settled in your room."

Marie Richards rose with a bright smile. "It's so nice to meet all of you. Good night," she said and accompanied her hostess.

Hallie laughed as Molly hurried to follow. "Eddie, you sure know how to end an evening."

He hesitated but returned her smile.

"I'll go get Jared so you can slip back in with the other gentlemen," she offered.

He shook his head. "No, I'll go with you. If my impression of Boyd Richards is correct, he'll want to help his wife with the children. It's been a long day for everyone. Travel will do that. So, please, lead on."

She inclined her head, gathered her skirt, and swept past him.

Chapter Three

NERVES GRIPPED EDDIE, but not the same feeling as waiting for a battle to begin. He'd learned to brace himself and dive into the fray. No, he'd never experienced this feeling.

Calling on the daughter of a well-established family had never before been a consideration. Mary McWhorter's quick response to the note he sent by messenger the day after the dinner at the Hawkinses' home surprised him. Her parents arranged for Mary and him to accompany them to a special dinner. *How would he manage the evening without looking absent of any social graces?* These thoughts unnerved him as he wrestled with his collar and tie. As his meeting with the War Department and the head of Indian Affairs didn't happen until Monday, and he remained on official leave, the major advised evening attire. He found himself hard-pressed not to utter a few choice words at a moment like this, but the Lord had helped him forebear on more than one occasion; though not always easy and a few slips occurred on occasion. He gritted his teeth, *not now.*

During the past few days, many events had transpired. He'd met the very diverse set of women residing in Hallie's House and reunited with his old friend, Micah, who now lived there. Hallie described Micah to him on the train, but she had no idea how much Micah differed from the boy Eddie had served with during the war. Distrust and caution filled the space between him and each of the house's residents during introductions. It would definitely take some time and effort if he decided to take the job offered to him.

The Richardses came by Hallie's House the day after the evening at the Hawkinses'. Mrs. Hawkins took her female guests on a shopping outing for the afternoon after a city tour, but Boyd and Ben convinced Eddie to rescue them with a manlier outing. It started with the prospect of a simple tour of the Georgetown area but somehow led them to Arlington and the cemetery[xiv] instead.

Walking those grounds overwhelmed him every time. He hadn't visited since the day they buried James. The choices of where to bury James had been the cemetery by the Soldiers' Home, the Congressional Cemetery, or Arlington. Even though he hadn't died a soldier, his military record—as well as working for the government since the war and being the son of a current military officer—were all considered. In fact, the President agreed James would have wanted to lay with his comrades.

Eddie had never shared such an experience—to walk that sacred ground—with two men who had served in the ranks of the enemy and held responsibility for some of the fallen men beneath their boots. They exchanged no words, only solemn looks, compressed mouths, and hard swallows as emotions threatened to overcome them. The distance to James's marble headstone seemed longer and, once reached, a cold monument to a man who had impacted so many. The hats each man removed upon first setting foot on the grounds were twisted, examined, and then held with solemnity between hands as Boyd prayed. The words resounded with gratitude and petitioned grace. Each knew the duty and honor of being a soldier, as well as the horror and loss; both were present here.

They rode back to Hallie's in silence. Micah took one look at them sitting on the porch when he returned from his job at the newspaper and offered to go procure a bottle of whiskey. His mouth twisted at Eddie's headshake, and he returned with coffee instead. Once he learned the identity of Ben and Boyd, Eddie thought he might have to prevent his old friend from starting a fight. Micah's bitterness continued; however, the fact that Ben also lost a leg seemed to satisfy him.

However, Micah couldn't resist telling them, "I'm stilled owed an arm from the Confederacy."

Ben gave a gruff response. "It was the war responsible for our loss of limbs not a contest of Yankees or Rebels. No one can be repaid."

Thankfully, Billy, who had chosen to stay and help Molly with a few chores after collecting the boys from Mrs. McDonald, joined them at this point, and his affable personality disarmed Micah. The topics soon moved to lighter subjects, and the ladies returned to find a companionable group.

Now he wrestled with getting ready for an elegant evening. He couldn't get the tie right on this collar. He turned from the mirror in frustration. A young voice drew his attention to the doorway.

"Need some help?"

He couldn't help grinning at his nephew's knowing look.

"Yes, please," he conceded, squatting down for Jared's nimble fingers to remedy the situation.

"There."

Eddie stood and returned to the mirror. His eyes noted everything in place and reached for his coat.

"Nicely done, nephew. Thank you."

Jared plopped down on the wooden chair by the window.

"Just returning the favor from the other night."

After a final look at his reflection, Eddie patted Jared's curly blond hair and turned his green gaze to meet the precocious brown eyes.

"You've been to formal parties at the Hawkinses'? They can't be that different from the dinner we had the other night. Right?" he asked and then laughed at the face Jared made. "That bad?"

"Well, I've only been to one. We normally get left with Mrs. McDonald. Everyone all dressed in finery and waiting to be received—are you sure you want to go?"

He angled back for a moment; to be sure no one passed in the hall to hear his response, and then leaned down to whisper, "Not at all. It's just there's a pretty young lady who wants to go, and I want to spend the evening with her."

Jared squinted in thought for a moment and whispered back, "If you just need an evening with a lady, go to Boston. The ladies who work with Julia—I mean Ma—are much nicer and your ears won't hurt."

Eddie hid his smile. "Thank you for your consideration, but the young lady I'm calling on this evening is very different from the ladies you mentioned. She's someone I might consider courting."

A look of panic crossed Jared's face. "Don't get married, Uncle Eddie."

"Why?"

"Because you won't have any time for me."

Eddie stopped his nephew from the quick exit he endeavored to make. "Now wait a minute, young man. Let's sit down and have a few more words." Once Jared settled in a chair, Eddie pulled another chair to face him and sat down. "Jared, until a few days ago, I didn't even know I had a nephew. You're real family, and if you haven't realized it, we only have Julia and each other in this world. That's pretty important. No one will come between us. If I marry, my future wife will have to welcome you in our home. Besides, if I ever have any children of my own, they'll need their older cousin to look up to and guide them."

He saw an uncertain smile spread on the boy's face. "So, when do I get to meet her? What's her name?"

Eddie whistled and laughed. "Hold on, I haven't even finished the evening. Her name is Mary McWhorter."

Jared's eyes widened. "I met her at the Hawkinses' once. She's so pretty."

Eddie smiled and stood. "Then I guess I'd better not be late, or someone else might take her to the party instead of me. Walk me down."

Two of the ladies in the house, Sara Brady and Margaret Elliot, straightened the parlor to his left as Jared and he reached the bottom of the stairs. They stared for a moment but soon ducked their heads. This could be the opportunity to bridge some of the awkwardness still present.

"Mrs. Brady, Miss Elliot, please tell me if I do not suit. This is my first evening out without my uniform, and I would welcome your opinion," he said.

"Tell him he should stay home," Jared said with a laugh.

The older of the two, Mrs. Brady, stepped forward. In her late twenties, she'd come to them from the hospital after recovering from a severe beating at the hands of her husband. Caroline, her little girl of six years, also stayed with them.

"Lieutenant Rigby, I think you look very nice. A real man-about-town in that suit. Please forgive our rude stares. You represent both a uniform and evening attire equally well. May we ask where you're off to?" she responded in a soft tentative voice, which lilted upward at the end of each sentence.

He smiled. "Thank you for your kind assessment, Mrs. Brady. I'm accompanying a young lady and her parents to a private dinner party."

"Oh, how nice," offered the delicate Margaret.

Hallie's familiar voice came from behind, disarming any tension.

"You ladies better not go on too much or the lieutenant might develop a painfully high opinion of himself. He's lucky to be in Washington now and not in the squalor of a few years ago. Although, the homes are something to behold. I'm surprised Mary didn't suggest an evening at the theater or opera."

"I had thought to escort her to such places, but her family invited us to this house-warming party for one of the senators, and she thought it was a good place to introduce me to Washington society."

Hallie's mouth twitched. "I see. Well, at least you won't be alone with the foxes and wolves. I believe Major Hawkins and Susannah are invited to the same party."

He sighed. "Good. Now where's that tall hat he left for me to wear?"

Jared disappeared for a minute and returned with the hat. "Here you go, Uncle Eddie. Try to survive it."

"I'll do my best. Good evening ladies."

An almost tandem, "Good Evening," echoed as he closed the door and headed for the hack rented for the event.

~~~

He approached the lavish home of Mary McWhorter with a sense of trepidation. This family far exceeded his class. The fact that Mary had written to him still astonished him. He looked up at their large house—twice the size of the Hawkinses' home. He found himself in a dazed state of disbelief as he lifted the knocker on the door. Their butler let him in with a look of haughty assessment. A movement on the large winding staircase caught his glance. His breath caught as he swallowed hard. Mary McWhorter took his breath with her dark hair pulled up with ornate combs on the sides while the remaining strands flowed down her back in curls. She wore a black velvet ribbon with a small brooch circling her neck. Her deep green gown had a bustle and a scooped, ruffled neckline. The tips of her delicate fingers skimmed the banister during her graceful descent.

"Lieutenant Rigby, how good of you to come this evening. My parents are looking forward to making your acquaintance," she said as she reached the bottom of the stairs and extended her hand. Her sapphire-blue eyes held appreciation.

He bowed over her hand for a brief moment and stepped back. "How lovely you look, Miss McWhorter."

"Thank you, sir. My parents will soon join us."

A moment of awkward silence ensued as Eddie looked up at the staircase, willing her parents to appear.

Mary approached him with a charming smile. "Would you be so kind as to escort me into the parlor while we wait?"

"Of course," he said, offering her his arm. He tried to mask his internal reaction to the richness of her home.

The parlor held velvet seating and rich tiny patterned chintz drapes, detailed moldings, a marble mantel, and a crystal chandelier.

"So tell me, Lieutenant, what are your plans for the future?" She eyed his attire. "Will you continue in the military?"

He met her clear blue gaze. "I'm in the process of making that decision. I have a couple of more prospects to consider."

"Might I ask what those other options are?"

He hesitated. Discussing it with Hallie felt natural even in the absence of full disclosure. This didn't. However, as he'd shown an interest in this young woman, he would try.

"The railroad or running Hallie's House."

Delight flickered at the first and a slight nose wrinkle at the second. *Interesting.*

"My, my, that decision should not be hard. The railroad surely offers a much better future if you choose to leave the military."

The loud voice of her father echoed, "Leave the military? Why Lieutenant Rigby, I didn't know you were considering it. Let us explore this topic further as we make our way to the party. Oh, please meet my wife, Lila McWhorter. I believe you met at James's funeral but, given the sad circumstances, we cannot expect you to recall it."

Eddie took Mrs. McWhorter's hand. "Forgive me. I believe your husband is correct. As I have had the privilege of speaking with your husband in the company of Major Hawkins, it's easier to recall him. However, please let me say the origin of your daughter's beauty is well found in you."

A pleased smile appeared on the poised face of Mary's mother. "How kind you are, Lieutenant. I do look forward to our evening."

"Ladies, let's gather wraps," Oliver McWhorter said.

They soon departed in a private family buggy after Mr. McWhorter dismissed the hack Eddie had rented. "I hope you don't mind. My man will take you home upon our return."

The conversation flowed with ease as they traveled. He discovered Mary's excitement about attending nurse's training in Connecticut. She demonstrated a quick mind and confidence, answering all his questions without hesitation.

He sensed a respect for Hallie's nursing skills as she shared experiences working with her at the hospital; however, he also detected a not so flattering implication in her comments. She spoke as if convinced her skills would soon surpass Hallie's.

"I understand Hallie will graduate from the program in Boston before Christmas. All the prior experience she's accumulated must have been helpful," he commented.

A brief flicker of surprise crossed her very composed face. "Oh, well, I'm sure she knows more than those who are just starting nursing. As do I. You see, I had the opportunity to start early at the hospital two years ago. We weren't ready for me to leave for school until now."

They pulled up to the senator's house at that moment. The large Federal Style home[xv] appeared in keeping in size with the McWhorter's home. Lovely grounds surrounded it, and many other guests arrived as they assisted the ladies onto the walk. A swirl of music and voices welcomed them as they entered through the grand portico.

Eddie took a deep breath on his way to meet their hosts and looked around in anxious anticipation for the Hawkinses. Multiple introductions swirled around him before he heard the low granite tones of Major Hawkins behind him, requesting a moment.

He turned, taking Miss McWhorter by the elbow to accompany him. Once they faced the major and his wife, Mary gave him a small smile and stepped forward to take Mrs. Hawkins's hands.

"How lovely to see you, Mrs. Hawkins. Mrs. Jackson told me you would be attending during our meeting with the Dames[xvi]."

"Likewise, Miss McWhorter. Have you shown the Lieutenant the gardens?"

Eddie caught the sparkle in the eye of the woman he viewed like a mother. She ignored his warning look at her interference.

Mary looked delighted. "Why, no. We have been so busy making introductions, but I would love to, if you will excuse us."

Mrs. Hawkins caught her husband's eye. "If you don't mind, Miss McWhorter, we would like to join you. They have made so many improvements, and my wife would love to implement some of them into our smaller garden."

Determined to take charge of the situation, Eddie offered his arm to Mary. "That's a wonderful idea. By the time we're done, our hosts may be through welcoming many of the guests and ready for the evening to proceed."

Their stroll along the lovely garden paths proved to be the most enjoyable part of the evening for him. They discussed community, family, and the beautiful foliage surrounding them. He recognized the way Susannah Hawkins tried to ask revealing questions of Mary, just as Mary turned each response to her own advantage with practiced skill. He and Major Hawkins suppressed the urge to laugh outright at their female stratagems.

As soon as they returned to the house, Mary pulled him away in search of her parents. The formality and confinement of the evening had almost suffocated Eddie by the time they bade their host goodbye. It took extreme restraint not to remove his collar as they rode toward the McWhorter's home.

"Here we are. George, please wait a moment. You will be

taking the Lieutenant home," Mr. McWhorter said as he stepped down.

Eddie waited to assist Mary as the man helped his wife. Once her mother joined her father, Mary made a graceful exit from the carriage and took his arm. As they climbed the stairs, he said, "Thank you for allowing me to be part of your evening."

"Certainly, my boy. We do hope to see more of you. We will say good night." Oliver McWhorter turned to his daughter. "Mary, I will expect you to follow us posthaste."

"Yes, sir."

Mrs. McWhorter smiled at Eddie as her husband escorted her into the house. Mary turned to face him as the door shut. The warm night breeze surrounded them. The sound of horse hooves and buggy wheels disrupted the air of intimacy.

"You have sparkled this evening, Miss McWhorter. Thank you for the privilege of being your escort," he said.

She gazed at him from under her eyelashes. "Thank you, Lieutenant. I don't know how I missed an attractive gentleman like you from our first meetings."

It would have been rude to say the first response forming on his tongue. He held no illusions. They both knew James swayed her first girlish adoration and not him. She'd barely even acknowledged his presence, but he couldn't blame her. The easy choice between the street rogue and the privileged son had warranted little discussion. At least now, he had potential as a suitor.

"The time wasn't appropriate for our acquaintance then. Even though my military activities delayed my response, I found your letter delightful. I'm glad for the welcome of my interest."

"You are very kind. Please call again soon. Good night."

He lifted the hand she offered to his lips. "Good evening, Miss McWhorter. I welcome the opportunity to call on you again soon."

She gave him a final smile and disappeared behind the ornate door.

Eddie strolled back to where George waited to take him home. He removed his tie and collar as soon as he settled into his seat.

~~~

Hallie laughed at the twins' antics as she raced after little Amanda Richards. She called to their mother, "Lucy, I'll get Amanda. Did you get Henry?"

The giggling little girl squirmed and tried to escape as Hallie caught her in the foyer.

"No, no, Hawi. No nap."

Hallie wrapped both arms around the small form and hugged her close. She then hoisted her up in her arms.

"Well, little miss, if you want to play with Jared and Charlie later today, you must nap now."

The little girl eyed her. After a moment of prolonged and serious contemplation, she leaned toward Hallie's ear and whispered, "Yes, ma'am."

Hallie breathed a sigh of relief. "Thank you, Amanda."

Footsteps sounded behind her, and she turned to find Lucy carrying Henry. They shared a smile and headed for the stairs. The sound of the doorknocker caused both of them to turn. Everyone had left the house for the day except for them and Mrs. Franklin, the cook. She didn't open the door at this time of day as dinner preparations were underway.

"I'll get it," Hallie said as Lucy waited at the foot of the stairs.

A contest of emotions coursed through her as she opened the door. The man leaned against the doorframe with his hat in his hands. His lips pursed then curled into a cruel smile underneath a well-trimmed mustache as his dark brown eyes flashed in recognition.

"Well, well, Hallie Price. Ted told me you were working for the Hawkinses. It just didn't seem possible for you to be living in Washington," he said with a slow, thorough perusal of her from head to toe.

This surprised and disgusted Hallie at the same time. "It's Hallie Hawkins now. I'm afraid Ted isn't the best source of information. I haven't seen him in almost seven years."

The man's eyes hardened. "I shouldn't have underestimated you. A woman like you could get anything she wanted from most men." His eyes went to Amanda. "Is this your daughter?"

Hallie moved aside as Lucy approached and jerked the door wide to view their visitor.

"If you cared about your family more than business, Jason, you would recognize your own niece." Lucy admonished her younger brother with her blue-green eyes flashing.

Lucy and Jason's similar heights and honey-gold hair linked them as siblings. However, a complete dissimilarity of personality and character existed between these two.

Hallie often wondered how Jason had emerged from such a good family. He'd ended Lucy's college education when he became a part of the first class at MIT in Boston. However, Lucy's return home had been as welcome as his departure. Jason Kennedy exhibited cruelty, even as a youth, and especially toward women. Ted brought him to the saloon for the first time as a youth of sixteen. He hurt young Erma, and she couldn't work for months. The other girls gave part of their earnings to keep the girl from ending up in the streets.

Hallie wanted to notify Mr. Kennedy about his son at that time, but Ted, as the Kennedy's top hand, convinced her to consider it a one-time incident. Jason only returned to the saloon one other time. None of the girls approached him. Hallie shut her eyes as she remembered. The feel of his lips on her neck still sent shivers of dread up her spine. She'd never been so glad to see Ted Dalton walk through the door. The entrance of the cowhand allowed her to turn with a fixed smile, full of false regret, and decline Jason Kennedy. She said Ted had already procured her services for the evening. Ted verified her claim and sent Jason home as his father wanted to see him. Although also a rogue, Ted had always protected her.

Jason's sarcastic voice brought her attention back to the present interaction between brother and sister. "I've been busy transforming the ranch into a thriving farm that's now an agricultural wonder."

"Congratulations, Jason. How did you know I was here?" Lucy said in a weary tone.

The twins both eyed the stranger and squirmed to get down. Jason smiled at them as he answered. "Mother wrote me about your trip plans last month. I wasn't sure of your itinerary, but the Hawkinses are well known and easy to find. Therefore, I thought calling on them might yield information. My plans to be here on business were set, so why not try to see my sister?"

Hallie decided to take control of the situation. "Jason, why don't you come in for a brief visit? Here, this is Amanda Richards, your niece. Amanda, this is your Uncle Jason," she said thrusting the little girl into his awkward arms. "We were just about to put them down for their naps. You go help Lucy, and I'll get some refreshments from Mrs. Franklin."

Lucy looked protective and fierce as she watched her brother holding her daughter. Hallie knew Jason now entered precarious territory and smiled as she shut the door.

Jason turned on the staircase. "Hallie, I mean, Mrs. Hawkins, would you please ask for coffee and not tea?"

"I can ask, Mr. Kennedy, but you'll drink what Mrs. Franklin prepares."

In the end, Hallie prepared their refreshments as she found the cook behind schedule with the dinner preparations. Lucy and Jason argued in angry whispers as she carried the tray into the parlor. They both grew quiet as she entered.

Jason smiled in satisfaction as she handed him a cup of coffee.

"Did the children protest too much?" she asked, taking a seat beside Lucy.

"I think their uncle intimidated them," Lucy said.

Jason glared at his sister. He then turned his attention to Hallie. "Lucy tells me you're a widow, a nurse, and run a home for the less fortunate."

"That's right. My husband was an exceptional man."

"He must have been to reform you," he sneered.

Peace settled on Hallie at that moment. "James's influence and love will always echo through my life, but it was God who transformed me."

Jason stared at her. "Oh, that's rich. You found religion. How convenient."

A deep southern voice cut through the room. "I wouldn't say it was a matter of convenience, sir, but more a matter of conviction."

Hallie fought the urge to laugh as she watched Jason turn, and the sneer on his face become a look of trepidation. Boyd

Richards advanced into the room to stand in front of Jason Kennedy. Although tall, Jason had to look up to meet the golden gaze of his brother-in-law.

"It's about time we met, Jason. Your mother proudly displays your picture," Boyd said.

Realization registered on the younger man's face. "So, you're the golden boy who married my old maid sister."

Boyd's eyes narrowed, and Hallie saw Jason take a step back. Lucy rose, placing a hand on her husband's arm. He turned and smiled as he put a protective arm around her.

"Yes, I have the privilege of having your sister as my wife." Boyd gestured to a chair. "Please, have a seat."

Once they all sat, Lucy turned to Boyd. "Where's Billy?"

"He's once again helping Mrs. Scott with chores."

"Where are Jared and Charlie?" Hallie asked.

"Well, Mrs. Scott gathered them from Amelia's as planned, and we met her at your house. Robbie and Jared just finished a fair game of chess. Very impressive for one so young. Lieutenant Rigby offered to bring them over with me if Billy wanted to stay and help Mrs. Scott."

"Where—" she started as the door burst open.

Eddie had both boys by their collars. "When I tell you two to stop throwing rocks, I mean it."

He released them as they became aware of the group in the parlor.

Hallie raised an eyebrow and motioned the disgruntled boys towards her.

"Charlie. Jared."

Both bowed their heads.

"Mrs. Hallie, you don't have to say nothing. I'm sorry," Jared said.

"Don't tell Ma," Charlie pleaded.

"We'll talk about it later. Now, meet our guest. This is Mrs. Richards's brother, Jason Kennedy from Texas. Mr. Kennedy, this is Charlie Scott and Jared Rigby."

Hallie noticed Jason staring at Jared and grew uncomfortable until he turned toward Eddie with a question on his face. Hallie gestured. "This is Jared's uncle, Lieutenant Edward Rigby."

"Nice to meet you young men and you, sir," Jason said as he shook hands with Eddie.

Charlie nodded and turned to Lucy. "Where are Amanda and Henry?"

"Napping and, yes, you may go wake them."

Jared and Charlie smiled at each other.

"Nice to meet you, sir," Jared said as they raced from the room.

Hallie shivered as she saw Jason's gaze follow Jared out the door.

He turned to Eddie. "Rigby? Please don't be offended by my next question, sir, but do you have a sister who works in Boston named Julia?"

The room grew quiet. Eddie didn't smile.

"I don't believe a gentleman should ask that question in mixed company."

Jason's level gaze moved to each person in the room and back to the lieutenant.

"As your answer could potentially impact others in this room, I do think it's appropriate."

"Jason, stop it!" Lucy said.

"Just wait, dear sister. I'll ask you again, sir. Is Julia Rigby your sister?"

Eddie stared at Jason for a measured moment. "Yes, sir, Julia is my sister, and if you know her, then you've frequented an establishment that might give your sister pause."

"I doubt that," Jason said.

"Why would you want everyone to know this information?" Eddie asked.

Jason smiled. "Because, Lieutenant, if my eyes don't deceive me and my calculations are right, I believe your nephew is my son."

Hallie's blood chilled as she remembered the story Julia had told her about Jared's father.

"What?" Lucy rose.

Eddie stared with hard eyes and compressed lips at her brother.

"Mr. Kennedy, I don't believe Julia is able to determine the parentage of Jared's father. Why would you want to make such a claim after all these years?"

Jason turned to Lucy. "Don't you see it? He has my eyes. His face is the same as mine when I was his age. The curly, lighter blond hair is the only difference. You talk to me about not recognizing my niece and nephew! You've been here and not recognized your own nephew."

Lucy sat down. "Jason, how could you?"

Boyd's face became grim as he put an arm around his wife. The situation continued to deteriorate. Jason always managed to cause havoc.

"Mrs. Richards, I'm afraid your brother must be mistaken," Eddie said.

Hallie found her voice. "No, no, I don't believe he is."

Eddie looked betrayed and startled. "Hallie, did Julia tell you that Jason Kennedy is Jared's father?"

"No—her words made more of an inadvertent disclosure. Let me explain. Jason, before I do, are you sure you want to pursue this?"

Jason paled and then eyed Boyd and Eddie with defiance. "If he's mine, the circumstances don't matter."

Hallie sat beside Lucy and took her hands. "I apologize in advance for what you're about to hear." She stood and faced them. "The reason I'm sure without final confirmation from Julia is because of another incident, which happened at the saloon in Texas. You see your brother did more than seek the services of one of the girls there. He beat her so badly that she couldn't work for months. I hadn't seen or heard of another incident like it until Julia shared about Jared's father."

She paused as she saw Eddie stiffen. "You see, she said it was rare, but she thought she knew who Jared's father was. She'd been sick and had some other problems the month before what she called the most terrible night of her life. Her first night of work after recuperating from her illness, a student at the new Technical Institute in Boston came to call. She didn't tell me his name, but called him a Texan and shared about his cruelty to her. He spent time with her and then beat her. She didn't work for two more months. After she discovered her pregnancy, the woman who owned the establishment allowed her to work in other capacities until after Jared's birth. Until now, it remained a familiar, but not a probable connection."

She stepped in front of Eddie as he started forward towards Jason. "No, he's not worth it."

Boyd and Lucy stood. Horror reflected in Lucy's eyes, and disgust shown in Boyd's golden gaze.

"It's time you left, Jason." Boyd took his brother-in-law by the arm.

Jason jerked away. "I'm leaving but will be back. My attorney will soon address this."

Eddie's breaths turned ragged. "You have no proof. Just probability."

"It's enough. I'll contact Julia," Jason said.

"No. You won't see my sister."

Jason laughed. "I don't think you have much say with Julia or she wouldn't be where she is."

Eddie lost restraint at that point and no one wished to help him find it. Jason hit the floor hard. He straightened, wiping blood from his lower lip. "I deserved that. Therefore, I won't report it to your superiors. I will, however, have my son. Good day, dear sister."

"Just leave, Jason," Lucy said.

Jason hesitated for a moment. Boyd stepped forward.

"Let me assist you."

Jason glared as he placed his hat on his head. "That won't be necessary. It's been a surprisingly productive day. I came to visit my sister and found a son. Quite the family man."

His cruel laughter continued until the door closed upon his exit. Numb silence settled on the occupants of the parlor. Eddie clenched and unclenched his fists. He turned to look at Lucy.

"Mrs. Richards, please pardon me, but I don't see how Jason Kennedy can be your brother."

Lucy crossed to take his hand. "I'm so sorry. My parents would be appalled at this behavior. My mother still has hope for him, but my father has learned Jason's true nature."

Eddie's face filled with compassion and concern. "If all this turns out to be true and they *are* Jared's grandparents, how will they feel? How do you feel about being his aunt?"

"Lieutenant, children are never responsible for their circumstances. I'm honored, as they'll be. Jared is a wonderful boy."

"We can't tell him. That's Julia's place," he said.

Lucy nodded. "I agree. In hindsight, there was something familiar about Jared. I just couldn't place it."

Hallie watched Eddie's face. She could almost see the thoughts rushing through his mind. It didn't surprise her when he looked at her.

"Hallie, my meeting with the officers was moved to this morning. That's why Major Hawkins came to get me so early. I've made one decision and am about ready to make another. The events of this day now necessitate it. Is the position still an option for me at Hallie's House?"

"Yes. Are you sure?"

He nodded, "We need to try to wire Julia, or I need to take Jared to Boston for a few days. When we return, Julia will be with us. Is there room for her?"

"Of course, and I'll let my friend at the theater know he might have the seamstress he needs." She smiled and then frowned.

"What is it, Hallie?"

Hallie hurried from the room calling, "Jared Hawkins Rigby."

~~~

Eddie wanted to stop her. "No, no. I must honor my sister. She should be allowed to tell him," he said, but Hallie had disappeared.

Boyd turned as his wife put a hand on his arm with determination burning in her eyes. "Boyd, I think my brother can be stopped before he begins. At least, from a legal standpoint. Don't forget who my father is. Let me contact his most prominent legal consultant here in Washington. Of course, my name will get me in the door, but you, my husband, will have to accompany me. I'll wire father and follow with a detailed letter."

Eddie felt grateful and cautious at the same time as he saw Boyd nod at his wife.

"That's a good start, but let me also wire Andrew in Virginia. Remember his status and contacts," Boyd said.

"You both are very generous. I know it looks like our

families may be linked, but we should wait until Julia arrives before you go to all this trouble and expense," Eddie said.

Boyd met his gaze. "Lieutenant, my brother-in-law is an unscrupulous man. It would be best to stay ahead of him in this potential legal battle. If you're concerned about our motives, don't be. We won't try to take Jared away from you. Protecting that innocent child is foremost on our minds even if he turns out not to be family."

Lucy's eyes widened. "Oh, no, no, Lieutenant Rigby, please don't think we would want to take Jared away, nor my parents. I grew up with Jason, and he'll push until things bend to his will. All of us must work together. The one thing Jason and I share is tenacity. Hopefully, I can use mine to work things out well for Jared. If he's my nephew, I at least owe him that. Besides, he needs to learn the good heritage of the Kennedy's, not just the ruthlessness of my brother."

Eddie felt ashamed. His life had made him cautious. "I'm sorry to have offended you. It's just the only real family I have are my sister and nephew."

The chiseled Texas rancher nodded as he clasped him by the shoulder. "I'll no longer stand on ceremony because, like it or not Eddie Rigby, your family relations may have to expand to include us."

The pressure clutching his chest released with the expulsion of a deep breath. "Thank you."

Hallie returned minus Jared and watched them. "What's on your mind, Hallie?"

She smiled, "I told Jared to avoid talking to Mr. Kennedy without one of us present. He wanted to know why, and I told him it went for him and all the children. It satisfied him for now as he promptly went back upstairs to resume his game, but I wouldn't be surprised if he pushes for more reasons from you later. Anyway, since I walked back in this room, I've been waiting for you to come to your senses, accept their help. Let's quit standing around talking. Believe me, Jason Kennedy is putting things in motion at this moment. Lucy knows this to be true. I'll have Mrs. McDonald watch the children so Boyd and Lucy can make those inquiries, and you can drop me by the telegraph office. Then you'll be free to see your superiors and ask for a discharge."

"I resigned this morning. This just confirms my decision."

~~~

As they rode in silence, Eddie thought about all his years in the military. It would be odd to not have someone telling him where to go and where to be each day. His life had pretty much been scheduled for him since his late teens. The first instance of him making a decision ruled more by his heart and not the military led to a command return to Washington. However, he refused to renounce his actions. It took all the influence Major Hawkins had, as well as his exemplary military record, to keep his discharge from being dishonorable. The military had controlled everything in his life except for his private thoughts and emotions all these years.

Now, just as he regained the freedom to decide the direction of his life, a new challenge had arisen. This time there would be no chain of command. The outcome for Jared depended on the decisions the adults in his life made.

Determination to protect his nephew and sister burned in him. He exhaled.

"What?" Hallie's voice reached him.

He shook his head and frowned.

She smiled. "You sighed. What's going through your head?"

He smiled. "Sorry, I'm just preoccupied with the many life changes happening in tandem. I hope to be able to make my way without being an army officer. Julia and Jared need me."

Understanding lit her face. "Change is intimidating. When I first came to the fort from Texas, all I wanted to do was get back on the next stage home. You didn't help."

He grimaced even as she laughed and continued.

"Your attitude challenged me, and I always like to achieve what others doubt I can do. Anyway, my point is, you need this change and challenge. Sure, Julia and Jared are your primary motivators now, but your resignation or acceptance of discharge this morning shows you knew it was time before this situation with Jason Kennedy occurred. God certainly knew. See how He made you available?"

Eddie shook his head at her ability to sum up any situation. His eyes glimmered in admiration as he said, "Hallie, you're a dose of what I've needed for a long time."

Her smile faltered a bit.

"Don't be so sure. Give yourself a few weeks of living under the same roof and dealing with all our ladies' challenges in an official capacity."

A newfound certainty settled on him. "You forget how long we were at the same fort and how smooth the situation has been at Hallie's House since my arrival. I know the job will change the situation a bit but not in a substantial way. My biggest challenge will be getting Julia to adjust once she's here, not you."

Hallie averted her gaze and licked her lips. She glanced back at him. "How is Miss McWhorter?"

This quick change of subject unnerved him a bit. He shrugged. "Still allowing me to call on her. At least one beautiful young lady appreciates my charms and dashing good looks." His eyebrow lifted in a challenge.

She stilled as she met his gaze for a brief moment. His pulse raced and his mouth went dry—what a dangerous path to try and unadvised for many reasons.

The buggy slowed, and the driver turned. "Telegraph office."

Hallie appeared grateful. The moment disappeared, and soon, so did Hallie as she jumped down without waiting for assistance.

~~~

By that evening, the confirmed changes in many lives began. Julia had wired an immediate response as Hallie had known she would. When it came to her son, Julia Rigby would sacrifice even the one livelihood supporting her survival.

Eddie visited the tailor to have a new suit made for work purposes. He also purchased a few ready-made shirts and pants. Although less formal than his uniform, the new clothes gave him a rugged appeal. A new wave of irritation rushed through Hallie as she watched him with the one who helped him choose his new clothes. Mary McWhorter fawned over him. Somehow, she thought the young woman would cease to be interested if Eddie left the military. Hallie didn't mind him calling on any young woman of his choice, but this particular one grated her nerves. He should find someone and marry. He needed a wife to love him well and bear him children. Jared and Charlie adored him. If James had lived, they'd talked about adopting a child from one of the orphanages, but Eddie could have a child of his own someday.

Hallie heard a knock at the front door and watched as Susannah Hawkins went to answer. As Mrs. Hawkins learned the details of the day's earlier events from Hallie, she appeared less welcoming and cautious as she opened the door. She responded with needed wariness as Jason Kennedy once again stood on the threshold. Jared and Charlie were in the garden with the judge's children. Hallie uttered a silent prayer of gratitude.

"Mr. Kennedy, I appreciate the introduction; however, under the circumstances, I cannot invite you into my home," Mrs. Hawkins said.

Lucy Richards started forward, but her husband stepped in front of her and strode to the door.

"Allow me to deal with my brother-in-law, Mrs. Hawkins." He reached a hand to widen the opening of the door. "Jason, let's step outside."

The door shut upon exit. Eddie seemed preoccupied as he stared at the door.

"Mrs. Richards, your brother is an attractive man. What is his full name?" Mary McWhorter inquired.

Lucy exchanged glances with Hallie, Susannah, and Molly before giving a reluctant response.

"Jason Kennedy. I would also like to advise you or anyone who has dealt with my brother, he's a dangerous man."

The last part must have penetrated Eddie's cloud of pondering. He frowned and placed a protective hand on Miss McWhorter's arm.

"You're not to worry. I can guard you from him."

A thoughtful look crossed the pretty face, and contemplation appeared in the violet-blue eyes.

"My dear Lieutenant Rigby—Oh, I can no longer address you as that. I mean, Mr. Rigby, I am sure that won't be necessary. It appears the man is merely interested in seeing his son."

Hallie's lips compressed into a firm line as she shook her head and said, "Tread into that pool at your own peril, honey."

Alarm, followed by confusion crossed Eddie's face. The

rest of the women shook their heads and excused themselves, leaving Hallie with Mary and Eddie. Billy took Molly's elbow and followed the women out to the garden where Ben and Marie Richards assisted Mrs. McDonald with the children.

Hallie stared at the couple for one more perplexing moment before it also became too much for her. She hoped Eddie figured it out soon.

"Please, excuse me," Hallie said. "I need to go help Molly get the boys ready to go home. I have to work at the hospital tonight. Mary, I know you need to be going home. Be so kind as to let Mr. Richards know we're in the garden as you leave. Just don't get into any conversations with Mr. Kennedy." She saw a slight flush on Miss McWhorter's face as she passed. She hoped Eddie noticed it.

~~~

The next week turned eventful and surprising in ways none of them could have imagined. Julia arrived within four days of notification, just as Hallie anticipated. However, no one expected Jason Kennedy and his attorney at the train station. Hallie's estimation of Julia rose as she watched her receive the legal papers they presented.

Julia remained calm and counter-produced legal papers from her handbag.

"My lawyer will be happy to discuss this with your representation, Mr. Kennedy. As you will find in the papers, my son and I are protected from your harassment until such a time as you're granted any legal rights, which I find doubtful."

Jason's face remained arrogant, and his lip curled as he responded. "Oh, I'll be granted rights, Miss Rigby."

His attorney shot him a warning glance before turning to Julia where she stood between Hallie and Eddie.

"Miss Rigby, we will review your papers, and I'll send a copy of ours to your lawyer in Boston. Good day."

Jason gave a mocking tip of his hat as he followed his attorney, Mr. Cook, off the platform.

Julia watched them depart and then turned toward Hallie and Eddie with a weary smile. "Now, I know you two wanted me out of the business, but this . . ." She sobered as she saw their startled faces. "No, no, no, I don't think you had anything to do with Jason Kennedy's actions except for Hallie's confirmation regarding Jared's parentage. I never thought Mr. Kennedy would ever be a part of our lives. The chance of his sister visiting the Hawkinses is still uncanny. What's she like?"

Eddie bent down to pick up his sister's satchel before putting an arm around her. "Lucy Kennedy Richards is nothing like her brother and very much on your side. Let me see you ladies to the wagon, so I can go fetch your trunk. We'll go home for a meal and talk about everything. Jared is going to be fine, even if I have to find a wife and adopt him." He emitted a tight laugh as he escorted them forward.

~~~

Talking over lunch at Hallie's House seemed an ideal plan. However, the other residents of the house made it impossible. All were excited to meet Jared's mother. They bubbled with stories about his and Charlie's escapades, leaving Julia doubled over in laughter. As the women all had different schedules, one would excuse herself to leave for work just as another either arrived or came downstairs. This continued for two hours after their actual meal.

The inhabitants of the house also had varied reactions to finding out about the lieutenant's new status in the house. Of course, Hallie had mentioned the possibility, but their complicated pasts included trust issues. Having a sister as a resident became the one thing in Eddie's favor.

They'd just finished washing the dishes when the door burst open accompanied by the exuberant voices of two little boys. The duo had spent the first part of the day playing at Amelia's house with Robbie and Clara under the watchful eye of Mrs. McDonald. It would've been easier if the regular school schedule had resumed. Mrs. Brady shooed them from the kitchen. Julia looked at Hallie and Eddie as she took a deep breath in preparation for greeting her son.

"Julia . . . I mean . . . Mother, what are you doing here?" Jared stood in the dining room with his mouth open and his eyes wide.

All adults involved had chosen to keep Jared in the dark

until Julia had a chance to talk to him in person. As Hallie took him to visit in Boston a few days each year, he didn't expect his mother here. On the few rare occasions when Julia had come, she'd stayed in a hotel and met them. Jared had a cordial relationship with his mother, but both maintained more independence than interdependence.

Charlie took a step back as Molly followed them into the house and shut the door. Jared's face now reflected a cross between apprehension and excitement.

"Well, Jared, seeing as your Uncle Eddie is here now, I thought it might be a good idea for me to come, too." Julia received a frown from her brother and continued. "That and there's the possibility of your father coming to see you."

They all should have known Julia would be blunt. She didn't often revise things to soften them a bit. All eyes watched Jared. Hallie crossed to sit in the dining chair closest to where he stood and reached for his hands to draw him to face her. His brown eyes darted from his mother to Hallie.

"My father? Do you know who that is, Mrs. Hallie? I didn't know I had one."

"Oh, Jared, everyone has one. The Indians killed mine, and you just never met yours," Charlie said.

Molly looked astounded. "Charlie Scott, we're going upstairs this instant. I'm sorry, everyone."

"What did I say? It's true, Ma." Young Charlie's voice drifted back to them as his mother assisted him upstairs.

Hallie waited until Jared's attention returned to her before answering him. "Yes, my darling boy, you have one. In fact, you met him the other day. Do you remember meeting Mrs. Richards's brother, Jason Kennedy?"

He frowned and bit his lip. She saw realization dawn as his eyes met hers. "That would mean Mrs. Richards is my aunt. She didn't seem too pleased with her brother. Why?"

She could only imagine how Julia would finish the tale. However, it belonged to her. But Hallie knew all the while that Eddie could at least frame it better for the boy.

"I think your mother and uncle would like to go outside and talk in the garden with you," Hallie said.

Eddie looked grim but grinned as his nephew let go of

Hallie's hands and came to stand in front of him. "Yeah, come on. Now don't look so serious. You have more family than you realized. That's fun, isn't it?"

A small smiled emerged. "Yes, I guess. I like the Richardses. Does this mean Henry and Mandy are my cousins?"

Julia looked confused, but Eddie nodded. "Yes, it does. Now, let's show your mother the garden and your swing. She'll tell you about your father."

Hallie remained in the chair as they left via the door off the kitchen. Life had finally settled into a regular rhythm over the past three years. She'd expected ripples, but why so many at once?

Eddie's homecoming, the visit from their Texas friends, her imminent departure to finish nursing school, and even Julia's new residence with them—something for which she'd prayed—would have been a joyful events if not under the shadow of Jason Kennedy's arrival.

God had a definite plan. She'd learned to trust despite circumstances.

A knock on the door jarred her from contemplation. She sighed as she stood and went to see the arrival. Delight and relief filled her at the sight of Billy Cooper's endearing grin and sparkling, multi-hued, blue-green eyes.

"Hello, Billy. Molly and Charlie are upstairs. Come on in."

He removed his stained Stetson as he ambled inside the formal foyer. "Actually, I'm here to see Micah. He's going to take us to see the newspaper office where he works. It seems Washington has many newspapers. You remember Lucy worked at the newspaper office before she married Boyd?"

"Of course, I do. You'll enjoy Micah's tour. Are the boys going?"

"Yes, and so is Mrs. Scott."

His eyes darted around as he smiled.

Hallie couldn't help smiling in return. "Micah must have arranged a tour for you. I know he'll be here soon, but I'll have to check with Molly about the rest. Also, I do know Jared won't be joining you as his mother just arrived. He's with her and his uncle now."

Billy nodded. "It's not right what Jason's doing, but we both know he never cared too much 'bout that. Doing what's right,

I mean."

"Unfortunately, that's true. Now, give me a minute, and I'll go get Molly and Charlie."

"Yes, ma'am."

The front door opened as Hallie reached the top of the stairs, and she saw Micah stick his head in the door.

"Hey, Billy, let's go."

Billy looked up with so much a resemblance to an anxious puppy it touched her heart. No matter her reservations about the fast progression of his relationship with Molly, he deserved the treasure he pursued.

"Billy, I'll take Charlie to the Hawkinses' on my way to the hospital," Hallie said. "Molly has been handling the house most of the day and deserves an outing. I'll leave Eddie in charge. He needs to give Jared and Julia some time. Micah, go on out to the wagon. I'll send Molly right down."

Micah winked at Billy before closing the door.

~~~

The beauty of the small, well-tended garden area behind the house hosted a small storm cloud in the form of a turbulent boy. His demeanor grew darker as his mother explained the situation in her straightforward way. His uncle interjected comments to avoid detonating the minefield of words. Eddie stopped her from giving the complete description of the injuries she'd suffered at Jason Kennedy's hands. The Julia he once knew would have tried to shelter a boy from the harshness of the realities. However, Eddie guessed that she figured it hadn't protected her brother. However, he knew better. Her efforts to shield him had helped him at the beginning. Jason Kennedy wouldn't steal his nephew's childhood.

"I don't want to know any man who hits women. I'll tell him so," Jared stated with his arms crossed as he sat between them on the decorative wooden bench.

Eddie raised an eyebrow. "I admire that feeling Jared, and what Mr. Kennedy did was wrong, but we must be fair."

"Edward Rigby, how dare you?" Julia shouted.

"Julia, wait and let me finish. Jared, there are many kinds of men in this world, and you'll learn the truth of them by their actions. However, I've learned to give everyone who has wronged me a chance to redeem themselves. That's all I'm saying. If your father has become a better man, we'll soon know. You should try to get to know him and watch carefully. We must let you decide what you think about him for yourself. But as our knowledge is limited to your mother's experience and my brief meetings this week, we'll protect you."

Jared nodded, sniffed, and then looked at Julia. "Mother, I'm sorry you got hurt."

"Do you know, I don't really think on that part of it so much because I got you? Jared, I . . . I love you, and I'm the one who's sorry for putting you through everything."

Julia's eyes were bright as she took her son in her arms. She gave Eddie a helpless look as the tough young lad buried his head against her and cried.

"Excuse me, Eddie, could I speak with you, please."

Hallie's voice beckoned him from the tree-covered path. He stood, dropped a kiss on Jared's head, and patted Julia's back as he left to follow Hallie to the side door.

"I'm so sorry to interrupt, but I have to leave for work now. Charlie decided to go to the Hawkinses' to play with the little ones there. I'll drop him by on my way. Molly has gone with Micah and the Texas group to the newspaper. I told her you would be in charge here," Hallie said.

He glanced back toward the garden

"Eddie, give them some time. I know she's a little too plainspoken, but she's his mother. He's used to her ways. They're all he's ever known. Things will get better, and they'll find their way." She waited until he looked at her and smiled. "Have some faith."

He closed his eyes and then startled her with a hug. "Yes, ma'am, and thank you for the reminder, as well as the work to occupy me at just the right moment."

He felt her stiff form soften for a moment as she returned his hug before stepping back and opening the door.

"You're welcome. I'll be home at eleven."

As he followed her inside, the time stated hit him. "You mean that you'll be arriving home at eleven tonight? Who sees you home?"

She laughed. "Eddie, I work this shift three times a week,

and you've been here."

He shook his head. "I guess too many things have preoccupied my mind."

She retrieved her handbag as they reached the entryway where Charlie waited.

"Mary McWhorter?" she said.

He grinned, "Sure. Pretty women always turn my head. That and a few other things have me distracted. Now, you still haven't answered my question. Who sees you home?"

"Dr. Jones or his new partner, Dr. Morrison, have their own buggies and see me home."

"Good. I'll take care of everything. There are some papers I need to prepare for the next board meeting. It'll be my first, and I need to start strong. You won't mind if I go over things with you tomorrow?"

"Not at all. Have a good afternoon and evening. Try to enjoy having your family under the same roof, and don't work too much. Molly will be back later in case we have any new arrivals. Come on, Charlie."

"Bye, Lieutenant Rigby." Charlie waved as he took Hallie's hand.

Eddie waved back as they walked to where Ian waited in the wagon. The old Irishman jumped down to help Hallie up after she boosted Charlie onto the seat. One of Ian's jokes sent the trio on their way laughing. Eddie smiled as he shut the door and headed to his office. It had only taken a few short days for him to establish a routine. His sister's arrival disrupted the day, but his work provided a set purpose to keep him focused.

He glanced in the dining room and parlor on his way to the door to his office; both were empty for once. Another indication of how well his best friend's vision for this refuge for women worked. None of the residents moped. All but two of the women were either at work, preparing to go to their job, or completing chores for the house. As the newest, Julia didn't follow the plan of the others for now due to the legal battle for Jared. The other woman, Bridget, remained in the hospital.

~~~

Bridget McAvoy crawled to their door five nights earlier.

Her fiancé, an established young man in the community with an esteemed career in banking, had beaten her. Bridget—a Scottish immigrant who'd lost her mother to illness during the journey across the ocean—fought to recover.

Her father had been pleased when she caught the eye of the man who had contracted him to complete the detailed woodwork in his new home. Liam McAvoy had been a skilled carpenter in Scotland. Hope for a better life drove them to America, but it took a period of grief and near starvation to drive the proud man to take his daughter and go door to door. He pled for the opportunity to demonstrate his skill for a day's wages.

Caleb Pierce looked longer at his daughter when he hired Liam than the work demonstrated on the new cabinets. However, the longer Liam worked, and when visitors to the house made complimentary comments, the man began to take more notice. So many future offers appeared from friends of Mr. Pierce that he had to acknowledge the man as a reputable tradesman. It also made his daughter a much more suitable consideration. The attentions of an established man flattered Bridget and honored her father. Delight soon turned to dismay after their engagement announcement. Caleb became jealous over any notice taken of Bridget during social outings and then even of gentlemen tipping their hats to her as they passed on the street. It started with a simple slap and escalated to a severe beating at the door to her home following an evening outing. They had dinner at the home of the bank president, and Bridget dared to say thank you and smiled a little longer than thought necessary at a compliment given by one of the unmarried associates.

Caleb beat her and left without a backwards glance. Too ashamed to knock on her father's door, Bridget lay there for hours before she crawled and stumbled the two blocks to Hallie's House. Her legs gave way as she mounted the steps to the porch. Molly heard the soft knock as she made the final check of the house for the night. Bridget couldn't reach the string of the brass bell kept by the door.

Micah came to get Eddie to assist them. "Rigby, get up. It's time for you to see why James opened this house."

He'd never slept too heavy as a soldier, and expected abrupt awakenings, so Eddie took no exception to his old comrade's manner.

Molly and Hallie lifted the new arrival off the floor as he came down the stairs. He intervened and scooped the slight auburn haired woman into his arms.

"Where do you want her?"

Hallie pointed to a sofa where Micah had spread a sheet. "There—for the moment. I need to get her wounds cleaned, but to be honest, we'll need to get her to the hospital after that. This is the worst I've seen this year. Micah, I want you to get to bed as you have work in the morning, and Molly you've had the late shift and need rest. I'll relieve one of my fellow nurses at the hospital and work the night shift. That way, I can get this one settled. Erma will work my hospital shift tomorrow if I relieve her tonight."

"But Hallie, you just got home a little while ago," Molly said.

"I'm fine. I can take the boys to Amelia's before going to bed after I get home in the morning."

Eddie's head reeled. "Stop this, ladies. Hallie, you tend to her cuts, and I'll get us to the hospital. Afterwards, I'll come home to rest for a bit before I take the boys to Amelia."

~~~

Hallie had shared Bridget's whole story with him two days ago after a much more alert visit with the recovering patient at the hospital. Her father agreed to their proposal of secrecy as to his daughter's whereabouts. Dr. Jones listed her as an unknown on the patient list, and Mr. McAvoy told Mr. Pierce that she recuperated with relatives in New York. What a blessing the marriage didn't come to pass because the rights of the husband often sent some of the women back into too many terrible situations. It seemed almost better to be a poor woman in need than an affluent one.

The situation came too close to what his sister Julia must have experienced at the hands of Jason Kennedy, yet still different enough to give Eddie the perspective he needed. It intensified his determination to keep his nephew from a daily relationship with his father and to protect his sister, as well as all the women now in the realm of his care. A much different battlefront than what he'd grown used to as a soldier, and in many ways more precarious because the rules of engagement involved social intricacies.

At present, he continued to learn the detailed backgrounds and circumstances of the residents. Hallie stated that they aimed to make these women safe, emotionally stable, and able to take care of themselves, whether they moved out as independent women or returned to their families. Reconciliation and forgiveness were encouraged unless the original situation remained dangerous. The myriad of issues propelling women to seek solace at Hallie's House included physical abuse, young widows doomed to the streets by a lack of family, wives abandoned by husbands, and girls who found themselves left to care for siblings after the death of their parents.

The last, both Eddie and Julia could relate to as it mirrored their past. Hallie's House didn't provide permanent residence for those it cared for, only a bridge to a better life. The ladies needed help to take the steps to the other side. Hallie, Molly, the supporting churches, the pastors, community volunteers, and now Eddie were vital in this process. They gave support, fostered accountability, and helped facilitate the emergent potential needed to succeed.

Eddie frowned as he sat at his desk and stared at the paperwork of Edna Thomson, one of the women leaving at the end of the week. A war widow whose husband came home with his health devastated by multiple bouts of dysentery and pneumonia. He survived but remained unable to work as he did before the war. She lived with his family during the war. However, once home, expectations were different. Work as a laundress and maid covered their basic needs until he became ill, and she had to care for him full time. The aftermath of his funeral proved too much, as it also involved the miscarriage of her child. Edna stayed at Hallie's House for six months and now worked for the post office. She now rented a room with another lady at a reputable boarding house.

Survival and navigating imposed changes to one's way of life; Eddie saw these framed in his own life, in the country during the war, in the soldiers he fought beside, in the struggling economy, and in the enemies he fought—especially the Indians. *Sunbeam.*

A brief knock on the door followed by Julia's entrance startled him out of his pondering.

"It's dinner time, my dear brother."

He looked at the clock on the mantle. "I'm sorry. I didn't realize so much time had passed. Forgive me."

She moved to sit in the chair facing him. "Eddie, once we get through this with Jason, we need to talk."

He moved the papers in front of him aside and smiled. "Certainly, but why wait? Do you want to talk now?"

Her observant eyes never wavered. "Wrong question. I meant about you. We were supposed to have lunch when you came back to Boston. Since then, you've learned the high and low points of my life, but haven't afforded me that same luxury regarding your life except for the war. I sense there's more to you leaving the military than you've allowed, and I want to know. We have sidestepped each other's lives for too long."

He propped his elbows on his desk and rubbed his hands across his face. He then faced her with absolute candor. "You're right, Julia, and I want to sit down with both you and Hallie to discuss it, just not today."

"Hallie? Why do you have to tell her? I mean she was the wife of your best friend, but that doesn't mean you owe her the details like you do family."

Eddie stood and circled around the desk to sit on its edge in front of his sister.

"Yes, I do, because of a promise I made to James on the day before his death. It concerned Hallie and because something happened in my life to prevent me from keeping it."

Julia narrowed her green eyes for a moment. "Fair enough, but don't keep it inside too long."

He grinned. "Deal. You always knew me so well. You haven't even been under the same roof as me for a day, and you're already making me feel like the little boy hiding his misdeeds. Just remember, I don't keep them all to myself any more. I pray."

She rolled her eyes. "Don't start on me. We'd better go. The ladies are waiting dinner on us, and Jared wants you to help him with a project."

He laughed and took her by the elbow as they closed his office door.

~~~

Julia changed dresses three times before accepting the

approving comments of Hallie and Molly. They'd arranged for her to meet the Richardses at the Hawkinses'.

Lucy and Boyd had chosen not to meet her when they dropped off Molly and Micah the previous evening. They had much to share with her and wanted it to be in private.

"Julia, relax. They're nice people. Be thankful Jared has some relatives besides us," Eddie said as he helped her into the carriage saved for special occasions. Ian had taken Sara shopping at the Market[xvii], so they couldn't use the wagon.

Hallie smiled, "Besides, the Richardses are nothing less than spectacular representations of true Texans. Jason is just an example of ruthlessness. Also, try to cover your reaction when you meet Boyd Richards."

Julia cocked her head. "Why would I need to do that?"

Eddie groaned. "Oh, here we go again. I swear Hallie would have married that man if it wasn't for James."

"Let's just say he's a man who makes you consider giving men a chance, but no, James was the one for me. Besides, the man was destined to marry Lucy."

"Don't worry; I've met more than enough men. Their ability to fascinate me has long since vanished. It's nice to consider an honest reaction, as I now won't depend upon them for the money needed to survive. I've even let myself start thinking about creating clothes again. When did you say I'm to meet with your friend at the theater?"

"This afternoon, but work on the next show won't start until September. That should give you time to resolve this situation," Hallie said.

Julia sighed and looked ahead with determination as the carriage jostled towards Georgetown. "Yes, that's good. Now, tell me all about the Kennedys so I'll be prepared."

~~~

Susannah Hawkins opened the door with a bright smile. "Miss Rigby, it is so nice to see you again. Please, come in."

"Thank you, ma'am. It's good to be able to tell you in person how grateful I am for all the help you've given my Jared," Julia said as she took the outstretched hands of the woman of the house. Her green eyes scanned her surroundings. "My, my—what a nice house this is. I mean the row house was very nice, too."

"Oh, my dear, that's right. The last time you visited our home James was still with us in Washington. Yes, this was my childhood home. I grew up in Georgetown. Thank you for the delight of being part of Jared's life. Now, if you will follow me, the Richardses are waiting."

Hallie and Eddie followed the two women into the music room without even a sideways glance or uttering a word between them. Lucy worked on a bit of stitchery with Marie. Ben and Boyd sat next to the window reading over some papers. All looked up as Julia entered with Mrs. Hawkins. Lucy handed Marie her needle, stood, and smoothed her dress. She hesitated but soon moved forward.

"Miss Rigby, I'm Lucy Kennedy Richards. Before you say anything, please allow me to offer apologies on the behalf of my parents and myself for what you've endured at Jason's hands and for the turmoil he's creating in your life at present. That being said, we're delighted to discover Jared is part of our family and want you to feel a part also."

All eyes watched as Julia completed a slow appraisal of the tall woman in front of her. A small smile emerged as her eyebrow lifted.

"I guess if you two stood side by side, it would be obvious that he's your brother. Same height and hair color, but those blue-green eyes of yours aren't his. I just realized my Jared may have his father's brown eyes, but they're not hard. No, they are kind—like yours. Thank you."

Lucy's dimpled smile erupted, and Marie hurried to stand beside her. "I'm Marie Richards. Lucy's husband is my Ben's brother. Things are going to go well."

The two brothers made their way to where their wives stood; both men burnished and strong; one with a limp and the other full of rugged strength. None could deny their brotherhood.

"Ma'am, I'm Ben Richards. We have much to discuss," stated the husky voiced younger of the two men.

"It's easy to see who the prettiest Rigby family member is. It's a privilege to meet you, ma'am," Boyd said, bowing before he moved to his wife's side. "I'm Boyd Richards, Lucy's husband."

Hallie watched his golden eyes, waiting for Julia to

respond. Julia turned and caught her gaze with such a knowing look that she had to look away to keep from smiling. Eddie had no such compulsion. He shook his head and grinned as Julia spoke.

"It's a pleasure to meet both you gentlemen and your sweet wives. I just wonder how you ladies manage to keep your composure when I know all the ladies must be close to swooning at the sight of your husbands."

Lucy and Marie shared tolerant smiles. "We're just two well-loved wives who are confident in their men," Marie said.

"Marie—," Ben started and then saw her protest-stopping smile.

"Please, everyone, have a seat, and I'll bring you some refreshments. I'll leave you to your discussions," Mrs. Hawkins said.

Once everyone settled, Boyd handed Julia a stack of papers.

"Miss Rigby, these are from my wife's father's legal representation, our legal consultants, and a telegraph from her father. Please take a moment to review them and allow your brother a perusal. Hallie informed me of your procurement of your own legal counsel and be aware these men will work with your attorney at your discretion."

Julia took the papers without saying a word. All waited in apprehensive and expectant silence. Marie jostled her knee in nervous anticipation until her husband placed a stilling hand on her rustling skirts. Lucy bit at the edge of a fingernail until Boyd also circumvented her by taking her hand.

Hallie stood to stretch her back. A rather large patient had required turning every two hours during her shift the previous night. The window beckoned her from across the room. The view overlooked the pristine garden James's grandmother had groomed through the years and his mother still tended with the help of a gardener. Many in Georgetown thought it compared to the gardens of Tudor House on 31st Street.[xviii] Many of the blooms drooped as the summer reached its end, but it remained a vibrant green. The bustle of the city sometimes kept Hallie from stopping for respites like this. James used to love to sit outside early in the mornings and early evenings. He used to say it would have been unbearable to have to stay confined within walls without taking time outdoors to appreciate God's creations. She turned to find Eddie looking over the paperwork.

The rustle of the pages broke the silence as he passed them back to his sister.

"Will your father truly be able to enforce this under these conditions, Mrs. Richards?" he asked.

"Mr. Rigby, my brother has underestimated my father, but others long associated with him in the area of business know better. He might have let my brother have his inheritance early, but he made sure protections and conditions applied. One such condition states my brother must marry and conceive legitimate heirs before the age of 35 years. My father has the rights to a life estate of his property with Jason as the proprietor. My brother can make all the profit off the land and business unless he breaks this or any of the other conditional requirements. Now, please, don't misunderstand. Jared's grandfather doesn't wish to exclude him as one of his heirs. He now has holdings in East Texas beyond the land across from our ranch. It's his nature to invest in land, and he's done so. He does have one stipulation though. Jared must wait until his eighteenth birthday before he tries to take the legal name of Kennedy. Is this insulting to you, Miss Rigby?"

Julia's green eyes narrowed as she leaned back against the chair. One foot kicked the bottom of her skirt from her crossed legged position. She stopped, placing both feet on the ground, as she leaned forward with a straight-backed posture.

"Not at all, Mrs. Richards. In fact, that's my preference. My son already has a fine name, Jared Hawkins Rigby. It reflects the most important people in his life and the families who have seen to his care. If I had wanted to make any claims on the Kennedy family, it would've been when my son was a baby.

"You see, I also took some legal precautions to protect myself from a situation such as this. After the terrible events of the night your brother visited my place of business, my employer wanted to press charges. If not for the personal damage and the loss of business, then for the damage he caused to the room and furniture. He also left without leaving payment. It put the chief of police in Boston in a rather unsavory situation. He chose to contact the dean of your brother's school and call a meeting. Your brother was left with the choices of writing his father to take care of the situation, making restitution on his own, being asked to leave school, or signing a paper to the effect that he would never frequent my business again and waived any rights if a child might have resulted. Most people wouldn't have cared if a girl like me died, but the police cared enough to prevent the exposure of some prominent people. Here's a record of the paper signed by your brother. My attorney provided a letter to his, disclosing this document. I'm sure they'll endeavor to discredit its validity, but it, along with your family's support, might be enough."

Boyd nodded. "Well addressed, Miss Rigby, but you don't understand. Our family does want to recognize and claim Jared as a legitimate part of the Kennedy family even before he's eighteen. In all other respects, Mr. Kennedy is claiming Jared as his grandson. The final paperwork will make provisions for Jared on a monthly basis either to be paid by his father or grandfather. The judge will have to make the best determination."

Julia looked perplexed. "But why? I've always seen to his needs and will continue to do so. My new job is to start at the theater in Washington next month. I've saved enough, so we're fine until that time."

"I'll also be helping my sister and nephew," Eddie added.

Lucy reached for Julia's hand and gave it a squeeze. "As we're family, Jared will never feel unwanted or rejected by us."

Hallie saw the moisture in Julia's eyes as she turned to look at her brother. Their shared history of loss and abandonment surged between them. Julia turned back to the compassionate woman across from her.

"Thank you, Mrs. Richards."

Hallie laughed as Lucy gathered a shocked Julia into a hug.

"You two had better quit being so formal. Julia, get used to the hugging. I've found it to be something these families do a lot of daily."

Julia laughed for the first time since entering the room, and everyone relaxed. "Thank you, Lucy and let me see if I have this straight – Boyd, Ben, and Marie."

"Perfect!" Marie beamed at her.

The door opened as Mrs. Hawkins entered with a tray. During the serving of the refreshments, Julia agreed to request her lawyer come for a meeting with their legal counsel at the end of the week. The Richards family planned to be back in Virginia for the last three days of their visit before returning to Texas. If any unforeseen problems arose, their cousin, Andrew Richards, would come from Virginia to assist Julia. Hallie watched Eddie and Julia share repeated looks of disbelief as lunchtime approached. Their discussions included the historic preclusion of the law to prevent or acknowledge a woman's rights. The precedents had always leaned towards the father's rights. However, with decisions such as "Pennsylvania vs. Addicks" in 1813[xix] and other more recent cases, mothers now had a chance. Boyd's cousin, Andrew Richards, had been so kind as to supply them with a listing of cases in America, as well as in England. Julia asserted her intention of reviewing these with all legal representatives involved in the case. Major Hawkins came home at lunch and readily participated in the group's continued discussion over the meal. He reiterated the advantage of Julia's imminent employment in a more acceptable position. The courts would have frowned at her prior occupation and the fact of separate residence from her son as possible conditions of being unfit and her not overseeing her child's care. Of course, this outraged Julia, but she acknowledged the legitimacy of the argument.

Hallie and Julia left soon after lunch for official introduction to her new employer. Julia would return after the meeting. Molly planned to pick up the boys and meet her there, as Hallie would be at the hospital after their trip to the theater. It would give Julia a chance to meet the Richards children, as well as Billy Cooper.

Julia turned to Hallie as Eddie assisted them into the wagon.

"What an unexpected family. I get the feeling Lucy can stand firm against her brother. She's both kind and spirited. I really like her and Boyd." She stopped to shake her head as a meaningful smile appeared. "You're right about that one. There's a handsome strength in him."

"You can't even imagine the story there. He was a lethal man of restraint when I first met him. Now, his faith strengthens him."

"Whatever it is, I'm just glad he'll be part of Jared's family."

Eddie nodded. "I agree with both of you ladies on the character of the man and his family, but don't start writing poetry. The resolution of this legal battle could take a while. It will truly try the bonds of family and friends. People sometimes will revert to siding with those from their past instead of new acquaintances."

Hallie frowned. "That's true in most cases, but this concerns Jared's future. I watched the Kennedy family try to justify Jason's earlier behavior as youthful indiscretions. His father doesn't abide violence against women. The incident in Texas contributed to Jason going away to school. His family hoped a less familiar environment would intimidate him enough to put him on a more responsible path. They now know how wrong they were. If the situation didn't involve Jared, it might be different. No offense intended, but they're protecting blood viewed as a grandson, nephew, and a cousin. It makes a difference."

Julia nodded. "I'm depending on that."

~~~

Eddie dropped the ladies off at the National Theater and decided to drop by the McWhorter's on his way home. Hallie said they would probably be there most of the afternoon. Her shift at the hospital didn't start until six o'clock, so she requested he send Ian to get them by five. The Irishman could drop her at the hospital where she had a change of clothes first and then return Julia to the Hawkinses' home as Molly and the boys would be through dinner.

Eddie had paperwork to do, and he needed to go by Calvary Baptist[xx], one of their church affiliates and the Hawkinses' home church. A young mother and her child—found in an abandoned building—would arrive at Hallie's House that evening. He wanted to get all the details from the head pastor. Mary lived near the church; therefore, it wouldn't be a detour to see her.

She planned to leave at the beginning of the coming week for Connecticut. Her exact affections for him remained vague. His pursuit began as a matter of practicality, but he did find her more attractive than he'd imagined. A slight bit of her sparkle dimmed when he received his military discharge. However, a new determination appeared as she shopped with him, and she seemed to enjoy his transformation into a businessman. He'd kissed her once—a pleasant experience.

He frowned as he pulled the carriage beside another parked in front of the large house. Just after lunch, so maybe she and her mother were entertaining. Hesitancy slowed his steps up the walk, but he found himself knocking once he reached the door. One of their maids opened the door.

"Good afternoon, Lieutenant, won't you come in?"

He removed his hat. "Yes, thank you. Is Miss McWhorter at home?"

"Yes, sir, the family has a guest, but I'm sure she won't mind me interrupting on your account."

"Please, don't. I'll just leave my card."

"No, no, sir. I'm sure she would be cross with me. Excuse me for just a moment."

Eddie watched the young maid hurry to the parlor door and as she opened it wide enough for her ample form to slip inside, he gained a glimpse of the other caller. He stiffened as he recognized the profile of the man seated in the chair. A flash of anger and betrayal went through him. This . . . he couldn't begin to understand.

Mary soon appeared in the company of the maid, wearing a look of guilt. She shut the door behind her. A forced smile appeared on her face as she made her way to him.

"Eddie, I wasn't expecting you. Hasn't your sister arrived?"

His green eyes narrowed. "The first is obvious given the caller now in your parlor, and the second is something I'll no longer discuss with you."

Her violet-blue eyes blinked at his tone. "Please allow me to explain."

"I wish you would do so, because it's beyond me as to the reason that man would be welcome in your home given our present relationship."

She licked her red lips as she spoke in a soft whisper. "My parents were intrigued by the situation and story. Mother thought it would be polite to ask him to lunch." She took a breath and lifted her chin a bit, as she added, "So did I. You have not gotten the story from his perspective. I thought it would be helpful for you. Mr. Kennedy was a bit reluctant when he discovered my association with you, and he didn't wish to discuss such a torrid occurrence with women. However, what he did say has led us to believe your sister's actions caused his outburst so long ago. He was just a young man, and his friends forced him to go to that place with them. It seems your sister tried to steal his wallet."

The parlor door opened, and Mary's flushed mother glided to where they stood. A smug-looking Jason Kennedy came to the doorway to watch the scene.

"My dear Lieutenant, I mean Mr. Rigby, I believe you know Mr. Kennedy."

City people were unpredictable with their motto to associate with the most appropriate people for the season. It appeared he no longer qualified, and for now, Jason Kennedy did.

"Yes, that's correct, Mrs. McWhorter, I do know Mr. Kennedy, but it appears my knowledge of your family was in error. Therefore, I withdraw from my present role as your daughter's suitor. Good Day to you, fine people."

Shock and distress, soon followed by outrage, mirrored on the faces of mother and daughter while the well-dressed man in the parlor doorway wore a look of satisfaction. Eddie turned and exited the stylish home.

He took deep breaths and thought about the lands of Kansas and Nebraska. A prayer for guidance occupied the rest of his thoughts as he traveled to the church.

~~~

The line of numbers on the page denoting the finances involved in the community-supported home amazed him. How Hallie had managed to stay in the black?

He discovered each woman sought the opportunity to donate a small amount once in residence. Many continued to send small contributions even after they left. They took ownership of their lives and were grateful for the ability to give back to the place facilitating such opportunities. Hallie saved every letter sent with the recorded amounts in a separate ledger.

The sound of the bell on the porch pulled him out of his calculations and planning for the next year. The board had scheduled a meeting for the end of the week.

Iris Walker came down the stairs just as he reached the door. She appeared the most timid of the residents, but always demonstrated a willingness to help. All reports indicated it had taken close to three months before she interacted with anyone. Then by four months, she responded to Molly and, after she procured a job at the library, she availed herself to others in the house.

Her parents had both been in the clutches of alcohol most of her life. The more she tried to please them and fix things, the more ridicule came her way. She held a poor view of herself the first day she entered Hallie's House at the age of sixteen. Her wispy brown hair and hazel eyes—hidden behind wire-framed spectacles—gave her semblance to a small sparrow about to fly.

"Mr. Rigby, would you like me to help you welcome them? I saw the pastor helping them out of the carriage from my window."

Eddie smiled at the soft-spoken woman. "I would welcome the help, Miss Walker. This mother and daughter would benefit from your tenderness."

A small flush of color rose in the pale cheeks. "Thank you." She joined him as he opened the door.

"Dr. Cuthbert[xxi], Reverend Parker[xxii] told me you would be bringing these welcome ladies," Eddie said as the pastor of the First Baptist Church ushered his two charges through the door.

If Eddie hadn't known they were mother and daughter, he would have thought two sisters stood before him. Both were skin and bones. The diminutive mother couldn't have been more than twenty-two, and her daughter looked to be about six. Their blue eyes widened as they looked around and huddled closer together. The kind pastor smiled.

"Mrs. Phillips, might I present Mr. Edward Rigby and— I'm sorry, my dear—remind me of your name," he said, looking at Iris.

"I'm Iris Walker. Welcome to Hallie's House, Mrs. Phillips. And who's this sweet young lady?" Iris knelt in front of the little girl who alternately hid her face in her mother's skirts and peeped at the strange man and woman before her.

The small blonde woman gave her a wan smile. "Thank you, Miss Walker. I'm Juliana and this is my daughter, Millie. How do you do, Mr. Rigby?"

The woman—with just a trace of a German accent— endeavored an appropriate social response, and he remembered the history in her file. Juliana Phillips came from an immigrant family.

She and her husband had lived with her parents. They'd owned a small restaurant in the city for the past year following a move from Pennsylvania. The building burned along with their residence above it six months ago. Only Juliana and Millie survived the fire. The fire department removed them, but they had nowhere to go. She mailed a letter to family in Pennsylvania but never received a response. They returned to the shell of their burned home and survived on small handouts. After a short period, the city decided to clear the building and restore it for rent by a new store. That's when the authorities discovered the pair.

Reverend Parker sent another letter to her aunt and uncle in Pennsylvania. He felt something must have happened to the prior correspondence and shelter at Hallie's House would be temporary.

Eddie smiled at them. "I'm well, thank you, and very glad to make your acquaintance, Mrs. Phillips and young Millie. Why don't you go upstairs with Miss Walker? She'll show you your room, and you can rest a bit before dinner. The other ladies will be home shortly, except for Mrs. Hallie Hawkins, our proprietress, who's working at the hospital, and Sara Brady, who works at a restaurant. Also, one of our ladies is still in the hospital, but I'll let Miss Walker share all the information about the house with you as she sees fit. Please get settled and look around." He squatted in front of the small girl. "There'll be some playmates for you here this evening. There's another girl about your age named Caroline Brady and a couple of boys. One is my nephew. So you won't be stuck in the house with no one to play with."

He received a small smile before she hid behind her mother's skirts again. Mrs. Phillips thanked the pastor and followed Miss Walker upstairs with little Millie in tow.

"Please tell Mrs. Hawkins not to look into employment or anything for a few weeks," the pastor said. "I really feel we will hear from her family. When I checked with the post office, they had stopped delivering mail to their address after the fire and returned any correspondence after no one claimed it. Juliana didn't think to check with the main office. So, her relatives can't know why she hasn't responded if they did write her."

"Certainly, I'm sure their time here will be restorative," Eddie said. "When you've been on the street for a time, you keenly appreciate a warm bed, clean clothes, and food more than anyone."

"Yes, and that sweet pair have kind hearts. Good afternoon, Mr. Rigby. We will notify you if her relatives write."

"Thank you, sir."

Eddie shut the door and returned to his office with a quick glance at the clock on the mantle. He had less than an hour before dinner. The house would soon be at its most active. The chatter of daily events as dinner plates filled, while delightful, could prove exhausting at the same time. Everything here differed from the dinners at the fort and over the campfires on the plains. All in all, almost too much to do within a small space for him, and it surprised him to find a couple of such adjustment problems since his return. As he'd grown up in a city, the return to city bustle didn't surprise him as much as his discomfort within the confines of a normal household. His non-conventional background and, in many ways, the war had provided an escape from the more social life he'd once established with the Hawkins family. The events at the McWhorter's went through his mind again, and he wiped a weary hand across his face. He found that he also needed a period of adjustment, just like many of the women in this house. He bent his head and strode to where his papers lay on the desk waiting.

Chapter Four

HALLIE WOKE WITH a small frown and a lingering feeling of puzzlement. She'd returned home last evening to find Eddie sitting under the tree just to the right side of the front yard. After a quick good night to Dr. Jones, she'd hurried over to him. His green eyes gazed at the stars, and he didn't immediately respond. The noted delay made her inquire if he'd been drinking. A frown and laugh preceded his emphatic denial. He'd then updated her about the events of the house, including his sister's excitement about the theater. She'd then given him a detailed description of Julia's exuberant experience at the National. Then he'd asked her to sit for a spell. Given the hour and lack of traffic, she'd complied. Soft laughter followed as she'd realized how conscious of social conduct she'd become.

Her mind replayed their short and confusing exchange after she sat on the soft grass:

"How was the hospital?" he asked.

"It was an exceptionally quiet night for a change. Thank you for welcoming Mrs. Phillips and her daughter."

"You're welcome. They'll be fine—given time." His voice faded as his gaze returned to the stars. "Hallie, do you ever miss Texas?"

"Well, I don't think about it too much, but I guess the openness of the land, not my life there."

He nodded. "Yes, I feel that way about the plains. Being with family and friends here is so welcome, but my fellow soldiers and the land there still call to me."

She picked at a blade of grass. "Are you regretting your decision?"

He sighed and adjusted to face her. "Hallie, it wasn't completely my decision, and I'm lucky to have an honorable discharge with my rank still intact."

Her eyes locked with his. "What happened, Eddie?"

"I would like to meet with you and Julia tomorrow morning after breakfast. It's time you know, but for tonight, I don't have the inclination to open that chapter. Sometimes, I wish to go back about three years and resign my post at a better point, but life doesn't always allow us to do things perfectly. "

He sighed and looked away for a moment. A slight breeze blew and his mellow gaze returned to her.

"How's Mary?" Hallie asked. "Did you update her about Julia?"

He smiled and gave a sarcastic laugh. "No, no, and I won't be in the future. I've withdrawn my hat from her list of suitors."

Surprise lifted her eyebrows. "Why?"

He shook his head. "I found Jason Kennedy at her home. Her mother had invited him for lunch."

"She has fewer scruples than I thought. Eddie, I'm so sorry."

He studied her face and reached to brush her cheek with his callused hand. "Hallie, it's for the best. Mary strives for different things in life than I do. This event just made me acknowledge it. My, albeit limited, experience has taught me real relationships develop in a natural way."

He leaned his elbow over his bent knee and sighed. "Go on in, Hallie. I know you must be tired. I'll make sure the doors are locked."

She sensed his restlessness. "Eddie, do you need anything? I bet there's a slice of pie left."

He smiled. "No pie, thanks, but one thing would give a little relief to my despondency. Promise me you won't think anything of it and will forget it tomorrow."

"You're worrying me a mite, Eddie, but I'll agree," she

said with a smile.

He leaned forward, pressed his lips against hers, and then released their captured softness with a sigh. Once her closed eyes opened to meet his, he stood and held a hand down to help her to her feet. He gave her his most charming grin.

"Don't start thinking, Hallie. We're both tired. This never happened. You helped an old friend let go of a perplexing day."

She took his hand and returned his smile. "Sounds like you're the one over thinking. I don't even know what you're talking about."

They parted ways once inside; she went upstairs, and he remained below to secure the doors. The demanding events of the day had drained all but the ability to slide into bed after donning her nightgown. Sleep overtook her as soon as she hugged her pillow, therefore negating further pondering about Eddie until the morning.

She threw off her covers and rose to dress for the day. A quick face wash with the cold water in the pitcher by the basin left her refreshed and awake. Her puzzlement stemmed, not so much from the kiss but from the other things he'd promised to share with them later that morning. He must have missed James during such a difficult time in his life. Their pledge on the train came to mind. The time had come for her to stand by her promise of friendship. After one quick look in the mirror, she hurried from her room.

Breakfast rushed by even faster than usual. Molly had left a little earlier to drop off the boys because Mrs. Phillips and Millie accompanied them. Today, they would find out about Millie starting school with the others in a few weeks. Sara Brady and her daughter Caroline left at the same time. Their two young girls had chatted throughout breakfast. Margaret Elliot, Iris Walker, Anna Gage, Frances Dickens, and Sally Morrison left the house for work after the small group's departure.

Sara would return after she dropped off Caroline with her minister's wife. She returned to the house to complete a few household chores and then planned to rest for a couple of hours before leaving for work at the restaurant. She worked a split shift, so she could leave work in time to pick-up Caroline in the afternoons. She tried to keep the same schedule year round. Once school resumed, it only differed in regard to place. Then she'd drop off her daughter at school instead, but still pick her up at the same time. After either afternoon pick-up, she spent about an hour at home with her daughter before returning to work for the evenings.

Hallie looked at Julia as they finished the last of the breakfast dishes. Eddie excused himself and disappeared into his office even before the others finished.

"Well, are you ready?"

Julia looked confused. "For?"

"Eddie has asked to meet with us this morning—something about events during his period away."

Julia wiped her hands on the towel one more time before she hung it to dry on the small hook by the basin.

"Let's go hear what my little brother has to say. I have a feeling it's going to be something unexpected. He always got this look about him when he was keeping things closely guarded, and it was never good even when he was a boy. He's had that look since I first saw him in Boston the last time you were there."

Hallie nodded and followed Julia to the door to his office. Julia knocked.

Eddie's tenor voice responded after a few moments. "Come in."

He stood as they entered. "I knew it would be you. Please have a seat. Is anyone else in the house?"

"No, not today," Hallie said as she sat in the soft brocade chair.

Eddie waited for Julia to sit in the soft chair before he crossed to close the door. He turned, his hands behind him, and leaned against its solid maple surface. He closed his eyes and bowed his head. A heaviness settled in the room as the silence reverberated.

His voice jarred them in its quiet intensity when he spoke. "I left Washington in a state of grief and confusion after James's funeral. By the time I arrived back at Fort Hays in Kansas, I was determined to finish out the few short months left of my assignment and return here. You see, I'd promised James. As you know, Hallie, our boy always had a vision of how things should be, but even saying that, he'd learned to be open to revisions. Both of us learned orders changed in an instant in the military. I just never imagined such would be the case for me at that time. You see things were changing in Indian Policy. Even before they officially swore in Grant, they started the plans for what would become his Peace Policy. Without going into all the failed treaties and previous efforts towards peace, including the one Hallie was aware of because of James's consultation, the Medicine Lodge Treaty, as well as Taylor's Peace Commission, just continues. The treaties didn't achieve the desired results for either side. And let's just say, transitioning from President Johnson's administration to President Grant's proved revealing. I'm a great admirer of President Grant and have had the good fortune to meet him more than once. He was a remarkable general during the war. Anyway, from the appointment of Ely Parker to the utilization of the Quakers after all the issues in the Senate and House, it's been one change after another. The generals I have encountered during these past years, including Miles, Custer, and Sheridan to name a few, would astound you. The one general I wish to have had the privilege to serve under is General Howard, but I guess—"[xxiii]

"Eddie stop. Hallie and I aren't interested in the things we've already read in the papers. The grand company you've kept doesn't impress us. We just want to know what detained you and what almost destroyed you." Julia gave Eddie a pointed look as he lifted his eyes to them.

He sighed and rubbed the bridge of his nose with his thumb and finger. After a moment, he returned to the chair behind his desk. "Forgive me. You always have a way of coming to the point, as does Hallie. So, I'll give you the condensed version. Once I arrived in Kansas, orders came for our special detail to remain there for at least another year. I immediately wrote Major Hawkins. He couldn't do anything. With it out of my hands, I left it in God's and continued. Close to the end of that year, we got a new interpreter and scout—a Cheyenne woman. At that time, our jobs included guarding the railroad workers from the settlers even more than the Indians. It seemed strange to me. It felt like being back at our old fort. Anyway, a minister and his family took in this young woman at the age of fourteen. She'd been very ill and thought to be dying. Her father had promised her to a young brave, and the boy became distressed when the chief told him nothing more could save her. He took her away during the night and found the camp of the minister who traveled with a regiment of dragoons,[xxiv] and left her there as they slept. The next morning they arrived at the military fort, and the minister's family took her into their home. The doctor there nursed her back to health, and she grew up at the fort. Anyway, after she came to our post, we became friends. My detail's orders dictated we remain there at the end of the year, so it continued. They sent us where needed—the area of Fort Scott[xxv] with the settlers who tried to prevent the railroad expansion; Nebraska; and even into our old area in Indian Territory. She was always there or at times was with us on our journeys. We became very close. I fell in love with her."

He stopped and when they didn't say anything continued, "Her name was Ese'he[xxvi], something to do with the sun in Cheyenne. The adopted name given to her was Sally Evans, but I called her Sunbeam. Her smile was as bright as the sun, and her joy of life amazed me. She'd become a Christian after a few years with her new family. We read the Bible together. The merging of her faith with the appreciation her native background has for all living things, gave me a fresh perspective. She believes the Indians appreciate the value of the animals and land more than the white man does. The greed and bloodshed saddened her heart. Through her work, she hoped to build understanding as peace didn't seem possible. I asked her to marry me, and she accepted, but my commander denied my request and said I'd be insubordinate if I persisted. Therefore, we decided to wait until I received a transfer to Washington. She planned to come with me, but then something unexpected happened the next year. A detail brought a group of Indians who'd left their reservation lands to hunt to the fort. They were defiant, and the soldiers killed some of the hunting party before they reached the fort. Three braves remained, and their consequences remained undecided. They brought them in as I walked Sunbeam to dinner one evening. She stopped as the three bound braves passed us and called out to one of the braves. He turned, his scowl turning to disbelief, and said her Indian name. They forced him to continue with the others. He turned out to be the young brave who'd sought help for her during her illness—her promised brave. We'd spoken about him, and I knew she loved him. The next few days were hard as she pleaded for a reasonable punishment with their ultimate return to the reservation lands. She received permission to speak with him, as well as the other two men. Then it turned into a disaster. The prisoners escaped, and they accused her of helping them. Sunbeam denied it, but they didn't believe her. They arrested her and sent my detachment to deal with the escaped renegades. Orders were to capture or kill them. My thoughts were more those of a man than a soldier. Honestly, following my orders in the most preferred way would have given me back the woman I loved and the respect of my military superiors, but it wouldn't have been right. Sunbeam had talked long with her brave about returning to the reservation lands but not about escape. He said he'd agree if she would come with him. She hadn't told me of this or given him her answer when the captives escaped. If the braves evaded capture, no one could verify the truth, and Sunbeam might go to prison. Therefore, I told my men to shoot to wound not kill if possible. I planned to capture them. We had another Indian scout with us, and it still took a few weeks before we returned with the prisoners. Two received wounds, but Sunbeam's man returned unscathed. During the trip back to the fort, I discovered, via our scout, that another Indian from the fort had indeed helped them escape.

"Technically, I hadn't disobeyed orders, but I hadn't followed the preferred option. Killing renegades often sent a message to other Indians: if you don't stay on the reservation land, this is what happens. I received suspended duty for a month without pay. I lost my pay but not my rank because of Sunbeam. Orders came for her release and an audience with the officers. The bargain she made secured protection for both of the men she loved. In the end, I had to stand and watch her leave with the three men from her former Cheyenne tribe in the company of my men. She sent a letter to me once they arrived via Corporal Case. Needless to say, my remaining time at my post even after returning to duty wasn't the same. I followed orders to the letter and had no further incidents but the powers in Washington still had some questions.

"My record prior to the incident and after the incident helped the War Department see fit to give me an honorable discharge after I met with the review board and Major Hawkins the day Jason Kennedy darkened our lives. That's what you needed to know." He gave a bemused smile. "The shorter version."

Julia went around the desk and hugged her brother. "I love

you." He stood and nodded as she headed for the door. Hallie sat stunned as Julia exited, but Eddie seemed to expect it. He crossed his arms and raised a knowing eyebrow.

"She's never been able to bear seeing me hurt when she can't fix it. That's when she leaves. But this time, I know she's just upstairs."

Hallie said the next thing on her mind. "I saw Red Cloud and Spotted Tail[xxvii] when they brought them to Washington for a visit. They showed them off while they saw the city. I always wondered what their impressions were. I saw intelligence and pride in their stance."

He nodded. "Hallie both sides have heroes, and both sides have savages. I think Red Cloud must have finally understood why the settlers and soldiers act as they do. Getting to know Sunbeam helped me see through my enemies' eyes. Perspectives and what each values are so very different. The thing is—the country is expanding, and the Indian can no longer be a nomad. He's contained or given freedoms under the laws of our government. As citizens, we understand our constraints. They don't because they didn't help establish our government. From what I understand of Red Cloud, he's been very smart in his dealings since his visit."

"Eddie, why did you try to court Mary McWhorter?" Her eyes pierced his.

He returned her gaze without flinching. "Sunbeam married her brave. I have to move forward. The dictates of society seemed to make sense."

"Once you know what true love is, how could you try to settle for less?"

His eyebrow went up. "Thank you." He looked toward the ceiling. "You hear that James? That's what I told you. Your wife just confirmed it. Now, I'm free to keep the promise of heading Hallie's House but freed from the rest."

The numbing details of Eddie's life since she'd last seen him reverberated. She hadn't asked the right thing, and now everything within her came to attention at Eddie's words. "What was the rest, Eddie?"

No hint of humor remained on his face as he answered. "He wanted me to marry you."

Anger, hurt, and confusion rushed through her. Her mouth

opened to shout at the man across from her, but understanding dawned. "We could take care of each other. His two favorite people."

One of the corners of his mouth lifted. "It's my fault really. He must have seen me take notice of you before we left the fort. It was really just his guilt from robbing me of the chance to compete for your affections when he allowed them to ship me off. No, no— I'm teasing. None of us had any control. Things happened as intended. However, he did say he thought I found you tolerable and that you viewed me as a friend. He hoped we could build on that."

"Reasonable but not feasible, is it?"

"No, as you said, once you've known true love—"

"Did Sunbeam love you?"

"Definitely, but she also loved him. He gave her the opportunity to live at the cost of the anger of the tribe due to his actions and the loss of the girl he promised to marry. Now, he'd married another during their years apart, but had lost her at the hands of the soldiers. Some Indians have multiple wives. Sunbeam always carried love and obligation toward him in her heart. Those feelings were there before hers for me, so no other choice existed in her mind."

"Eddie, why would you make such a promise to James?"

His eyes grew moist. "He was dying, and it gave him peace."

The magnitude of his experience hit her, and she felt horrible about questioning him in this way.

"Eddie, I'm so sorry Sally Evans didn't become your wife. It's a joy to know you're loved for you, and it sounds like she did. It's hard to understand, but God will work this for good. Is there anything I can do for you?"

He shook his head. "Thank you, Hallie. You'd better go get some rest before your shift tonight. I have the board meeting."

She nodded and exited as he turned his attention toward the papers on his desk.

~~~

She traversed the distance from Eddie's office to the foot of the staircase in a daze. Heaviness made the ascent of the stairs a drudgery. Hallie kept her head down until she saw two feet on the next to the top stair. She lifted her head to find Julia sitting there. A weary sigh escaped as she lifted her skirt and turned to sit in the space next to the blonde woman. Julia shifted to give her more room.

"Hallie, he's different in so many ways. Eddie would always fight to make things the way he wanted them. He became more determined when things were harder. The night we got word of our father's death, he told our mother it would be fine. We were a family, but she left. Then he did all he could as we tried to make it alone, but I could see him sacrificing for me.

"He would pretend to have eaten and bring me all the food he could find. After I lost my job at the tailor, he insisted on being the one to take care of us. I knew he wouldn't abide the choice I'd made, but it would allow him to survive. That sounds odd; yet he made enough to get by alone. Therefore, I didn't give him a choice. I knew he was angry and wanted to change it. I didn't sense any anger in him about what he told us today—just resignation."

Every nuance of her prior recollections of Eddie from the first moment they met rushed through Hallie. She compressed and released her lips a few times before responding.

"You know Eddie didn't like me much when we first met. In some way, he sensed my ilk without knowing me. It had something to do with you and a lot to do with protecting James. Your brother is very loyal and protective of those he cares about. We became friends, and I came to know your brother better after I accepted Christ. The war taught him and James there are things you can't change. They followed orders without question. Time also taught them to look beyond their own plans to God's plans even before they unfolded. If they did the right thing, and things still didn't go as expected, I watched them both accept it with a shrug. Like Eddie going to Kansas when we came to Washington. What happened this time was a product of Eddie trying to do what he thought was right as a Christian man, and it got him in trouble as a soldier. He accepted the consequences, including losing his love. The one thing I question is his attempt to court someone like Mary McWhorter."

Julia smiled. "That just shows how ready he is for a home

and family of his own. But at the same time, I sense restlessness in him."

Hallie laughed.

"After being out on the plains, I'm sure city life is very confining for him."

"I'm sure you're right. It's just that a busy city used to be all Eddie knew, and it seems like being back would calm him. I mean Washington isn't Boston, but still—"

"You're afraid he'll leave?" Hallie asked.

Julia nodded and then laughed. "I once left him on his own, but now I would like to keep him around. There was a time when we made each other laugh even during hardship. My little brother was always a prankster and loved to make people smile."

Hallie reached over and covered Julia's hand with her own. "Don't think so hard right now. So much has happened. All of us need to treasure the time together each day and stop trying to see tomorrow before it gets here."

She received a smile. Julia stood and waited for Hallie to join her.

"Hallie, you need to get some rest, and I need to freshen up a bit. Lucy and Boyd are picking me up in a little while."

A stream of sunlight reached them as the front door opened, and Sara entered in a rush. She closed the door behind her, stuck her head in the parlor to check the clock on the mantle, and dashed up the stairs. Their presence at the top made her stop.

"I'm running so late. It took longer to help Mrs. Phillips get young Millie enrolled for the coming term. If Caroline hadn't been with us, I don't think Millie could've entered the building. I've never seen eyes so big. She asked to stay with Caroline at the minister's house, so I'll fetch both of them this afternoon."

Hallie looked down the stairs. "Where's Mrs. Phillips?"

"She went on to the market with Molly after Ian dropped me here. I barely have enough time for a rest before I need to leave for the restaurant." Sara smoothed back a stray strand of brown hair as she studied Hallie for a minute. "Are you getting one of your headaches? You're eyes have that look."

Hallie rubbed between her eyes. "Just a little, but I'm headed to my room to rest for a bit now. Thankfully, I don't have to be at the hospital until three. Excuse me, ladies."

She heard Julia and Sara exchange a few more words before the sound of Sara's footsteps and swishing skirts followed her. The woman gave her a small wave when she passed Hallie's door. Hallie shut it, closed the draperies, removed her dress, and placed a thin robe over her undergarments. The sheets were cool as she slid beneath them and closed her eyes. If she could sleep before the headache took hold, she could dissipate its intensity.

~~~

Eddie finished compiling all the documentation needed for the board meeting by one o'clock. He had a vague awareness of Julia leaving with the Richardses, Sara leaving for work, and wondered at the delay in the return of Molly and Mrs. Phillips. However, his sustained concentration reached such depths as to preclude the event of lunch and overlook the absence of Hallie. He thought about the coming school term for the children.

Schoolwork had always been drudgery for him, not because of difficulty, but due to the tedious amount of time it took to complete. He'd preferred being outside even before his abbreviated school experience. James helped remedy the shortcomings in his education by lessons written in the dirt at fireside or in muted oratory during marches between battlefields during the war. Afterwards, first in Boston and then as they moved to Indian Territory, actual books were introduced. His friend could have been a professor if so inclined. Eddie paused as the terrible tangles of *What-ifs* circulated his mind. He looked up and laughed as he sent a thought to his departed friend: *James, this may be worse than schoolwork.*

He stacked the ledgers and papers to the side of his desk and stood for a good stretch. The rumble of his neglected stomach moved him out the door. Just as he closed the maple barrier on his morning labors, the echo of voices emanating from the foyer reached him. They grew stronger as he moved down the passageway but came to an abrupt stop as he emerged. There stood Molly Scott and Billy Cooper.

Billy clutched his hat tighter. "Lieutenant."

Eddie shook his head. "I know it will take time, but please call me Mr. Rigby or Eddie."

"Mr. Rigby, is Miss Hallie here?"

A voice drew their focus to the top of the stairs. "Here I am."

He watched a somewhat pale Hallie descend in her hospital dress. Molly stepped forward and took the hands of her friend as she reached them.

"Hallie, Billy and I need to talk to both of you."

Eddie watched Hallie search Molly's pretty face for a moment; tilt her head, and then smile.

"I bet I know what's coming, but I do want to hear it from you," she said. "Let's go get something cool to drink and sit around the table to talk."

Hallie brought glasses of refreshing water with a little lime and small plates of gingerbread for each of them balanced on a tray. Billy looked like an out-of-place scarecrow with his lanky, angular limbs sticking out from the elegant dining chairs. He smoothed his straw colored hair several times as his multi-hued eyes darted from Hallie and Eddie to Molly. His Adam's apple bobbed a few times before he spoke.

"It's like this. I've asked Molly to be my wife, and she's accepted."

Billy took a quick gulp of his tame drink as he watched the man and woman across from him. Eddie looked at Hallie and found her smiling at Molly. The magnitude of what this could mean didn't seem to bother her in the least. This meant *he* must forge ahead.

"I can see you both are very happy in each other's company, but I must ask your specific plans from here," Eddie said. "It would be unreasonable to think you haven't looked at all the lives to be impacted by your decision."

Molly looked at Billy, and he nodded.

"Mr. Rigby, you know all about my journey," she said. "In fact, you've been a part of it, and I want to, once again, express my gratitude for your kindness and care at the fort. I've lost much, but God has restored my mind, and now He's sent this wonderful man to be my husband. He's also sent him to be a father to Charlie. Our paths crossing after Hank's death was not a coincidence. Those thin threads connecting us had purpose. God meant them to become thicker and more interwoven later—now. I've had many concerns as we've discussed the direction for our lives together, but in talking with Billy, as well as my mother and Charlie, those are now laid to rest. We also have the support of the Hawkinses, the Jacksons, and the Richardses. Now we want your support and understanding. I must apologize for the impact this will have on Hallie's House and more than anything on Jared. He and Charlie have become more like brothers than just friends. Jared must be allowed to visit for all our sakes."

Eddie felt a pang of hurt for his nephew, even as he felt hopeful for the young couple. He drew in a deep breath and exhaled. "So, you'll be moving to Texas?"

Billy nodded, "Yes, sir. Mrs. McDonald will also go with us."

Hallie's warm words sounded like a blanket of blessings. "I'm so happy for you. Molly, you belong on a farm not in this enclosed city. It's the life you knew before tragedy struck. Charlie will be sad to leave here more than you will because it's all he remembers, but he'll soon relish the freedom there. Your mother needs to slow her pace a bit. She's a strong woman, but the responsibilities she has taken on working for the Jacksons and the Hawkinses have been immense. Billy, you're a good man to extend care to her. You and Molly deserve each other. Both of you have endured great loss and now have been given a great love. I'll miss Molly and Charlie, though. All of us will."

She quirked an eyebrow at Billy. "I knew you'd been taken in hand when I heard you went to the Richardses' farm with the Kennedys after the last time I saw you."

Molly jumped out of her chair and circled to hug Hallie. Eddie took it as his cue to stand and shake Billy's hand.

"I'll talk to Julia about letting Jared visit. She'll want to wait until this legal battle is over."

Billy grabbed his hand with a strong return grasp. "Of course, but let me assure you, Jared's grandparents are good people. They'll help Julia to the extent she allows."

Hallie hugged a red-faced Billy before turning to Eddie.

"I have to leave for the hospital now. Please forgive me for not finalizing things for the board with you. I wasn't feeling well. Please let me know the outcome of the meeting, and we can review plans tomorrow."

He frowned. "Let me take you to the hospital as Ian isn't

back."

Molly turned. "Yes, he is. He was just showing Mrs. Phillips where we store our preserves. She loves to cook. He left the wagon ready to take Hallie."

The blue-tinged shadows under Hallie's eyes and the pallor of her skin bothered him. "Are you sure you should go today?"

A perplexed look mixed with a wry smile accompanied her response. "I've been going to work feeling worse than this on many days throughout these past years. Unless it's impossible for me to walk, I go to the hospital. I owe Dr. Jones my best efforts. I'll see you tomorrow." She turned back to the newly engaged couple. "Molly, I'll help you with your packing in the morning. I gather you'll marry in Texas."

Billy smiled. "No, ma'am. We'll marry here in two days. Everyone here has become family for my Molly and Charlie."

Hallie glanced at the clock. "Oh, I have to run. We'll get everything together."

She dashed out the door, calling for Ian. Eddie felt Molly's kind, blue gaze as he turned. "She's very thankful for her life here. The only thing she'd change is to have James. However, I pray for her every day because she doesn't give herself permission to ever rest. She takes care of everyone else first."

Eddie didn't give a response, and she didn't seem to want one. Molly took Billy's hand and informed him they needed to bring in the items Ian had unloaded.

~~~

Eddie heard the footsteps on the wooden floor outside of his office a few minutes after the front door closed for the second time within the hour. After the first time, the echo of the exuberant voice of Charlie mingled with Molly's laughter, and Billy's Texas drawl drifted through the house. Now he sat anticipating the sound of a knock. It soon came with the door opening in tandem. His nephew entered and plopped down with dejection radiating from his youthful face.

Eddie cleared his throat. "You're supposed to wait until I tell you to come in after you knock."

The brown eyes flickered up for a brief moment. "Sorry."

"Accepted. Now, do you care to tell me what has your

mouth so turned down?"

Jared shifted and bit a fingernail. "Charlie's going to Texas."

"That's true. We're also losing Mrs. Scott and Mrs. McDonald."

The gate of emotion opened. "It's not fair! Why did Mr. Cooper have to fall in love with her? I want them here. Charlie's my best friend."

Eddie let his mind and heart wrestle with his nephew's feelings before he spoke. He stood and moved to the chair next to the one occupied by Jared.

"You know James Hawkins was my best friend. I had to let him go more than once, but we always remained friends. So will you and Charlie."

The skeptical brown eyes appraised him. "Really?"

"Absolutely. You'll see him from time to time as you have relatives living there."

"So you think Julia, I mean, Mother, will really let me visit?"

Eddie nodded. "Not right away, but I bet within the next year."

"Will you go with me?"

Eddie felt a lump in his throat. "Sure, if you want, but your mother might want to travel with you. She's never been anywhere besides Boston and Washington. Just like you. Her new job looks like there might be some time between the shows for which she'll be sewing. If I do go, I'll have to make sure things are taken care of here."

Jared's face brightened. "Miss Hallie will take care of everything. She always does."

Eddie nodded and leaned forward. "Jared, since you've been living here, who do you feel takes care of you the most?"

A small frown followed by a slight thoughtful tilt of his nephew's head followed. "Well . . . everyone has helped, but I think Miss Molly and Miss Hallie in different ways. Miss Hallie makes me feel safe, and Miss Molly treats me like she does Charlie. Now that Mother is here, I hope she'll take care of me."

"Do you remember James?"

"A little. He made Miss Hallie happy. I remember her

laughing and smiling more then."

Eddie smiled, "He could do that." His nephew stood up and gave him a solemn hug. "I'll be your best friend, Uncle Eddie."

Moisture filled his eyes. "Thank you, Jared. I'll be here for you. Now, you'd better go find Charlie. You don't want to waste any time."

A big smile erupted. "Yes, sir!"

The door soon slammed as the boy made a quick exit.

~~~

Eddie headed home tired after his meeting with the board members. Politics and Society in Washington were a maze. His ears hurt from all the discussions prior to the review of the business pertaining to Hallie's House. They approved the extension of the endowment funds after he presented the success stories of so many of the women. They had focused on the failures until he presented letter upon letter from employers, friends, and family members extolling the positive impacts and avoided missteps due to having a haven with a bridge to change. In so many of the cases, a true life or death situation existed, where having a choice other than the grim reality of hopeless despair, made the difference.

He stressed why the ones termed "failures" had in many ways chosen not to succeed. A few found change too frightening. Some had lived in negative circumstances for so long that it caused them more anxiety to live any other way. They were at home in poverty and abuse. You couldn't force anyone to accept a better life. The new lives of the women who stayed weren't lavish. Employers didn't pay women well, but the ones who walked through the doorway of change offered by Hallie's House gained a clear perspective about their previous circumstances. Better didn't mean richer. They grasped the reality of a life beyond where they'd started.

The gaslights in the parlor were dim, and he could just make out the silhouette of his sister curled up in a chair next to the window with a cup of tea.

"How were the wolves of society?" she asked.

He gave her an indulgent smile as he collapsed into the chair opposite of her. "Tamed now. We're approved for another year."

She nodded as he yawned.

"Why are you still up?" he asked.

"I was stewing about all the information the lawyers shared with me today. Hallie came home from the hospital with a bad headache. She told me she's always had headaches since she was a little girl—just like her mother. This one was so bad she couldn't stand the bright lamps. We dimmed them, and I took her upstairs. She didn't even put on her nightclothes and requested to sleep without being disturbed. I did all checks and accounted for everyone in the house. Now that you're here, I'll retire. Molly offered, but I told her it was time to pass the torch as she's leaving. I like feeling useful. If any late new arrivals come, wake me."

She stood and bent to kiss his forehead before taking her cup to the kitchen. He waited for her at the bottom of the stairs. "I'll walk you up and then check on Hallie."

"I checked on her a few minutes ago and brought some cool rags. She was grateful but groggy. I'm sure she'll be fine. You need rest, Eddie."

He quirked a warning eyebrow at her with a grin, "Sister, dear, I'm fine and will check on Hallie."

She sighed. "Fine."

They climbed the stairs in comfortable silence, and she patted his arm as she opened the door to her chamber. He lifted his hand and continued down the passage to Hallie's door.

Julia had left it ajar. The door creaked as he pushed it open. Hallie lay on her back with an arm flung over her eyes and forehead on top of a rag.

He walked to the bed and reached down to smooth the dampened hair away from her temples. Her hair lay like a dark shawl around her shoulders.

"Hallie?" he whispered, sliding the rag away. No longer cool—he placed it in the bowl of water on the bureau, squeezed it out, and returned it to her forehead.

Hallie shifted. "Eddie?"

She reached to hold the rag in place as she started to sit up, but he eased her back down with a gentle touch.

"No, no—you rest. I sent Julia to bed. The ladies are asleep, and the meeting went well. Can I get you anything?"

She stared at him in the darkness. The lamp light from outside the door provided a dim illumination of her face.

"No, I just have to get still until sleep comes. If I can sleep, the headache will be gone when I awake. It's been a while since I've had one like this."

He kept his voice soft as he fingered the ends of the long, silky strands of hair on the pillow. "I'll let you rest then."

He stood, lingering for a moment before moving to the door.

Pain laced her soft voice. "Thank you, Eddie. I'm sorry to be a burden."

Regret tingled. "Hallie, you've never been a burden since the day I met you. I just wish there was some way for me to take away your discomfort. Good night. Call out if you need anything."

He pulled the door to, leaving a small crack.

~~~

Dawn emerged from the night as Hallie eased open her eyes with a complete feeling of refreshment. Wellbeing registered in every fiber. It always amazed her to experience this state in the wake of terrible pain and healing sleep. If she didn't sleep, the headache could linger for a few days at varied degrees of intensity. Thankfully, rest came not long after Eddie visited her the previous evening. The throbbing in her head had made his words and actions hard to register at the time. Now she pondered his gentle concern and kindness as she stretched like a lazy cat, enjoying the extension of her no longer tense muscles. She sighed and sat up to face another busy day.

The peculiarity of timing depended on perspective, and she saw God's hand in it. The hospital seemed to need her to increase her hours just as Eddie took over the administrative duties of the house. Dr. Jones had shrugged, reminding her how the influx of patients came in small ripples or large waves. Besides, she planned to leave for Boston in just a couple of weeks.

It would be odd being away. In order to save money, she'd decided to stay the first month without coming home. There were more concerns now that Molly would be in Texas, leaving Eddie with the complete responsibility of running things. However, Julia showed a willingness to help. Once her job with the theater started, it would be daytime hours until the week before and during the run of the show. Hallie saw creativity spark within Eddie's sister as she talked with the head of the theater. The talents she'd abandoned long ago were still present, just a little rusty from lack of use. There again—the timing factor.

Hallie looked up. "Thank you."

By the time she made it to the dining room, she discovered the clock showed an hour later than she thought. Eddie and Julia sat alone at the long table. The other ladies had departed for the day, and the distant sound of laughter signaled the presence of Jared and Charlie playing in the yard. The siblings smiled as she joined them. Eddie rose and returned with a fresh cup of coffee for her.

"Thank you for this and the rest, but I really needed to get up earlier, before dawn. It's a big day. Bridget is coming home today. Also, the final dinner with the Richardses is tonight."

She took another fortifying sip of warm coffee and sighed. "Oh, Eddie, I forgot to tell you one other item on our agenda today. A gentleman, Professor Grierson, is stopping by at eleven this morning to see you. He's trying to decide the best placement for his wife, Rebecca, either here or at the asylum. I met the couple the other night at St Elizabeth's and discussed it with Molly. She definitely felt Hallie's house warranted as the first consideration for Mrs. Grierson. I'll let you visit with him, and then we can decide."

Eddie nodded. "Fine. Might I ask the nature of the case?"

Julia stood. "I don't need to know this, so I'll take my leave. Let me clear the dishes." She gathered the plates with expedient precision and disappeared into the kitchen.

Hallie looked down for a few moments. "Mrs. Grierson is a woman who's at the point of mental and emotional exhaustion. She's always been a strong woman, and her husband is beside himself. Their children are grown, and he thought she'd be more relaxed. Instead she's sad, lacks confidence, and is anxious about many things to the point of exhaustion."

"Have they talked with their pastor?"

She nodded. "Yes, and, from what I could tell, Rebecca feels guilty about not being able to release everything."

He gave her a level look. "Hallie, this may be more than we

can handle."

She didn't blink. "Maybe, or it might give her permission to rest for a while. That perhaps will help. It's worth trying."

"We'll see. Well, are you up to reviewing the information from my meeting with the board?"

He stood, waiting for her to take a final sip of her coffee, and helped her from the dining chair. She preceded him to his office.

~~~

Eddie decided to be the one to open the door for the professor. About half an hour before time for the appointment, he left his office in search of a small bite of something from the kitchen. He'd just inhaled three slices of fresh baked bread, washed down by a cold glass of buttermilk, when he heard the knock.

A well-dressed man in a dark suit and a felt hat stood at the door. He wore spectacles over dark brown eyes and had distinctive black eyebrows. Removal of his derby revealed hair as dark as his brows, sprinkled with gray. Eddie stretched out his hand toward the somewhat shorter man.

"Professor Grierson, I presume? I'm Edward Rigby. Please come in."

The returned handshake held firm. "Thank you, Mr. Rigby. Yes, I am Ivan Grierson. It's kind of you to see me."

"Not at all. My office is this way."

He let the man precede him and, once there, watched the man lay his hat in the adjacent chair.

"If you get warm, please remove your jacket. There's a hook behind the door."

Eddie received a grateful smile.

"I believe I will. It's rather warm today."

Eddie waited until the man found his seat before he began.

"Professor, would you care to tell me about your wife?"

A frown appeared as the man removed his spectacles but then merged into a softer expression. The professor had a rich, expressive voice capable of capturing the attention of the listener. Eddie saw the man's life through his canvas of words as they painted a beautiful love story.

"My Rebecca was the loveliest seventeen-year-old the day I

first saw her at a picnic. A year lapsed before our paths crossed again. By then, she had blossomed into the most beautiful eighteen-year-old starting college, and I was a twenty-five-year-old teacher. If I had not returned for further studies needed to teach at the university, I would never have met her again. It took me two more years of courting to convince her to marry me. We both loved art, theater, history, and music. However, we also had differences. Rebecca has a fierce drive to complete her pursuits at the best level, often to the exclusion of many things. I am very competitive but love to enjoy things in tandem. Work never kept me from seeking enjoyment. Hers did. She is very hard on herself. When others see her as exceptional, she finds an insufficient performance. This got worse and then better as the children came. We went through many triumphs and trials. I think things started to crumble for her emotionally when her mother died just as our youngest daughter started college. Insecurities multiplied and she relived old failures. She seems to be trying to sabotage each area of her life—even our relationship. Mr. Rigby, there is no way I can convey to you what an extraordinary woman she is. Her former students and other teachers would tell you if they were here. It's as if she is afraid everyone will find out she is *not* extraordinary, because that is reality for her. If she keeps on as she is, I am afraid others may start to doubt her, and it breaks my heart."

Eddie couldn't think what to tell the man who had so much more experience in life—until his last statement stopped him. He fingered the small school slate Jared left on his desk the day before while contemplating a response. The man facing him replaced his eyeglasses. Eddie leaned forward.

"Professor, the whole world may start to doubt her, and I know they'll talk about her if she moves anywhere besides remaining at home. I can tell this will bother you. If you think a brief meeting with me will change her reality, you're wrong, sir. Please forgive me if this sounds harsh, but you must understand that your wife is at a dire point in her life. It's more than you losing her. She could lose herself if something doesn't change. I saw this with some of my soldier friends, and they were men. I can't imagine how hard this is for both you and your wife."

The man appeared taken aback and then angry. "She is my wife, and it is my job to protect her."

"Yes, yes, but how do you protect her from self-destruction? I truly believe God alone can do that."

The man put on his coat. "So, you cannot help her? The hospital at least felt they might."

Eddie looked down. "Please sit down, Professor. On the contrary, I think Hallie's House is exactly where Mrs. Grierson needs to be right now. Let her get away from all the expectations that her life currently holds for her. She needs to be in a place offering stillness. Let her regain spiritual, emotional, and physical stability. Hopefully, she hasn't fallen into the abyss of those who are now living within the walls of the asylum. One of our ladies lived there but is now restored. Personally, I feel the good Lord did the bulk of the healing in her case. I would suggest you meet her, but today is the day before her wedding and move to Texas."

"Really? How exceptional." The man stood again and retrieved his hat. He went to the door and turned with his hand on the knob. "I will bring Rebecca on Monday. Thank you."

Eddie fingered the pen in its holder, removing and replacing it several times before dipping into the ink to make notes about his meeting with the Professor. He would request Molly's input this evening. It served as another example of a hard lesson he should have learned after he first met Hallie—his first reactions could be wrong.

When Hallie first told him about the case, his old feelings from his mother's abandonment surfaced. He thought the woman wanted to find a way to leave her family. After visiting with the professor, he felt compassion for the woman.

~~~

The knock on the door took a moment to register as the group left the dining room. Hallie continued her conversation with Molly. Susannah started for the door, but Ben Richard's gruff voice stopped her.

"Allow me to get it, Mrs. Hawkins."

Susannah smiled at him and returned to where Lucy Richards waited to resume their discussion on the way to the parlor.

During this final night of the month-long visit of their friends from Texas, all present determined not to waste a moment.

They expressed thoughts and sentiments only the Richardses could appreciate. The sense of urgency increased more due to the imminent departures of Molly, Charlie, and Mrs. McDonald. The move to Texas necessitated by the planned nuptials tempered the excitement and joy surrounding Molly and Billy's marriage.

Ben opened the door. Conversations trickled away and ceased as an unusual silence followed.

An unmistakable southern voice with a tenor timbre uttered a hesitant inquiry, "Is this the home of Major Hawkins?"

Major Hawkins started toward the door just as Ben sent the man sprawling on the doorstep with a well-aimed punch to the chin. The women gasped, especially Marie Richards.

"Benjamin Leon Richards, what's come over you?" she demanded.

Major Hawkins helped the startled man into the foyer as Ben ignored his wife and glared at the newcomer. The man touched his jaw and shook his head. He then stepped forward and returned the blow with sufficient force to knock Ben backwards towards his brother.

Boyd's voice held a mixture of irritation and humor as he made introductions. "Everyone, please meet my best friend's brother, Jack Johnson. Jack, I'll make complete introductions of all here after you officially meet my ill-mannered brother, Ben."

Hallie could tell she would like this young man. His green eyes twinkled with goodwill and flashed a challenge as he spoke.

"Good evening to all. Actually, Ben, I'm glad we got that out of the way. I've wanted to do that since my brother and his wife left Arkansas to help you run your farm in Texas. If you're steamed because he's finally returning to Arkansas, that's fine. Call us even. Just remember, he's my brother."

Boyd went very still. "Jack, it's good to see you again. You sure do look like Marcus did when I first met him during the war. Your brother Will is shorter and stockier. Anyway, this exchange between my brother and you is ill aimed. Both of you should be taking me outside. I caused your brother and Florence to move. Marcus knew you were secure and safe. He also knew my brother was in a precarious situation. I was too selfish to remedy it." He turned to his brother. "And Ben, sure Jack could've stayed home, and maybe Marcus wouldn't be returning to Arkansas, or maybe it was just time for them to be with their families."

Jack grinned, Ben frowned, and then they shook hands. Marie and Lucy rushed forward apologizing. Soon, the ladies ushered Jack into the kitchen and fixed a plate of food. Once satisfied, Susannah Hawkins took him to the study where the men waited with varied patience.

After Mrs. Hawkins joined the ladies—now in the parlor— Hallie asked the question looming in all their minds.

"Do you know why Jack Johnson is here?"

Susannah hesitated. "Here in Washington, or why is he here tonight?"

Her mother-in-law didn't tend to be evasive unless in a difficult situation.

Hallie sighed. "Both."

"He's in Washington due to railroad business. Also, as his brother wrote to him of the Richardses' trip, he arranged his business here to coincide with their visit. There were delays preventing his scheduled arrival three days ago."

Julia licked her lips as she cut her eyes at Hallie. "What exactly is his business here with the railroad?"

The older woman took a sip of cooling tea from her delicate cup. "He's hiring men to help with the expansion in the Southwest."

Julia stood but stopped as Hallie pulled her down beside her. "Julia, he didn't come for Eddie. Your brother wouldn't leave right now. He knows I'm leaving to finish my training. If he's interested in anything Mr. Johnson has to say, it'll have to wait until at least the spring."

Amelia's firm voice drew everyone's attention. "Julia, our brothers were best friends. If you do not mind an observation, as one sister to another, I might be able to help. Enjoy your time with him now. Different events and circumstances took years away from both of our brothers and us. It's hard as many of those years were our own choice—yours in your way and mine in mine—but both are irretrievable. I would give anything to have James back here and support him in any way possible. He still had plans and dreams up to the day he died. Hallie's House was just the start. James wanted to give Eddie a bridge in returning to civilian life after the military, but he would never expect him to abandon his own dreams. Have you even asked Eddie what those are?"

Julia shook her head. "No, I haven't. I just want our family together."

Hallie felt the effect of her sister-in-law's words but knew their truth. "Amelia is right. Eddie should have a choice. If he's thinking about leaving again, it won't be now. He loves being here with his family."

Mrs. Hawkins reached to pat their hands. "My dears, our Eddie has come such a long way from the street boy I first met. He's a fine man, and all men must find their own way. James always wanted Eddie to know he had a home. The major and I think of him as a son. Julia, you and Jared are family. You won't be alone."

Julia took a handkerchief from Amelia and dabbed her eyes.

"I want to know if Jack plans to go through Arkansas on his return trip. He needs to see his family and, depending on the timing, see Marc and Florey when they arrive," Marie said.

"We must invite him to the wedding tomorrow. I bet Boyd and Ben will find out everything and let us know, Marie. He sure does look like his brother but seems more light-hearted," Lucy said.

"Well, he hasn't been through everything Marc has."

Hallie had missed meeting Boyd's friend but wanted more details. "Lucy, please tell us about Marc and Boyd's friendship."

The women listened to the captivating story and then the topic turned to the wedding. Billy knocked on the door and asked to see Molly home, ending the evening.

~~~

The next morning, Hallie's House bustled with activity. All the women arranged to be off work so they could attend Molly's wedding. Even Bridget finally agreed to go. Molly and Billy went to her when they returned home the previous evening. The young woman's residual bruising and the idea of a wedding—after the incident with her former fiancé—worked against her participation in the day's festivities. In the end, a kind heart triumphed—that and the honor of being escorted by Mr. Edward Rigby. He approached her as the young couple awaited her reply in the parlor.

Then Micah Gallagher asked if he could escort her. The pair of friends agreed to each take a side, leaving the young woman blushing. She needed protection during the outing to the church.

Hallie had retrieved the men's pressed suits and shirts from downstairs and started up the stairs when she heard Eddie's protest, Jared's exclamation, and Julia's call of distress.

"Jared, I've told you to knock before you enter a room. Julia, I'm in the tub."

"You have a bunch of scars, Uncle Eddie."

"Oh, my dear Eddie . . . Oh, Oh . . . ."

Hallie shook her head at Sara and Juliana who ran out of the music room. After one more glance toward the upstairs, they returned to their little girls. She looked up and saw curious souls emerge from their rooms at the commotion.

"Please go back to your rooms and finish getting ready. Amelia and Mrs. McDonald have just left with Molly. We don't want to be late. I'm sure the Rigby family can resolve whatever has caused these outbursts."

The way soon cleared, and Hallie continued to Eddie's room where Julia stood with her arms around her still gaping son.

"Where'd you get that?" the boy asked.

Eddie continued to list the origins of the multiple scars on his chest and arms. Some from the Civil War and some from Indian battles. He stopped and rolled his eyes.

"Ladies, this water is very cold now. Would you mind turning around? As my clothes have seemed to disappear, Jared, bring me the sheet off the bed."

The boy extricated himself from his mother's hold to do his uncle's bidding as the ladies complied with modesty. The sound of splashing water signaled Eddie's emergence from the tub.

"Goodness, Uncle Eddie, that one on your back is the best of all."

Eddie's voice remained indulgent. "Ladies, I'm decent enough if you must turn to see. Jared, this one I got two years ago. An Indian arrow got me during a retreat. Thankfully, we had an Indian with us who knew how to tend it. It healed fine. Now, go see if you can find my clothes."

Hallie stepped forward and laid his evening attire on the chair. "I was bringing these to you."

His green eyes twinkled at her. "Thank you, Hallie. Please take my sister and nephew downstairs so I can get ready. They don't realize how tough I am."

"You've never talked about these."

His eyebrow went up. "Why should I? It's part of being a soldier. Just as writers have ink beneath their nails, soldiers often have scars beneath their clothes. Hallie, please."

She shook her head and turned. Julia walked across the room to place a kiss on her brother's cheek.

"Julia, I'm fine. Please stop fussing. You need to head on to the church with the others. Micah and I will bring Miss McAvoy as soon as I'm ready."

Hallie's hands went to her face. "Oh, dear, I have Micah's suit, and he's at Ian's house out back getting ready. Jared, run this to him." She passed him the other suit on her arm.

"Yes, ma'am."

The women stared at Eddie a moment longer. Julia started for the door, but Hallie held back.

"It was Sunbeam who doctored you after the last arrow wound?" she asked.

He nodded. "She removed it and put some mixture of plants and dirt on it. The poultice had to stay on it for a long time. She would check and tend it." He shrugged. "Still don't know what it was, but it healed faster than any other injury I've had."

Julia moved from the doorway and took Hallie's arm. "I'm glad she was there, little brother. We'll leave you in peace. See you at the church."

~~~

The simple and beautiful wedding charmed everyone in attendance. Four surprise guests entered the church just as the ceremony started: Boyd's cousin, Andrew Richards, his wife, Liza, their daughter, Mary, and their aunt, Elizabeth Richards. They had come from Virginia after Boyd sent them an invitation by special messenger. Andrew arranged for the group from Texas to leave by train from Washington the next day without the need to come back to their house in Virginia. They also arranged for a room for Molly and Billy at the esteemed Wormley's Hotel[xxviii]. Andrew's status as a diplomat made procuring their room, as well as lodging for his family for the week at the establishment, easy. Amelia seemed to feel it necessary to inform the new couple about the Negro ownership of the hotel. The pair gave her a blank stare. They dismissed her misguided concern as they informed her of the shared ownership of the Richards ranch in Texas by Daniel Richards, a former slave and childhood friend of Ben and Boyd. The extravagant gift of the room took the couple aback, and they accepted it due to the gracious insistence of Liza Richards. Andrew introduced himself to Julia after the wedding and placed himself at her disposal through the next week to assist with legal matters. The English couple contrasted copper and gold; he had the golden hair of the Richards family and hers glistened red. Both possessed blue eyes shining with intelligence and good will. Their nine-year-old daughter, the primmest little lady Hallie had ever seen, delighted everyone.

Jared introduced her as his cousin to all the other children in attendance. The small imp seemed to find him worthy and took his arm after receiving a nod from her mother.

Molly and Billy glowed with happiness. Charlie beamed when Billy took his hand to walk down the aisle after he kissed his new bride. Mrs. McDonald shed tears of joy throughout the exchanging of vows. A time of new beginnings and endings but no regrets. Everyone seemed to be at a loss due to the change in the original plans. The group had planned to leave for Virginia right after the unusual morning wedding, but due to Andrew's arrangements, all of the day's activities changed. Judge Jackson suggested the ladies help prepare a quick picnic, and they all adjourned to Rock Creek Park[xxix]. He promised to reward their diligence with a dinner at Mr. Welcker's[xxx] fine restaurant in the evening. All showed enthusiasm for these plans.

No one seemed to mind the warm temperature of the day. The beauty of the trees and a few residual blossoms captivated the group. Their fun attempts to play baseball exhilarated the group. Knickerbocker's rules reigned.[xxxi] Eddie and Boyd were naturals with a bat. Ben surprised them with his pitching, and Andrew, who made clear his preference for the game of cricket, displayed tolerable skill each time he caught the ball. Micah made it through, but bent the rules a few times. Billy made up for his less than stellar batting with the ability to field and take the bases when he did chance a hit. The biggest surprise of the day—the identity of the young coaches. None of the men had played before, and the young boys instructed them. Jared, Charlie, and Robbie rolled their eyes during the first attempts. Judge Jackson gave a serious recounting of the one professional game he'd seen played. The ladies laughed and cheered as much as politeness allowed. It came time to leave to change for dinner quicker than any of them wanted, but all loved the delightful day.

Everything would have been perfect if Bridget's former fiancé hadn't happened to be at the restaurant when they arrived. Caleb Pierce's face became a canvas of dark emotions as he watched their approach to the table. Bridget noticed him at once and alerted Eddie and Micah of his presence. Eddie used discretion as he left Micah in charge of seating Miss McAvoy and made his way to the table of the spineless creature, who glared their way. The man sat next to the well-known banker, Henry D. Cooke[xxxii]. Eddie's surety of the equal status of the rest of the table's occupants found quick confirmation. He nodded at one of the men on the board of the foundation for Hallie's House.

"Good evening. I beg your pardon for interrupting your dinner, but I have a matter of the utmost urgency to discuss with Mr. Pierce. Mr. Pierce, might I speak to you outside for a moment."

The tall, handsome man rose and excused himself to follow Eddie's path, which took a wide berth from where Bridget sat with her head down. As soon as the doors closed, the man tried to pull Eddie toward the back of the building, but he hadn't counted on the muscled resistance. A slight shrug of Eddie's shoulders released the man's grip.

"Mr. Pierce, I'll make this brief. I'm the head of Hallie's House where your former fiancé is now recuperating from the brutality you inflicted upon her. Her father has informed the authorities of your actions, but he hasn't chosen to press charges unless you try to have contact with his daughter. The facts of her medical status after you harmed her are a matter of private, but well documented record by the doctors who treated her. I'm well aware of the prestigious company you're keeping this evening, and you should be aware of the highly prestigious legal and political men at my table. You may make inquiries once you return to yours. Perhaps none have recognized Miss McAvoy in her present state. Only the guilty one would recognize her with her still swollen face. Do we have an understanding?"

The man's eyes narrowed and he chewed on his bottom lip a moment. He nodded. "Yes, Mr.—"

"Rigby, Edward Rigby." Eddie smirked without restraint "Oh, do pardon me for not introducing myself before."

The man's face registered surprise. "James Hawkins's friend? I should have recognized you from the eulogy you gave at his funeral."

"Yes. I didn't realize you knew him."

"Not directly. My older brother was at Harvard with him."

"Pity. It would have made you a better man if you'd known him."

The man blanched. Eddie nodded and walked away. He noticed that Mr. Pierce returned to his chair without a sideways glance at them a few moments later. The remainder of the evening went well, and even Miss McAvoy joined in the laughter.

~~~

Eddie awoke close to dawn with a very dry throat and the call of nature from the water he drank right before bed. He took care of the more pressing of the two needs first and then went in search of some water. As he tried to find his way back to the stairs, the dark shape outside the curved front window alerted him. The person sat on the wooden settee on the porch. After a quick assessment of his attire—pants and an old shirt of Micah's—he opened the door. His heart calmed when he saw Hallie there. Her hair cascaded over her shoulders, and she had on a plain cotton day dress he seemed to recall from their time at the fort. She managed a wan smile as he sat down next to her.

"You're worried about Molly tonight?"

She nodded. "I've been praying for them both. Billy understands more than most as he also lost his family to an Indian raid."

He shook his head. "Forgive me, but I don't think I knew that. I'm sure you ladies have discussed it. Imagine that."

"But what will he do if she can't handle truly becoming his wife in a physical way? What will happen if she has a breakdown in that fancy hotel? She'd be devastated."

Eddie took her hand. "Hallie, this isn't like you. Let it go. You're not in charge. Tonight is between them and God. I haven't known Billy long, but I'm willing to gamble on his love for her. He won't move faster than she directs."

"Of course, you're right. What are you doing up?"

He held up the glass.

"Well, I guess it's close enough to the new day to start it. I'll go change and start breakfast."

"I'm fair at making biscuits. Let me finish this, and I'll change and join you."

Hallie smiled. "Thank you."

~~~

The train station bustled with people, trunks, and noise. They brought all of Molly and Charlie's trunks with them. Hallie wove through the people as Eddie went to check in the trunks. Mrs. McDonald stood with the Hawkinses and Jacksons. Jared had spent the night with Charlie at the Jacksons, and the boys sat on a bench with Robbie and Clara, looking restless. The Richardses had left the Hawkinses' home early to meet their relatives and the newly married couple for breakfast at the hotel. Their arrival appeared delayed, but Hallie turned as she heard Molly's voice behind her.

Molly's face glowed as she hurried to catch up to her, and Hallie could see the rest of the late arrivals close behind her friend.

Hallie embraced her with relief. "Good Morning, Mrs. Cooper."

Molly blushed and laughed. "I'm still getting used to that." She leaned close to Hallie's ear and whispered. "He's the most wonderful man, and I'm so blessed. I was afraid I might have a breakdown but—well as a lady, I can't say more—I'm fine and my husband is a gift."

Hallie clutched her close and whispered. "I'm so glad. Now I can let you go without concern."

She looked over Molly's shoulder. Billy waited a few feet away. "Mr. Cooper, you'd better come give me a hug, and then get your wife and new son on that train quick or I won't let them go."

Billy grinned and ambled over to comply. "I'll take good care of them, Miss Hallie."

"You'd better." She wiped away a tear, and Molly hugged her again. Charlie ran up and gave her a fierce hug around the waist. She squatted down. "Charlie, I love you. You'll like Texas. There's lots of space. You'll make a good cowboy."

His tear-stained face stayed serious as he stated, "I'm going to be a farmer, too."

"Yes, you are. I might have to come see that sometime."

His face lit up. "Really?"

Eddie's voice responded beside her. "I promised Jared a visit. Maybe Miss Hallie can come with us."

They both received hugs before the adults started their remaining goodbyes.

Boyd Richards boarded last. He hugged his aunt and shook hands with his cousin before he returned to the spot where Hallie stood with Eddie, Major Hawkins, and Susannah.

Hallie continued to mop her face in the wake of telling Mrs. McDonald goodbye. The woman felt like a grandmother to her. She blew her nose

"Mr. Richards, thank you for all your help with Julia and Jared. I know we'll be seeing each other as we're kind of related," Eddie said, shaking the tall man's hand.

"Our nephew is going to be fine. Don't be surprised if his grandfather turns up during this legal battle."

"I'll look forward to meeting him."

Boyd's golden eyes moved to Hallie. "I'm so proud of you, Hallie Price Hawkins. We want to hear about your graduation. A nice long letter please. I've had to hear mainly from your mother-in-law and father-in-law these past years. Lucy and I want to hear directly from you."

He turned his eyes on the small woman next to her. "No offense to your delightful letters. Thank you for your kind hospitality this month."

Susannah Hawkins burst into tears and reached up for a hug. Boyd picked the small woman clear off her feet before letting her down beside her husband.

Major Hawkins reached out his hand. "Once again, it's a privilege. I know our paths will cross again, my friend."

Boyd nodded, "Major, you've been one of the most unexpected friends of my life. It's been—"

The major reached and grasped his shoulder. Hallie loved how men communicated without words.

An exuberant voice called, "Boyd, Boyd, wait a minute." Jack Johnson ran to reach them. "I've done some checking, and it looks like I can arrange a visit to Arkansas by the spring. Tell Marcus I'll see them there."

Boyd nodded and hugged the younger version of his best friend. "I'll tell him. Thank you, Jack."

Boyd gave the group one more devastating smile and received one more hug from his aunt before he disappeared onto the train.

The mixture of friends and relatives on the platform stood waving to the faces pressed to the windows as the train began to move. Hallie couldn't help but think about being on the train to Boston the next Thursday.

~~~

His laughter and light washed over all the older ladies in the back pew. Hallie watched Eddie stop and marveled as he delighted in assisting the widows as they filed into the aisle. Their eyes sparkled like schoolgirls as he spoke to each with respectful charm and deference. A sigh, a smile, an added spring in their steps emerged as they moved forward to shake hands with the pastor on the way out of the church. Eddie had let them know they were viable and mattered. He acknowledged the sparkle of youthful charms still noticeable for those who looked. The most impressive part lay not in his ability to charm but in his ability to allow himself to be charmed by the treasure of the varied lifetimes of experience and uniqueness of those with whom he took time. He meant it.

Micah's words to Bridget at the breakfast table about Eddie and James ran through her mind. James had been goodwill with an intellectual intensity driving him, while Eddie had been the practical street smarts to figure out a way to survive when the odds were against it during the war. Both from different backgrounds but both were seeking God's guidance. They'd been quite a combination to serve with then.

Looking back to the days at the fort, Hallie could see how they both learned from each other.

"Hallie?" She blinked and saw Eddie now in front of her.

"I'm sorry; other things are on my mind. Are you ready? The Hawkinses will wonder where we are."

He smiled. "I'm sure the children are keeping them busy."

He took her elbow as he guided her to the door. They spoke to the pastor and then hurried to the carriage. Julia had chosen to go with the Judge and Amelia.

Eddie helped Hallie into the shiny black carriage and soon settled onto the seat beside her. He flicked the reins and they rode in silence for a few moments, enjoying the sunny day. Hallie fanned herself and wished for autumn to come. She anticipated the changes it would bring, not just in the weather but also in her life. Nursing school had been a welcomed challenge when she first started, and the necessity of coming home before her final three months disappointing. She had to finish it to fulfill a promise to James.

Then just one unfulfilled vow remained—to keep her heart open to love. She might never be ready.

"Might I interest you in a walk along the Potomac after lunch?" Eddie asked.

Hallie blinked in mute astonishment for a moment and then started to laugh until she saw his earnest expression. He continued. "We'll take the boys. It'll give everyone, especially little Clara, a break from them and afford us an opportunity to be outside."

An inner sigh of relief went through her as he clarified his reasoning. She smiled and nodded.

"That would be nice, but we'll need to change clothes. Let's go by the house and do that before we go to lunch. They'll just have to allow us to be less formal. I'll also get a change for Jared, and I'm sure there are some old clothes of James's at the Hawkinses' for Robbie to borrow. He's getting so tall."

Eddie gave her a bright smile. "Good. I'd better get this horse to hurry."

She held her hat as he urged the mare into a trot.

Everyone gave their approval of their plans once they arrived with apologies for being late. The boys were excited and lunch completed with more expediency than usual. At the last minute, they entreated Julia to go with them, but she declined. She wanted to visit with Amelia about helping with Clara since Mrs.

McDonald would no longer be available. Robbie no longer needed constant supervision, but they'd continue to welcome Jared's after school visits for at least this school year not unlike their accustomed arrangement. Robbie, however, approached his fifteenth birthday and, due to the void left by the absence of Charlie and Mrs. McDonald in their daily routine, it would feel more normal with Jared there. However, in light of his exceptional marks, Robbie might finish his studies early and be off to Harvard before his sixteenth year.

Hallie sensed a big brother attitude as she watched Robbie with Jared. Of late, Robbie had announced that he preferred his proper name of Robert.

Due to the small starting salary at the theater, assisting Amelia would also help Julia's finances. Hallie had also asked her to take on some of Molly's paid duties at the house. Much of Julia's savings now covered legal fees, so she needed every opportunity for employment.

A mood of gaiety grabbed the group as they embarked on the afternoon outing. The boys wore wide legged cotton trousers and light, long sleeved shirts. Jared wore a simple cap and Robbie a tilted straw hat. Hallie carried an umbrella as a shield against the sun. Eddie chose to forego social protocol for his present social station and looked more the part of a port worker. Amelia threw up her hands the moment she saw him, in contrast to Julia, who resounded her approval.

They decided to walk from the house, and as they neared the water, Robert turned.

"I'd like to walk ahead with Jared to see some of the boats. May I?" His eyes focused on Eddie.

"Certainly, we'll soon follow."

Jared grinned, "Thanks, Uncle Eddie."

"You really should call him Uncle *Edward*," Robert said in a serious tone as they quickened their pace away from the adults.

Hallie noticed no one walked beside her after a few more steps and turned to find Eddie watching the boys with an incredulous expression. She walked back. He continued to look past her.

"Hallie, *look* at them."

She complied and then frowned. "What?"

He put his hands in his pockets, turned to pace back, and then returned to her. "They look like James and me. Just with a few more years between them—and I was the oldest by an important six months. From behind, Robbie is a replica of his uncle, and when he turns around, the Hawkinses' features are more dominant than the ones of the Jacksons. Moreover, Jared looks more like a Rigby than a Kennedy no matter what Jason says. It's amazing. We've almost come around in time. Where did the years go?"

Hallie's hand went to her mouth. She'd been living so close to the boys the obvious failed to become apparent. Now thirty-five-years old, this must overwhelm Eddie, She took his arm.

"Shall we walk, Mr. Rigby?"

The skin around his green eyes crinkled as he smiled and shook his head one last time. "Yes, Mrs. Hawkins, we shall."

The still waters were peaceful and the silence companionable. Hallie felt herself relax.

"Georgetown or West Washington, it's still lovely now. I much prefer it to the Washington I saw upon our arrival. Let us just say it's now much improved."

"Regardless of many things, it was a very grand sight during the Grand Review[xxxiii] of the army down Pennsylvania Avenue at the close of the war."

"I've been told and, believe me, the buildings in Washington overwhelmed me; they *are* grand. This is just a bit slower."

"How do you find Boston in comparison?"

Her face lit up. "I adore it. Have you seen the Women and Children's Hospital there?"

"No, but Julia says it's a good place. A lovely building."

"Yes, you should come visit me while I'm there." Her steps faltered a bit, and he steadied her.

He walked in silence beside her for a moment. "We'll see. Now, I wonder what they're up to."

Jared and Robert hurried toward them.

"Come on, the man on that boat said we could have a look and go out with him for a while if you two agree," Jared said, breathing hard from running.

Hallie smiled as Robert tried to keep the excitement off his face.

Eddie quirked an eyebrow at Hallie, and she nodded. "Yes, I think it would be permissible."

Jared hurried ahead whooping as Robert whistled and kept pace with the two adults who had also quickened their steps.

The small boat appeared sturdy with a billowing sail unfurling as they approached. Although, Hallie found it hard to determine the age of the sailor manning the deck with his back turned to them. When he turned—to her surprise—he appeared no more than twenty-five years of age. Deep auburn hair and a close cut beard framed a sun-reddened face with snapping blue eyes. The man extended a hand attached to a well-muscled arm to greet Eddie even as he assisted Hallie aboard with the other.

"Welcome aboard. My name is Nehemiah Gallagher."

Hallie tripped and a deft arm caught her. She smiled in gratitude.

"I'm Mrs. Hawkins. Hallie Hawkins."

Eddie saw Hallie to a seat. He then turned to finish introductions. "I'm Edward Rigby. I assume you've met our respective nephews."

Nehemiah scratched his head. "I'm confused. When the lads said they needed to get their aunt and uncle, I assumed you were married."

Hallie and Eddie laughed.

"Oh, no. I'm the widow of his best friend. Our families are close. Robert is my nephew by marriage, and Jared is Mr. Rigby's nephew."

The blue eyes sparkled.

"Now, I'm seeing the picture of it. Anyway, thank you for consenting. It's my pleasure to show the boys the water. Much more enjoyable than the moonlight boat rides I've been giving for pay this week."

Eddie cleared his throat. "It's generous of you. My one concern is your willingness to do it on a Sunday." He hushed the boy's initial protests with a stern look.

Nehemiah gave Eddie a good-natured smile. He propped a foot on a small box and pulled a pipe from his pocket. He took his time filling it from a tiny stringed pouch. It took mere seconds to light it and take a few thoughtful puffs, but to those waiting, it seemed like an eternity.

"As a matter of point, I did find my way to Mass this very morning, but I've also found my rest can be on or off of the water. When you're a fisherman or a sailor, all days are spent on a boat, even Sunday. If in port, I'll still hoist the sail, and if the good Lord sees fit to fill it with wind enough to move across the water, I see no reason not to bless others with a relaxing free jaunt. Your leisure is assured, and I would be delighted in the company."

Eddie nodded. "Thank you, Mr. Gallagher. It'll be a treat."

Excitement laced Robert's voice. "Can we help guide it out?"

Nehemiah's posture relaxed as he took his position at the helm. "No, no, but you two lads sit here. I'll instruct you as we go. You might come back another day for a lesson."

The boys peppered the man with a barrage of questions as the wind filled the sail of the unfettered boat guided by the Irishman. Hallie looked outward with a sigh and smiled at Eddie as the wind began to loosen strands of her hair and its covering. She reached up and removed the pin anchoring her battered hat. Eddie removed his cap, but his short, curly hair stayed in place. He shrugged as she gave his locks a pointed look.

"What can I say? I had an Indian once compare my hair to Custer's. However, Sunbeam said mine was more the color of the wisps at the top of the wheat, and his more like the silks on corn."

A gentle curiosity overcame her. "Would you describe her to me?"

His green eyes reflected hesitancy for a brief moment. "Well, her hair and eyes are much like yours, but her skin is bronzed whereas yours is fair. You're about a head shorter than I am, so she'd about reach your chin if she stood next to you. However, her small, slight stature belies the height of her nature: strong and resolute."

"Her life sounds hard."

He looked out and then back to her with a glow in his eyes.

"Honestly, she would disagree with you. You see, she had a very stable life as a child within her tribe before her illness, and then a loving life with the Evans family thereafter. She received a good education and easily utilized it to put her in a position to help her people.

"Hallie, you must understand how the inevitability of the changes for the Indians doesn't change the facts of who they were long before our people came. They're loyal, fierce, and provide for their families off the animals and food yielded. They moved as needed and respected the rhythm of the land and all of nature.

"I've come to understand how all the misunderstandings couldn't help but occur. We have expected them to understand our ways, our needs, and surrender a way of life we didn't give them. Both sides made mistakes, but there's no way to stop it now. She understood it."

"But her life could've been so much better if she'd married you. If she knows, why would she choose life on a reservation?"

"Thank you for that, but heritage goes deeper than conformity or comfort. Loyalty to blood more than love. My head understood those things from the time she made her choice; it just took my heart longer. God took care of working it out within me, and now I look ahead without regret. I do think of her and am so grateful to have claimed her affections for a time. The one thing without change is the friendship we shared. If our paths ever cross again in this life, I'll always be her friend. I keep hoping to get a letter, but she won't put her hand to touch my life now she's chosen another. Maybe in time. I pray her husband will come to share her faith, and they might get word to me."

"So you don't know if she's well or anything?"

"On the contrary, Mr. and Mrs. Evans traveled to the reservation to witness her marriage. They wrote to tell me she was doing well."

"I'm sorry, Eddie."

He shook his head and blew air from his lips. "Hallie, it was God's will. I'm at peace. Look at the current state of my life. I'm finally out of the military and well employed. My prayers regarding my sister have been answered. I have a wonderful nephew and friends more like family than acquaintances, and my opportunities keep opening. I'm blessed."

"Would some of those opportunities involve your conversations with Jack Johnson?"

"Hallie, I won't discuss any future considerations with you right now. I'm aware of my obligations and promises to my family and friends. These will be fulfilled." He gave her a level look before turning his attention toward the activity on the other side of the boat. "Mr. Gallagher, how long have you been in the area of Washington?"

"Just a few months. I plan on remaining here through the autumn before returning home to Maine."

"Yes, many men have had to find work away from home to make money in this economy."

"Actually, I came to Washington for a different purpose. I just knew I needed employment during my time here. The men in my family have been fishermen for generations even before immigrating. I came in search of my oldest brother. My Da had led our family to believe he had died after his hospitalization close to the end of the war. During my father's final illness, he revealed the truth. Needless to say, we were all devastated, especially my mother. You see Da had traveled to see my brother in the hospital but returned with news of his death."

Hallie felt goose bumps form on her arms, and she gave Eddie's hand a light touch. He turned and his eyes widened as realization dawned.

"Mr. Gallagher, what's your brother's name?"

"Micah Gallagher."

The boy's mouths fell open. Hallie shook her head at them. Eddie's voice remained calm as he continued in casual conversation.

"I served with Micah Gallagher. He helped us find laughter even after the darkest battles."

Nehemiah's voice choked. "That is what I hear of him. I am the youngest and was but a wee one when he left. Were you with him when he was wounded?"

"Yes, I was. He sustained immense damage to one of his arms and one of his legs."

The young Irishman composed himself with a show of fortitude before he asked the expected question. "Mr. Rigby, would you be knowing where I might find my brother? I went to the Soldiers' home but was unable to get a current address."

"Why don't we turn the boat and you come with us for the rest of the day?"

The man nodded, and the boys were quick to provide many questions as distractions with Robert understanding Eddie's purpose. Hallie could almost guarantee Eddie's thoughts mirrored her own in praising God's divine appointments.

"The water is wonderful. I would love to try another boat ride sometime," she said.

"Yes, I think the boys could be easily persuaded to join us again."

"We'll have at least one more joining us in the future if it's on this boat."

"I hope all goes well," Eddie said. "He's been so much more like himself this past month. The man I met when I first saw him again the day I returned was not the comrade of old."

They kept their voices quiet. "You're one of the reasons for the change, and the group from Texas also helped. He's had work but not friends."

"Nor family."

They continued in silence the rest of the way to the place where Nehemiah kept the boat docked. Polite conversation continued on every subject except the apparent one as the group walked to the Hawkinses' home. Their new friend whistled as they approached.

"Your clothes belie your station."

Hallie smiled. "This is the home of my in-laws."

Eddie looked at the boys. "Robert, would you mind asking your parents to drop off Jared and Julia?"

"No, sir, and thank you for a fun excursion. I'll be happy to make your apologies and express your need to assist Mr. Gallagher at this time." He turned to the sailor. "Mr. Gallagher, thank you for your kindness and a pleasant outing."

In contrast to Robert's mature compliance, Jared started a bit of a sullen protest. Eddie leaned down and whispered in his ear. Jared turned and extended a hand.

"Thank you, sir."

Once the boys disappeared into the house, the three adults settled into their carriage. Hallie knew there would be a stir at the house with Nehemiah's arrival. All the ladies were home on Sunday afternoons. It didn't matter.

Micah liked to write in his room after worship. The newspaper had even utilized some of his smaller pieces, demonstrating awareness of his talents beyond setting type.

They learned Nehemiah's three other brothers and four sisters still lived in the area around their home in Maine. The family fishing tradition continued. Their mother had suffered poor health since her husband's death and longed to see the son she'd thought to be dead.

Neither Hallie nor Eddie chose to share anything else about Micah. He should tell his story to his youngest brother. They did tell him about Hallie's House so he would be prepared by the living situation and of the expected wary reception awaiting him.

Ian met them to take care of the carriage and horse upon their arrival. He didn't flinch during the introduction to Nehemiah, but he did grunt and spit at the ground with a meaningful look at Eddie.

As expected, a few women sat in the parlor and in the music room, and the others were sure to be resting upstairs as they entered the house. Greetings died on lips, and silence filled the space instead of chatter.

Hallie excused herself as Eddie ignored the stares and took Nehemiah to his office.

Eddie looked at the uncertain man sitting in front of him.

"Mr. Gallagher, in a few moments all will become clear. Hallie—"

He didn't get to finish as the door opened. Micah had either been sleeping or writing as his eyes looked tired. He grumbled about having to see Eddie about business on a Sunday as he entered behind Hallie. The sailor stood, his hat in hand. Micah's eyes went from the man to Hallie and then to Eddie.

"Who is this?"

"Micah, this is your youngest brother, Nehemiah."

Both brothers stood still. Nehemiah swallowed hard a few times, and Micah's eyes reflected slight moisture. The eldest stepped forward extending his prosthetic arm. The youngest grasped it after an awkward pause. Then Micah turned and left with his unsteady gait thumping down the corridor.

"He has the look of my brother Samuel," Nehemiah said, sinking onto the chair behind him.

The sound of thumping returned, soon followed by the reappearance of Micah.

"Would you be wanting to walk a ways with me, brother?"

Nehemiah stood. "That I would, Micah." He smiled at Hallie and Eddie as he followed his brother out the door.

Hallie stood. "I'd better get Sara and start setting out the meal we made yesterday."

"I'm afraid I won't be here. I'm meeting Jack Johnson at his hotel. He leaves in the morning, and we have Mrs. Grierson arriving."

"All right. Also, Eddie, I'll be working days this week at the hospital until Wednesday. It's my last day. You do remember I leave on Thursday?"

He stood. "No, for some reason, I thought it was on Friday. Will you have a chance to go over matters for the house tomorrow evening?"

"Yes, after dinner would be fine. Amelia and Susannah are coming to help me with my packing after work tomorrow. I'm borrowing a trunk as mine—brought from Texas all those years ago—has seen better days."

She reached for the door.

"It's been a good day, Hallie."

"Yes, yes, it has. I'm so happy for Micah."

He nodded. "I'll follow you. I need to change clothes and leave to meet Mr. Johnson. What will you tell the ladies?"

"Nothing. I'll let Micah introduce Nehemiah when he's ready."

"That's my Hallie."

She stopped and watched him head up the stairs. *His Hallie?* She called Sara to help her put the food on the table.

Chapter Five

REBECCA GRIERSON surprised Eddie. He didn't expect a petite woman who looked at least five years younger than her almost fifty years. Wisps of shiny, dark brown hair escaped from the neat coil at the nape of her neck, and eyes the color of forget-me-nots reflected an array of emotions during his first meeting with her and Hallie. Inner apprehensions plagued him about handling this case without Hallie to help him.

However, the minister's wife, who took care of little Caroline Brady, had offered to assist as needed. The look of defeat mirrored in Mrs. Grierson's expressive blue eyes reminded him of the Indians upon their surrender to the reservations, but sparks of fight and victory peeped through as she talked about the Lord. A grand battle raged in the woman. She loved her husband, but the combination of her work, his work, and his longer hours overwhelmed her. The empty house hadn't seemed so isolated until after the children were grown. Her husband's absence when he had to stay to grade papers or meet with students became more apparent. The running of their household and seeing after their responsibilities with minimal input from him served as another small portion of the issue.

Their family had endured much difficulty during the war, followed by the loss of her mother, the leaving home by their children, and a culmination of many past regrets. Mrs. Grierson expressed embarrassment at her emotional struggles; however, she could no longer deny their presence. She gave God the glory for her ability to continue to this juncture and prayed for healing and restoration. Eddie had never heard anyone apologize so much or take responsibility for so much.

No wonder she suffered from exhaustion. The high degree of her intelligence showed; however, unbalanced emotions affected her view of the situation and a much-skewed self-perception resulted.

Her entire body stayed tense. She sat with a rigid upright posture with her back away from the chair, and her knee moved in agitation beneath her dress. Eddie breathed a sigh of relief when Hallie reached over and covered the woman's hands with her own. Much like watching a plant perk up after a drink of water, one kind touch meant so much. A kind word backed with actions meant more.

"Mrs. Grierson, we're so glad you're here. This week I don't want you to do more than rest, read, get to know the other ladies at your discretion, and pray. Let us take care of you. I can tell it'll go against your instincts, but you must. It's the only way for you to see the world will *not* fall apart if you don't attend to it. God has sent you here, and you must learn to trust others."

"I know. The scariest part is I've stopped trusting myself."

Silence followed but Eddie understood. He'd felt those same feelings after James's injury, which left him on his own for the remainder of the war. That time deepened his trust in God.

"Coming to the end of yourself is the beginning of truly trusting God in everything," he said.

The bright eyes filled with tears, and she nodded.

Hallie stood. "Let me show you to your room. I want you to rest."

"Thank you both for allowing me to come here. Please express my gratitude to your supporting churches and board. I'm so sorry."

Eddie wanted to shout at her in frustration but knew it wouldn't have the desired result. Instead, he stood and met her eyes with one word, "Stop."

Hallie placed an arm around the diminutive form and left the room. Strength and fragility were mirrored opposites but just a breath from each other. James's legacy in this place went forth with each person they helped.

He thought about Micah and Nehemiah, now reunited and

planning a trip home to Maine at the end of September. Both had obligations to their present occupations. Nehemiah would be free of his before they left, but Micah wanted to return to his position. The editor at the newspaper asked him to assist in finding a temporary replacement. Much to their surprise, he mentioned Bridget McAvoy. It wouldn't be easy for him to persuade his boss to allow a woman to fill his position, even for a short period, but if anybody could do it, Micah would. Things sure moved at a faster pace in the city than on the frontier. In many ways, Eddie found it more unnerving than waiting for an Indian attack. At least then, you knew what you'd be dealing with once it happened. Here, you never knew. After a few more minutes of pondering, he stood for a good stretch and went to check on the activities of the house. Visibility and availability, both in the house, as well as in the community, were as important as the office work he did during the day. He made perfunctory visits to key patrons in the afternoons and then completed the expected monthly meetings with the employers of each of the ladies to check on their performance and job stability. Before the ladies left Hallie's house, they preferred each to have at least six months in a stable job. It still amazed him how Hallie and Molly had kept up with everything. Hallie had juggled her duties at the hospital and Molly her responsibilities as a mother with the ones he now did full time. The house would feel both women's absences by the end of the week.

~~~

Hallie's excitement danced within as they approached the train station. It had been ten o'clock last evening before Susannah and Julia had helped her shut the new trunk provided as a gift by the ladies of the house. As she didn't plan to come home until December, per Eddie's edict, more items were packed. He'd sent her a note as he left for a meeting yesterday. She remained unsure if he'd be at the station.

Major Hawkins and Susannah picked her up at seven, right after her final goodbyes with the women at breakfast. Emotions had vacillated like a broad pendulum swing during the expression of well wishes. Julia, while still supportive, exhibited obvious distraction at her brother's noticeable absence. He'd left the house early, and no one seemed to know where he'd gone.

The gentle hand of her mother-in-law covered hers. "James would be so proud of you. He wanted you to complete formal training. You are so smart."

Hallie smiled. Susannah shared coloring so much like her own that onlookers might think the woman to be her mother instead of her mother-in-law. "Thank you. I have to finish. It would dishonor James and the opportunities your family has made possible to do otherwise."

Major Hawkins cleared his throat. "Hallie, you've also done much for us. Losing James would have been hard under any circumstances, but your presence and fortitude have strengthened all of us."

Tears clouded her eyes. The major looked so much like an older version of James. If only . . . This couple had become the parents she needed, as well as cherished friends.

"I love you both," she said.

The carriage stopped. Major Hawkins unfolded his tall form as he stepped out and turned to assist the ladies. They waited as he arranged for her trunk to load.

The bustle of movement, mixed with voices overtook them as they approached the platform beside the train. Each served as reminders of their recent farewell to their friends from Texas.

"I hope Molly and Elizabeth are both enjoying their journey," Susannah said.

"I'm sure Charlie's excitement will give all of them new eyes," Major Hawkins said.

"Little Henry and Amanda will love showing him things. I—"

The major turned to see what had caught her attention. Eddie walked toward them carrying a shiny new leather satchel.

"Well, son, we had decided you weren't going to wish Hallie a good journey."

Eddie gave him a sheepish look as he reached to shake his hand. "I had a few last minute things to do. My apologies for any appearance of rudeness."

He placed a quick kiss on Mrs. Hawkins's cheek and turned to Hallie. "I ordered some special items, and they weren't ready until this morning. Hallie, this is for you to keep all your notes and school items together. Inside you'll find a bottle of ink, pens, a bound leather book of blank pages bearing your initials for notations from your studies, as well as stationery and envelopes for personal correspondence."

He held a leather case out to her. She looked from his smiling face to the case and back a few times. She reached out with unsteady hands to take the extravagant and thoughtful gift.

"Eddie, it's much too nice. I don't know what to say." Her now moist eyes went to his.

He quirked an eyebrow. "Thank you will do."

She laughed. "Thank you, Eddie, but—"

The major took the case from her. "No buts, Hallie. Eddie wants you to have this, so use it and the other things inside well."

Mrs. Hawkins nodded as she hugged Eddie. "Yes, and we will expect regular letters. It's nice to know I might have helped fashion you into such a thoughtful man. Did you remember to put postage in the case?"

He gave the small woman an indulgent smile. "Thanks to you I did, and, yes ma'am, there are stamps in a small packet."

The voice of the conductor beckoned to passengers to start boarding.

"We'll see you in December, Hallie. Come, Susannah." Major Hawkins gave Hallie a warm embrace and then waited as his wife did the same.

"I love you, dear," Mrs. Hawkins whispered close to her ear.

Hallie kissed the soft cheek of the woman she loved as a true mother.

Major Hawkins turned to Eddie. "We'll expect you to call this evening."

"Yes, sir."

They watched the quick departure of the couple who were the only parent figures in their lives. Eddie took her elbow to escort her to the steps of the train.

"Eddie, you shouldn't spend your money on me."

"Hallie, allow me this. If it makes you less beholding to me, you should receive pay for the earnings held for me all these years. This is just a small token of gratitude and friendship. It gave me joy to be able to do this for you."

His green eyes sparkled with sincerity. She nodded, and he

raised her hand to his lips.

"Now, get on this train and come back an official nurse. I'll take care of everything here."

"Thank you, Mr. Rigby."

She turned and gave him a final wave. Once settled in her seat, she searched the faces of the people waving from the platform but couldn't find Eddie. Even as she dismissed it, disappointment fluttered in the base of her stomach followed by guilt. He'd always managed to keep her off kilter from the first time they met. Irritation replaced all previous emotions as she sat the thoughtful gift on the seat beside her.

~~~

Eddie arrived at the lawyer's office just as his sister went inside. They'd met with both him and Andrew Richards the previous week. Julia's attorney from Boston sent everything he had on the case to this associated office. Mr. J.A. Oxley, a distinguished looking man with graying at the temples of once coal black hair, had a stellar reputation. He wore spectacles down on his nose when reading but removed them with a flourish during prolonged periods of rhetoric. His relaxed posture put others at ease until the intensity of the intellect in his eyes unbalanced those within the parameter of steady regard. Candor and canniness typified the man. The Washington attorney and the distinguished British envoy collaborated like two pieces of flint; they sparked and flamed into an agreeable fervor full of common purpose. Andrew had returned to Virginia but promised to avail himself as needed. Eddie and Julia remained optimistic at this point.

He smiled at his sister as he entered the prestigious office. "Hello, Julia. Is he ready for our meeting?"

She smoothed the back of her dress and completed an elegant descent onto one of the leather chairs outside Mr. Oxley's inner office.

"His secretary just went to announce me. Did you catch Hallie before she boarded the train?"

He eyed the polished door as he responded. "Yes, yes, I arrived just in time."

"I still don't quite understand your need to special order items for her," she said.

He stroked his upper lip as he reflected with definite distraction. "It's complicated," he said, crossing his arms.

Julia lifted an eyebrow. "So you say."

The door opened and the secretary bade them enter. "Mr. Oxley will see you now."

Eddie met the man's eyes as they entered and sensed something wrong as he greeted them.

"Good morning, Miss Rigby, Mr. Rigby. Please have a seat. We have much to discuss."

Julia shared a nervous sidelong look with her brother as they occupied the chairs in front of the oak desk. The lawyer removed his eyeglasses and cleaned them with a few quick swipes of a finely embroidered handkerchief. After replacing the spectacles and unnerving them with a few frowns, he leaned back in his chair with a frank stare in their direction.

"There has been a new development impacting your case. I am afraid it could sway the judge to find on behalf of Mr. Kennedy. Our office was notified of the change this morning."

Eddie's mouth pressed into a grim line. Julia bit her lip.

"Mr. Oxley, what's changed?"

The man sighed and sat forward with his hands clasped on the desk. "It seems Mr. Jason Kennedy is marrying Miss Mary McWhorter at the end of this week. They have asked the court date for this case to be set for next Monday as Mr. Kennedy is needed at his ranch in Texas."

Julia remained still. She didn't look at Eddie. Her voice held no emotion when she spoke. "This case shouldn't be resolved by the simple fact of him taking a wife. If the judge's decision is based on my less than conventional living circumstances compared to the appearance of a more socially acceptable living situation, that's not just. In my opinion, the judge should talk to Jared. Let him see the fine young man he's becoming—living as he is now. Let him talk to Jared's teachers. I've done the best possible for my boy."

Mr. Oxley pursed his lips. "A child will not be allowed to tell the judge what is best. The law will not recognize his voice over the adults in his life. It will be a dispassionate decision based on the ability to provide stability and opportunity for the boy. I had previously thought your recent move and efforts to lead a more stable life would impact the judge. Especially, as there is no solid proof of paternity. However, I must tell you, this will change things."

Eddie stood and strode to the library shelf with his back to them. Anger simmered in the pit of his stomach.

"This isn't right. It's not fair, and Jared shouldn't have to have his life torn apart because of a chance meeting of his possible father." He turned. "Are you telling me we should concede?"

The man pushed the eyeglasses up on his nose as he picked up a telegram on the desk. *"Will arrive by train in a week. Have court date set for Tuesday,"* he read. He looked at them. "This is from Mr. Joe Kennedy. Jared's purported grandfather. Andrew Richards had anticipated Joe Kennedy would try something along these lines. He sent for the elder Kennedy after his first meeting with you. He sent this during his journey. We will not be pushed to comply with the Monday court date. I will request Tuesday."

Julia stood. "Thank you, Mr. Oxley."

Eddie held up his hand.

"Wait a moment, Julia. I don't think the resolution of everything is Mr. Kennedy's responsibility. Mr. Oxley, we have many people who will testify to the facts of Jared's life in Washington during all the years when his father was absent. Jason Kennedy didn't even give an after-thought to my sister once the school authorities resolved his troubles. The slight potential of him becoming a father didn't seem to concern him after he harmed my sister. Jason signed papers under the astute care of my sister's employer and should have no rights. Will the judge not even take these things into consideration?"

The lawyer looked at him over his spectacles and nodded.

"Of course, but from a conventional and fact determined view, Jared's father does not propose harm to the boy. He is offering a life full of provision and opportunity within a stable and family oriented environment. Why would the judge want to deny such an amazing future for your nephew?"

Heat filled Eddie's face. "Jason Kennedy is a dangerous and violent man. Would the judge want to subject Jared to the potential for harm?"

The distinguished man gave them a sly smile and sat back in his chair. "Exactly. That picture must be well painted and more important, proven to be a possibility, but we need testimony beyond your sister. Mr. Kennedy will be able to provide some, but he is bringing two other people who may be able to render testimony that is more important. Without Jared's grandfather's provisions for legal restraints with Jason's inheritance and testimonies, I don't think the judge would give much credibility to your sister due to her past." He sent an apologetic glance toward Julia. "Begging your pardon, ma'am."

"Who are these people coming with Mr. Kennedy?" Julia asked.

"A lady named Erma Franklin who worked at the saloon in the Kennedy's hometown in Texas and a young cowhand recently fired from the Kennedy ranch. I personally think the trail hand will be the most impacting."

Eddie met the man's intelligent eyes. "Why?"

The man motioned for Eddie to have a seat and as soon as he complied, he leaned forward, glancing from brother to sister. "The young man is fourteen and was severely beaten at the hands of Jason Kennedy before he was fired. The reason for the beating is disturbing. The boy had taken in a hound pup and shared his food with him at night. Ted Dalton, the foreman of the ranch, had laughed about it and told the boy to make sure he took care of the mutt with his own pay and provisions, which the boy did. However, Jason Kennedy was furious. He shot the dog and beat young Samuel Perkins. He then ordered Ted to get him off his ranch. Mr. Dalton dumped the young man at the saloon. The women there got him to the town doctor. He had a broken arm, a broken nose, and three broken ribs. If Jason Kennedy has shown a history of violence involving not only women, but toward youths and innocent animals, well—"

Julia paled and interrupted him. "Mr. Oxley, please protect my son from that man."

Eddie realized the man had wanted them prepared for the worst before he allowed them to hope within reason. He hated the court's way of handling things but knew its necessity.

"Is there anything else we need to know, Mr. Oxley?"

"No, no, well, you may or may not be aware of Major and Mrs. Hawkins' visit to me this week."

Eddie frowned. "Not beyond your preliminary meeting

with all those involved in Jared's life. Why did they come to see you?"

"They have offered to become Jared's legal guardians if necessary."

Eddie stood. "I need to go talk to them."

Julia stayed seated. "Eddie, they came to me and offered. It'll be a last resort. They're people I trust. They've been like parents to you and grandparents to Jared."

Mr. Oxley stood and came around the desk to assist Julia as she rose, escorting them to the door. "We won't meet again until I see you in court on Tuesday. I want the witnesses and Mr. Joe Kennedy to seem impartial to you. It will present better. We will protect Jared."

"Thank you." Eddie shook his hand, and they made their way through the lobby and out to the street before Julia spoke.

"Will you drop me by the theater?"

He nodded. Julia—never one to talk when heartsick—preferred to get busy. He understood as he tended to be the same way. For once, he welcomed the stack of papers awaiting his attention. However, even as he helped his sister into the carriage, he spared a sad thought for Mary McWhorter.

~~~

The rest of the week and weekend passed without incident. Everyone went about their daily routines without complaint, and no new residents appeared on their doorstep. In fact, they only had one visitor to the house. Professor Grierson appeared on Sunday afternoon, and although Eddie could tell the man tried to be a loving and supportive husband, his visit seemed to agitate and depress Rebecca. She went up the stairs muttering about how she'd ruined her husband's life by not being strong enough. Julia caught Eddie's eye and followed the petite woman up the stairs. The house felt a little suffocating, so he welcomed the opportunity to go and collect Jared from the Hawkinses.

After a detailed visit with Major Hawkins in his study, Eddie entered the parlor. Jared laughed as he looked at an ambrotype photograph with Mrs. Hawkins.

"What's so funny?"

"You are, Uncle Eddie. Look at you and James in this

picture. You look a bit like me, but I'm going to be taller."

Eddie couldn't help grinning. "And who told you that?"

His nephew shrugged. "No one. I just know. The Kennedy's are tall."

Eddie's smile faltered a bit. "I'm not sure if all of them are. If I remember right, Mrs. Richards said her mother was short. But you may be right, and I'm not short."

Jared eyed him. "I guess not, but you're shorter than all the other men around here except for Micah and Ian."

He caught Susannah's look—it told him to surrender or the boy would persist.

"Touché, nephew. Now it's time to go home. Thank Mother Hawkins for a wonderful afternoon."

The boy turned and hugged Susannah. She handed him the picture and he placed it in the display case by the window. Eddie walked over and let his gaze linger on the images. Mrs. Hawkins's firm voice drew him.

"I'm so glad Robert sent this picture of you boys. Do you remember the night of James's birthday celebration at the fort when we gave you the package?"

Eddie glanced at the captured moment of his best friend and him in uniform at the beginning of the war one more time. He turned and met the brown eyes of the only mother figure in his life.

"Yes, yes, I do. It was the night Mr. Kennedy's trail hands came through on their way home to Texas and also the night Hallie accepted Christ."

Susannah Hawkins gave him an unflinching look of speculation. "That's right, and I seem to recall you treating her differently in the days leading up to our departure."

He looked down and then gave a causal response. "She *was* different."

Mrs. Hawkins inclined her head. "Do I need to say it, Eddie?"

He exhaled in gratitude when Jared interrupted. "Are we staying for supper?"

Eddie placed a hand on his nephew's head and smiled down at him. "Nice try, but no, we aren't. Your mother is expecting you home." He ignored the waiting look on the face of his dear friend's mother. "Thank you for letting Jared come home with you after church. I know he's enjoyed himself. We love you."

Susannah put her arm around Jared's shoulders and walked with them to the door. "Jared, this is a big week for you. Just remember to listen to your mother and uncle. We will be in court every day."

"Yes, ma'am. Good night."

Jared opened the door and dashed out as Eddie turned with guilt mixed among many other emotions. "There have been many events and people in my life since the fort. I'm not the same and, even if I did have some feelings for Hallie then, it was not meant to be."

She stood on tiptoe to kiss his cheek. "I have prayed for you for many years, and God has answered in many ways. Sometimes as I hoped and sometimes not, but in retrospect better. He always has plans better than our own. I do not know what He has planned for your life or for Hallie's, but I have my opinions. I'll just pray for the best for you both. I love you. Now, get Jared home and know this week will work out the way it's supposed to. We have to trust either way."

He closed his eyes and exhaled. "Thank you for reminding me. Good night."

~~~

Mr. Joe Kennedy struck an impressive figure as he strode into the courtroom with confidence and a look of dismissal thrown towards the chair where his son sat with his legal counsel. He arrived thirty minutes before the scheduled hearing. Julia and Jared sat with their attorney but stood as the broad figure of the rancher from Texas approached. Eddie and the Hawkinses also stood. They waited as he completed a visual summation with a piercing brown gaze that softened once it fell on Jared.

The man didn't wait for an introduction. He gave his grandson his full regard. "You must be Jared. I'm your grandfather, Joe Kennedy." He turned at the opening of one of the doors to the courtroom, and a diminutive woman with graying hair made her way to stand beside the bulky man. "And this is your grandmother, Agnes Kennedy."

Eddie saw the woman's blue eyes fill with tears and watched in amazement as his nephew moved to hug the unknown woman. The woman hugged Jared even as her kind eyes looked to Julia. His sister's stiff posture softened for a moment, and the two women shared a kindred smile.

"You must be Julia Rigby?"

Julia faltered as she lifted her chin and nodded with a quick look of trepidation sent toward Jason Kennedy, who glared at them with a mixture of disbelief and anger.

"Yes, sir, I'm Julia Rigby. Thank you for your help and for traveling all the way from Texas to be here. I didn't realize Mrs. Kennedy was accompanying you, and I know this is a precarious family situation. However, I think you'll find your grandson to be worth all of our efforts."

The rancher grunted.

"I believe you'll do, Miss Rigby. Now, do they expect Jared to have to sit through this spectacle, or will we be able to spare him, Mr. Oxley?" The man's attention shifted to the lawyer who watched the first meeting with calculated interest over his eyeglass frames.

"Your presumption of our identities is astute, Mr. Kennedy. The judge expects Jared to be here during the preliminary opening of the case, and then Mrs. Hawkins and the major will take him home. Oh, let me introduce you to Major Ronald Hawkins and his lovely wife, Susannah."

Major Hawkins rose and assisted his wife as they moved forward. "Mr. Kennedy, I had the privilege of hosting your cowhands at our fort in '67 and then, more recently, your daughter and her family in our home."

Joe Kennedy gave the major's hand a firm shake. "Yes, you've been a good friend to my son-in-law; therefore, I'll also consider you in that light. Would you mind if my wife accompanied you once they excuse Jared? Even given the circumstances, it's still hard for her to deal with our son in this situation. Her grandmother's heart is firm in regard to Jared, but—"

"We understand, and she is welcome. Right, Jared?"

The boy's brown eyes, so like his grandfather's, widened as he tilted his head to look up at the woman who still held him to her with tears streaming down her face. "Yes, sir, Major Hawkins."

Agnes Kennedy smiled down at her grandson and then

sought Julia's hand as she stepped forward with one arm still around Jared. "I'm so pleased to meet you, Miss Rigby, and I'm so sorry for this situation."

Julia gripped her hand with warmth in her emerald eyes. "I think I just realized how important you'll be to Jared's life. Forgive me for not thinking of you before now."

Eddie couldn't believe he heard those uncharacteristic words uttered by his sister, but he agreed. Julia looked up at him as she released the small woman's hand.

"Mr. and Mrs. Kennedy, I would like you to meet my brother, Edward Rigby."

Joe Kennedy extended his hand. "Yes, Boyd told us about you, sir. I can see a great mixture of both our family's in this fine young man. Jared, I do hope we can get you to Texas for a visit by next summer."

Jared threw a look at his mother, and she nodded. A wide grin erupted. "Yes, sir."

His grandfather chuckled but soon sobered as he caught his son's glare. The judge's entrance followed, and all parties returned to their respective seats.

As the morning progressed, Eddie's face grew grimmer. Jason Kennedy's lawyer and the read testimony of former patrons of the establishment in Boston—who wished to remain anonymous—painted his sister as a shameless harlot. Julia informed them at break that these were men angered by her departure from the profession as they were weekly visitors. Mr. Kennedy's lawyer knew the names of the men, and the judge requested the list. Then, Julia wrote down the names of the men she thought had provided such testimony, and passed the list to the judge after Mr. Oxley protested the anonymous nature of these witnesses. The judge sustained his objection after he reviewed the lists. This confirmed Julia's suspicions and worked in their favor.

Jason Kennedy then took the stand and tried to paint his violent actions as overstated and defensible during his evening with Julia on the night of Jared's conception. He said he missed his wallet as he prepared to leave that evening, and she wouldn't return it to him. Furthermore, she'd demanded payment for her services before he left. Mr. Oxley submitted the reports from the doctor who treated Julia, her former employer, and the agreement signed by Jason Kennedy after the fact as evidence of her innocence and the brutality she'd experienced. His counsel then countered with the success of his client in the farm and ranch business, his high graduating status, and lack of any other incident of this nature. Mr. Oxley then presented the two young people from Texas who had suffered violence at Jason's hands. It shocked Jason to see Erma Franklin and Samuel Perkins enter the courtroom. Of course, Jason's attorney dismissed Erma's case as an act of teenage defiance and Samuel's as a response to a non-compliant employee. Joe Kennedy then took the stand to review legal documents regarding Jason's inheritance. He had Jason's hands tied there.

Mary McWhorter Kennedy took the stand. She made a convincing presentation on her husband's behalf and of their desire to raise Jared in a loving and respectable home in Texas. She proved mesmerizing to watch, and Jason looked very smug as she swept by in an elegant exit. Eddie felt ill, and he could tell his sister felt likewise. However, the judge's face remained unreadable as he dismissed them for the day. He would deliberate and return his findings the next morning at nine o'clock.

The inevitable occurred as they left the courtroom. Joe Kennedy came face to face with his son and his new daughter-in-law.

"Father, I'd like to present my wife, Mary."

Mr. Kennedy's eyes turned on Mary to the exclusion of Jason. "My dear, you're very lovely. Jason has chosen well. However, it pains me to say, *you* have not. I apologize in advance for the misery you'll be sure to experience."

Mary's violet eyes had batted in the initial flattery and then narrowed at the insults. "Mr. Kennedy, as this is our first meeting, I will try to excuse your harsh judgment of my marriage. I assure you of my ability to be the wife and partner your son needs. We definitely understand each other."

Joe Kennedy removed a cigar from his coat pocket and made a slow production of lighting it. He gave no more of a response than to chuckle as he walked away.

Eddie and Julia bade Mr. Oxley goodbye and followed him. Mr. Kennedy helped Julia into the buggy, waited for Eddie to join him on the front seat, and then slapped the reins wearing a sideways smile, the cigar held in his teeth. The man inspired Eddie's respect.

~~~

Agnes Kennedy and Susannah Hawkins—they reflected two sides of the same coin. Agnes had grown up on a vast farm in Texas and Susannah in the elegance of Georgetown privilege, but both women had hearts mirroring love for their families and husbands. If Susannah had never lived at the fort, she might not have been able to identify so readily with the rancher's wife; both were strong women with an elegant manner. Jared still seemed a bit intimidated by his robust grandfather, yet demonstrated no hesitancy with his grandmother. They chatted about everything. The Richardses arrived home a day before the Kennedys left for Washington. Jared received assurance of his friend Charlie's wellbeing.

The end of the evening arrived before anyone expected. The men exited the major's study to find Jared asleep—his head on his mother's lap and his feet in his grandmother's lap—in the parlor as Mrs. Hawkins played the pianoforte. Eddie scooped up his growing nephew and Julia received one more hug before they left. They persuaded the Kennedys to stay at the Hawkinses instead of at the hotel with Erma and Samuel.

Julia waited for him in the dining room as he put Jared to bed. He removed his coat and shirt collar and went downstairs to join her. She looked up as he entered and pulled out a chair.

"Here's some buttermilk."

"Thanks."

Her eyes held uncertainty, whereas, her erect shoulders appeared braced for a battle.

"What do you think of our chances, Eddie?"

He took a large, cold gulp of the thick milk and wiped his lips with the back of his hand.

"Honestly, presentations were pretty balanced. It'll depend on the judge's view, but I think Mr. Oxley had it right. The actual presence of Mr. Kennedy, Miss Franklin, and Samuel Perkins made more of an impact than written testimony. I'm praying. Now stop it, Julia. Don't look at me that way. I've not pushed, but you need to listen. God isn't like all the men you've known and won't die as our father did. He won't abandon you the way our mother did or be inadequate in his provisions the way I was. Now hardships still come, but He *will* stand by you no matter what this world throws at you. If you'll trust Him, you'll understand the difference."

Weariness masked his sister's face as she stood. "I love you, Eddie, and know you mean well. I'm going to church with you, so let's just leave it there for now. Thank you for standing beside me. Oh, and your provisions weren't inadequate, they were just too hard earned for you to have to share them."

He took her hand and pressed it to his cheek. "Sister, don't you know the one thing that gave me joy during that time—when I found a provision for you. Those meager items meant something. When you left, it became just survival."

Her eyes widened in understanding and tears glistened. "Oh, Eddie, why didn't I realize that until now? You see, that's the way providing for Jared has changed my life. Before him, it *was* just survival. Knowing he had what he needed has given me purpose. I can't lose him."

He kissed her hand. "I know. Now, go to bed. I'll turn off the lights before I turn in for the night."

~~~

The sick pendulum of emotions, vacillating between anticipation and trepidation swirled around and within all the people in the courtroom. Mrs. Hawkins twisted her delicate handkerchief. Eddie sat at the edge of his chair with his arms propped on the wooden rail in front of him. Those beside him bit their lips, jostled their legs, and uttered soft prayers. Eddie moved like an uncoiled spring when the judge entered, triggering the rising of all in the room.

Absolute silence followed the tandem volume of everyone resuming their seats after the judge took the bench. The creased face behind the gray beard wore a somber expression as he scanned the room with his hands folded beside his resting gavel. He looked down for a moment. His voice startled all to attention as his eyes lifted and pierced those within his address.

"There are many lives to consider in this case, and all interested parties will now be assured of crossing paths again. If

Mr. Jason Kennedy had not pursued a visit with his sister at the Hawkinses' home, this case may never have come to be. However, he did and it is. Therefore, this court is ready to make a ruling in the matter of the custody of the child, Jared Hawkins Rigby. This young man is not the first to have unusual—less than conventional—circumstances surrounding his birth and upbringing. Due to the war, I have found many mothers left to raise their young ones alone and doing an adequate job. Therefore, the point of Miss Rigby being unmarried does not mean her son is at a disadvantage. However, her previous source of profession and residence are a poor environment for raising a child, yet there again, she arranged placement for the boy in a better situation with the Hawkinses and the schools chosen. Upon reviewing Jared's school performance and medical records, they are both excellent. He has been surrounded with a nurturing environment. However, a real family has not been a part of his life except for the past few months with the return of his uncle and the subsequent arrival of his mother. Miss Rigby is now in a more respectable, if not as lucrative, a profession." He stared at Julia. "I commend you for these facts. However, this court takes exception to your delayed pursuit of an alternative profession before now. You saw to your son's care, but you withheld yourself from him. Your ability to continue to provide for all his needs on your own is indeed in question." He turned his eyes from Julia's grave face and settled on the smug face of Jason. "Now, Mr. Kennedy, you are *not* to be commended for any effort to acknowledge or care for your son until this point. The one decent act was to want to acknowledge the boy and provide for him when faced with his existence. But in reviewing the terms of your inheritance, this court finds your motives may be less than paternal. You will gain your full benefits if the boy takes on your name and becomes a part of your family today. However, your father must know you well, as, outside of my ruling today, he has specified you must have a child within the confines of marriage. You and your new wife can still meet the requirements on your own if so blessed; however, you could be assured of it if I so decide to give you custody." He turned his attention on Joe and Agnes Kennedy, Eddie, the Hawkinses, and Jared. "Then we come to the other relations and friends involved. In all honesty, these are the people who offer the boy the opportunity for stability even more than his parents. I have reviewed their offers to be guardians and provide financial and physical support. However, I find the boy's parents must be the first scrutinized, and if possible, held responsible. Therefore, my initial determination as of ten o'clock last evening read: Jared Hawkins Rigby is best served to live within a stable family home in Texas with his father and step-mother. A legal representative will make regular checks and inquiries into his status to be sure no physical harm has befallen him." He glared as Jason slapped his attorney on the back. "However, a new development, which bore consideration, came to my attention this morning. Moreover, Miss Julia Rigby and Mr. Edward Rigby, I apologize for the presentation of this information in this manner. A legal representative, on behalf of your mother and her late husband, received notification of this hearing via Miss Rigby's former employer and the newspaper article about this hearing. Anyway, we will review the Will and its terms in detail at the close of this matter in my chambers. They concern the Rigbys alone and none of the other parties in this courtroom—except for the way they change Miss Rigby's ability to provide for her son. This court now finds young Jared Rigby can stay with his mother and have more than adequate provisions. Furthermore, this change in status has many implications for Miss Rigby that should prevent her seeking less than honorable work in the future. The presence of Jared's uncle, grandparents, and friends here today is evidence of their intention to surround this young man with family. Now, all of this should render Jared's status in the custody of his mother as best. However, I still find the boy and his father should have the opportunity to know each other. Therefore, my ruling is that primary custody of the minor, Jared Hawkins Rigby, will remain with his mother, but he will travel to Texas each summer, spending one month with his father and three weeks with his grandparents each year once he is twelve years of age. Until he reaches that age, visitation will be at his mother's discretion. His name will remain Jared Hawkins Rigby until the age of eighteen years. He can then petition for the change to Kennedy, if he so desires, to inherit his grandfather's provisions. This matter is resolved." He hit his gavel to punctuate the end of the hearing.

A stunned silence ensued until Jason Kennedy's lawyer

blurted out, "I object and would like to be apprised of the legal documents to assure their content and legitimacy."

The judge gave him a severe look. "So noted, and once they are reviewed and probated, you will be allowed to view them. My ruling still stands. Now, I will have Mr. Oxley, Julia Rigby, Edward Rigby, and Jared Rigby in my chambers."

Eddie took his young nephew's elbow as the boy gazed at him with wide eyes and confusion. The solemn lad reached for his mother's hand. Julia turned a pale face toward her brother, which mirrored his shock. He knew they faced more.

An hour later, numbness permeated every part of him. It seemed their mother had worked many jobs after leaving her children and had barely survived on her own until the beginning of the Civil War. She'd worked at one of the nicer restraints in New York by the end of the war. While working there, she caught the eye of a wealthy French businessman visiting from England. A man ten years older than her and well established as an art dealer and part of a shipping company. Initially, she refused to marry him, but he determined to have her and demanded to know why. She shared how she'd deserted her two children after the death of her first husband. The man wanted to help her find them and take them in until she let him know they'd be grown by that time. He still wanted to find out what happened to them but couldn't locate Julia. However, he did find Eddie's enlistment in the war. Marta Rigby had agreed to marry him when he insisted on making provisions for Eddie and Julia and any grandchildren to come through his Will in the future. Philippe Rousseau didn't have any other children and agreed. If Julia and Eddie weren't located within two years of his death, the provisions for them would go to Marta, in addition to the generous provisions made for her and the upkeep of his estates in France and England as long as she chose to live in Europe. The tragic part of the recounting of his mother's life after her marriage regarded the most recent events. After the death of her husband, Marta sent a representative to find Eddie and Julia in America. She oversaw the sale of his business holdings, minus the retention of shares so designated to her, and both estates before leaving for America. She wanted to purchase a home and be available if her children decided they wanted to see her. However, she grew ill on the ship and required hospitalization upon disembarking. Her representative managed to locate Julia's former employer a week before the ship arrived last month. Then he had to wait for Marta Rousseau to become lucid enough to direct his actions. She requested a transfer to a hospital in Boston so she could speak with both Julia's former lawyer and former employer.

After the judge's review of the documents and story, the door to the judge's chambers opened.

"Mr. Rigby, Miss Rigby, meet Monsieur Rosen, your mother's legal representative."

The siblings inspected and, in turn, received inspection by the small Frenchman during an appraising silence.

"Mademoiselle, Monsieur Rigby, it is my pleasure to make your acquaintance. This must be Madame's grandson, Jared, no?"

Julia found her voice first. "Yes, this is my son, Jared. Jared, say hello."

Jared swallowed hard before speaking. "Hello."

The small, mustached man in the well-tailored suit smiled and reached out his hand. Jared took it.

Eddie stood. "Excuse me. I want Jared's grandparents and the Hawkinses present for this."

No one protested as he made a quick exit. He ignored Jason Kennedy and his attorney as he took purposeful strides toward the older couples still waiting in their seats. They rose and followed him without question. Eddie shut the door to the room as soon as all were inside. He made brief introductions to Monsieur Rosen and requested Major Hawkins and Joe Kennedy be allowed to view the legal documents before proceeding. Major Hawkins read them and then passed them to Mr. Kennedy. Eddie could tell the legitimacy of the information by their expressions.

Eddie shared a look with the major.

"Eddie, these provisions will take care of your family for the rest of your lives, if handled well. I believe Mr. Kennedy can help guide you. Also, remember, Andrew Richards is familiar with all European dealings and should be made your legal guide in this. I had a letter from him today, and there's been a delay in their return to England due to some business requiring his attention here until the end of the month. We're meeting for breakfast tomorrow."

Monsieur Rosen gave a confident smile. "I know Andrew

Richards. If you will allow me the pleasure of breaking my fast with you, I am sure we can conclude all of the necessary papers."

Eddie gave the man a hard look. "First, know, for the sake of my sister and nephew, I'm grateful. Personally, I would rather not accept it—"

Mrs. Hawkins took his arm, and he relaxed a bit, tittering between yelling and weeping. He looked back at the man. "This doesn't make what she did go away."

The man failed to give immediate defense. "No, no, you are correct, Monsieur. Madame would be the first to agree. However, it is something much needed at this time. Fate has smiled on you now. If you cannot forgive your mother, perhaps you agreeing to receive these provisions will be enough. In time—maybe yes or maybe no—only you can decide."

Julia's emotion-laden voice drew him. "Where is she?"

The man's face softened. "Madame Rousseau is at the New England Hospital for Women and Children in Boston[xxxiv]."

An emotional wave of shock spread over the entire room. The man frowned. "Is this not a good hospital? I will have her moved—"

Susannah Hawkins's calm voice stopped him. "It's a very good hospital. It's just that my daughter-in-law, the wife of my late son, is in nurse's training there. She's a very good friend to Julia, Eddie, and Jared."

The man beamed. "Providence, oui?"

Eddie ran a weary hand over his face. He knew more than providence had a hand in this, and because he did, he knew the ultimate might be required of him—forgiveness—and he might not be ready or willing. His green eyes met the brown ones watching him, and he stood.

"Monsieur Rosen, we'll see you in the morning. I need to speak with my family and friends at home. This day has been overwhelming in more ways than expected."

The man blew air threw his lips. "But of course. For now, I require your and your sister's signatures on this letter, confirming my presentation of these documents and your intent on accepting—pending review by your legal counsel. Therefore, the judge will be able to close today's proceedings in protection of your nephew's interests, as his inheritance is a separate item than yours. Miss Rigby, I will require your signature as your son's legal guardian."

The judge saw Eddie's hesitancy. "I assure you everything is in order, Mr. Rigby. Otherwise, my decision today would have been different."

Major Hawkins and Mr. Kennedy nodded their agreement. Eddie sighed and took the pen. He and Julia signed where directed. The last page awaited their signatures after Andrew Richard's review the next day.

The judge directed them out the back entrance of the courthouse. Major Hawkins drew Eddie aside as they approached the carriages.

"Son, we're going to take Jared home with us. You and Julia need to talk. I cannot fathom all that the two of you must be feeling. Just remember, you are no longer that abandoned boy. You moved past him with God's help, but I am not sure Julia has. Now is the time to decide if you will commiserate in bitterness or let her see forgiveness reign."

Anger welled up inside of him, and he walked a few steps away. "I know what I should do, but—"

"But? That one will get you into deep waters. His strength goes beyond yours. James would be the first to tell you that bitterness never wins."

Eddie heaved a sigh, turned back, and gave a reluctant nod. "Yes, he would. I can almost hear him in your voice."

Major Hawkins gave his shoulder a firm pat and crossed to assist his wife into the carriage with the Kennedys and Jared. Julia moved to him and took his hand just as she had the first day after their mother left all those years ago, but this time he could sense her hurt and fear. She'd tried to be so brave for him back then; now his turn had come. He placed a comforting arm around her and led her to where Ian waited for them in the buggy.

"We need a long ride, Ian, and your discretion."

The Irishman moved his pipe to one side. "I can see that you do, so you'll have it."

Julia leaned against him as the large wheels turned and the hoofbeats echoed off the streets as they rode in the silent companionship of grown siblings. Neither needed words for the moment; they would come. And they did.

They returned to the house four hours later. Amelia Jackson met them.

"Mother sent for me as she knew you wouldn't be back for a while. All is in order in the house. I had to turn Mr. Grierson away because his wife was resting and didn't need to be disturbed. His status as a gentleman finally outweighed his effort to defy me."

The determined expression on her face looked so like James. Eddie smiled. "Your brother would be proud of you, Amelia."

The blue eyes widened, and a pleased smile followed. "Thank you."

"No, thank you, for coming. Ian can drive you home."

She smiled as she pulled on her gloves. "No, need, I have my carriage. Good evening and I'm happy Jared will still be around. Clara and Robert would have been sad to lose him, as would I."

She hurried out before they could respond. Amelia never expressed so much. Julia shook her head. "Wonders never cease. Well, I don't know about you, brother dear, but I'm exhausted and want to retire for the night. Forgive me for leaving everything to you, but I must."

Eddie felt the same but would give everyone the barest information—the fact that Jared would be staying with Julia—over their evening meal first. Nothing could have prepared them for today and this perplexing and bitter blessing. He gave up trying to wrap logic around the events. Once he crawled into bed for the night, he said a prayer for guidance and let the rest go as quick slumber overtook him.

~~~

At about ten o'clock, the sound of the bell outside of the front door roused him. He fumbled in the darkness to pull on his pants and a shirt. He found Mrs. Brady opening the door as he started down the stairs. Still dressed, he suspected she still read late in the parlor.

"Why, Jared, I thought you were gone for the night," she said.

"I wanted to come home." Jared stepped into view, followed by Major Hawkins.

Eddie reached the last step. "Mrs. Brady, thank you. I'll take care of him."

She laid a tender hand on Jared's head and gave an understanding smile. "Excuse me," she said and returned to the parlor. Her young daughter adored Jared even though he often treated her as a tag-a-long.

The major caught Eddie's eyes and shook his head. He understood the meaning: no reprimands as his nephew continued to struggle with all the day's events. Eddie nodded.

"Thank you for bringing him, Major. We'll see you in the morning."

Major Hawkins squatted, gave Jared a hug, and bid them goodnight. Eddie sat on the bottom step and patted the place beside him. Jared sat down without a word. He turned to look at his uncle with tears in his eyes.

"I got what I wanted today, but you and Mother got something you didn't want because of me."

Eddie felt a lump form in his throat, and it took him a moment before he could choke out a response. He frowned and leaned his elbows on his knees with hands clasped as he turned to look into the heartbreaking face.

"Wait a minute, Jared. We got what we wanted today, too—you."

"But you got your mother back, too, and I don't think you want her. I kind of understand, and I kind of think I don't. Julia—I mean—Mother once told me my grandfather died, and my grandmother had run away and left the two of you afterwards. That's all she told me when I asked if I had grandparents during one of her visits. She didn't want to talk about it. But you know what I think, Uncle Eddie?"

"No, but I wish you'd tell me."

"I think mother wanted to keep me and see to my care because she didn't want me abandoned in the way you were. Sure, we haven't exactly had the same relationships my friends have had with their mothers, but I've always known she was there looking out for me. She made sure a family surrounded me by bringing me to the Hawkinses. I've been happy. Your mother must have been very sad, scared, and without any help whatsoever to run away like she did. She was wrong to leave you, but she didn't have a place like this to help her, and neither did you or my mother. You know Johnny Ponder ran away and abandoned his parents, but they forgave him and let him come home. Don't you think God would want you to forgive my grandmother? She's helping us now."

Eddie looked at the almost ten-year-old boy. He knew too much for his age. Still, how did you explain that adults sometimes cling to the injustices done to them to justify their own choices? And to feel like they're somehow better than the one who has wronged them? The simplicity of Jared's logic brought him to his knees within the confines of his soul. He put an arm around his nephew and hugged him close to his side.

"You're right, Jared. It's hard, but I'll try."

Jared pulled away and stood up with a glance up the stairs. "Do you think I could go sleep on the cot in Mother's room tonight?"

Julia had moved to Molly's old room, and she'd left the cot Charlie used at the foot of the bed. Jared had never used it as he had his own small room, unlike the other children in the house. His room, on the third level, had once been a nursery for the first owners before the war.

"I know you can, and it'll please your mother to know you're there." He grinned, pulling Jared back as he started to dash up the stairs. "Remember, most of the house is asleep. We need to be quiet."

Jared grinned. "Sorry."

In answer, and to his nephew's delight, Eddie swung the boy up in his arms and carried him up the stairs.

~~~

The next morning, Julia's expression and posture evidenced renewed determination and maternal protectiveness. She stood at the door with her hands on Jared's shoulders. Eddie could see the proud tilt of her profile as he shut the door to his office where he'd worked since before the first ray of sunrise. He wanted all the bills and schedules for the ladies in order for the week before the morning breakfast meeting at the hotel. One of the many things he'd discussed with Julia during their long ride yesterday included the possibility of a trip to Boston. Neither one wanted it, but knew their mother's representative might request it. After his morning prayer time, he'd felt convicted to go if asked. However, from the clarity reflected in his sister's eyes as he approached, he knew she didn't.

He looked down at the beaming face of his nephew. "Good morning, Uncle Eddie. Mother says I can come with you to the hotel, and then she's taking me to work with her today at the theater. It'll be the last chance for me to go with her with school starting next week. She doesn't have to work tomorrow, and we're going to Harper's Ferry for a picnic and swim. It's normally our day at the Jackson's, but mother is going to ask if Robert and Clara can come with us."

Julia rolled her shoulders and tilted her head as she spoke. "There have been too many fast changes for my son, and I'm not about to go dashing back to Boston right now. I've decided to sign the documents for Jared and me to receive our inheritance. You can decide for yourself. If Mum gets well and decides to come see us, I'll face her then. She walked away, and I think she needs to come to me."

Eddie couldn't argue with any of her reasoning, but he knew it wouldn't be that simple for him.

"I support you in your decision, Julia. We'd better go, or we'll be late."

Her shoulders relaxed, and she gave him a grateful smile and a nod.

~~~

Everyone waited at the table when they arrived. Major Hawkins expressed surprise at seeing Jared.

Julia requested a pen from the waiter and asked Monsieur Rosen to direct her where to sign after she asked Mr. Richards one question: "Are things in order?" Once he nodded, she signed, bade them all a good day, and departed with Jared without waiting for breakfast. She paid a waiter and took the basket presented to her at the door leading to the lobby. Eddie realized she must have somehow arranged to have something ready. Her new status as a self-sufficient woman afforded her an opportunity to have a true relationship with her son and a different life.

Admiration radiated from Monsieur Rosen's face as he stroked his mustache. "Your sister has an even stronger resilience than her mother, and Madame Rousseau is very—how do you say—a tough woman."

A wave of bitterness caught Eddie. "I never thought of my mother as tough, just a weak coward."

"Eddie, that's very harsh of you," Major Hawkins said.

"Do you realize who your mother has become, Mr. Rigby?" Andrew Richards asked with a lifted eyebrow. Then he continued before Eddie could respond.

"She is well respected in England and all of Europe for her work with her husband as an art dealer. The Rousseau name is linked with many of the top art traders like Paul Durand-Ruel[xxxv]."

As Eddie gave him a blank look, he rolled his eyes and looked at the major for help.

Major Hawkins sat forward. "Eddie, the Corcoran Art Gallery[xxxvi] here in Washington has been anticipating her arrival, and they were disappointed to learn of her illness. Your mother is not the same person you once knew."

Eddie's lips pursed. "Money and prestige buy you influence, but they don't change character."

"I think you would be surprised by the things your mother has done for some of the orphans in both London and Paris. She knew she could not take back the wrong she did by leaving her own children, but she has tried to fix her eyes forward each day," Monsieur Rosen said.

Eddie ignored the man and turned to Andrew Richards. "Are there any conditions to be imposed upon my sister, nephew, or me beyond what's plainly stated? The maze of legal terms is enough to hang a man without him even realizing there's a noose around his neck. I trust your knowledge of law on both sides of the pond enough to rely on your determination."

Andrew took a sip of his tea and shook his head. "Rather suspicious of your Mum given the generosity she is showing, old boy, but no, there are no hidden traps in these documents. I would suggest appointing a business advisor to guide you both as this is a substantial endowment."

"Mr. Kennedy and I met with my son-in-law, Judge Jackson, last evening, and he wants you to meet with the man managing his assets. It's your decision, Eddie, but we can help guide you."

"I sure wish James was here. He had an astute mind with the law and figures," Eddie said.

"Who is this James?" Monsieur Rosen inquired.

Major Hawkins smiled at the man's confusion. "James is my late son and was Eddie's best friend."

The man gave a solemn nod. "I am so sorry for your loss."

Andrew placed the papers, pen, and ink in front of Eddie. "Sign it, my boy, and let's break our fast in celebration of the blessings sent your way."

Eddie sighed and put the pen to the paper. He stared at his name at the bottom for a moment and passed it to Monsieur Rosen. The man checked the now dry pages Julia had signed and stacked Eddie's on top of them, laying them on the small table the waiter had brought with the ink and pen. He gave Eddie a speculative look, and before he could even ask, Eddie responded.

"I'll go, Monsieur Rosen. What time is the train?"

A new look of respect appeared on the small Frenchman's face. "Eleven o'clock this morning. I had hoped your sister would come, but no matter for now. They are holding tickets for us and I have rooms at a hotel in Boston. We will see your mother tomorrow evening."

The major gave him a proud slap on the back just as their meal arrived.

~~~

Hallie re-read the telegram for the fourth time. She still found it hard to believe. The woman who had become one of her favorite patients . . . Eddie and Julia's mother? She leaned against the wall outside the door leading to the ward where Madame Rousseau rested after an afternoon of delighting some of the younger patients on the porch. Hallie had taken her for her first outing since her arrival. The quick-witted woman had a captivating smile. Her gray-streaked, light brown hair and sparkling green eyes made an attractive contrast.

Something familiar and likable about her, struck Hallie from the moment she met her. Now she understood why. However, there were also differences, beyond the difference in hair color. Marta Rousseau embraced life even in illness. She had a tendency toward self-deprecation and frankness. Except in the moments when a haunted look appeared in her eyes. It disappeared as she inquired about other patients and staff. Near death with pneumonia upon her arrival, she'd only had one visitor since her transfer from New York. The small man hadn't returned in a week. Mrs. Hawkins's telegram arrived midmorning:

Marta Rousseau is Eddie's mother. Eddie is coming to Boston. My letter will follow. So much to learn, and Hallie knew she would need to be prepared before Eddie arrived. She pushed away from the wall and hurried into the ward. The lovely eyes opened as she approached the bed. The woman's accent—a mixture of British with French nuances—endeared her to Hallie. She remembered Julia telling her that their parents came to America from England. Julia had been two and her mother had made the trip while pregnant with Eddie.

"My dear, Mrs. Hawkins, I thought you had left for morning class."

Hallie sighed as she took the soft hand. "I was called out to receive a telegram from Washington. It seems that we have much more in common than our love of children and things of beauty. I'm friends with both of your grown children, Eddie and Julia."

The woman paled, and the haunted look appeared for a moment before one of candor replaced it. "And how do you know this?"

After Madame Rousseau donned her spectacles, Hallie handed her the telegram. The long fingers on the aging hands shook as she returned the message to her. "This is all you know?"

Hallie nodded. "About your identity. My late husband was your son's best friend and enabled him to leave street life."

Marta Rousseau gave a regal nod. "Then we have much to discuss. I need to know about my son before he arrives. Perhaps we can start anew and leave the unchangeable past behind."

Hallie frowned. "I'm not—"

The generous mouth compressed. "Can anyone change the wrong I did or the lives any of us have lived?" After receiving a headshake, Marta continued. "We start now then. *Oui?*"

Hallie sat down next to her and smiled. She wanted to learn the woman's side of the story. She just hoped Eddie would listen.

Chapter Six

THE REGAL ARCHITECTURE of the hospital—austere and welcoming at the same time—with its multiple peaked roof and well-tended grounds. Eddie swallowed as he removed his tall hat upon entering the facility behind Monsieur Rosen. During the time they spent together traveling to Boston, the gentleman managed to gain Eddie's grudging admiration and respect.

The Frenchman began with Monsieur Rousseau as an apprentice at the age of fourteen and received an education in England. He then returned to his benefactor's full time employ. His parents lived in a small village in France where his father worked as a watchmaker. He first met the new Madame Rousseau after he turned twenty-seven. His employer had lost his first wife and child during childbirth seven years before he met Marta on a trip to America. Monsieur Rosen smiled as he described the joyful reciprocal transformation in both individuals, making up the new couple over the ensuing years.

Monsieur Rousseau also made provisions for him in his last papers, and he acquired twenty-five percent of the business interests retained with Marta having the other twenty-five percent. The remaining fifty percent of the interests sold at a substantial profit, especially with all the economic issues present in both America and Europe. Eddie listened but chose not to reveal much until he spoke with his mother. They arrived in the late afternoon.

He looked about in apprehension as much from the setting as the circumstance. Hospitals were never a place he sought. Too many of his friends had lost their lives within such walls. He turned at the sound of quick footsteps approaching them. Relief and ease flooded him at the sight of Hallie wearing a plain dress covered with a long pinafore type apron. Everything stilled inside, and he knew he could bear the situation.

"Good afternoon, Monsieur Rosen and Mr. Rigby. Please follow me. Madame Rousseau is expecting you."

Eddie frowned and received a quick look from Hallie. It spoke volumes, and he knew not to ask questions. The row of beds in the ward filled with women suffering from diverse illnesses unsettled him. To his surprise, Hallie led them to the last bed beside the window. His heart raced, and a lump formed in his throat upon seeing his mother again. The picture in his mind—the over pondered reflections of an eleven-year-old—of a lovely, full-faced woman putting him to bed with grief in her green eyes the night of her husband's death at sea. She assured him everything would be fine, but when he went into the kitchen of their small house the next morning, he found his sister alone. He'd run to the door calling for his mother. Julia placed her hands on his shoulders and told him they were alone.

Even though much changed, he would have known his mother without the introduction Monsieur Rosen gave.

"This is Madame Marta Rousseau, your mother, and Madame, may I present—"

"Edward Thaddeus Rigby—my son. You have the build of your father and from behind I might mistake you for him. But your face is my reflection in younger days."

Her voice sounded different, but the same; the unique prosody of a mother's voice remained a lifelong connection to her children. An unexpected comfort sparked somewhere inside of him.

"Mum, it's unexpected to see you. How are you feeling?"

Moisture sparkled in the slanted eyes as a tentative smile shone on him.

"Much better, thank you." She stared at him for a prolonged moment before turning to Hallie. "Mrs. Hawkins, would you please leave us. Monsieur Rosen you may also go. Please come see me tomorrow. *Merci.*"

The abrupt dismissal resulted in no offense as Hallie bent to hug her, followed by the Frenchman's exchange of kisses on both cheeks. Hallie patted Eddie's arm as she followed the small man on the path out of the ward.

His mother motioned toward the chair beside her bed. "Please sit, Edward."

He placed his hat on the small table beside a pitcher of water and complied. She reached for his hand, and he flinched upon initial contact but didn't pull away.

"My son, we have much to discuss, but I will not waste this time on regrets, however unforgivable, of the past. Your friend, Hallie Hawkins, was kind enough to supply me with some of the events and conditions of both yours and your sister's lives."

She shut her eyes for a moment and opened them to reveal pain reflected in their depths. "I would do things much differently, but I cannot. Therefore, I have written each of you a letter, filled with my heart. Please open the drawer in the table next to you."

He complied.

"Good. Now," she continued, "I want to thank you for accepting the generosity of my late husband and for coming to see me. He found me worthy of his love, and his gift is an extension of his affection. Please use it to make your past stay in yesterday and your future secure. Once I am well, I will go to your sister, if you think she will receive me for a visit. I would like to meet my grandson. Whether you choose to allow me to be part of your lives in the future will be your decision. Please do not feel any obligation."

She sighed and a momentary look of self-loathing appeared. "You would be correct to think this is no more than what is rightfully owed you."

He modulated his deep tenor voice in softness.

"Mum, to be honest, I've been very angry and bitter against you for years. Now, I'm just confused on what to feel and convicted to forgive you, but it's hard. Not so much because of the hardships I faced, but for the life Julia's lived to survive."

She covered his hands with both of hers.

"Thank you for being honest."

He sighed and reached inside his coat pocket. "I also wrote

you a letter last night. The possibility of my turning and leaving once I got here existed, so I wanted to have something to give you."

Her understanding smile tugged at his heart.

"I wouldn't have blamed you, but I am glad you didn't leave," she said. "Will you stay and visit with me until the nurses force me to rest?"

"I'd like that." It surprised him to find his words were true. Almost half an hour later, Hallie returned.

"Madame, I must apologize, but it's time for your evening meal, and you mustn't tire yourself."

A regal tilt of the head and a gracious smile accompanied his mother's response. "But of course, my dear." She reached for Eddie's hands, and her eyes widened in surprise as he bent to place a kiss on her lined cheek.

"Good night, Mum. I'll be back in the morning. My train doesn't leave until one tomorrow afternoon."

He waited for Hallie and his mother to say goodnight with a sense of satisfaction, gratitude, and impatience. A pervading restlessness overcame him as he waited for Hallie to accompany him after one more parting smile. He loosened his collar and tie upon reaching the foyer.

"Eddie, wait a moment. I can't keep up with you."

Realization hit him as he turned to find Hallie trying to keep pace with his rapid strides. He gave her an apologetic grin.

"Sorry, I just need to get some air. Have you ever played four-pocket billiards?"

"What? No, but I've learned croquet."

He smirked. "That's too slow. You need to go change clothes and come with me. We'll grab a meal at the hotel restaurant, so I can also change into less formal attire. Then I'll take you to my old friend's pub and game room. You won't have to worry about anything."

A moment of hesitancy passed. "Eddie, I normally work from dawn until nine or after at night. However, I'm due for my bi-monthly afternoon off. Maybe the head nurse will let me take it this evening instead. I'll have to check. Will you wait?"

He noted the dark circles under her eyes for the first time and gave her a bright smile. "Of course."

Thirty minutes later, Hallie returned, wearing an apologetic smile—combined with an attractive brown, cotton dress with a high, lace-trimmed neckline.

His gave her an appreciative smile. "That color complements your eyes."

A warm smile appeared on her face. "I'm glad it pleases you, seeing as you've had to wait. If your mother hadn't charmed my supervisor, I wouldn't be here. You have to have me back by ten o'clock."

He frowned. "Where are your quarters?"

She gestured behind her. "I have a small room off of your mother's ward."

He shook his head. "Very well, I'll now take you away. Shall we?"

She took the arm he presented, allowing him to usher her out of the hospital with quick steps just short of a run.

~~~

They found Monsieur Rosen dining at the hotel, and he asked them to join him. After their meal, Eddie excused himself to change clothes, leaving Hallie to converse with the very interesting European gentleman. The man's intelligence and knowledge about art, architecture, and the world fascinated her.

"I've heard the artist Monet is amazing. My sister-in-law and her husband traveled to France last year and saw some of his work."

"Yes, yes, I have met him. He has a different technique. His canvases mesmerize your eyes. The time of day, season, and weather are captured in such a way . . . " He shook his head, pursed his lips in a kiss directed towards his fingers on his right hand. They made a bursting motion as they spread, leaving his hand open. "Perfection."

He pulled out his pocket watch. "Please forgive me, Madame Hawkins, I hate to end our delightful conversation, but I must leave for another engagement. Please express my regrets to Monsieur Rigby."

Hallie smiled. "Of course, I enjoyed visiting with you. Good night."

She watched him leave the lobby and smiled as she turned

back to watch the stairs for Eddie. A few minutes later, he walked toward her with all traces of the formal gentleman removed. He wore a casual brown coat over a collarless shirt, brown pants, and shoes. A worn derby hat completed his rogue look. The desk clerk frowned in their direction, and Hallie laughed as Eddie took her arm to usher her out the door. He heralded a buggy and gave her a challenging look as the driver confirmed the address given to him with an apprehensive glance.

"Stay close to me, and I'll keep you safe. Do you trust me?"

A momentary chill followed by secure certainty followed. Her brown eyes met his intense green ones. "Yes, I do, Edward Thaddeus Rigby."

His gaze darkened, and then he wagged a finger at her. "My mother is the only one who has ever used my complete given name. "

She licked her lips and hummed a little tune one of the children in the ward had taught her as she sent a teasing look his way. "Maybe I should just start calling you Thaddeus. Then I'll be the only one who claims you by that name."

"Hmmm. What's your second name?"

She crossed her arms in satisfaction. "I don't have one. My mother wanted one, but my pa said Hallie was enough."

He rubbed a finger across his lips. "Then, no, you must continue to call me Eddie. Besides, I don't look like a Thaddeus."

Hallie laughed. "No, you don't. Now where are we going?"

He removed his hat and looked down at the brim as he ran his fingers across it.

"Tommy, the man who fed Julia and me a meal on a few cold nights, was able to acquire this place after the war in a well-played game of cards. Tommy's son was my friend. He served with James and me. Therefore, the place is special because of my friends and because it's where I met James during a less than well-turned card game. It turned out to be the luckiest losing hand I ever had. Julia told me they now have a billiard table, and I want to teach you the game. What do you say?"

It sounded so different from anything she'd done since traveling east. Part of her thought it foolish for a woman of her age and status to consider, but the idea thrilled her.

"Sure, Eddie, it sounds like fun."

He sighed and smiled. "Good."

The moonlight bathed the street as Eddie helped her to the ground. Bright light and laughter emanated from the corner establishment. It had the feel of the saloon in Texas, but no girls of her former ilk were part of the atmosphere.

She spotted a poker game in the corner, a few lads around the touted billiard table, and an older man behind the bar. A few fleeting glances were sent their way as they navigated the small maze of tables, stopping at the bar.

The exclamation of welcome from the barkeep made it worth the effort. He whooped and hurried around, grabbing Eddie by his upper arms.

"Eddie Rigby! I never expected to see you again, but I'm glad you're here. Did you leave the military? I heard Julia moved to Washington. Do you live there?"

Eddie laughed. "Tommy, Tommy, give me a minute. I would like a long chat. But first, I need to have a go at your billiard table."

Tommy gave him an appraising look. "You'd better be good if you want to win money off the lads back there; especially the short one with the beard. He's closer to your age than the rest."

"No, no, I'm not here to gamble. This is Mrs. Hallie Hawkins, the widow of James Hawkins. You remember my friend? I think you met him the day we left for the war when you came to see Jake off."

The man glanced her way. "Ma'am." He looked back at Eddie. "Jake has told me all about James Hawkins. I understand you met him in this very place, and I'm glad to have you here. Still, you'll have to talk to the short gent over there if you wish to work the pocket table."

The small man in the rear turned and leaned against a tall slender pole. Hallie knew the men used it to knock the balls on the table about with, but she remained unsure of the particulars.

"Hey, Tommy, is your friend interested in a game?" called the small man with muscled arms beneath a cotton shirt pressed tight against his chest by suspenders. He reached up to sweep his longish hair out of his eyes and then scratched at his beard.

Eddie turned and strolled toward the man. Uncertain of the

wisdom of his idea, Hallie could only watch.

All the attention of everyone in the room fixed on the two men. Eddie stood over a head taller than his challenger. They stood in silent appraisal. Then Eddie kicked the stick and pulled it out of the man's hand as an echo of gasps and throat clearings filled the room. How in the world did he expect to keep her safe if he got into a brawl? Hallie crossed her arms as she sent an irritated look toward the barkeep. Her ire increased as the old man gave her a knowing smile.

The sound of laughter erupted from the back of the room, and Hallie turned back to see Eddie slapping the smaller man on the back.

"Jake McDonald."

"Eddie Rigby. Or is it still what—Corporal, Sergeant, or Lieutenant Rigby?"

"No, it's just Eddie to you. I got my discharge last month. Come. Let me buy you a coffee or something stronger to drink, and we'll catch up on things."

Tommy winked at Hallie as he went behind the bar and grabbed a bottle, as well as some coffee.

Eddie took her elbow, and they moved to prop on the counter rail.

"Jake McDonald, please meet Hallie Hawkins. She's James's widow and my good friend. Hallie this is Jake, Tommy's son."

Jake gave her a respectful nod. "Your husband was a good man."

Tommy raised an eyebrow. "What will it be?"

Hallie and Eddie took the coffee, but Jake opted for whiskey. They spent the next hour sharing stories and experiences. Then they finally made it back to the billiard table. The real fun began as soon as the old friends picked up their cue sticks.

Eddie and Jake were amazing during the first few games, but she floundered a bit until she gained confidence and won the next three. The men protested, but she suspected they'd let her win. They laughed and just as Hallie surrendered her cue stick for the evening, a hush filled the rest of the room, and all eyes turned to the police officer at the door.

Hallie recognized him. He'd brought an injured young

woman to the hospital the first night she arrived and had been by a few times since then. However, he didn't acknowledge her. Instead, he sent Eddie a look of pure hatred.

"Well, well, I wondered how long it would take for you to return to where you first started in life, Mr. Rigby. Things sure changed after you left. I came home from the war and made something of myself. I'm not surprised to see you, but I warn you not to try any of your old swindles."

"Officer Calhoun, I think you're out of line. You're making assumptions," Hallie said.

The officer seemed to notice her for the first time. "Why, Mrs. Hawkins, I'm shocked to see you here and keeping such company. I'm sure your instructors would frown on such an outing. And I believe my childhood experiences with your companion give me to believe my so called assumptions are correct."

Eddie leaned over, whispered in Jake's ear, and received a nod. Eddie took her by the elbow and saluted Tommy as they approached the doorway.

"Officer Calhoun now, is it? Well, sir, let me take the time to assure you of your misconceptions. Things aren't always as they seem. This is simply a reunion with old friends. Now, if you'll excuse us, I need to escort Mrs. Hawkins home."

"So, you aren't staying in Boston?"

Eddie's eyes were guarded and hard. "No, I'm not and no laws have been broken. May we go?"

He received a curt nod.

Once underway, Hallie looked across the carriage at Eddie. His fixed gaze focused out of the window, and then he turned as if sensing her attention.

"Calhoun always thought he was better than everyone else. Even when I was still in school before Mum left, he was the boy who received the praise of the teacher and reveled in humiliating others. Until the war, when other men showed him true valor and true brutality. What really galled him—my friendship with a man like James."

"But why? I'm sure James treated him well."

Eddie gave a knowing laugh and shook his head. "You'd better stop making your late husband a saint. Sure, he tried to be fair, but James was fiercely loyal and Calhoun purposefully tried to sabotage me on the field during the heat of battle a few times. I'm pretty wily and took care of myself, but James saw it. There's no place on the field for anyone to work against a fellow soldier or to create a distraction. It could have meant our lives. James suggested a transfer for Calhoun, and when asked my opinion by the general, I agreed."

"But James always refused rank, why would a man be transferred at his request?"

"Hallie, there's still things you don't know. It goes beyond Mrs. Hawkins's view of her son's humble preferences. Initially, James felt he shouldn't be a candidate as he'd refused West Point in favor of Harvard, but as the war progressed, it was for another reason. They used James for intelligence and planning. He often disappeared behind enemy lines for the generals. A missing private isn't noticed within the ranks as often as an officer."

Her mouth went dry and her voice decreased to a mere whisper. "They sent him alone? He could've been captured." Her eyes flew to his face. "But he wasn't alone, was he? "

"No, and it felt good to slip on civilian clothes and become a less visible target for a bit of spying. We were both very agile, and James was like a fox in his tactics. Just remember, I didn't advance in rank until after James got hurt. Then his father made sure I received continued military training at the academy after the war. I'd just finished before being sent to the fort where we first met you."

"Legally lethal and devastatingly handsome."

A suffocating tingle of something in the silence followed her words. His soft response increased it.

"Who?"

Confusion gripped her. "Both of you. Stop it, Eddie. You have a way of unbalancing me." She couldn't look at him as she wished to withdraw her words. "I sure enjoyed meeting your friends tonight and thank you for the billiard games."

"Hallie—"

The hack driver alerted them to their arrival at the hospital. Eddie assisted her to the ground and paid the driver.

"Eddie, you need to get back to your hotel."

He started walking and turned when she didn't join him.

"Hallie, I'll walk you to the door and see if I can sneak in to check on my mother."

He grinned in the moonlight, and she caught her breath. She quickened her steps to pass him. He slowed and took her by the hand.

"Whoa, where's the emergency?"

"Eddie, I promised my heart protection, and I promised James the opposite before he died. He wanted me to feel again. I've managed to protect myself and reasoned he would understand because of my love for him."

Eddie pulled her into the shadows beneath a tree. "Hallie, we talked about all of this on the train when I returned, and I've tried to be your best friend, but right now—"

She couldn't deny their feelings as he bent his head and kissed her, not the same as the brief, meaningless meeting of their lips in front of the house a few weeks earlier. The strong haven of Eddie's arms and his quicksilver kiss devastated and excited her like a splintered bolt of lightning across the sky. His breath intoxicated her as he pulled back and whispered her name. Her eyes opened—now unguarded—searching his. Her hands crept around his neck, and she found her fingers toying with the hair curling at the base.

When had the door to her heart cracked open, and when had he managed to step inside? Why now?

"Hallie, stop trying to reason with yourself. Nothing has changed beyond discovering something amazing. I'm not even sure I'll believe it tomorrow unless you remind me, and that'll be up to you. You need to finish your training, and I've got to get back to Washington. Too many surprises and changes during the past month for us to add anymore, but I feel pretty blessed." He stroked her cheek before he once again captured her lips with his.

His full lips released hers, and then he gathered her in a hug for a moment in which she felt at home. Once he released her, he took her hand and guided her back into the mixture of moonlight and lamplight next to the street. Contentment filled her heart in that moment, and she didn't want to move beyond it. Therefore, she allowed her hand to remain in his until they approached the hospital door. She knew a churning swell of uncertainty waited on the other side. Therefore, she took hold of Eddie's other hand as she turned to face him, feeling the impact of who his past and his present made him. They had several things in common in their lives from their difficult childhoods, James, and the now intertwined lives of their family and friends.

He placed a crooked finger under her chin and lifted it for a brief kiss as he gazed down at her and spoke with candid certainty. "Hallie, you're more than my best friend. Would you be interested in going to the opera with me at the National in December? Julia tells me they'll be doing the *Marriage of Figaro*."[xxxvii]

She laughed in delight. "Why, yes, Mr. Rigby, if I'm finished here. Do you know the dates?"

He shook his head. "No, but I'll find out and write to you posthaste."

"Please do, sir." She dropped his hands and gave him a gentle push on the chest. "Now, *Edward*, I must bid you goodnight. Wait here and I'll send someone to let you in if it's possible for you to sit with your mother. I have to rest for a couple of hours. I had a lovely evening."

She went to the door and turned. *My, my, he was handsome.* The reason why it had taken her this long to acknowledge still fought a battle within.

"Hallie, you decide what you want. "

She gazed at him. "What do you want, Eddie? Have you decided?"

Eddie's candid gaze hid nothing.

"You. My heart has known for a while; tonight just allowed me to admit it. I love you, Hallie." He bridged the space she'd put between them and kissed her cheek. "Good night."

The shield held over her heart since James died threatened not to hold. She would decide whether to let it crumble or resolve to repair it, but it might not be her choice. The unmasked love in his eyes caused her to hurry into the building.

~~~

Eddie basked in the summer's end breeze on his face as he paced the grounds of the hospital. Everything within him called out for Hallie. The intensity of the alchemy between them surprised even him.

His heart continued to pound, and his breaths remained

uneven, and those were just the physical results. The wonderful confirmation of the love within his soul for Hallie overflowed and left him undone.

He overcame the temptation to compare his feelings for Sunbeam with these multi-faceted emotions for Hallie as he realized the complete truth. In many ways, he'd run from the first spark of attraction at the fort all those years ago, and he'd continued to run until now.

He stopped and stared at the impressive hospital for a moment as his thoughts went to Jared the night after the hearing. His nephew returned home to be near his mother.

The same advice applied now. Just as Julia drew comfort from her boy's choice to sleep on the cot next to her bed, perhaps his own mother would like him to sit next to her bed as she slept in the antiseptic ward. If only they'd allow him to see her at this late hour.

A young nurse appeared at the door. He put on his best charm, explained his limited time, and need to sit with his mother for a bit. She gave him a compassionate smile as she told him he could have an hour. Before leading the way, she warned him not to disturb the other women.

He progressed toward his mother's hospital bed in his most stealth manner, but grimaced as the chair creaked when he took his seat. Marta slept with uneven breaths. He frowned as she coughed and turned on her back, opening her eyes. Another cough followed, and she struggled to sit up until Eddie stood to assist the young nurse who bent to help her. The startled look on his mother's face turned to one of tenderness as recognition occurred.

"Edward, what are you doing here? What *are* you wearing?" Her eyes went from him to the young woman who now listened to her chest with a stethoscope. "Dr. Dimock[xxxviii], what brings you to my ward?"

Eddie's eyes widened. *The woman must still be in her twenties.*

The attractive young physician straightened. "Mrs. Hawkins returned as I prepared to leave for the evening. She explained the unusual circumstances of your son's visit, and I decided to make an exception for you, Madame Rousseau."

The doctor turned toward Eddie. "Mr. Rigby, you have one

hour before one of my nurses will come for you."

Marta reached for the young woman's hand. "Thank you, Dr. Dimock."

"You are welcome. Good night."

Eddie stared in amazement as the doctor departed. His mother laughed until a fit of coughing ensued.

He placed her pillow, plus the extra one lying on the foot of the bed, in a vertical position behind her back. As she adjusted to the soft prop, he turned to pour her a drink of water from the glass pitcher on her bedside table. He helped her take a ginger sip and answered her greeting questions in a soft voice.

"I saw Hallie home and wanted to check on you. I took her to meet Tommy McDonald and Jake in the old neighborhood. It looks like I'll leave in the morning instead of the afternoon."

Her familiar green eyes narrowed. "Why? What has happened?"

He placed the glass back on the table and resumed his seat. "I just need to get back, Mum. My job is there, and Julia needs me there in case Jason Kennedy decides to try anything before he leaves town."

Eddie squirmed and looked away as her eyebrows lifted in challenge. "What?"

"I know I missed a significant amount of your life, but I can still tell when you're not saying the real reason," she said. "How is Mr. McDonald? Did you tell him about me?"

Irritation flickered. "Mum, let's both allow ourselves the right to reserve things until we're ready to discuss them," he said. The resignation on her face extinguished his resentment. He swiped a hand across his mouth and sighed. "Tommy is fine, and I didn't mention you, just where I've been since I last saw them. It's up to you to let old friends know you again if you choose."

She folded her hands. "That is fair, and I thank you. Now, I know you have not read my letter as you were out this evening, but I did read yours. Thank you for your honesty and everything you chose to share. I realize your sister is the one who has really lost the most since I left. It breaks my heart. She has known the least true friendship and love of any of us. Your Da adored her, and we wanted so much for her. I take responsibility and must face her. I hope her life will be much easier now. You were truly blessed by your friend, James, and his family. I must come and thank them in person."

He stiffened. "That's not necessary. They don't expect it."

She gave him a sad smile. "But I do. Son, I am so sorry about your friend. I found myself wanting to meet him as I read your letter. He must have been an extraordinary young man."

His smile faded as a lump formed in his throat. "Yes, yes, he was. I'm sure Hallie has spoken of him to you."

A thoughtful expression crossed her face as she tilted her head and nodded. "Only to mention she was a widow and to tell me about your friendship. She is a woman who does not like to volunteer information if not asked."

"Mum, I want you to rest. I didn't come to talk tonight, just to sit with you and let you know your son is here."

Her eyes fluttered closed and were moist as she opened them and reached for his hand. "Thank you. It means so much." She leaned back against the pillows. "I would like to try to sleep. Promise me you will receive my visit when I come to Washington."

His eyes met hers. "You're coming?"

She squeezed his hand. "Once I am well, nothing could keep me from my family if they will allow such."

On impulse, he stood and kissed her damp forehead. "Yes, ma'am. Please try to rest now."

He helped her adjust on the pillows and straightened her covers. Her eyes met his.

"I love you, my son."

He held back tears. "I love you, too, Mum. Now sleep. I'll be here until you do, unless they force me to leave. Please give my apologies to Hallie. She doesn't know I'm leaving in the morning. Tell her to write if she wants."

"I will tell her, but . . . I will tell her. Good night, Edward."

"Good night, Mum."

Twenty minutes later, a nurse came to escort him from the building.

~~~

The route home didn't follow what the railroad listed. Eddie took a few detours of his own at the stops. He needed time to think about a good many things. Therefore, when he arrived in Washington and found his way to Hallie's House, it occurred at a time when no one expected him.

The unplanned episodes of life often yield a very candid view of situations. The first involved the Griersons. They conversed on the bench in the garden as he approached unnoticed from the side street.

"My dear, you should have said you understand, and I'm doing the right thing," the professor said.

Rebecca's face and eyes looked weary. "I know. I know. I never say what you want."

"That's not true. It's just sometimes you try to be so honest and forget I need to hear something different from my wife."

"Did you just hear what you said, Professor?" They both turned at the sound of Eddie's voice. "If she can't speak honestly to you and more important, if you can't receive it, then you'd better ask yourself if you truly love Rebecca to the degree you proclaim. Do you just want this lovely shell you value and wish to puppet?"

The professor's face turned red as he jumped to his feet. "How dare you, sir?"

Eddie's quick eyes didn't miss the confirmation of his words on Rebecca's face. She must have felt the same thing.

Eddie moved to face the refined man. "I dare because she won't. Professor, unless you just want a female mirror to reflect your own views back to you, you'd better start listening to the real woman before you. Part of this culmination of stress may be due in part to aspects of her relationship with you. Furthermore, she might not have told you, but the doctor says she's not physically as strong as she should be. Her fatigue and emotional breakdowns aren't so much mental, but an inability to handle all aspects of her life due to true physical weakness. She's demonstrated fortitude, not breaking down before this point. Now, the doctors will work to help her, and we have to make sure she gets plenty of rest and the right nutrition. I for one don't want any woman I love to be less than honest with me ever, even if I have to walk away or allow her to walk away. If you're as smart as all your university degrees indicate, you'll find a way to listen and find the extent of the treasure in front of you. Now, if you'll excuse me."

The second situation he encountered—the one he feared might occur—involved Julia and Jason. He heard them yelling at each other through the opened kitchen door. As he opened the screen, he could see Jared in their midst. Mr. and Mrs. Kennedy rushed into the room. Mrs. Kennedy pulled Jared out of the room with him screaming for his mother. Mr. Kennedy pulled Jason to one side as Eddie entered. Julia turned with a look of relief as he crossed to put his arms around her.

"Jason, Julia has been fair. She even let us take Jared to the dinner at the McWhorter's last night. What in the world are you doing here? Your mother and I were on our way to the train station and wanted to stop to say goodbye. Of course, you knew we were leaving today, and you didn't expect Mr. Rigby to arrive. I hate to think what you would've done."

Jason's brown eyes flashed dark flint. "I would've taken my son home to Texas for a visit. It's not fair for me to have to wait until he's twelve."

"Son, you'd better follow the law if you don't want to lose everything. Do you really think Jared would want to go with you right now?"

"She's poisoned him against me."

Eddie cradled his sister close. "No, Jason, I think you're doing it all by yourself. I can't believe she let him go with you last night. She won't allow anything extra for a while now."

Julia turned with her composure now intact. "Jason, I would like you to leave now. "

Jason grabbed his hat off the table. "Goodbye, Pa. Please apologize to Ma for me. We leave in the morning."

Julia excused herself to rush from the room. Joe Kennedy crossed to the kitchen door and watched his son traverse the lawn to the carriage where Mary McWhorter Kennedy sat waiting. He turned back to Eddie with a ruthful expression.

"To think I thought things were going to be manageable after the success of the supper last night. It was really a nice evening overall. I guess part of every parent hopes their prodigal will somehow come home."

"I understand," Eddie said. "You'll have to wait and see. Believe me; I never expected to see my mother again."

The older man's expression held compassion. "How is your

mother?"

"Healing in many ways. "

"And you?"

"Working on it with the help of the Lord."

Mr. Kennedy slapped him on the shoulder. "That's all you can do. I admire you for going to see her."

"Thank you, sir. It was the right thing." A sense of urgency filled him. "Come, you can't miss your train. Let's go find the ladies and Jared."

Jared looked relieved as they entered. They visited for a few moments before Joe Kennedy stood and took his wife's arm to prepare for their departure. Promises of letters and a planned trip for the summer emerged as they walked them to the door.

As soon as the door closed, Eddie checked the time—almost three. He pulled Julia's letter from their mother out of his coat pocket.

"Julia, I'm taking Jared with me to the church. I need to check on a few items. While we're gone, read this and get some rest. We can talk whenever you're ready."

She stared at the folded stationery affixed with a seal. Her fingers toyed with the curls on her son's head.

"How is she?"

"She's different, but the same—older and still recovering from her illness at the moment. She plans to come to see you."

Julia's eyes took on a distant glaze. "We'll see. Now you two go on."

Eddie caught the look on Juliana Phillips's face as she headed toward the kitchen with a wide-eyed little Millie in tow to help with dinner preparation. What a blessing—the other women were out of the house and the professor and Rebecca remained in the garden. Eddie exited via the front door with Jared to avoid any more unpleasant exchanges.

~~~

They'd almost reached the church before Jared spoke.

"Uncle Eddie, I don't like my father very much right now. He was much nicer at the McWhorter's last night, but I think today is the truth."

Eddie didn't reply, and the boy turned to him.

"How was my Grandmother Rigby-Rousseau?"

The simple question startled Eddie. He realized his words could affect the boy's mental picture of a woman he'd never met.

"Well, Jared, she's still getting well, and Hallie's helping her."

Jared frowned. "I meant how did she behave toward you?"

"Very honest."

"Do you forgive her?"

Eddie smiled. "Yes, because she made me realize that it can't be undone, and she's sorry about it."

Jared slumped in the buggy seat. "Maybe I'll forgive my father when he's sorry. I don't think he is at all."

"Give it time, Jared. Things are a little different because my mother and father both loved and cared for your mother and me until Da died. I knew both my parents, and when I saw Mum in Boston, I realized how much I missed her. Even then, it was hard to let go of the hurt. It's going to take some time for us to develop a new relationship, but we have a start. You still don't really know Jason Kennedy."

"I'm not sure I want to. Is your mother coming here?"

"Yes, once she's well. She wants to see you, if Julia will allow it, but you need to let them talk first."

Jared gave a solemn nod. "I want to thank her for helping to keep me with my mother."

Eddie jumped down, followed by his nephew. "Good."

They entered the church, smiling.

~~~

As they entered the house ready to sit down for a normal evening, Eddie thought he either should have stayed in Boston or never gone. The sound of shouts once again greeted him upon his second entrance of the day. The sound of his sister's voice didn't bode well.

"You won't enter this house again!" Julia yelled to Caleb Pierce. "Bridget informed me my brother already had one talk with you, but evidently it wasn't enough."

"Miss Rigby, your brother isn't here, and he doesn't give me directions regardless of the number of important people he knows. Miss McAvoy remains my fiancée; therefore, I do have rights."

Bridget's Scottish brogue thickened with emotion. "Mr. Pierce, you had no right to come to the newspaper today or to follow me home. Our engagement became broken the night you put me in the hospital. *Ach*, let me go!"

Eddie uttered a prayer of thanks. Jared had stayed to play with little Caroline Brady and young Millie Phillips as they struggled to construct a playhouse out of fallen limbs. He missed Micah, Hallie, and Molly at moments like this. They'd dealt with these situations, and he didn't feel very diplomatic in this instance.

He strode into the fray at the foot of the stairs. "Let her go and leave, or I *will* send for the authorities."

The long fingers of the refined man were slow to unfurl as he sneered a response. "I can make sure her father never gets another job in this town."

Bridget pulled away, rubbing her arm. Julia placed a protective arm around her and led her toward the kitchen. Once they disappeared, Eddie responded.

"You can try, but I can make sure he does get work. Now, you're trespassing and need to leave. If you approach Miss McAvoy at her job or come here again, charges will be pressed. I have the right to remove you from these premises and will if you don't comply."

The tall, angular blond man curled his lip. "You are no different than I am, Mr. Rigby. Violence sometimes gets us what we want."

"It does when dealing with other men, and when it's a last resort but never with women. Real men protect women."

"This isn't over."

"You've made the wrong choice."

The man made a quick reach for the door. "You have no idea of my status. I can destroy this house and shut the doors."

Eddie reined in his self-control. "Get out. The authorities will be notified."

The man scurried off the porch as Eddie advanced forward. He shut the door and headed for the kitchen.

Julia and Bridget watched Mr. Pierce's departure from the window. "I need to call on the police and board members. I'll be back late, so once the others get home, continue with the evening as normal. Have Ian stay in Micah's room tonight, and lock the doors."

~~~

Eddie started with the police and made a report, but their response didn't encourage him. His visits to each of the Hallie's House board members proved more assuring. One of them held a position over Caleb Pierce at the bank. He would have to wait until the morning to visit with Bridget's supervisor at the newspaper, but he didn't mind the wait. He wanted to procure an escort for her each day first. Last, he went to the Hawkinses'.

Mrs. Hawkins's smiled in welcome as she opened the door.

"Eddie, when did you return from Boston?"

He hugged her. "Just today. Is the major home?"

She frowned. "Yes, he's in his study. Is something wrong? How are your mother and Hallie?"

"Fine, Fine. Both of them are fine, and I'll visit with you after I see him."

Major Hawkins stepped out of his study. "I thought I heard your voice, Eddie. Have you eaten? We're having our meal a bit late tonight as I just got home a few moments ago myself and had to finish some correspondence."

"No, I haven't and would love to stay after we visit. I need to talk to you."

The astute blue eyes met his. "Of course. Susannah, have another place set, and we'll try to be brief."

Eddie collapsed into the leather chair by the bookshelf as Major Hawkins closed the heavy study door.

"I need another man at the house to help me protect the ladies from irate fiancés and husbands."

Major Hawkins sat across from him. "Is this general or due to a specific problem?"

A smile erupted. "You know me well. Caleb Pierce bothered Bridget McAvoy at work and the house today. He's threatened the foundation of Hallie's House, so I visited all the board members, as well as the police."

"When will Micah return?"

"Next month."

The still fit soldier rose and lifted the lid on the humidor on his desk. He quirked an eyebrow at Eddie—who shook his head—and retrieved a cigar and a match. The pungent but sweet aroma filled the room. The skin around the blue eyes crinkled as they narrowed at the smoke following the first draw.

"You know, I couldn't ever do this around James, and I still only indulge on occasion." A few more thoughtful puffs followed. "Caleb Pierce comes from an old family and could prove a real problem if we do not handle this correctly. It's my personal opinion that a bank in Chicago, Boston, or New York would benefit from his skills and might even give him the opportunity to advance posthaste."

"I don't think either one of us can influence something like that."

The major gave a sly smile. "My influence is limited in some areas, but my wife's extends farther than you realize. Susannah and Caleb's mother have been friends since childhood, and their families have long been associated. With your permission, I will advise her of the situation and see if she might appeal to his mother's sure desire to avoid scandal."

Eddie chuckled. "Your family never ceases to amaze me. However, until they have a chat, I still need another man at the house."

"Well, let me see. I think Sergeant Case might work. You know and trust him. His recent assignment to my office will make him available. He can escort Miss McAvoy to work on his way in the mornings and home in the evenings. He can use Hallie's House as his lodgings until Micah returns. Now you are home, you'll be there during the day."

Relief flooded him. Nathan Case—perfect. They'd served together so long; they could communicate without saying a word.

"He'll do, except he might get a little irritable with all the women. Mr. Case always runs if women are talking. He says their cackling is too noisy."

The major laughed. "He'll survive." He stood. "I'd better snuff this cigar, and we need to get to the table. My Susannah will get impatient."

~~~

By the next week, everything settled into an uneventful

routine. Bridget appeared relaxed with the sergeant as her escort. Mrs. Hawkins had tea with Mrs. Pierce and no further incidents occurred. Even though Eddie wouldn't breathe easy until they notified him of Caleb Pierce vacating Washington, but he guessed it would take time. The children were in school, and the ladies of the house were doing well. Even Professor Grierson allowed his wife some room to breathe, with his visits now reduced to twice a week. The lack of mail from Hallie—to him or the Hawkinses— bothered him. However, Julia received a short letter from their mother. They'd scheduled her release from the hospital for the next week, but she couldn't travel for a month. Tentative plans for her journey to Washington were set for October. Monsieur Rosen finalized all the inheritance paperwork. Eddie and Julia met with the financial consultant recommended by Amelia's husband. They remained in the process of making decisions.

Hallie's silence served as a sign for him. He wrote a letter of his own, not to her but to Jack Johnson. The time had come for him to direct a few events.

Chapter Seven

THE EVENTS IN the wake of Madame Rousseau's departure from the hospital included an increase in the influx of patients and the intensity of Hallie's studies. She remained ahead of the rest of the class due to her previous enrollment, and it appeared she might finish by mid-December or sooner. The month of September rushed by like a train, and October swirled in with the downward flight of emblazoned leaves. The hospital stayed busy, and Boston bubbled with activity. The most recent news of concern involved a fire in the Hyde Park area at the beginning of October. After the horrible fire in 1872, the city became nervous when any notable flames erupted.[xxxix] Many things merited discussion, but of late, not much time or inclination existed to write home about them.

The pages of the leather book Eddie gave her held the notations she made from her training; however, the pages of stationery remained blank as she neglected correspondence. The once joyful task of composing long letters ceased as Hallie decided to focus on the concerns of the hospital and school. Guilt pricked her as the many letters from Susannah went unanswered. At a little past eleven one night, the little letter bundle overwhelmed her, and she decided on at least a short response. She owed her mother-in-law so much. The blank sheet taunted her as she began:

Dear Susannah,
I must apologize for being so neglectful of you. My studies

and work have taken all my thought and energy. Please know I'm well and hope the same for all there. It appears my endeavors will result in a return to Washington before Christmas. Please keep a caring eye on Julia as I know the impending arrival of her mother will be difficult for her. Madame Rousseau is a fascinating person and will in no way be what you would expect of the woman who left her two children so long ago. My heart is still confused by the contradiction at times; therefore, I know Julia and Eddie must find it hard to reconcile.

I must close, as it's late. Please send my affection to the rest of the family, and give Jared a special hug.

Your Forever Daughter-in-Law,

Hallie

She stared at the abbreviated narrative as she bit the end of the pen. After a moment, she dipped the writing implement into the ink well one last time to address the less than complete endeavor. She released a deep, involuntary sigh upon standing and then shook her head at the weary reflection in the mirror above the basin. Her eyes closed as she tried to capture the image of James's dear face. Their love always burned with steady warmth and comfort when she pulled inward and basked in it. Whenever she looked beyond the confines of her room or the daily rigors of the hospital, another face started to flash with irritating frequency, and she wouldn't have it.

A quick lift of the window to allow in a rush of autumn air—rich in the aroma and sounds of night—helped clear her inner battle. She grew still as the full moon stole her gaze and then directed it upward beyond the stars and another voice spoke to her soul.

"I know Lord, but how?" She closed the window, turned down the lamp, and slid into the bed. Drowsy comfort overtook her and she drifted off in the middle of her continued prayers.

~~~

The next morning flew by, and Hallie rushed from task to task at the bidding of the doctors. Many new patients filled her ward, so it surprised her to hear a familiar voice call her name.

"Yes?"

Her eyes fell on an elderly woman to her right. It took a

moment before recognition flooded her.

"Mrs. Matthews, what are you doing back here? I thought we were done, following your discharge."

The weathered face held a wan smile. "My dear, at my age, a discharge is just a temporary pass to go home for a while. I see Madame Rousseau has left. There is a fascinating story in her life if I'm not mistaken, but I know you won't be the one to tell it. However, do tell me, dear one, what happened to her handsome son? He came for only two visits."

Hallie hesitated but decided no harm could come from a partial answer.

"He lives in Washington and had to return to his responsibilities there. I believe she's traveling to see him and other family this month."

The wrinkled hands folded and smoothed her covers in satisfaction.

"Good. Now meet my curiosity on one other point. He seemed very fond of you. Has he contacted you?"

Hallie smiled. "No, ma'am, but we're old friends. You see, my late husband was his best friend."

"The pair of you must have been wonderful support for each other."

"Yes and no. He had to leave right after the funeral and has recently returned after years away."

The faded eyes watched her with a reflective look. "Mrs. Hawkins, did I ever tell you about my first husband?"

Hallie looked down at the small watch on her bodice pin. She had a few minutes, so she sat on the chair next to the bed.

"No, ma'am."

"Well, he was my best friend and forever-love. I was a girl of fifteen, and he was twenty-five when we married. We had nine children before he died at the age of fifty with pneumonia. He took such good care of me and made me laugh. We lived simply and tried to help others, as we were able. Such a good life, and then my life became very hard once he died. I had to work cleaning and doing laundry for others. My eldest son helped finish raising the youngest of the children before he left home. Then I was alone. A childhood friend tried to court me about ten years after I first became a widow. He came in and out of my life until I spurned him. That man would have helped with the children and relieved my son of some of his duties, but all I could see were my responsibilities and the still lingering love in my grief-filled heart. I understand he married years later. We never spoke again. I have regretted my actions because our long friendship could have made a good marriage. Anyway, after my children were all gone, the emptiness became unbearable. I married a man I met at church, but whom I found preferred a bottle to a Bible after our wedding. We had a few laughs, many disagreements, and then he too was gone, killed by the whiskey. My choices have led me to a lonely place."

Hallie stared at her in stunned silence. "But your children—
"

"They're grown with their own families and visit when they can. My house is empty. I find myself rising early to walk— seeking visits with neighbors because my walls have no voice. Those visits, my church, and my time with God are my life. It's a good life, but I still think of my dear friend."

"I could arrange to visit you."

A crackle of a laughter erupted. "My dear, it's a kind thought but not my purpose in telling you."

Hallie frowned and the woman patted her hand.

"Madame Rousseau's son looks at you with great affection, and I saw it when you looked at him."

"No, no, I—"

Mrs. Matthews sighed and slid down on her pillow. "I need to rest now. Just think on it. Allow me to meddle. It gives me purpose."

"Yes, ma'am, I'll be by to check on you."

For the next four hours, she worked with expeditious intensity at all tasks both menial and care related in an effort to block out all other thoughts. Her muscles and mind ached when she entered her room at the end of the day. She wanted it to be like that until she finished.

~~~

Hallie swallowed hard as she paid the hack driver. The roughness of the neighborhood became even more apparent in the daylight. She looked out of place in spite of her plain cotton day dress. An ironic smile lifted her lips, and she shook her head, gathering the courage to move forward. However, once she went through the door, Tommy's smile put her at ease as he straightened from cleaning a table by the window. He wiped his hands on the towel and threw it across his shoulder.

"Mrs. Hawkins, I must say this is a surprise—a pleasant one. What brings you to my neighborhood?"

Hallie liked his directness. She crossed to stand in front of him. "I wondered if you or Jake might have time for a little chat."

She glanced at the handful of men drank at the tables. It reminded her of the days at the saloon in Texas, but the looks of curiosity here weren't propositional ones.

Tommy waited for her eyes to return to him. He gestured to the table. "Certainly, ma'am. Jake's picking up a shipment and should be back in a few minutes. Would you like a drink?"

She smiled and shook her head. "No, thank you."

He nodded and slid into the chair across from her. His knees popped as he sat. "Getting up and down has become a noisy affair at my age." He folded his hands on the table and leaned forward. "What's on your mind? Is Eddie doing well? I got a short letter from Marta, I mean, Madame Rousseau, the other day—what a shock, at this point. Our families were once close. Anyway—"

Hallie covered his hand for a brief moment. "He's fine, as far as I know. Yes, he didn't expect his mother's return. I came here to see if you could tell me more about Eddie before and after his father's death. He's been a good friend, and I just want to understand him through someone else's eyes."

Tommy gave her a speculative look and a twinkle appeared in his eyes. "Would you believe he was a choir boy and at the same time a mischief maker?"

Hallie gasped. "No . . . yes . . . my, my."

He chuckled. "Yes, they were a solid family even being poor before they lost his Da."

"Tell me about his father."

"Tad Rigby was a robust, brawny man who loved his family and the sea. He really enjoyed being a fisherman. He once told me the ocean was his first sweetheart. Then he met Marta when he was eighteen, and she won his heart. He brought his family across the sea for more opportunities. Little Julia was the laughter of his heart, and Eddie was the adventure in his soul. His spells at sea were hard on Marta, but she glowed during his times at home. He always made sure their needs were met. Marta was . . . I might not . . . "

Hallie watched the man struggle before he decided to continue. "Marta grew up without a mother, and her father died right before she married Tad. Her older sister married young. Marta wasn't equipped to be a caretaker without the support of a husband. It doesn't excuse it, but it's the truth. My dear wife often stopped by to help Marta when Tad was working. Marta loved her children but life overwhelmed her. In many ways, Tad's family sank at sea with him."

Her heart ached for the loss. "Might I ask why friends didn't take in Julia and Eddie?"

"Mrs. Hawkins, families in this neighborhood do well to keep their own fed and clothed. However, we helped when we could, and besides, Julia and Eddie often refused. They didn't want to be a burden on anyone. My Martha did ask them to live with us, and then Julia got the job with the tailor. If it had lasted, things would have been much better." He stopped and looked past her to the door. "Here's Jake. Let me help him get in the crates. I'll send him to you. He knows about both James and Eddie."

Hallie watched the collage of diversity out of the window as she waited; skin color, different languages, and varied accents drifted through the door as people passed. They all had one thing in common—their humble status in life.

"Mrs. Hawkins?"

Hallie turned her head to find Jake beside her table. She smiled at Eddie's friend. This man returned to the old neighborhood after the war. He seemed content.

"Please join me, Mr. McDonald."

"It's just Jake," he said as he turned the chair around so he could sit with his arms propped on the back.

Handsome in a rugged, devil-may-care way, but not concerned about it.

"Father says you want some insight on Eddie."

She nodded.

He drummed his fingers on his propped arm. "You're not going to find much more than what you see. Eddie had it rough and survived it. He's solid. I've been with him on these streets and in battle. "

"Did he ever have a girlfriend?"

Jake grinned. "Yes, one for a short time. She's now married to our wonderful Officer Calhoun. It's another of the many reasons the man dislikes Eddie so much. Eddie's street smarts fascinated her. Her family didn't like him at all."

"What happened?"

"Your husband. Eddie left the neighborhood to work for the Hawkins. That was that."

"Were you friends with James?"

"I didn't meet him until the war started and, no, not at first. I resented his friendship with Eddie and the changes in my friend. Then, I got to know James. He was the smartest man I ever met, but he could get on the level of each person. I never felt judged or considered less by him. Do you know what I mean?"

"Yes, I do. My own background is pretty humble."

Hallie saw a spark of respect enter the man's eyes. He readjusted his arms on the back of the chair.

"Good. That confirms my first instincts about you. Anyway, war throws a bunch of men together from different backgrounds. What's interesting is how much we learn, not just about others but also about ourselves. I discovered myself to be a bit prejudiced toward the more privileged, like James. And I watched him learn to trust the instincts of people like Eddie and me. You see, your husband was a wonderful strategist, but at first couldn't anticipate the unexpected. War is a bit like chess, but the war we fought didn't have a precedent. Eddie and I were used to scrapping on the streets and no rules fighting. The point is—we all needed each other. Most of the time, Eddie could feel when something was off-kilter, even if he wasn't sure what. Because of it, he often took the field first. That's why he blames himself for what happened to James. Normally, he would've taken the first step out of the trees, not the man in front of James."

"But his cartridge box dropped off of his belt?"

He nodded. "Yeah, a real mess that day. Eddie didn't talk to anyone for a few days except our superiors. He finally talked to me the week following James's transfer to the hospital. Still angry at himself and grieved for his best friend, he'd spent more than a few nights, as he put it, wrestling it out in prayer. I tried to stay as close as he would allow for the remainder of the war. Eddie found he had an identity apart from being the rescued youth. Lieutenant Hawkins was proud of him. Once he knew James would live, his focus returned. He was a good soldier."

He paused and watched her for a moment. "I'm afraid you already know most of what I've told you. Might I take the liberty to say something without offending you?"

Hallie met the honest eyes. "Sure."

"You're looking for the one in the other, and that won't work. I've never been as proud to call two men my friends. Their friendship may have been unlikely, but it was the best kind. I'm guessing, in some ways, kind of like your marriage to James. But, Mrs. Hawkins, in my observation of you with Eddie, it's obvious."

She blinked. "What?"

He grinned and stood. "You can answer that one without me. I wish you luck. Bring Eddie back for a re-match of billiards sometimes. Now, if you'll excuse me."

All of Hallie's emotions went still. "I will, Jake. Thanks."

He nodded and walked away.

Her heart pounded, and warmth coursed through her. The truth filled her. She thought back to that last night before Eddie left Boston. Her head now admitted what her heart knew then. *No, it's unwise to write him.* She must talk to him in person. She just hoped Eddie would listen once she returned home.

~~~

Close to the end of November, all requirements for her certification were satisfied. Her instructors and the hospital staff were pleased. Dr. Jones sent an affirmative response to her letter about a job with increased pay in Washington. She wrote the Hawkinses and the head of the board at Hallie's House. A letter from Julia the previous month gave a brief description of the updates on the ladies in the house, Jared's school activities, and the reunion with her mother. The description of the last, summarized it as difficult but improving. She found it strange, but none of the letters mentioned anything about Eddie.

A knock on her door interrupted her packing. A friend and fellow nursing student, Shannon O'Connor, entered at her response. A secretive smile emanated from the young woman's face and an extra twinkle shone in her hazel eyes.

"Hallie, you need to either finish or take a break for a while. Your train doesn't leave until Monday. I hear there's a picnic in the park at the Commons and Gardens[xl] by the water. Come with me, and we'll go together. If you don't want to stay, we can go shopping. It's Saturday, you're finished, and I'm not on duty. We should have this outing."

She looked at her friend's pretty, green dress and hat. "Let me change first, and then I'd love an outing."

Twenty minutes later, they left. The crisp air tinged with the burnished smell of autumn leaves invigorated Hallie. She laughed as Shannon retold the escapades of some of the children at the hospital.

"I knew the patient was ready for discharge when he could jump out of the bed and kick the doctor in the leg."

The driver reined the horses and turned to let them know they were at their stop. They paid him and expressed gratitude as he assisted them to the ground.

People strolled amidst the trees and played with their children and dogs; the sight delighted her. Hallie looked around as they neared the water.

"Shannon, who are we meeting for this picnic? I should've asked before now, but I expected to see Martha or Leah as they're the only others free today. No familiar faces so far."

Shannon just smiled. "We aren't there quite yet; you'll recognize them."

Close to the water, a well-dressed woman sat on a blanket with a basket beside her. Hallie didn't recognize her until she turned and stood as they approached.

"Madame Rousseau, how nice to see you."

The woman crossed and kissed both her cheeks. "My dear, Mrs. Hawkins, I wanted to do something special to celebrate your completion of the nursing program. We dropped by and had Miss O'Connor assist in this little surprise. I came to town to help with the planning for the new art museum. The board of trustees has worked to raise the money needed for the construction and hope to have it open within two more years.[xli] We must beg your forgiveness for not notifying you of our arrival at the end of last week, but there has been much to do. However, as I believe we will leave on the same train on Monday morning, there will be time for a more extensive visit."

Hallie couldn't get over how healthy and strong she looked. "You look wonderful. This is so kind of you. Did Monsieur Rosen come with you?"

The green eyes twinkled back at her. "No, he has sailed for Europe. My son is with me."

Hallie's heart jumped and her eyes looked around. "Eddie? Where is he?"

Gentle hands led her to the blanket. "Please, have a seat, my dears. I have sent him to the bakery for our dessert. The hotel packed a wonderful luncheon for us in this basket, but I wanted some special sweet to celebrate today."

They settled their skirts around them and helped her unpack the basket. Hallie set the basket to the side as they finished.

"Ah, here he is." Madame Rousseau rose to take the bakery box from her son. "We have surprised her."

Eddie escorted his mother back to them and settled her on the blanket before he followed, propping his arm on one knee as he assumed a casual posture. He gave a broad smile as he removed his hat.

"Congratulations, Mrs. Hawkins, and thank you for helping us with this surprise, Miss O'Connor. I believe my mother plans to take you to a few shops before the day is at an end."

Shannon blushed. "You're very welcome. Hallie needs a few more happy surprises."

"Hello, Mr. Rigby. How have you been?" Hallie waited for his slanted green gaze to fall on her.

"Wonderful. Things have gone well. I'm even working on songs for the Christmas service, and we plan a caroling. Julia and Jared are well, but you may have heard from her, so let me know. I don't want to give repetitious news."

Hallie stared at him, realizing only she felt awkward. She blinked. "Yes, she updated me on the ladies in the house. Mrs. Grierson went home, Mrs. Phillips and her daughter went to live with family in Pennsylvania, and Micah is home."

Madame Rousseau and Shannon filled the plates and passed them around as they talked.

"Yes, and I'm thinking he's close to courting Miss

McAvoy. Now, let's eat. I'll say grace."

All heads bowed until he finished. They resumed their conversation and enjoyed the small feast.

"Bridget and Micah?"

"We'll see," Eddie said with a shrug. "Also, Mrs. Brady and her daughter will leave us before Christmas. She has a job as the cook for the Spencer family, and they'll live with them. What are your plans?"

Hallie startled. "I'm coming home, of course, and will soon work with Dr. Jones again. I wrote the Hawkinses a few weeks ago. "

Eddie tucked his head. "I'm afraid she neglected to tell me. Both she and my mother are a bit perplexed with me of late, as they can't get me to tell them everything."

Hallie caught the gaze of his mother who shrugged. "He is a man, and they do not always feel we must know."

Shannon laughed. "My father is a banker, and he never tells my mother and me anything. We find out things as we go."

The meal proceeded. After it, they consumed the wonderful pastry. Eddie stood as the women began to pack the basket.

"I need to walk after such a meal, or I'll fall asleep. Mrs. Hawkins, would you care to join me?"

Madame Rousseau gave him a fond smile. "Yes, you two take a stroll. Miss O'Connor and I will finish."

Eddie held down his hand and assisted Hallie to her feet. They walked in complete silence for a few moments, the leaves crunching beneath their feet. He tipped his hat to the ladies they passed, and Hallie inclined her head to the many hats tipped her way. He sighed and glanced behind them.

"I think we're out of range. I didn't know if Miss O'Connor knew of our longtime friendship, so I've kept it formal. I'm so proud of you, Hallie. You kept your promise to James and yourself. Well done."

Hallie relaxed. "Thank you, Eddie."

"I want to apologize for infringing on your journey home. This trip wasn't planned to coordinate with your leaving. In fact, until Miss O'Connor told me your plans when we came by yesterday to discuss this surprise, I still thought it would be at least another week before you returned."

"Are you still taking me to see the *Marriage of Figaro*?"

Eddie slowed his steps. "Of course, if you want to go. It's on December 10th. I took mother to see *Mary Stuart* on October 5th. The newspaper displays in the *Lorgnette*^{xlii} are large. Julia is delighted in her work with the theater."

"Yes, I'd love to go."

He looked at her with a small lift of his brow. "Thank you. It'll be wonderful to escort you."

Silence once more resumed until Hallie spoke. "Where's your mother living?"

He inclined his head toward a large tree and removed his hat. He leaned against the trunk. "It's been interesting. Julia left upon Mum's arrival at the house and refused to see her for a week. However, Jared enjoyed his grandmother tremendously during her visits. During that time, she took me to meetings with art dealers and to the gallery. One day we arrived home, and Julia was waiting. They disappeared upstairs and re-emerged three hours later with red eyes. Then—without a word to me—they purchased a house. Julia and Jared now live with Mum in Georgetown—close to the Hawkinses. I'm told I have a room there, but that's not in my plans."

"What are your plans, Eddie?"

He removed his coat and placed it at the base of the tree. "Please, have a seat."

She complied without protest. He joined her and turned with a serious look.

"Hallie, I still consider you my best friend, even though I know my last visit to Boston might have compromised that standing. Your lack of correspondence gave me the answer I needed in regard to any other course for us. Let's return to our former state. I need the advice of a dear friend at this moment."

His words stirred a mixture of emotions within her. She bent her head.

"Hallie, I haven't offended you, have I?"

Her brown eyes lifted first, followed by her chin—tilted in determination. "No . . . I'll always be your friend, Eddie, and I must apologize for not treating you as one of late. I'm afraid my correspondence hasn't been what it should be with anyone. So, tell me what advice might I provide?"

"I've been in touch with Jack Johnson." He stopped at her swift intake of air and then continued. "The railroad has expanded in Arkansas, and he's trying to get closer to home. There are a couple of positions available, and he wants to know if I'm interested in one of them. It wouldn't start until this summer. In fact, if I take it, Jared could go with me and then maybe Mr. Kennedy would meet us and take him the rest of the way for his visit in Texas. Then my mother has been educating me on the residual business interests she has retained and wants me to manage them for her. It would mean some limited travel, but I would be able to remain in Washington and continue part of my work at Hallie's House, or I can simply continue in my present position. The investments I'll soon make, will yield a profit for the future even if I don't choose to pursue further job opportunities. Due to my past, I'm cautious and will retain access to most of my assets. Several knowledgeable men, including Mr. Andrew Richards, have advised me on the best way to manage things in order to secure a stable future. I can also pay you back for the work you did in my stead."

Hallie stared at him with a lump in her throat. "Why would you consider the move to Arkansas?"

He picked up a leaf and twirled it. Then he looked at her and replied in a soft voice. "The city confines me at times and . . . "

She held her breath as he crushed the leaf and let a gust of wind sweep away the residual. He stared ahead as the particles dissipated.

"You. I've made it uncomfortable for you to return home even if you won't admit it." His gaze captured hers as he turned his head. "Hallie, you've taken care of so many people. I would like to be the haven you run to when needed, but I'm not sure you'll ever let anyone be that for you again. The empty space created in my life when James died remains. I still think of him every day, and I know the same is true for you, but we have to move forward, Hallie. He wanted that, but the thing is . . . I feel free to walk forward toward the people and things God has put as the desires of my heart. Never forced or obligated. You must also allow yourself this. Hallie, if you want to get your own small house and live away from Hallie's House, you can. Amelia has taken an interest and the minister's nephew just returned from the university, and he wants to help. Yours and James's dream will continue and help many people."

"Eddie, I'll admit being uncomfortable, and you've always kept me unbalanced, but I've not wanted to face why. Since your return home, we've gotten close. Our feelings took me by surprise the last time you came, but I don't want you to leave Washington. The opportunity with your mother balanced with the work at Hallie's House sounds the best to me. Your family is there."

He stood. "You don't understand, Hallie. My feelings for you haven't changed from what I told you my last evening in Boston. I meant it when I said I would always be your friend, but I'll also always love you. The thing is, Hallie Price Hawkins, our backgrounds are more similar than different. If James hadn't fallen for his nurse, I would have and did. Honor and friendship kept me away all those years. I even grew to love another, but my heart keeps coming back to you." He turned and she stood.

Her voice shook as she admitted the truth. "And my heart has run from yours. Eddie, you have the most candid view of me, even when I don't like it. You give me permission to laugh and relax a little when I think I have to hold on too tight. I went to see Tommy and Jake to ask them about you."

"Hallie, you shouldn't go there unescorted. Did you learn anything?"

"A little, but it made me admit something to myself. Then, when I saw you today, I knew."

Eddie guided her toward the back of the tree, facing the water. His sage green eyes burned with intensity as he took both of her hands in his. "What did you know, Hallie?"

She shut her eyes, too overcome with emotion. His gentle voice reached her. "Hallie, look at me, please."

Her fawn gaze met his. "Eddie, you've been there for me, and I want to run to you. I don't know why you would want someone like me when you could have someone without a past such as mine. I can't even have children. You deserve so much more."

She backed against the tree, and he leaned his shoulder against the trunk to one side of her as he glanced to be sure others didn't watch them. He leaned to whisper in her ear.

"Hallie, I love you." He lifted a hand to trace the line of her cheek.

She turned her head and whispered back. "I love you, too, Eddie. Please stay in Washington, or take me with you."

He leaned in, and she gasped as he brushed his lips across hers. "Eddie, we're in public."

He wiggled his eyebrows and received a smile. "I don't care, but I'll restrain myself. So, you'd go with me?"

She nodded and reached for his hand. "I see people lose their lives every day, and I want to live, Eddie. Besides, you might get into trouble without James, the military, or me to look out for you." A self-effacing smile appeared as she added, "Or maybe I would without you."

He laughed. "You're probably right. But we can talk about our choices later. Although Washington doesn't seem as confining at this moment as it did yesterday. Right now, I just need to know one thing. If I take a knee, will we be noticed, and do you mind?"

Hallie gave him a level look with a lifted brow. "I prefer right where you are with us on equal footing."

He took both of her hands and kissed each in turn. "Forgive me for the lack of propriety by ignoring a courtship, but we have acquired our place in life. Will you do me the honor of becoming my bride, my wife, and forever friend?"

Her eyes never left his. "Yes, I will, Edward Thaddeus Rigby."

For the first time, no barriers and no hesitancy existed. The binding thread in the echo of James's life joined the golden cords of theirs, interwoven by eternal mastery for a higher plan.

Research Resources For Sunbeams at Twilight

**There are no quotes from any of these works. This is a list of research resources and information for the reader to access for more information related to historical people, places, or things. I did extensive research in order to establish a true historic setting for my fictional characters. Please remember this story is a work of historical fiction. Any adjustments or errors made for the fictional plot or story are my own. A complete list of "Research Resources" including places I have visited, all the reading resources and websites (these are listed per dates visited and may have changed) I have researched are included. Some Duplicate listings appear in the Endnotes and Resources. The Endnotes are in the order of numbered notation per history related items in this fictional story.

Sources Located through The Historical Society of Washington, D.C./ Kiplinger Library (visited the library July 2010):

Winchcole, Dorothy Clark, Church Historian, First Baptist Church, Washington D.C., 1952, *The First Baptist in Washington D.C. 1802-1952.*

Tiller, Carl W. and Tiller, Olive M., copyright 1994, At Calvary: *A History of the First 125 Years of Calvary Baptist Church,* Washington, DC, 1862-1987, Trinity Rivers Publishing, 1994.

Special Report of the Commissioner of Education, District of Colombia, Filed September, 1875.

Archive Newspaper Resource: *The Lorgnette*, Vol. 11 No.55, Advertisement for The National Theater for *The Marriage of Figaro,* performance December 10, 1874, Thursday.

Archive Newspaper Resource: *The Lorgnette*, Vol. 11, No.1, Advertisement for performance Monday October 5, 1874 at The National Theater, *Mary Stuart Queen of Scots.*

Whyte, James H., *The Uncivil War: Washington During the Reconstruction 1865-1878,*Twayne Publishers, New York, copyright 1958, Library of Congress: 57-14776.

The Junior League of Washington's, *The City of Washington: An Illustrated History,* copyright 1977 by The Junior League of the City of Washington, D.C., A Borzoi Book, published by Alfred A. Knopf, Inc., New York, 1977, first paperback 1985.

Other Historical Research Sources:

Alcott, Louisa May, *Civil War Hospital Sketches*, Dover Publications, Inc., Mineola, New York, Dover edition first published 2006, original work published 1863 by James Redpath, publisher, Boston, under the title, *Hospital Sketches*.

Barnes, Joseph K., Surgeon General, *US Surgeon General's Office, The Medical and Surgical History of War of The Rebellion (1861-65), University of Texas at Tyler Library, Microfilm #s LAC 22396-405, Med V 2pt1; p. 425-465 Chapter IV "Wounds and Injuries of the Spine",* Vol. 2, Book 1 #LAC 22399, Vol. 1, Book 2 *"Appended Documents" p.10-13, p.84-85, p.206-208.*

Christian, Mary, Editor, *Treasures of the Museum of Fine Arts Boston,* introduction by Malcolm Rogers; chapter introductions by Gilian Wohlauer, "A tiny folio", copyright 1996 The Museum of Fine Arts, Boston; Museum Editor: Peggy Hogan, Designer: Kevin

Callahan, Production Editor: Meredith Wolf, Production Manager: Lou Bilka.

Davis, Deering; Dorsey, Stephen P., and Hall, Ralph Cole, *Georgetown Houses of the Federal Period*, Dover Publications, Inc., Mineola, New York; copyright 1944, 1972 by Architectural Book Publishing Co., Inc., New York; Dover edition, first published 2001.

Howe, Julia Ward Howe, 1861, Listed "#510 Mine Eyes Have Seen the Glory", Tune "Battle Hymn", American Folk Song, 19th Century, as found in the *Baptist Hymnal, 1975 Edition*, Convention Press, Nashville, Tennessee, copyright 1975, Convention Press, church Services and Materials Division, Nashville, Tennessee, Eighth Printing.(***Note Julia Ward Howe's poem published as "The Battle Hymn of the Republic". See Robert J. Morgan reference).

Hutton, Paul Andrew and Ball, Durwood, editors, *Soldiers West, Biographies from the Military Frontier, Second Edition*, copyright 2009 by the University of Oklahoma Press, Norman, Publishing Division of the University.

Johnson, Paul, *Art: A New History*, copyright 2003 by Paul Johnson, Chapter 26 "The Internal Conflicts of Nineteenth-Century Art", pp.581-607, (** p.600, found information about Paul Durand-Ruel a famous art dealer during this period), Harper Collins Publishers, New York.

Kuhl, Isabel, *Impressionism: A Celebration of Light*, Parragon Publishing Book, 2010, copyright Parragon Books Ltd 2008.

Morgan, Robert J., Ebook pp 154-155, *Then Sings My Soul: 150 of the World's Greatest Hymns Stories,* "Battle Hymn of the Republic", Published in Nashville, Tennessee by Thomas Nelson, Inc., copyright 2003 Robert J. Morgan.

Morse, Joseph Laffan, Sc.B., LL.B, LL.D. Editor in Chief, Standard Reference Works Publishing Company, Inc., New York,

The Universal Standard Encyclopedia, volume 2, Argon-Bedstraw, an abridgment of the New Funk and Wagnalls Encyclopedia, "Baseball", pp.693-700, Universal Standard Encyclopedia copyright 1956 and 1957 by Wilfred Funk, Inc. copyright 1954 and 1955 by Wilfred Funk, Inc., New Funk and Wagnalls Encyclopedia copyright 1949 and 1952 by Wilfred Funk, Inc., Funk and Wagnalls New Standard Encyclopedia, copyright 1931, 1934, 1935, 1937, and 1942 by Wilfred Funk, Inc.

Rhodes, James Ford, *History of the United States 1850-1909, Vol., VII, 1872-1877, From The Compromise of 1850 to The End of the Roosevelt Administration*, copyright 1906 by James Ford Rhodes and in 1934 by Daniel P. Rhodes, published by The MacMillan Company, New York.

Richards, Linda, *Reminiscences of Linda Richards: America's First Trained Nurse,* Whitcomb and Barrows, Boston 1911, copyright 1911 by Linda Richards, Thomas Todd Co, printers, 14 Beacon Street, Boston, Massachusetts for Book. "The Story of This Reprint" by J.B. Lippinott Co., (Philadelphia, London, Montreal) 1948 reprint with Foreword by Anne L. Austin, Los Angeles, California as a Facsimile Reproduction; Facsimile Reprint was reproduced by Levering Riebel Co., Camden, New Jersey.

Rutkow, Ira M., *Bleeding Blue and Gray: Civil War Surgery and the Evolution of American Medicine*, Random House, 2005.

Utley, Robert M., *The Indian Frontier 1846-1890, Revised Edition*, copyright 1984 by the University of New Mexico Press, revised edition first published in 2003.

Wiatowski, Claude, *Railroads Across North America: An Illustrated History,* first published 2007 by MBI Publishing and Voyageur Press, Minneapolis, MN, copyright 2007 Mountain Automation Corporation.

Websites
(Per date last visited)

http://
www.gale.cengage.com/free_resources/whm/trials/addicks.htm
Women's History - Rights on Trial - "Pennsylvania v. Addicks:
1813."(Site visited 2/1/2011)

http://www.boston.com/yourtown/news/jaimaica_plain/2011/01/hi
story_time_the_new_engl . . .
Reiskind, Michael, Guest Columnist, "History time: The New
England Hospital for Women and Children", posted by Matt
Rocheleau, January 1, 2011, 09:00 A.M.

"A Brief History of Cambridge, Massachusetts, USA"
http://www.cambridgema.gov/~historic/cambridgehistory.html
(site visited 9/12/2010)

Historic Medical Sites in the Washington, DC Area, "19, site of
Columbia Hospital for Women", 2425 L Street, NW, Washington,
DC 20037.
http://www.nlm.nih.gov/hmd/medtour/columbia.html
(site visited 2/23/2011)

"Photography During the Civil War,"
http://www.encyclopediavirginia.org/photography_During_the_Ci
vil_War(site visited 9/24/2011)

"Indian Wars"
http://www.globalsecurity.org/military/ops/indian.htm
(site visited 2/11/2011)

http://www.native-languages.org/cheyenne_words.htm
"Vocabulary Words in Native American Languages: Cheyenne"
(site visited 11/20/2011)

http://libraries.mit.edu/archives/exhibits/wbr-visionary/

Andrews, Elizabeth; Murphy, Nora; and Rosko, Tom, "William Barton Rogers: MIT's Visionary Founder", October 2004, pp.1-10,(last accessed 7/10/10)

http://www.bostonfirehistory.org
(Site last visited 11/29/11)

http://www.nps.gov/archive/fosc/posofsek.htm
"Fort Scott National Historic Site – Soldier Vs. Settler: Railroads in Southwest Kansas." (website visited 8/2/2008)

Story Related Places Visited in Boston, Massachusetts in October 2000:

Boston Common, founded 1634
Boston, Massachusetts

Boston Museum of Fine Art
Ste. 140, 100 Hunington Ave.
Boston, MA 02116-6511
www.mfa.org/

Harvard in Cambridge, Massachusetts
www.harvard.edu

MIT-Massachusetts Institute of Technology
77 Massachusetts Ave., Cambridge, MA 02139-4307
www.mit.edu/

Story Related Places Visited Washington DC, July 2010:

Historical Society of Washington DC, 801 K St. N.W., Washington, DC
www.historydc.org

Information on the History of Medicine from displays at the National Museum of Health and Medicine; Related Brochures: "Battlefield Surgery 101: From the Civil War to Vietnam", "To Bind Up the Nation's Wounds: Medicine During the Civil War", "Abraham Lincoln: The Final Casualty of the War" (located behind Walter Reed Hospital-visited in 2010, has now moved), 6900 Georgia Ave., NW, Building 54, Washington, D.C. 20307. www.nmhm,washingtondc.museum

Information from Displays at the Smithsonian National Museum of American History, Kenneth E. Behring Center, Washington D.C.: Exhibition "Abraham Lincoln: An Extraordinary Life" and brochure developed by the museum and *American Heritage magazine,* Museum Director of *National Museum of American History:* Brent D. Glass, President and Editor-in-Chief, American Heritage Publishing: Edwin S. Grosvenor; and "GM Motor Transportation Exhibit"
14th St. &Constitution Ave. NW, Washington DC
www.americanhistory.si.edu

Tudor Place, Historic House and Garden, 1644 31st Street, NW, Washington, DC 2007 (Georgetown area)
www.tudorplace.org

The Dumbarton House, Museum and Headquarters, The National Society of The Colonial Dames of America, 2715 Q Street NW, Washington, DC 2007 (Georgetown Area)
www.dumbartonhouse.org

The National Theatre
1321 Pennsylvania Ave. NW, Washington, DC
www.nationaltheatre.org

The National Museum of the American Indian
4th St. & Independence Ave. SW, Washington, DC
www.americanindian.si.edu

Arlington National Cemetery and Arlington House, the Robert E. Lee Memorial www.arlingtoncemetary.org

Ford's Theatre, National Historic Site, 511 Tenth Street, Washington, DC 20004
www.fords.org

ENDNOTES

**There are no quotes from any of these works. This is a list of research resources and information for the reader to access for more information related to historical people, places, or things. I did extensive research in order to establish a true historic setting for my fictional characters. Please remember this story is a work of historical fiction. Any adjustments or errors made for the fictional plot or story are my own. A complete list of "Research Resources" including places I have visited, all the reading resources and websites (these are listed per dates visited and may have changed) I have researched are included. Some Duplicate listings appear in the Endnotes and Resources. The Endnotes are in the order of numbered notation per history related items in this fictional story.

i Boston Fire 1872, Research sources included: James Ford Rhodes, LL.D., D.Litt., *History of the United States 1850-1909, Vol., VII, 1872-1877, From The Compromise of 1850 to The End of the Roosevelt Administration* Chapter XL, pp.112-113, copyright 1906 by James Ford Rhodes and in 1934 by Daniel P. Rhodes, published by The MacMillan Company, New York.

ii Chicago Fire 1871, Research sources included: James Ford Rhodes, LL.D., D.Litt., *History of the United States 1850-1909, Vol., VII, 1872-1877, From The Compromise of 1850 to The End of the Roosevelt Administration,* Chapter XL, pp.112-113, copyright 1906 by James Ford Rhodes and in 1934 by Daniel P. Rhodes, published by The MacMillan Company, New York.

iii Louisa May Alcott, A wonderful writer and early nurse during this period. See: *Civil War Hospital Sketches* by Louisa May Alcott; Civil War Hospital Sketches, Dover Publications, Inc.,

Mineola, New York, Dover edition first published 2006, original work published 1863 by James Redpath, publisher, Boston, under the title, *Hospital Sketches*.

iv Sanitary Commission, this was learned from research included: Rutkow, Ira M., *Bleeding Blue and Gray: Civil War Surgery and the Evolution of American Medicine*, Random House, 2005; also information learned at the National Museum of Health and Medicine during my visit there.

v Louisa May Alcott, A wonderful writer and early nurse. See: *Civil War Hospital Sketches* by Louisa May Alcott; *Civil War Hospital Sketches*, Dover Publications, Inc., Mineola, New York, Dover edition first published 2006, original work published 1863 by James Redpath, publisher, Boston, under the title, *Hospital Sketches*.

vi Economic Collapse of 1873, The economy during this time period has similarities to today's economic issues. See James Ford Rhodes, LL.D., *D.Litt, History of the United States 1850-1909, From The Compromise to the End of the Roosevelt Administration, Vol. VII, 1872-1877,* Chapter XL, pp. 107-128, copyright 1906 by James Ford Rhodes and in 1934 by Daniel P. Rhodes, published by The MacMillan Company, New York.

vii Generals, research from Soldiers West; Hutton, Paul Andrew and Ball, Durwood, editors, *Soldiers West, Biographies from the Military Frontier, Second Edition*, copyright 2009 by the University of Oklahoma Press, Norman, Publishing Division of the University.

viii Linda Richards: Researched her life from her own book: *Reminiscences of Linda Richards: America's First Trained Nurse,* by Linda Richards; Whitcomb and Barrows, Boston 1911, copyright 1911 by Linda Richards, Thomas Todd Co, printers, 14 Beacon Street, Boston, Massachusetts for Book. "The Story of This Reprint" by J.B. Lippinott Co., (Philadelphia, London, Montreal) 1948 reprint with Foreword by Anne L. Austin, Los Angeles, California as a Facsimile Reproduction; Facsimile

Reprint was reproduced by Levering Riebel Co., Camden, New Jersey.

ix Dr. Susan Dimock, A good resource mentioning her: Chapter 2, "The First American Training School for Nurses", *Reminiscences of Linda Richards: America's First Trained Nurse*, by Linda Richards; Whitcomb and Barrows, Boston 1911, copyright 1911 by Linda Richards, Thomas Todd Co, printers, 14 Beacon Street, Boston, Massachusetts for Book. "The Story of This Reprint" by J.B. Lippinott Co., (Philadelphia, London, Montreal) 1948 reprint with Foreword by Anne L. Austin, Los Angeles, California as a Facsimile Reproduction; Facsimile Reprint was reproduced by Levering Riebel Co., Camden, New Jersey.

x Shepherd, Alexander R.: He is well known for many achievements in Washington, especially in the advancement of the way it looked. See *The Uncivil War: Washington During the Reconstruction Period 1865-1878* by James H. Whyte, Twayne Publishers, New York, copyright 1958, Library of Congress: 57-14776; and The Junior League of Washington's, *The City of Washington: An Illustrated History*, copyright 1977 by The Junior League of the City of Washington, D.C., A Borzoi Book, published by Alfred A. Knopf, Inc., New York, 1977, First paperback 1985., pp. 201, 235-237, p. 267, p.341.

xi Howe, Julia Ward: Researched origins in *Then Sings My Soul: 150 of the World's Greatest Hymns Stories* by Robert J. Morgan, Ebook pp 154-155, "Battle Hymn of the Republic", Published in Nashville, Tennessee by Thomas Nelson, Inc., copyright 2003 Robert J. Morgan.

xii Howe, Julia Ward, Her work is listed as "Mine Eyes Have Seen the Glory" in the Baptist Hymnal, #510, Howe, Julia Ward, 1861, Tune "Battle Hymn", American Folk Song, 19th Century, as found in the *Baptist Hymnal, 1975 Edition*, Convention Press, Nashville, Tennessee, copyright 1975, Convention Press, church Services and Materials Division, Nashville, Tennessee, Eighth Printing.

xiii Ambrotype: The picture referenced for my fictitious character

"James" was made during the Civil War and therefore, could have been this type, See: http://www.encyclopediavirginia.org/photography_During_the_Civil_War "Photography During the Civil War." (Site visited 9/24/2011)

xiv Arlington: Visited Arlington House and Arlington Cemetery in July 2010

xv Georgetown Houses in the Federal Period, See: Davis, Deering; Dorsey, Stephen P., and Hall, Ralph Cole, *Georgetown Houses of the Federal Period*, Dover Publications, Inc., Mineola, New York; copyright 1944, 1972 by Architectural Book Publishing Co., Inc., New York; Dover edition, first published 2001.

xvi Dames: *The Junior League of Washington's, The City of Washington: An Illustrated History*, copyright 1977 by The Junior League of the City of Washington, D.C., A Borzoi Book, published by Alfred A. Knopf, Inc., New York, 1977, first paperback 1985, p. 44 Shows the Dumbarton House, Headquarters for the Colonel Dames of America.

xvii Market Square: It is mentioned on p. 90, of *The Junior League of Washington's, The City of Washington: An Illustrated History*, copyright 1977 by The Junior League of the City of Washington, D.C., A Borzoi Book, published by Alfred A. Knopf, Inc., New York, 1977, first paperback 1985.

xviii Tudor House, visited in July 2010, Also, shown on p. 88 of Davis, Deering; Dorsey, Stephen P., and Hall, Ralph Cole, *Georgetown Houses of the Federal Period,* Dover Publications, Inc., Mineola, New York; copyright 1944, 1972 by Architectural Book Publishing Co., Inc., New York; Dover edition, first published 2001.

Xix Pennsylvania vs. Addicks See: http:// www.gale.cengage.com/free_resources/whm/trials/addicks.htm, Women's History- Rights on Trial- "Pennsylvania v. Addicks:

1813."(Site visited 2/1/2011)

xx Calvary Baptist: Tiller, Carl W. and Tiller, Olive M., copyright 1994, *At Calvary: A History of the First 125 Years of Calvary Baptist Church,* Washington, DC, Trinity Rivers Publishing, 1994.

xxi Dr. J.H. Cuthbert 1869-1887: ***Utilized with fictional characters for this story, however, he was a Washington preacher during this period. See: Winchcole, Dorothy Clark, Church Historian, First Baptist Church, Washington D.C., 1952, *The First Baptist in Washington D.C. 1802-1952.*

xxii Reverend Dr. J.W. Parker ***Utilized with fictional characters for this story, however, he was a Washington preacher during this period. He is mentioned on page 14 of Tiller, Carl W. and Tiller, Olive M., copyright 1994, *At Calvary: A History of the First 125 Years of Calvary Baptist Church, Washington, DC, 1862-1987,* Trinity Rivers Publishing, Inc., 1994.

xxiii References for Fort Hays, Medicine Lodge treaty, Taylor's Peace Commission, and Generals See: Utley, Robert M., *The Indian Frontier 1846-1890,* Revised Edition, copyright 1984 by the University of New Mexico Press, revised edition first published in 2003.

xxiv Term dragoons used before the Civil War and referred to as Cavalry after. Research found their early usage on the Frontier in chapter on "Stephen W. Kearney", by Durwood Ball, p. 43-71 in Hutton Andrew, Paul and Ball, Durwood, editors, *Soldiers West, Biographies from the Military Frontier, Second Edition*, copyright 2009 by the University of Oklahoma Press, Norman, Publishing Division of the University.

xxv Fort Scott: See "Fort Scott National Historic Site—Soldier Vs. Settler: Railroads in Southwest Kansas." http//www.nps.gov/archive/fosc/posofsek.htm(website   visited 8/2/2008)

xxvi Ese'he is the Cheyenne word for "sun", http://www.native-languages.org/cheyenne_words.htm, "Vocabulary Words in Native American Languages: Cheyenne" (site visited 11/20/2011)

xxvii Red Cloud and Spotted Tail, Their First visit to Washington in 1870. See: pp144-152 Utley, Robert M., *The Indian Frontier 1846-1890*, Revised Edition, copyright 1984 by the University of New Mexico Press, revised edition first published in 2003.

xxviii Wormley's Hotel mentioned in *The Uncivil War: Washington During the Reconstruction Period 1865-1878* by James H. Whyte, p. 180-181 and 259, Twayne Publishers, New York, copyright 1958, Library of Congress: 57-14776.

xxix Rock Creek Park: Is mentioned on p. 105 and several times in *The Junior League of Washington's, The City of Washington: An Illustrated History*, copyright 1977 by The Junior League of the City of Washington, D.C., A Borzoi Book, published by Alfred A. Knopf, Inc., New York, 1977, first paperback 1985.

xxx Welcker's restaurant mentioned in *The Uncivil War: Washington During the Reconstruction Period_1865-1878*, by James H. Whyte, pp.180-181, 193,Twayne Publishers, New York, copyright 1958, Library of Congress: 57-14776

xxxi Baseball: See a recount of the long history of baseball: Morse, Joseph Laffan, Sc.B., LL.B, LL.D. Editor in Chief, Standard Reference Works Publishing Company, Inc., New York, *The Universal Standard Encyclopedia, volume 2, Argon-Bedstraw, an abridgement of the New Funk and Wagnalls Encyclopedia*, "Baseball", pp.693-700, Universal Standard Encyclopedia copyright 1956 and 1957 by Wilfred Funk, Inc. copyright 1954 and 1955 by Wilfred Funk, Inc., New Funk and Wagnalls Encyclopedia copyright 1949 and 1952 by Wilfred Funk, Inc., Funk and Wagnalls New Standard Encyclopedia, copyright 1931, 1934, 1935, 1937, and 1942 by Wilfred Funk, Inc.

xxxii Henry D. Cooke, He is mentioned several times throughout because he was a very wealthy and influential man in Washington. He had a history in banking. *The Uncivil War: Washington During the Reconstruction Period 1865-1878* by James H. Whyte, (Twayne Publishers, New York, copyright 1958, Library of Congress: 57-14776).

xxxiii Grand Review: represented on p.229 of *The Junior League of Washington's, The City of Washington: An Illustrated History,* copyright 1977 by The Junior League of the City of Washington, D.C., A Borzoi Book, published by Alfred A. Knopf, Inc., New York, 1977, first paperback 1985.

xxxiv New England Hospital for Women and Children See resource: Mentioned in Chapter 2, "The First American Training School for Nurses", *Reminiscences of Linda Richards: America's First Trained Nurse,* by Linda Richards; Whitcomb and Barrows, Boston 1911, copyright 1911 by Linda Richards, Thomas Todd Co, printers, 14 Beacon Street, Boston, Massachusetts for Book. "The Story of This Reprint" by J.B. Lippinott Co., (Philadelphia, London, Montreal) 1948 reprint with Foreword by Anne L. Austin, Los Angeles, California as a Facsimile Reproduction; Facsimile Reprint was reproduced by Levering Riebel Co., Camden, New Jersey. (Also see my website list for another resource.)

xxxv Paul Durand-Ruel: See *Art: A New History,* by Paul Johnson, copyright 2003 by Paul Johnson, Chapter 26 "The Internal Conflicts of Nineteenth-Century Art", pp.581-607, (** p.600, found information about Paul Durand-Ruel a famous art dealer during this period), Harper Collins Publishers, New, York.

xxxvi Corcoran Art Gallery mentioned several times in *The Uncivil War: Washington During the Reconstruction Period 1865-1878_*by James H. Whyte, Twayne Publishers, New York, copyright 1958, Library of Congress: 57-14776.

xxxvii National Theater and the Marriage of Figaro, Newspaper Resources: *The Lorgnette,* Vol., 11 No.55, Advertisement for The National Theater for "The Marriage of Figaro", performance December 10, 1874, Thursday.

xxxviii Dr. Dimock, A good resource mentioning her: Chapter 2,

"The First American Training School for Nurses", *Reminiscences of Linda Richards:* America's First Trained Nurse, by Linda Richards; Whitcomb and Barrows, Boston 1911, copyright 1911 by Linda Richards, Thomas Todd Co, printers, 14 Beacon Street, Boston, Massachusetts for Book. "The Story of This Reprint" by J.B. Lippinott Co., (Philadelphia, London, Montreal) 1948 reprint with Foreword by Anne L. Austin, Los Angeles, California as a Facsimile Reproduction; Facsimile Reprint was reproduced by Levering Riebel Co., Camden, New Jersey.

xxxix Fires in Boston: James Ford Rhodes, LL.D., D.Litt, History of the United States 1850-1909, from The Compromise to the End of the Roosevelt Administration, Vol. VII, 1872-1877,pp.112-113 A Good website is http://www.bostonfirehistory.org

xl Boston Commons: Boston Common, founded 1634, Boston, Massachusetts, Visited Boston in 2000

xli Boston Museum of Art: See: Christian, Mary, Editor, Treasures of the Museum of Fine Arts Boston, introduction by Malcolm Rogers; chapter introductions by Gilian Wohlauer, "A tiny folio", Museum Editor: Peggy Hogan, Designer: Kevin Callahan, Production Editor: Meredith Wolf, Production Manager: Lou Bilka

xlii Plays at the National Theatre: Newspaper Resources: *The Lorgnette*, Vol., 11 No.55, Advertisement for The National Theater for *The Marriage of Figaro,* performance December 10, 1874, Thursday; *The Lorgnette*, Vol. 11, No.1, Advertisement for performance Monday October 5, 1874 at The National Theater, *Mary Stuart Queen of Scotts.*

ABOUT THE AUTHOR

Lana Lynne Higginbotham (writes historical fiction novels and blog under the pen name: *Lana* Lynne): Lana is a Speech-Language Pathologist and a writer/author. She is the author of three other historical fiction novels (listed by Titles: subtitles) under her pen name, Lana Lynne: *Home Always Beckons (subtitle: A New Sunrise)(*First Publication 2009; Revised/Second Edition coming in 2018*); Trails of Change (subtitle: A New Sunset)* (First Publication 2010; revised-Second Edition coming in 2018); and *Sunbeams at Twilight (subtitle: A Life's Echo) (First* Publication 2012; revised-Second Edition 2018). *A Compass of Stars in Her Eyes (*First Publication 2018*)* is her newest historical fiction romance.

Her first contemporary Christian novella is *Whimsy Michaels and Her Amazing Room (*First publication 2018).

Other writing credits include: A creative nonfiction novel, written with a coauthor: *Life Between the Letters: The Chuck and Mary Felder Story (*First Publication 2014*)* by Lana Lynne Higginbotham and Mary K. Felder. She wrote a weekly blog post (2012-2014) and was part of the new "Venture Galleries Author Collection" blog team (2013) under her pen name, Lana Lynne, for Venture Galleries (February 2012- January 2014).

Lana lives with her husband in East Texas. They are empty nesters and proud grandparents. Learn more by visiting www.lanalynne.com.

www.ingramcontent.com/pod-product-compliance
Lightning Source LLC
Chambersburg PA
CBHW020550180626
46810CB00007B/2451